T0083477

JUDGE ANDERSON
YEAR ONE

An Abaddon Books™ Publication
www.abaddonbooks.com
abaddon@rebellion.co.uk

This omnibus first published in 2017 by
Abaddon Books™,
Rebellion Intellectual Property Limited,
Riverside House, Osney Mead, Oxford, OX2 0ES, UK.

10 9 8 7 6 5 4 3 2 1

Editor: David Thomas Moore
Cover Art: Garry Brown
Design: Sam Gretton, Oz Osborne and Maz Smith
Marketing and PR: Rob Power
Editor-in Chief: Jonathan Oliver
Head of Books and Comics Publishing: Ben Smith
Creative Director and CEO: Jason Kingsley
Chief Technical Officer: Chris Kingsley

Judge Anderson created by
John Wagner and Brian Bolland.

ISBN: 978-1-78108-555-4

Printed in Denmark by Nørhaven

JUDGE ANDERSON
YEAR ONE

ALEC WORLEY

ABADDON
BOOKS

WWW.ABADDONBOOKS.COM

Introduction

I FIRST MET Judge Cassandra Anderson in 1991 within the pages of the comic book *Judgement on Gotham*. Her first scene had her answer the phone before it rang. What a perfect introduction to Mega-City One's premier psychic. It was the promise of a bust-up between Judge Dredd and Batman that made me buy the book, but it was the supporting character of Anderson that had me hooked. Written by her co-creator John Wagner and long-time chronicler Alan Grant, she brought a goofball energy to every scene in which she appeared. Superstar artist Simon Bisley was also tuned into Anderson's eccentric frequency and drew her more like a musclebound Tori Amos than the chic Debbie Harry lookalike she had been under Brian Bolland, who drew her first appearance 11 years before in *2000 AD* #150.

I started tracking down the books and annuals that collected her older adventures while discovering her more recent and edgy psychotropic epics, which were then running in the monthly *Judge Dredd Megazine*. Reading all these alongside Judge Dredd's regular adventures in *2000 AD*, I felt that Anderson had become almost as much a part of the Dredd saga as the legendary lawman himself. Her continued adventures in comics, her appearance in the 2012 *Dredd* movie (essayed with jittery toughness by a terrific Olivia Thirlby), and the character's various cosplay incarnations at comics conventions around the world testify to Judge Anderson's continued—if not increasing—popularity. But Anderson is more than just Dredd's sidekick or a pin-up for the *2000 AD* set.

Judge Anderson is a writer's dream: funny, smart, tough, cool and our moral compass in the world-gone-berserk of Mega-City One. She's a dynamo of emotions, conflicts and abilities and—unlike Dredd—doesn't need other characters around to bring her to life. While Dredd is a monolithic embodiment of 'justice'—you may as well try and relate to your refrigerator—Anderson is driven to redeem the city by something more than a sense of duty. She wants to prove not only that good exists (despite the odds), but also that the people are worth fighting for—and she does so not just because the law says she must but because she wants to.

Did I mention she was funny? Oh, man, she's funny. It's always a joy seeing characters poke fun at the paternal gravity of the Justice Department, and Anderson takes her colleagues' tolerance for the quirks of Psi-Division to the absolute limit. She insists on calling an irate Chief Judge "CJ" then "Baby" (she had the hip patter of an off-duty rock star back then) and treats Dredd himself like an endearingly cranky uncle. (I love that panel in *Judgement on Gotham* where she sticks her fingers in her ears as Dredd bellows at a suspect.)

And to top it all, she's psychic! What the hell must that be like? To have the ability to tune into the thoughts of someone else and hear what they think of you as plainly as if they were telling you to your face? Never mind the psychos and criminals. You don't need to be psychic to know they despise you. Never mind the citizens and all that avalanche-of-pain stuff. You hear that all the time. What about those closest to you, your superiors, colleagues and friends—the people you rely on to do your job and reassure you that you're doing the right thing? The people who have the strongest influence on you as a human being. They may be telling you that you're too full of yourself. That you're too cocky, or maybe even crazy, and that one day it will get the better of you. Maybe they don't care enough to have any kind of opinion about you except how hot they think you look in that uniform.

What kind of human being could possibly carry the weight of all that ghastly truth and still think people were worth a damn? How powerful would that person's mind have to be to not lose themselves in the maelstrom? In terms of strength of character and force of personality, Anderson is pretty much a Hercules.

And yet Anderson is no superwoman. In fact, she's often a complete screw-up. She's reckless, erratic, and treats rules and regulations the way Led Zeppelin treated hotel rooms. At times it's hard to tell if Anderson is even sane. (In the comics, she once gave up being a Judge altogether and took a sort of intergalactic gap year. At one point, she was having acid visions in the desert with help from a witch playing the bongos in her underwear. Well, it *was* the '90s.) Yet heroes need such quirks and vulnerabilities—*Die Hard* wouldn't be half as thrilling if John McClane were bulletproof. For me, Anderson's imperfections make her even more appealing.

All this and more made me want to write this trilogy of Judge Anderson novellas. The character has collected a lot of baggage over the years and I wanted to get back to the conflicted wisecracker she had once been in the early strips. But I also wanted to dig deeper than a five-page comic strip in *2000 AD* would allow. I wanted to see the whole world through the eyes of a woman who can read minds, and treat that concept as though it were real. I wanted to put her through the rigours of desire and depression, to give her the space to think for herself, find out what she really wants and watch her go after it.

Above all I wanted to treat Anderson like a human being rather than a sexy cartoon. My Anderson farts. She stinks of sweat. She doesn't have time to shave her legs. She cracks jokes about being on her period. And no more of those daft kick-boxing moves she did in some of the comics just to show off those shapely legs. This bitch mixes it up like Gina Carano in the movie *Haywire*: chokeholds, thumbs in eye sockets, broken teeth, violence at its most ugly and magnetic. I have a friend frighteningly well versed in the science of fisticuffs and when I asked him whether a petite woman with Mossad-equivalent training could take out a room full of hostiles he proceeded to show me exactly how (and has since apologised for breaking that table-lamp).

Anderson's psychic gifts made her a nightmare to write. Dramatic tension is commonly achieved by characters withholding information and/or their true feelings; ergo: Anderson is a character with the potential to suck the life out of every scene she walks into. Dear God, but she was hell on a stick to write, but I'm glad I got to know her as closely as I did. It's made me love the character all the more.

I'm honoured to have been given the opportunity to provide the foundation for her debut adventures in *2000 AD*, so a thank you is most definitely in order to the initial commissioner Ben Smith, Abaddon editors David Moore and Jonathan Oliver, and *2000 AD* editor Matt Smith.

P.S. It's all canon, baby.

Alec Worley
February 2017

PART ONE
HEARTBREAKER

Finding love in the city is hard. Soaring crime rates keep everyone indoors. Living life on the right side of the law keeps everyone busy. These days, who has time to make that special connection? Is romance dead?

MEET MARKET don't think so. We're Mega-City One's most popular in-house dating agency. Our auctions can get you a great deal, whether you're bidding on the date of your dreams or listing yourself as part of a romantic evening that goes to the highest—and hopefully hottest—bidder!

Sign up before Valentine's Day and we'll upgrade your first listing for free.*

Whoever you're looking for, you can find them on MEET MARKET.

*subject to 36-month contract; offer excludes robots, mutants and aliens.

'Meet Market' Tri-D commercial,
first aired 01.02.2100

MEGA-CITY ONE
2100 A.D.

One

Zak placed Reena's synthi-caff on the table and smiled. Reena snarled and thrust her fork into his eye. He staggered backwards, open-mouthed, barging into the table behind him, spilling hot drinks into the laps of another couple, who stood and cursed him. The table capsized as Zak sprawled onto the floor. He sat up, touching the utensil protruding from his eye. A woman screamed.

A plate shattered against the wall by his head. Then a cup glanced painfully off his skull. Reena was a lot bigger than her profile picture had suggested. She was standing now, snatching glasses, plates and cutlery from the other tables and hurling them at him, shrieking obscenities, as though he were a rat she had cornered in her kitchen. Other couples were grabbing their coats and bags and hurrying past her out the door. Some just sat and stared. One of the guys behind the counter was babbling into a vidphone. Reena grabbed an empty loomanade bottle and pointed it at Zak, screaming.

"One-eighty tall, my ass. You lying sack of stomm!"

A big guy began to rise from a chair beside Reena, appealing to her to calm down, and she smashed the bottle across his face. He cried out and fell to his knees, clutching his cheek. The few remaining onlookers fled. The surrounding windows were now crowded with people, some filming the scene on their vidphones. Reena stared at the broken bottle in her shaking hand. Her chest heaved as though she were pausing to catch her breath. She turned to Zak, her teeth bared.

Zak's habmate Marty had warned him that there were way too many crazies out there. Didn't he read the newsfeeds? Zak had just told him that a cute girl on Meet Market had accepted his 75-credit bid to take her for an afternoon stroll around a holo-park. Marty advised him to wear a stab-vest; he had read about this chick who murdered this guy she met through one of those agencies. You gotta watch out for those futsies.

Marty was right, of course. The feeds were full of stories about futsies, those citizens whose minds could no longer resist the overwhelming madness of day-to-day life in Mega-City One. Some threw themselves off buildings or under trains. Others vented their outrage on their fellow citizens, using hastily purchased shotguns or the biggest cleaver they could find in their kitchen drawer. Having claimed the lives of several unlucky citizens, these spontaneous episodes would invariably conclude with a couple of well-placed bullets courtesy of the Justice Department.

"Listen to me when I'm talking to you!"

Zak held up his hand to placate Reena, edging towards the door as he did so. But the gesture only seemed to incense her. She snorted like a maddened bull and ran at him, clutching the broken bottle like a dagger.

Zak yelped, feeling the fork wagging in his eye as he turned and scrambled for the exit. The automatic doors parted and several onlookers backed away outside. Reena grabbed a fistful of Zak's hair, throwing her weight on top of him and pushing him to the floor. Scrabbling wildly, he pulled over an ornamental plant, spilling stones and soil. Reena stabbed him in the throat three times before the rest of the bottle shattered in her hand. Zak grabbed the largest of the scattered stones and rolled over to swing it at her head. He felt it connect and she fell to one side with a groan. The onlookers watched as Zak staggered to his feet and lunged towards them with bloodied hands. They retreated and he fell to his knees, clutching his throat.

Through his remaining eye, he squinted at the afternoon sun glowering through the vast windows of the Meet Market plaza. He could feel blood pulsing warm against his fingers, drenching his shirt. Someone would help him. Any second now. He would be okay. Zak felt himself topple and roll onto his back, his hand falling away from his spurting neck. From here he could see the indoor holo-park where he and Reena had paid to take a stroll, maybe rent a boat on the lake.

"Drop your weapon, citizen."

Bemused, Zak turned his head. Across the spreading pool of blood in which he lay, he saw a Judge approaching from across the plaza, his Lawgiver raised. Zak heard screams, then feet pounding towards him from the caff-bar. The Judge paused, then fired twice. More screams as someone landed on top of Zak, driving the breath from his body. It was Reena. A large stone slipped from her dead hand and rattled on the ground beside him.

Zak shivered as he felt Reena's body dragged aside. Strong gloved hands pressed down either side of his throat.

"Control, this is Montana," the Judge said. "I need a med-wagon, code three, at Meet Market Block, level six at the caff-bar on Valentino Plaza."

Zak looked up at the red and blue visor glaring down at him.

"Hang on, citizen," the Judge said. "You're gonna be okay."

Zak felt a wave of helpless gratitude. He shivered again and felt as though he were falling backwards. He hoped his sisters would take care of Mom.

Then the world according to Zak Mahoney disappeared.

* * *

EXPERIENCING THE DEATH of another person through their eyes was routine post-mortem work for a Psi-Judge, but Cassandra Anderson always worried that it moved her more than it should. She figured she would get used to it soon enough. At least the technical term 'reading for latents' no longer felt as shockingly indifferent as it had when she first heard it as a child. Zak's body was cooling more rapidly than usual, thanks to the blood loss. It was time for Anderson to vacate the premises. Principal Randall, a leading telepath at the Academy, liked to scare cadets with the story of the Psi-Judge who had lingered too long in the fading mind of a dead subject, the Judge's consciousness drowning in darkness when the lights finally went out.

Anderson withdrew her fingers from the dead man's temples and opened her eyes.

"You okay?" Montana said. "What did you see in there?"

"Same thing your witnesses saw," Anderson said. "One minute these two're making nice, next minute she's riding the overzoom to Nutsville."

The med-wagon had arrived and Anderson moved aside to let a pair of spindly droids start bagging Zak's body. The two Judges had the plaza to themselves now. Montana had released the last of the witnesses, who were now being ushered elsewhere by Meet Market staff. Meet Market was required by law to accommodate Judge patrols, although the company filed constant objections on the grounds that it spoiled their expensive ambiance. Thank Grud Montana had been finishing up a sweep when he heard the screams. Anderson had just finished a routine cult bust-up two blocks south at Robin Hardy when she caught a patrol call about an assault in progress. She arrived five minutes later to find Montana guarding the two bodies and confiscating a citizen's vidphone, threatening to bust the creep for obstruction.

"Sane one minute, crazy the next," Montana said, watching

the med-droids lift the bodybag containing the woman. "Sounds like a standard futsie to me."

"Wait a second," Anderson said, standing in the droids' way as they tried to load the body into the med-wagon. "Don't you wanna know why this woman flipped out?"

"She flipped out because she was crazy."

Anderson shook her head.

"There's gotta be a reason."

Montana gave her a sympathetic look.

"The other week, there was this mall manager up in Michael Douglas Block," he said. "Gets his hands on a flame-thrower, torches everyone in menswear before the Jays can take him down. No priors, no reason. People just snap. You'll see this kind of thing every other day around here, rookie."

"Rookie?" Anderson said, standing her ground. "That's cute, Montana. Now let's see..." She touched her temple.

"You made full eagle a whole month before me. Gee, I'm surprised you haven't made Chief Judge yet with that kind of experience."

Montana tried to interrupt.

"Passed by Judge Landsman, right? Although you almost blew it for failing to submit the correct address on an incident report. Oh, and there's an 'o' in 'perpetrator.'"

"That's real clever, peejay," he said. *Peejay*; Street-Div's latest epithet for a Psi-Judge. "I'll bet that one goes down great at kids' parties. But, y'see, there's this thing we need in the real world called 'evidence' and—Hey, what're you doing?"

"Gathering evidence," Anderson said, lowering Reena's bodybag to the floor as the droids chirped their annoyance. She ignored them and unzipped the bag, revealing the dead woman's blood-streaked face.

"I need to know whether we're looking at a plain old futsie flip like you say, or something else. Now keep these droids quiet, I'm trying to concentrate."

Anderson touched the dead woman's forehead and tuned out before Montana could answer.

The other Judge, the droids and the plaza in which they all stood vanished as Anderson slipped into silent blackness. She reached out, drawn by the psionic afterglow that remained inside the dead woman's congealing brain.

Reading the minds of the dead was really no different from reading those of the living. With a living subject, you just locked onto their cerebral cortex and fired psionic impulses into their synapses in order to access whatever memory you were after. Psi-Judges called it 'lock and shock.' Unlike living minds, the dead ones did not wriggle about like a mess of eels when you tried to grab hold of them. Provided the brain was reasonably fresh and had not been sucked inside out by a Lawgiver round, post-mortem subjects took a lot less 'locking' but one heck of a lot more 'shocking.' The Psi had to jumpstart the dead brain by flooding it with psionic energy. This temporarily revived the inanimate mind and illuminated the neural pathways last used by the subject. The Psi then had to maintain a steady flow of energy into the subject's brain in order to keep the lights on while they had a look around.

Anderson let her psi-energy flow and felt the woman's blackened mind light up like a city block returning to life after a power cut, although the synapses in the right hemisphere kept flickering. She remembered the woman had suffered a head trauma when Zak clocked her with that stone, and Anderson had to increase her bandwidth into the dead brain in order to maintain a steady link.

The first thing Anderson heard was hate. Super-fast gamma brainwaves, screeching like a zillion tortured violins. No steady beta-waves here to rationalise or restrain, just a torrent of terrified loathing. She heard wild commands to claw out the eyes of the man cowering before her, rip the flesh from his cheeks, beat his head against the floor until his skull cracked like an egg.

Anderson listened. Psi-Division telepaths were trained to regard the human brain as a radio with every station playing at once. Some stations played fast; others plodded. Some sang shrill and staccato; others produced bass notes so deep they felt like an earthquake. Anderson could tune in and out of different thoughtwaves as easily as if she were flipping channels on the Tri-D. But she was struggling to hear her way through this cacophony. So insistent were the woman's hateful thoughts that the moment Anderson tuned one out another replaced it. The thoughts weren't fried in the telltale backwash of drugs or stims; nor were they slurred by alcohol. The only thing the woman appeared to be high on was nerves and caffeine. Anderson was eventually driven back, forced to tap the more rational core of the woman's long-term memories.

Anderson struggled to sustain the immense flow of energy into the dead woman's brain. That tap on the noggin had caused a post-mortem haematoma, a 'black spot' that was now leaking psi-energy. Anderson quickly tapped into the woman's revived synapses and several long-term memories rang out at once. The woman's name was Reena Stanhope. She had a mother in Sector 72, whom she called every Saturday. She kept lots of houseplants. She lived in fear that the Judges would find out she had an illegal Tri-D hookup, which her last boyfriend had set up for her and which she couldn't figure out how to disconnect. She was an account manager at an ad agency. She hoped people liked her. She worried about her weight. She was lonely, dissatisfied, and fearful that her next birthday would prove another tick of the clock counting down to spinsterhood. Anderson had heard it all before, of course. Everyone's private fears sounded remarkably similar.

It was here in the forebrain chatter that you heard the 'screamers,' the psychotic or predatory urges, the long-term damage wrought by abuse or trauma. This was the stuff of which futsies were made and it usually started yelling at you the minute you tuned in. But here inside the rational core of Reena Stanhope's memories, there was nothing of the sort. So what had made her flip?

Anderson was unsure how much longer she could maintain the psi-link, especially with that black spot leaking energy like a punctured tyre. Better hurry up and read those latents before the lights go out. She sank herself into the cockpit of the woman's consciousness. Two holes glowed in the blackness, converging and widening until the light enveloped Anderson and she found herself peering through the eyes of Reena Stanhope, viewing the last few minutes of the woman's life.

Reena was eating a forkful of brandycake. Anderson could feel its soft sweetness mashing between her tongue and palate. She heard the clink of Reena's fork against her plate. She and Zak were talking about tomorrow's Valentine's Parade, a weekend-long festival that flooded the city streets with exotic dancers and lavish floats. Reena had never attended. She had been put off by too many stories of Judges busting heads at random. Zak said it could get pretty crazy, but was a lot of fun. Maybe they could check it out together. Yeah, maybe. It turned out they both lived in Carey Mulligan Block. She lived three levels down from him, but they both used the same gym, the one where the air conditioning kept breaking down and that girl with the piercings was always on reception, but never said hello.

The conversation was a breeze, each topic revealing a shared interest or giving Zak a chance to show off his cool sense of humour. Reena worried about filling her face with cake while they were talking and wondered what her mom would make of him. Reena had only just subscribed to Meet Market. The first two bidders she accepted had not impressed her. The first was at least 40 years older than his profile picture and had forgotten to bring his teeth. The other guy, who called himself 'JudgeCuddles2072,' had suggested they skip the bat-gliding lessons secured by his bid and Reena's listing fee, and instead go back to his hab. But this time Reena appeared to have stuck man-gold. Maybe not 24-carats—he was way shorter than the 180cm he had stated on his profile—but definitely worth another date.

Zak asked if she would like another caff. She did. The bar was warm and comfortable and their coupon for the holo-park was good for another month.

Anderson heard a thought shriek out of nowhere like a bolt of lightning.

He's playing you, Reena.

Unrelated thoughts always bubbled up from the cauldron of a person's mind, but they rarely lingered, or struck with such violence.

Anderson listened, horrified, as that single thought—*he's playing you*—consumed Reena's mind like a virus.

You think a guy with arms like that struggles for a date, Reena? He's probably bidding on twenty other girls right now. And look how you're falling for it, bitch. Are you really that stupid? Are you really that desperate? Tomorrow morning that drokker will be high-fiving his buddies and laughing at pictures of you on his vidphone.

Reena was glaring now at Zak as he queued at the bar. She stabbed her fork into the table, rattling her caff cup, drawing glances from the other couples. Her heart was racing. Anderson did not have to be an empath to feel the volcanic hatred gathering inside Reena's body.

From nought to 'I wanna kill you' in 60 seconds? No way was that a normal train of thought. So what had caused it? Some long-forgotten trauma? Dormant psychosis? Nothing Anderson had heard so far in the mind of Reena Stanhope suggested any such thing. Anderson was now convinced Reena was no futsie, but would have to dig even deeper if she were to find any evidence to the contrary. If evidence existed at all.

Zak smiled as he returned with Reena's caff. The image

flickered. That damn black spot was now haemorrhaging psi-energy as fast as Anderson could pump it. One minute more and her body, kneeling somewhere out there in the Meet Market plaza, would pass out under the strain, severing the psi-link, and leaving her consciousness stranded. But did Reena deserve to be remembered as a murderous futsie, another reason for citizens to hide behind their hab doors, her breakdown a conundrum that would torment her family for the rest of their lives?

Anderson held on, as Reena's view of Zak and the caff-bar dissolved into a black sea that repeatedly whispered the words *he's playing you*. Anderson focused on the source of the sound and pitched a final round of synaptic commands into Reena's deepest memory centres.

An image flashed through Reena's mind: a black arrow, gleaming as it drilled through the air. Anderson felt it burn with hatred. The image was not a memory. It was a bolt of negative psionic energy shaped—visualised—in the form of an arrow, and fired into Reena's mind. There it had detonated, confirming every insecurity, igniting every secret terror, obliterating all sense of judgement and sending her aggression impulses somewhere north of thermonuclear. Reena Stanhope was not insane; she had been driven to murder by a powerful psychic.

Anderson let go, releasing herself from Reena's dwindling mind. But instead of surfacing in her own body, Anderson felt herself sinking deeper into the surrounding darkness. She took a second to realise, grasping at emptiness, that she must have passed out, her body keeling over out there in the real world, leaving the rest of her to evaporate. Anderson felt a flush of panic before her memories vaporised and she forgot what panic was. She felt herself dissolving. Where was she? Was she in trouble? What is 'trouble'? Who am I? Anderson? Anderson.

"Anderson!"

Someone was shaking her by the wrists. Then a gloved hand slapped her face so hard that she cried out in rage. Anderson caught her attacker and threw him to the ground, locking his throat with both arms, a reflex burned into her by fifteen years of daily training in the Academy dojo.

"You're welcome," Montana said through gritted teeth, as the world returned to Anderson's senses like a refreshing tide.

"I'm sorry," she said, releasing him as the med-droids retrieved Reena's body.

Montana sat up, rubbing his throat.

"You nearly broke my neck, peejay."

"And you're breaking my heart, Montana. Now listen up. I think we've got a psychic psycho on the loose."

Two

"That all sounds very interesting, Judge Anderson," said Sector Chief Hauser. "A clear case for Psi-Division right there. However, Psi-Div has signed you over to me for the next three days, which makes me your acting chief. And the only psychic phenomenon of interest in my sector house is the ability of my boot to materialise up the ass of any rookie who sees fits to waste my gruddamn time."

Anderson had barely finished helping Montana to his feet when she received the call from Psi-Division. She was among two-dozen peejays seconded to Hauser and due to report to Sector House 7 for briefing at 16:00. The entire city was preparing for tomorrow's Valentine's Parade, and Hauser's was one of several sectors that required more Jays on the street. What the citizens called 'annual festivities,' the Justice Department called a 'barely containable riot.'

Upon Anderson's arrival at the Sector House, the battered droid on reception advised her to hit the sleep machine. Hauser liked his Judges to be wide awake when he was yelling at them during roll call. She ignored the robot and instead performed a 'skip and dip' through the minds of the various clerks and Judges passing through reception. Soon she had gained enough information to pinpoint Hauser's whereabouts.

She found him in the hangar bay where he was brandishing a wrench at a delivery droid that had apparently mislaid a shipment of cuffs. She weathered a barrage of vitriol before apologising for the interruption and pitching her case that a psychic murderer was at large in their city.

"Your Chief Ecks owes me a favour, Anderson," Hauser said, thrusting a clipboard into the droid's pincers and shoving the robot aside. "I suspect he believes he's repaying me by sending you. I hear you're what passes for a star pupil up at that kook farm."

Psi-Judges were forbidden from eavesdropping on the thoughts of senior Judges, but Hauser's were too loud and self-important to go completely unheard by Anderson.

These peejays gimme the creeps, she heard him think.

Anderson said nothing, letting him launch into the monologue she could hear him preparing in his head.

"Tomorrow morning every street in this city is going to be filled with parade floats that contravene every known vehicular regulation and health and safety law, and they'll be accompanied by an army of maniacs hell-bent on dancing their way into an obscenity charge."

Anderson waited as Hauser continued.

"By midnight tomorrow there'll be a queue outside every iso-block in this sector and every bed in my med-bay will be carrying a wounded Judge. In other words, I have a ton of stomm in front of me and I need a few extra hands to help me shovel it."

He looked Anderson up and down.

"I dunno what you're used to in Psi-Div, but we work the frontline, down here in Seven. We got some of the highest unemployment rates in this city, and that means more perps than we know what to do with."

Anderson spoke.

"Which is why the Department needs to do more to protect employers, as you said yourself in your address to the sector's Business Federation last month. I believe you pointed out that Meet Market provides sixty-eight percent of all employment within a ten-mile radius of their block."

Hauser's eyes narrowed.

This here's a restricted area, she heard him think. *Give me the slightest reason to think you're picking facts outta my head, rookie, and you'll be facing an investigation.*

"Sir, I had Control feed me some information on my way over here. I also spoke to Accounts Division," she said. "According to Meet Market's published revenues and the company's recent fall in share value, Accounts have predicted with 94% accuracy that the company will have to lay off a significant number of staff by the end of this quarter."

Anderson activated a holo-reader from her belt and handed it to Hauser, who read the title of the newsfeed article she had selected: *THIRD MEET MARKET FUTSIE. CAFF-BAR KILLING SPARKS SHARE FREEFALL.*

Anderson waited, but Hauser refused to take the bait.

"Third futsie...?" she prompted. "Sir, last month one of their subscribers strangled his date in the Meet Market butterfly ranch. The following month a couple are enjoying an afternoon in a plastic surgery spa when the woman suddenly decides to crank up the dial on her date's liposuction machine."

Hauser handed back the reader, unimpressed.

"Anderson, maybe you haven't had the slab under your boots long enough to know this, but we have over two hundred futsie incidents every week in this sector alone."

"But none of them have occurred in Meet Market until now," she said. "This company has screening protocols, psych-evaluations, record checks, the works. Their safety record has been spotless since the company was founded. Then, boom, three futsies in as many months? It's my feeling that—"

"We're Judges, Anderson," Hauser said, losing patience. "We can't afford to feel anything. And what you're talking about here is coincidence. Once the weekend's over, feel free to go tell Psi-Div about your magic arrows or whatever it is you saw in that woman's head."

"Someone is causing these attacks," she said. "They want us to think we're dealing with random futsies, and not some psycho with an agenda."

"Sounds to me like a rival company, if it's anything," Hauser said. "I'll have Accounts look into it next week."

"If anything's gonna happen, it's gonna happen this weekend," Anderson said. "And if it does, Meet Market will have to cut their staff, and that'll leave you with another few thousand unemployed cits in your sector."

Hauser paused, reluctant.

I really hope you're reading my mind right now, rookie. I want you to know that you've yet to impress me.

Anderson resisted a frown.

"You've got fourteen hours of my precious time to find me a plausible suspect," he said. "Or the case is closed and I'm putting you on report."

ANDERSON SAT ASTRIDE her Lawmaster, parked on a balcony of the hangar bay overlooking the western sprawl of the Meg. Dusk was creeping over the city and the blocks of Sector 7 were lighting up like vast glittering mushrooms. She ignored the view, absorbed in studying Meet Market's surveillance footage on her Lawmaster's data-screen. The suspect must have been within ten to five feet of the victim; any closer and Reena would have surely noticed him, any further away and you were talking about a psyker with one heck of a throw. Anyone packing that kind of heat would not have gone undetected by Psi-Div's own psychic surveillance unit.

She shuttled through the security footage, back and forth, switching angles, studying every face. Access to Meet Market Block was limited to staff and subscribers. Unless the suspect had somehow psyched his way in, they would not have made it through the front door, which required both a pass and facial recog.

Most dating agencies in Mega-City One were virtual. People met online and agreed to meet someplace in the city. But with the city being what it is, Meet Market found they could make a lot of money by providing citizens with a safe area, as well as ironclad screening processes that prevented them from bumping into a psycho. Subscribers listed themselves and bid on each other, and the money went towards one of Meet Market's in-house activities, anything from synthi-plonk tasting to zero-G bowling.

Anderson saw countless couples enter and leave the 200-seater caff-bar before Reena Stanhope went berserk. She watched them fixing their hair and puffing out their chests as they greeted their dates. She watched them queue at the counter, sip caff and talk. She also spotted a couple of quick-witted suitors darting towards the exit upon catching sight of their date in the flesh.

Anderson felt strangely helpless before the crowd encased inside her data-screen, their thoughts beyond her reach. She had to resort to what she remembered from body language classes, in which Psi cadets had been drilled alongside Street Division trainees. Most of the guys in the bar looked around and rubbed the backs of their necks, while the women folded their arms or fondled their jewellery. Everyone appeared more engaged in themselves than anyone else. The suspect, theory suggested, would have sat back, relaxed, feeling like a wolf among sheep. Judging by the hate-bomb that had been fired into Reena Stanhope's mind, the suspect was somewhere on the aggressive empath spectrum, and therefore unlikely to have the ability to read peoples' thoughts the way she could. So the suspect probably knew their targets, selected them prior to attack. But Anderson had no time to study the victims' files and decipher a connection.

Wait a second.

Anderson hit pause, then rewind and play. She saw what appeared to be an elbow belonging to someone just out of shot as they raised their arm to take a sip of their drink. She switched angles. In a far corner there was a small table, beneath which she could see someone's leg shifting back. Whoever was sat there had moved their chair so their back faced the window. Now why would someone not want to look at that lovely view of the holo-park opposite the bar?

From this position, the person was out of shot from one angle and obscured by a pillar from another. How many times must this creep have been here to have figured out where to sit without being caught on camera? Maybe someone on the inside had told him?

Anderson watched her suspect edging around just out of shot. I can see you, creep. *Now let's see if we can get a better look at you.* She shuttled the footage forward, then hit play. The suspect left the premises three minutes before Reena Stanhope plunged her dessert fork into Zak Mahoney's eye. Three minutes. Enough time to make it out of there before the psionic payload infected the victim's brain. The suspect had even made a show of looking at his watch before departing. *Nice touch, creep.*

Anderson tapped the pause key. He was male, Caucasian— unusually pale, in fact—around 183cm, maybe 73kg, with a mop of black hair, and wearing a long elegant coat. He pulled a flat cap low over his eyes just at the point when one of the cams would have clocked a close-up of his features. The suspect was not wearing gloves and he had left behind an empty cup, but the crockery would most likely have been destroyed during Reena's rampage. He must have been sat there for well over an hour, and Anderson was dismayed to see his features hidden by the brim of his cap when he was served at the bar. However, security cams were not the only form of recording to which a Psi-Judge had access. Anderson had an idea...

She jumped at the sound of a Lawmaster revving its engine behind her.

"Montana?"

"You know, for a Psi you're pretty easy to creep up on," he said, pulling alongside and killing the engine.

"Just don't forget to keep your guard up when you do it, though, okay?" Anderson said.

Montana pretended to wince.

"I heard you managed to win over Hauser."

"Shortly before he called you up and told you to keep an eye on me, right?"

Montana gave her a look. "You're all about cutting to the chase, huh?"

"Montana, I can hear everything rattling around inside your head."

"Everything?" He looked alarmed.

"I just mean you can skip the formalities."

"Just trying to be civil, Anderson." He almost looked hurt.

"Hey, it's appreciated," she said with a smile. "Most people treat Psis like we've got tentacles or something."

Montana laughed.

"And thanks again for the assist back at the plaza," she said. "Hope I never have to return the favour."

"So is Psi-Div's star pupil leading this investigation or what?"

Anderson tried not to feel irritated. Her tutors at the Academy had regarded her as a prodigy; the higher-ups, as one of their most valuable assets. To them, she was living proof of the validity of Psi-Division, and as such her judgement and reputation must remain as flawless on the street as it had been in the Academy. But ever since she made full eagle, it felt like everyone made a game of trying to catch her out. Guys like Hauser. It sure would feel great to show that doubting old fart what this rookie could do.

"I got a lead off Meet Market's security files," she said. "But I couldn't get a mugshot. So I figure we find whoever served him at the caff-bar and get a description. Either verbal or, you know..."

She wiggled her fingers at her temples and made a ghostly noise.

"Hauser was right," Montana said, amused. "You guys really are creepy."

They ignited their Lawmasters. The huge motorcycles lit up, their engines growling.

"I got names and addresses of everyone who was on duty at the bar this afternoon," Montana said. "They all live in employee habs in Meet Market block."

"Great, I know a short-cut," Anderson said. "So keep your eyes on my tail."

She ignored the quip Montana had thought better of making and took off down the hangar bay ramp. Montana chased her into the darkening city.

ANDERSON'S LAWMASTER FLASHED past the streetlights, weaving through the evening traffic on the Bonnie Tyler Expressway. Montana closed in behind her.

"Access to the block is limited to staff and subscribers, right?" His voice crackled through Anderson's earpiece. "You think this guy could be some kind of hacker?"

"I doubt it," Anderson said. "Meet Market's securityware is almost as good as the Department's. Any hacker with that kind of talent's gonna be hitting banks not a dating agency."

A munce-tanker moved aside to let Anderson pass.

"Meet Market receive profile alerts direct from the Department," she said. "Anyone with a serious record doesn't get in and we know about everyone who tries."

Montana accelerated to keep up with her as she swung off onto an overzoom feeding into the belly of Meet Market Block, which now rose into view, a mountain of neon.

"Then maybe someone's opening the door from inside," he said.

"A possibility," Anderson said. "But we've got way more possibilities than we can handle right now. This guy's fresh meat, Montana."

They passed beneath a Meet Market banner: 'IT'S FACE-2-FACE FRIDAY—SIZE UP THE PRIZE AND BUST THOSE BIDS.'

"I checked the files of every other Division and couldn't match anyone on record with our guy's MO," Anderson said.

"Which is?" Montana followed Anderson down towards the entrance of Meet Market's main lobby.

"Well," she said. "If he's behind the previous two 'futsie' cases that occurred here, I'd definitely say he has a thing about dating couples, wouldn't you? I think we're looking at a sexually neurotic sociopath, intelligent but maybe not much of a thinker. And he's probably got some kind of grievance or fixation with this place."

They glided unopposed through a security checkpoint and entered a brightly-lit garden dominated by a pink statue, which rotated on a plinth outside the main doors.

Anderson parked beside the statue, recognising it as an enlarged replica of an old Brit-Cit landmark: a winged Grecian youth poised on tiptoe, clutching a stub gun in lieu of the original's bow and arrow. Nearby speakers hummed an instrumental version of 'Shooting Spree In My Heart' by Ramona Rae Cash as the statue's gun squirted intermittent volleys of holographic hearts.

"Classy," Anderson said.

Montana dismounted, laughing.

"You should meet the simp that runs this place."

Anderson studied the huge revolving figure. It turned towards her, its unblinking eyes meeting hers for an instant, before dowsing her with blood-red hearts.

Three

MONTANA WATCHED IN fascination as Anderson closed her eyes and listened for the thoughts of any living being who might be hiding behind the apartment door.

"He must be out," she said eventually. "No one in there but the cat."

"You can read cats?" Montana said.

"Not really," she said. "They don't speak human."

Montana pondered this for a moment then regarded the hab door. They had questioned the staff at the caff-bar that afternoon, and had the name and address of the guy who had been working the cash register at the time of the murder: Pablo Greggs, Hab 428, Food & Drink quarter of the Meet Market employee hab-zone. The walls of the corridor outside Greggs' front door were decorated with candy-stripes so vivid they shimmered if you stared at them for too long. But the air smelled like fresh laundry and the only sound that broke the surrounding hush was the hum of an approaching carpet-cleaner. As far as in-house employee habs were concerned, Anderson had visited a lot worse.

Judges must be here for Pablo, thought the guy on the carpet-cleaner.

Anderson turned and planted her foot on the hood of the cleaning buggy, forcing the man to brake.

"You got something to tell us, citizen?" she said, probing the man's thoughts.

"Nothing, Judge," said the man, a Mr Nubert Sully, his thoughts radiating a desire to finish his shift in time to catch drinks with his buddies. "I just figured you was here for Pablo."

"Why would you think that?" Montana said.

"I just heard Pablo got fired this afternoon," Sully said.

Montana glanced at Anderson.

"Why?" Anderson said.

"Got caught pocketing creds out the cash register after that poor guy got murdered," Sully said. "By the size of the greedy bastard, I'd say he stole his fair share of cupcakes too."

Didn't figure the company would press charges, he thought.

"Why wouldn't the company press charges?" Anderson said. "He stole money from them."

Sully looked bewildered. "No offence, but the company don't like getting the Judges involved unless it's something major."

"It's not up to the company to decide which crimes are major, citizen," Montana said, looming over him.

The poor guy was rattled, his thoughts coming fast but honest.

We look out for each other around here, he was thinking. *You work for Meet Market, you get treated like family. Oh, Grud, please don't bust me. I didn't do anything.*

One of the first things Anderson had learned about streetwork was that everyone lies. All the time. Witnesses, suspects, innocent cits, Judges, everyone. No wonder most Psi-Judges had a little swagger about them when dealing with the public. Being a walking lie detector was something of an advantage. Anderson could only imagine what it must be like for the grunts in Street-Div, patrolling the city with little more than a gun and hope.

"You know where Pablo is right now?" Anderson said, feeling bad for riding the poor guy so hard.

"No idea, Judge," Sully said. "But if he's out of a job he'll have twenty-four hours to find someplace else to live. That's the way it works around here."

"Thanks for your help, Nubert," she said, removing her foot from the buggy and standing aside. "And pay your Tri-D license before you get caught."

Sully stared at her, confounded, before trundling away down the corridor, his head down.

Montana hit the judicial override on Pablo's front door. It hissed open and he and Anderson peered inside. A small suitcase lay open on the bed, half-filled with clothes and toiletries. Several bin liners full of laundry were spilled about the floor. A cat, a clunky-looking synthetic, mewed at her from inside a pet carrier.

"Guy left his cat in the carrier," Montana said. "Was he in a hurry?"

Anderson found two sets of doorfobs in a bowl in the hallway and a pair of well-worn shoes by the door; it looked to her as though Greggs had not left the apartment. A cold breeze streamed through the living room, knocking an empty noodle carton to the floor. Montana appeared and beckoned her into the bedroom, motioning for her to be quiet. He pointed to a window forced open by the wind, curtains billowing. She could already hear the jangle of panicked thoughts emanating from outside.

Grud, please don't let them find me. I'm sorry I took that money. Dunno what I was thinking. Lemme live through this.

Anderson peered out the window, the night wind whipping at her hair and billowing in her ears.

"Pablo?" she said.

Pablo Greggs shuffled away from her, tiptoeing along a thin metal ledge, struggling to flatten his ample belly against a sheer wall of glass. The wind rippled the back of his T-shirt as he sobbed.

"Get away from me. I ain't going to no gruddamn cube."

"It's okay, Pablo," Anderson said, probing his temporal lobe for some reliable short-term memories. "We're not here about the money. We just need to talk to you."

Greggs ignored her, shuffling just out of her reach.

The boy's head was a blizzard, his thoughts shrieking, racing faster than Anderson could make sense of them. There was no way she could lift a coherent memory from that mess, although she managed to decipher a few basic facts. Minutes ago he had been packing his things, cursing himself for not calling his hated line manager an asshole, and wondering whether pawning his cat would raise enough money for a week in a hostel. Then he received a call from a buddy on front desk. Two Judges were on their way up to see him. Pablo panicked, suddenly possessed by the belief that hiding was his only option. Why not hide on the ledge outside the window? The Jays would never think to look for him out there. So far so awesome, until the initial terror wore off and Greggs realised he was just as scared of heights as he was of Judges.

Greggs paused and gazed at the world below, a chasm crisscrossed with bridges, each one streaming with tiny lights. The cold winds churned about him. Anderson heard the boy's thoughts start to swirl with vertigo. She would have no hope of reading a latent memory from Greggs' corpse if it was pasted to the slab two hundred stories below.

"I got this," Montana said, grabbing Anderson as she went to step out onto the ledge.

She tried to shrug him off.

"We need this guy's memory, Montana."

She lunged for Greggs' hand as he moved another inch out of reach.

"If I can touch him I might be able to read him."

Montana pulled her inside and removed his eagle and shoulder pad. He was a good head taller than her and had arms like a weightlifter. He tossed his helmet onto the bed along with his Lawgiver. Anderson realised it was the first time she had seen his face.

Montana moved out onto the window ledge as she dragged the sheet off the bed and looped it around his chest, winding her hands around either end of the makeshift rope.

"Okay, I got you," she said, as Montana extended his hand towards Greggs. Anderson held either end of the blanket as she reached out with her mind, wrestling Pablo's squirming thoughts, aiming to project a calming mantra into his frontal lobe.

"Hey there, buddy," Montana said, taking Greggs' trembling hand gently, as if about to lead him in a dance.

Greggs flinched, slipped and dropped screaming from the ledge.

Montana snatched the boy's wrist as the two of them fell. Anderson slammed her foot against the wall as she was jerked forwards, still clutching either end of the twisted blanket looped around Montana's chest. She heard the other Judge roar with pain as she braced her legs, locked in an impossible deadlift. Her arms felt like they were being torn from her shoulders. Greggs was screaming like an animal.

Montana yelled. "He's freaking out. I can't hold him."

Anderson felt Greggs jolting like a fish on a line.

"I gotta let go," Montana groaned.

Anderson ignored him, focusing instead on penetrating the boy's frenzied mind. She clawed her way through the hurricane of thoughts and burrowed into his frontal lobe, flooding it with a terrifying declaration.

You are going to die, Pablo Greggs.

Anderson felt the boy's thoughts flash like a popped light-bulb, then melt into silence. He had fainted with fright.

His burden no longer struggling, Montana managed to lock his arm around the ledge. Anderson grabbed him, and together they eventually landed Pablo Greggs on the bedroom floor like a fishing net full of Black Atlantic toona. The two Judges flopped beside him, panting.

"What the drokk has that kid been eating?" Montana said, grabbing his shoulder and wincing. "Rockrete?"

Anderson rose and shook the feeling back into her fingers. Montana watched as she pulled off her gloves and touched the boy's face, immersing herself in the silent blackness of his mind. Greggs' sleeping thoughts sounded like whalesong, slow and sonorous. She tuned them out, locating the hippocampus, which let out a barrage of short-term memories: screams, lights, bellowing wind, a breathtaking drop. She felt a pang of guilt for having to terrify the kid into submission.

Like a technician soldering circuits on a motherboard, Anderson inserted a dozen subliminals into the boy's mind, framing the episode with the Judges on the ledge outside as nothing more than a wild dream. She and Montana would place him on the bed, where he would wake up with nothing on his mind but the problem of where he was going to be sleeping tomorrow night.

Anderson hurried on, focusing hard to recall the mundane events of Greggs' working day. The memory she was looking for, that of the suspect's face as he had ordered his drink, would be barely encoded, just a routine detail blurred among countless others.

Memory retrieval was tricky at the best of times. The brain was not a filing cabinet in which everything was stored neatly in categories. First kiss? You'll find that in the occipital lobe. Mother's funeral? Have you tried the limbic system? No way. Memories had to be conjured using the entire brain, zapping a thousand different synapses all over the joint before you got a clear picture. And even then only the most skilled telepath could trust what they saw. Memories were living things, constantly evolving, constantly accommodating new information and experiences. They also mutated on contact with stuff like nostalgia, peer pressure, even advertising. Last month Anderson had been called in to scan a reluctant witness who genuinely believed the murder suspect they were after looked like the guy on the Umpty Candy commercial.

Sure enough, Greggs' memories of working at the caff-bar had blurred into a drone of taking orders, typing at the cash register and trying to flirt with the new girl. Anderson had to rely on visual cues to distinguish dates and times. Today, Greggs had returned from his lunch break ten minutes late, ignored an earful from his manager and logged into the cash register at 12:13. Over an hour later, Zak Mahoney and Reena Stanhope would be dead.

Anderson immersed herself in Greggs' memory until she could see it as her own. A girl with curls and dark eyes had stuck in Greggs' mind. So had the bearded guy who complained about the length of time he had spent queuing, as if he expected Greggs to do something about it. Greggs had taken this guy's order with barely concealed contempt before the suspect stepped into view. Same coat, same cap, same mop of black hair. He was even taller than Montana, but thinner: around 188cm, she guessed. His face was long, with sculpted cheekbones that emphasised his gauntness. His skin looked unnaturally pale and somehow stiff, like that of a corpse. His almond eyes did not seem to blink as he gazed like a serpent at the boy before him. The man had reminded Greggs of a radiant saint whose portrait his grandmother had on her kitchen wall when he was a child.

Anderson memorised the face, taking care not to let the image become moulded by her own preconceptions of the suspect. Once out of her trance, she would psychically transmit his likeness back to Psi-Div to compare with their records. But even with the technological advances in surveillance and facial re-cog, matching a suspect to a mugshot was not easy. Not in Mega-City One. Citizens changed their bodies as casually as they changed their clothes. Face-changing clinics were bound by law to provide before-and-after photos, but such paperwork was often either wilfully incorrect or got lost in the Justice Department's labyrinthine filing system. These days, many clinics were unlicensed and even the most lightweight criminal gangs had a surgeon on their books. The creep Anderson was looking at right now could last week have been a hundred-and-fifty-kilo woman named Delilah.

Anderson knew that a face summoned out of the ether would not be enough to convince Chief Hauser, and she had less than 10 hours in which to find something concrete. She knew she could not wait for Psi-Div to compare records and give her a file, if one even existed, or for surveillance to give her a GPS of the suspect's current location. She heard Greggs take the creep's order and ask if he would like a ticket for tonight's 'Face-2-Face Friday' event.

"Thank you," said the man, smirking at a private joke. "But I have one already."

"WE HAVE EVIDENCE this man will be attending your gathering tonight," Anderson said, standing over the Meet Market technician. "So with that in mind can you explain exactly what you mean when you say this guy doesn't exist?"

Anderson could feel one of her headaches coming on. The technician swallowed.

"The picture you've given me," he said. "It matches the one on this account right here. But the account's not real. It's all made up. It's a bait profile. We create them ourselves to attract subscribers."

He looked up at Montana, pleading.

"All dating agencies use them. We work strictly within the legal limits."

"What about the face?" Montana said, tapping the screen, indicating a profile picture that was the exact likeness of the image Anderson had retrieved from the memory of Pablo Greggs.

"It's computer-generated," the technician said. "Along with everything else."

"And yet someone with that face and using that account accessed this building at 10:48 this morning," Anderson said. "They got past a membership scan and a facial re-cog. How?"

"I don't know, Judge," the technician said, helpless. "I work surveillance, not profiling." *Please don't cube me*, he thought. *I got kids. I can't afford to lose this job.*

Montana gripped the man's chair and swung him round.

"Then give us the names of everyone in charge of membership, profiling, and tek," he said. "Anyone who might know who activated that profile and who might be using it right now."

The technician grabbed the vidphone and started making calls to the other departments. The rows of monitor-jockeys surrounding them in Meet Market's Surveillance Hall were doing their best to ignore the two Judges in their midst. Holographic displays dilated and shifted on every wall, mapping the various levels of the block. Anderson could hear nervous thoughts pattering about her like rain. One guy had clocked her Psi badge and was desperately trying to think of anything other than the score of unpaid parking tickets he had dumped in the recycling shredder that morning. Montana took her to one side.

"I hate to ask, Anderson, but..."

"No, Montana," she said. "I'm not imagining this guy. How else do you explain him showing up on the security cams?"

"I know," he said. "I just had to hear you say that."

Anderson said nothing, deep in thought.

"So this guy somehow activated a dead account," Montana said. "An account that was only accessed once and that was today. So what about the previous two murders?"

"He could have more of these ghost accounts floating around," Anderson said.

"And changed his face to match every one of them?" Montana said. "Is this guy a mutie? Some kind of shapeshifter?"

"Uh-uh," she said. "Our guy's too camera-shy. Why make the effort to hide if you can shapeshift? No, he's a norm."

"A norm who has someone on the inside?"

Anderson nodded.

"So what's our play?" he said. "If this guy's coming tonight, he could be here in less than an hour."

A tall man in a gold frock strode into the Surveillance Hall on heels so high they may as well have been stilts. His hair was a mushroom cloud of pink curls teased into the shape of a huge pair of wings.

"Cupid Van Doren," he said, sidling up to Montana. "Welcome to the block that love built, Judge..." He peered at Montana's badge. "Montana? Why, you sound suitably mountainous."

Montana stared at Van Doren's beard, which had been dyed crimson and woven into the shape of a heart, covering the man's chest like a baby's bib.

"Now I hear you're conducting an investigation," Van Doren said. "May I ask into what? It was my understanding that the woman responsible for today's tragedy was killed."

"I'm afraid it's a little more complicated than that," Anderson said.

Van Doren turned and looked down at her, his smile tightening.

"Well colour me intrigued," he said. "So long as it doesn't clash with my shoes."

Aren't you a little young to be a Judge, blondie? Van Doren thought.

Anderson frowned.

"We're looking for a man in connection with our current investigation," she said. "We believe he may be attending this event you're hosting tonight; 'Face-2-Face Friday,' is that correct?"

Van Doren nodded, his thoughts quickening. *Another futsie? What the drokk is going on? What do we have to do to keep these crazies out?*

"Could you explain what tonight's event entails?" Anderson said.

"Of course," Van Doren said, preoccupied. "Every Friday we run an open house where our guests can bid on each other face-to-face instead of online. Tonight's our busiest night of the year, it being Valentine's Weekend an' all. So we open up three extra levels to accommodate demand."

Can't have Judges trampling around here tonight, Van Doren thought. *The little one's a Psi. Can she hear what I'm thinking?*

"Might I ask what is the nature of your investigation?" Van Doren said, indicating the stairs. "In my office, perhaps?"

The Judges stood their ground as Anderson explained how the suspect was using a false account.

"We can detain him once he's been identified by your security staff on the front door," she said.

Montana looked unsure.

Anderson could see Van Doren's frantic thoughts blossoming into images: Judges rampaging through the building, shots fired, screams, newsfeed headlines, a profit margin continuing its nosedive into the red.

"I assure you, there'll be no risk to your staff or guests," Anderson said. "Now, if I could speak to your Head of Security?"

Van Doren nodded, causing the wings in his hair to flap, and turned to a vidphone on a nearby console. Montana nudged Anderson.

"You sure about this?" he said.

"Creep doesn't know we're coming," she said. "If we can get the drop on him, I can contain him, no problem."

"We gotta be sure, Anderson," he said. "We don't want this guy lighting up anyone carrying a piece, whether that's us or their security guys."

"I'm not taking any chances, Montana. I wanna nail him straight away."

"Hey, it's your call," he said. "I'm just not sure going head-on is the best way to deal with this guy. I've seen psychos go for broke the second they see the uniform."

Oh, Grud, they might cube me for this.

Anderson turned to Van Doren, who looked back, stroking his beard and trying to appear defiant.

"What did you just do, citizen?" Anderson said, approaching.

"I cancelled the party," Van Doren said. "All the guests are going home."

Anderson thrust her finger in Van Doren's face and bellowed.

"Get on that vidphone right now and cancel that order."

Everyone looked up from their monitors; a few removed their headsets. Montana hesitated, confused, as Van Doren stamped his foot and glowered at the Judges.

"I am legally entitled to protect my guests and staff," he said. "And I am not about to allow another crazy onto my premises."

Anderson glanced at a nearby surveillance screen. Vehicles were turning away from the building. Staff were starting to clear tables and shut down bars.

"Van Doren, you're turning away our suspect," Anderson said.

"You're also looking at six months and counting," Montana said, producing a set of cuffs.

"I doubt it, Judge Montana," he said. "I'm confident my lawyers will have little trouble arguing my decision was in the best interests of public safety. He might even question the possibility of rash decisions being made by a couple of unseasoned Judges."

Anderson glanced again at the surveillance screen. A queue of vehicles were now in retreat. Her suspect could be among them, disappearing back into the city, saving his strength for some future atrocity.

"You've already lost half a day's revenue on level six after what happened at the caff-bar," Anderson said. "How much more do you think this little stunt will cost you?"

"It'll cost me a lot less in the long run, Judge Anderson," Van Doren said. "If I let you go chasing another futsie around my premises, then the headlines alone will ruin me."

Every technician in the room was listening, murmuring in awe as the boss faced down a couple of Judges.

"Meet Market is a sanctuary, Judge Anderson," said Van Doren. "One of the few places in the city where people like us don't have to fear people like you."

"I think you've forgotten who you're talking to, citizen," Montana said, moving in, cuffs poised.

Anderson held him back.

"Van Doren," she said. "The man we're after isn't a futsie. But we believe he may have orchestrated the previous incidents that have taken place on these premises."

Van Doren listened, appalled, as Anderson continued.

"Those crazies that somehow got past your securityware? One man's to blame. He's targeting your business, and if we don't catch him tonight, we may not catch him until he's killed a whole lot more, maybe even brought down your entire company."

Anderson heard Van Doren's mind racing, seeking the sanest possible option.

"Now there's a way we can do this quietly," Anderson said. "Without the uniforms, but we'll need your help."

Montana looked at her.

"Bring your guests back here," Anderson said. "Host your evening as planned. We can take this creep down without firing a single shot and none of your guests will know it even happened."

Van Doren hesitated.

"Undecided?" Anderson said. "Wondering if your lawyer

49

can still back you up? Not now you're obstructing an official undercover operation."

You can hear me, right? thought Van Doren, staring at her.

Anderson nodded.

Thanks to those futsies or whoever you're telling me is behind all this, my company is now on the bones of its ass. Another repeat performance, so much as a single shot fired in this block tonight, and half the people in this room are going to lose their jobs by the end of next month. Think about that while you're out there gambling with our future.

Van Doren smiled, as though nothing had passed between them, then spoke into his vidphone.

"Yes, that's right," he said. "'Face-2-Face Friday' is back on. Tell them we apologise for the mistake and the first one hundred guests to reach the bar will find a free drink waiting for them. And tell wardrobe we have a couple of special visitors that require a change of clothes."

He looked the Judges up and down, a malicious smile creeping across his face.

"Nothing too subtle," he said. "They'll need to blend in, after all."

Four

ANDERSON FINISHED STUFFING her Lawgiver into her purse.

"Now where am I supposed to put these?" she said, holding up her badge, cuffs and an extra clip. Montana struggled for a reply. She couldn't blame him; the way he had been dressed by Van Doren's people reminded Anderson of a cross-dressing pimp she had once arrested for loitering.

She tried to ignore the thoughts whispering in Montana's head whenever he looked at her. Her own outfit seemed to consist almost entirely of windows.

She called to Miss Falcone, Meet Market's Head of Surveillance, who was perched on the sofa typing into a handheld computer.

"Hey, can I at least get a bigger purse?" she asked. "And maybe another earpiece. This one keeps falling out."

Falcone answered without looking up.

"Not now we're moving," she said.

Another floor swept into view, moving left to right behind the window of their portable suite. This level appeared to contain a Splurgeball maze, in which Meet Market guests wearing armour scampered through neon-lit corridors blasting each other with paint-loaded bazookas. The Judges' suite had previously passed through a sky-surfing arena, graffiti classes, and something involving trampolines and cake.

"How many guests you got here tonight, Falcone?" Anderson said, tugging down the hem of her skirt and frowning at a box containing a pair of spike-heeled shoes.

"We're predicting only around eighteen thousand, that's three thousand on each floor," Falcone said. "Numbers have been slipping every Friday since we had our first futsie."

Montana shook his head.

"That's a lot of ground, Anderson," he said. "And we can't rely on our boy using the same account twice."

"It doesn't matter what he looks like, Montana," she said, struggling with her shoes. "It's what he'll be thinking that counts. He's gonna be the only one who didn't come here looking for a date."

She stood up, grabbing the arm of her chair for support.

"That'll make it real easy for me to pick him out."

Falcone looked up and spoke.

"Also, we're analysing the accounts of every guest who checks in. If we find anyone who shouldn't be there, we'll use facial re-cog to pick him out so you guys can move in. Our internal security also know you're here. They'll be on hand if you require assistance."

"Best if they stay out the way," Montana said.

The Splurgeball maze was replaced by a colonic irrigation hall. Couples lay on their sides and chatted, seemingly oblivious to the burly hoover-bots labouring behind them.

Anderson blinked.

"Who says romance is dead?"

"Okay, your Halos are ready," Falcone said, detaching a small box from the side of her computer.

"My what?" Anderson said.

Falcone opened the box and picked out a flexible metal disc the size of a penny.

"Hold still," she said, as she pressed it against Anderson's forehead. "I've only just inputted the activation code. It takes a few seconds to kick in."

Anderson felt the disc magnetise to her brainwaves, extracting a stream of psi-vapour as gently as a kiss. A holographic band sprang to life, encircling her head like the brim of a hat. Lettering revolved around the circumference.

<<<HI! I'M BLONDIE LEWIS. I'M 20. I'M A HAIRDRESSER FROM MEG RYAN BLOCK<<<

"It's basically a low-level psionic amplifier," Falcone said. "Completely legal, of course. It can't reveal what you're thinking, just changes colour depending on your mood. Helps break the ice among the guests. The rest is just your profile information. Mr Van Doren insisted on writing that for you."

Montana's Halo appeared as Anderson looked again at the words circling her head.

<<<I LIKE KITTENS, PILLOWFIGHTS, AND GUYS IN UNIFORM<<<

Anderson frowned, her Halo turning from black to red.

The suite came to a stop. Falcone retrieved something from her pocket and handed it to Anderson. It was a smooth black handle with a wristband dangling from one end and a trigger embedded at the other.

"You'll get the idea," Falcone said, hurrying her towards the door.

"Keep in touch, Montana," Anderson said. "And remember, don't go near this creep unless I'm with you."

"Roger that," he said, his Halo turning from black to blue.

Anderson toppled into a lamp. Cursing, she pulled off her shoes and threw them aside.

"You wanna walk around in bare feet, Anderson?" Montana said. "You're supposed to be inconspicuous."

"Believe me, Montana," she said. "In this dress, my feet are the last thing anyone's gonna be looking at."

* * *

ANDERSON STEPPED ONTO an indoor street. Musclebound guests in revealing gym-wear laboured beneath weight machines lining the pavement. They were observed by the passing crowds, whose coloured Halos jostled like umbrellas. Anderson shivered, her feet already cold upon the gritty floor. Huge air vents whirred in the ceiling.

"Sorry it's a little fresh in there," Falcone said through Anderson's concealed earpiece. Anderson discreetly pressed the device more securely into her ear canal.

"We have to regulate the temperature in there. Body heat interferes with the Halos."

"Where's Montana?"

"Level one-oh-one," he said. "I'm on a bouncy castle."

Anderson stifled a laugh.

"Okay, I'll work my way up. Call me if you find anything. I'm starting my sweep."

Falcone and Montana signed off as a huge holographic image of Van Doren's head appeared above Anderson, the wings of his hair spreading over the crowd as he boomed down at them like a cheerful god.

"I'm seeing a lot of new faces here tonight," he said. "But don't be shy. Pull those triggers and bust those bids."

Anderson ignored him and headed towards the bar. The weight machines clanked like robots amid a confusion of bleeps, whistles and *ker-chings*. The guests appeared to be aiming their trigger devices at the people exercising, scanning them like groceries at the checkout. Anderson looked up as her Halo rang with a *ker-ching*.

<<<CURRENT BID: 80 CREDS<<<

A handsome young man finished scanning her and waved.

"Hi, I'm Royce," he said. "See you later, maybe?"

He departed with a smile. Anderson regarded her own trigger

for a moment, then tossed it towards the trash. She missed the bin, and as she stooped to pick up the device, a dozen *ker-chings* sounded above her head.

<<<CURRENT BID: 1,793 CREDS<<<

She cursed, wriggling and tugging at the hem of her skirt as she hurried to the bar.

A bartender resembling a shaved gorilla recommended some kind of protein shake. She declined and ordered a blue tea instead. A bulky man wearing probably the only tasteful suit in the building stood by an exit. He nodded at her. One of Van Doren's security guys. She looked away. She had done undercover work as a cadet, but the experience had not been to her taste. Listening in on people's thoughts while wearing a badge was one thing, but sneaking into people's heads without their knowledge felt downright creepy. She took a long sip of her warm tea and tuned out the incessant *ker-chings*, laughter, whoops and catcalls. The guests' excited thoughts sounded like a monsoon on a tin roof.

Talk to her. Keep your shoulders back like the article said...

Hope Xavier finds out I'm here. Maybe then he'll know what it's like to...

Can always take out another loan. Just keep bidding...

But Anderson was looking for a train of thought in a much deeper register, brisk but steady, a predator seeking prey, not a citizen giddy with excitement at the prospect of a three-day weekend. The suspect had done this before, and would be feeling calm and secure in the knowledge that no one was yet onto him.

"Excuse me, are you a Judge?"

Anderson's heart leapt and she turned to catch a man with a moustache staring at her cleavage.

"Because my heart feels like it's been arrested."

He looked up and grinned.

Two drinks, Byron, my man, and she'll be good to go, he thought.

"I don't think so, Byron," Anderson said. "Now go home before your girlfriend finds out you're using all your lines on someone else."

Byron's face dropped, his Halo swirling from green to yellow. Anderson handed him her empty glass and patted his cheek, before departing to continue her sweep.

THREE HOURS LATER, Anderson emerged from an aquarium containing underwater baking classes, and entered something called 'The Fitzgerald Suite.' The area appeared to be a ballroom designed by someone who believed the 1920s was the era of flower power. She picked her way between the bob-haired flappers dancing to Jimi Hendrix, until she found the ladies room.

Anderson set down her purse with a clunk, drawing glances from the women retouching their make-up at the sinks either side of her. The inescapable fresh air had soaked into her joints. She was trained in the use of a Tibetan breathing technique that could raise the body's temperature, but this made it even more difficult to maintain her scan, so she had given up and let the cold sink in. Her feet ached, her temples throbbed, and she had left her aspirin in Van Doren's changing room.

Falcone had not been in touch; Anderson had kept checking her earpiece to make sure it had not fallen out. No one had anything to report. Evidently, the suspect had not checked in with the same account they had used before. Nor had Falcone's people found a ghost profile attached to anyone who had entered the building. Anderson figured everyone who was going to arrive tonight would have done so hours ago. Maybe the suspect had decided not to show. After all, why risk another hit so soon after the last one?

Anderson splashed her face with water and heard something rattle into the sink. She opened her eyes in time to see her earpiece disappear down the plughole. She swore and slammed her hands on the counter.

"You lose an earring, honey?" said the woman beside her, her Halo nodding. "I hate that."

Anderson stared at her, her own Halo boiling red.

She felt as though the entire case was crumbling around her. The more she tried to compute what little evidence she had, the less it seemed to make sense. She had clearly got carried away, led everyone on a bug hunt. You can't afford to feel anything, Hauser had said. Kinda tricky when you had a direct line into the head of every single person living in this madhouse of a city. That was something the gorillas in Street-Div would never understand.

Anderson heard something whistling in the same angry frequency as her own thoughts.

Eros, child of love and strife...

The words were perched on a screaming gamma note, the kind you heard when the subject was in the throes of spiritual revelation or psychotic breakdown.

God of love now turned to hate, reborn corrupted by a corrupt world...

It sounded like a prayer, recited in devotion—to one's self, or someone else; Anderson could not tell. The speaker was male, older, and his thoughts seemed to sparkle with hatred, just like those of Reena Stanhope. Anderson looked up, then leaped onto the counter, as the other women nervously retrieved their purses and stepped back. Anderson touched the ceiling and listened again.

Punish those who have scorned me, who desecrate love's perfect sanctity.

The thoughts were coming from the floor above, but they were fading. The target was moving. If she was going to catch him, she needed to do so now. She did not have time to relay a message to Falcone or Montana. Anderson realised the other women were staring up at her.

"You okay?" said one.

"I thought I saw a rad-rat," Anderson said.

The women shrieked, scattering the contents of their makeup bags, as Anderson leaped down, peeling the metal disc from her forehead and dissolving her Halo. She grabbed her purse with both hands and ran outside, searching for the nearest set of stairs.

MONTANA WAS PATROLLING the outskirts of the dino-polo arena, his Halo clouded purple, deep in thought, when he got the call from Falcone.

"We've found something," she said. "It's another bait profile. The guy who's using it is in the Rave Hall. That's suite three-oh-two, east quad, level one-oh-six."

Montana was already jogging towards the nearest elevator and smacked the call button.

"Our guy?"

"His face doesn't match the one you gave us, but it's somehow the same as the CG picture on this account."

Montana stepped inside the elevator, closing the doors before anyone could join him.

"Where's Anderson?" he said, hitting the directional key for 106, east quad.

"She's not responding," Falcone said. "We lost her somewhere in the Fitzgerald Suite on one-oh-six, not far from your man."

"Keep looking for her. Let me know as soon as you find her. I'm en route to the suspect's position."

"We already have security in the area."

"Don't crowd him. He'll know you're onto him."

Montana groaned with impatience as the keypad light crawled from button to button towards level 106.

* * *

ANDERSON PEERED OUT at the man she had followed through a darkened, open-plan office. She had crept from desk to desk behind him, her purse clamped between her teeth, dance music thudding up through the carpet from the suite below, throbbing against her bare feet. The man finally switched on an overhead lamp, activated a console, and pulled up a chair. She watched from behind a filing cabinet as he withdrew something from his pocket, plugged it into the console and sat down, clasping his hands. That same prayer had been stuck on repeat in his head for the last five minutes, every word sounding to Anderson like a knifepoint scribbling on a chalkboard.

Eros, child of love and strife, whose arrows once inflamed the hearts of the Hellenes...

Sitting alone in an empty office reciting prayers to forgotten gods was a pretty weird thing to do, even for a tek guy. So feverish was his recital, so unbreakable his belief in every word, Anderson struggled to distinguish the guy's name. Time to break his concentration. She withdrew her badge and Lawgiver from her purse, and sidled up behind him. Peering over his shoulder, she could see his console had several applications running, but could not determine what they were doing. She placed her Lawgiver within reach on a table behind her, just as she caught his name amid the din of prayer inside his head.

"Randall Rockfeather," she said.

The man jumped and spun around in his chair.

She grinned and brandished her badge.

"Mind if I ask you a couple of questions?"

THE RAVE HALL engulfed Montana in a riot of coloured lights. The bass line pounded inside his chest. He surveyed the room and clocked the suspect straight away: the only good-looking guy in the room who was drinking alone. He was sat at one of the tables near the bar that surrounded the dancefloor. A tall, elegant man, his Halo radiating innocent white.

Montana saw two of Van Doren's security guys standing nearby, covering the exit. One of them kept glancing at the suspect. Montana grabbed a discarded drink from a nearby table and sauntered along the bar towards the suspect's opposite flank, maintaining a discreet view of both the suspect and the imprudent security guards. Anderson had said the suspect was not a mind-reader, but he wouldn't have to be to notice the two vultures lurking over his shoulder. If these guys weren't careful, the suspect would be forced to make a move before Anderson got here.

The suspect pretended to watch a girl leave the dancefloor, turning his head just enough to confirm the presence of the two goons standing behind him, both of whom were dumb enough to glare right back at him. The suspect returned his attention to the dancefloor.

Game over, thought Montana. *Sorry, Anderson. This is my show now.* Move in, hold the guy's shoulder and throw a right into his chin. That was how Street-Div tackled rogue psykers. Montana would have him dazed and bundled out the exit before any of the guests knew what had happened. Pretty cool, huh, Anderson? He felt for the Lawgiver tucked uncomfortably down the back of his pants as he shouldered his way more urgently through the drinkers and talkers in his path.

The suspect gulped the last of his drink and left his glass on the table as he stepped down onto the dancefloor. One of the security guards, drokkhead that he was, moved after him, but his buddy hung back. Montana watched as the hesitant guard suddenly drew a zap-stick from his belt, jammed it into his partner's throat and lit him up. The guy jiggled on the spot for a moment, then dropped to the floor, still twitching.

Montana barged through the crowd, as the guard caught a man standing nearby, grabbing him by the neck of his shirt and hurling him down onto a table, scattering glasses. Montana looked for the suspect, but he had disappeared into a pool of swirling lights and dancing bodies. Montana heard screams pierce the pounding music as the maddened guard went to stab his zap-stick into the face of the struggling guest.

Montana caught the guard's arm before it could descend. Locking the man's head, he then swung him around into a nearby pillar. The guard's face connected with the rockcrete and he dropped to the floor, senseless.

Montana searched the floor; he had felt his Lawgiver slip from his belt as he turned. The weapon had bounced under a nearby table. Everyone was too busy staring at the unconscious guards to see it lying there. Everyone but the suspect, who stood looking at the Justice Department weapon, then at Montana, his face registering the connection. Montana sprang towards the suspect, grabbing his collar as he turned to flee. Montana wrenched him backwards, but the suspect turned and clapped his hands either side of Montana's face.

Montana felt something like an electric current pass through him, and the shifting lights above him seemed to blacken, as though veiled by a sheet of descending arrows. He felt the curious sensation of pins and needles in his head. He looked at his hands and dimly realised the man he had been restraining had vanished.

"Judge Montana, he's getting away," Falcone was yelling through his earpiece.

Irritated, Montana picked the device from his ear and tossed it away. He remained on the dancefloor, suddenly fascinated by the bodies whirling around him. So free. Montana felt overwhelmed. He watched the girls, their long hair sweeping their faces, their hips swaying, breasts bobbing, their bodies bathed in the light of their coloured Halos. He stared helplessly at a girl with short blonde hair as she draped an arm over the shoulder of her dancing partner, drawing him in for a kiss. Montana's stomach tightened. He felt as though a gulf had opened up inside him, a chasm that could never be filled. His Halo turned vivid green as the man moved his hand around the girl's waist, pressing her body against him. Montana went to retrieve his Lawgiver.

"LESSON ONE," ANDERSON said, hauling Randall Rockfeather off the floor and back into his chair. "Never try and hit a lady around the head with a table lamp, especially when she can hear what you're thinking. And lesson two, never try and run from a Judge."

Rockfeather whimpered, clutching his bloody nose as she cuffed him to the desk.

Interesting. A hate-filled crazy would have gone for her throat, not made a break for the nearest exit. This guy appeared curiously sane. He was around 160cm, pot-bellied, late fifties. Not even close to the image of the psyker she had pulled from the memory of Pablo Greggs. Rockfeather had one of those logical angular minds, a lot like the guys in Tek Division. His thoughts rang with the tenor of certainty and experience, but also with a note of anxiety and bitterness, of never being listened to despite his obvious talents.

"What are you doing up here, citizen?" Anderson said.

"Overtime," Rockfeather said.

The guy's thoughts felt like blades, although not as sharp as those Anderson had heard inside the poisoned mind of Reena Stanhope.

Rockfeather swore and struggled as she caught his wrist and placed her hand on his head, reaching into his memory core. His mind bristled with tiny black needles, dozens of them. Instead of giving Rockfeather both barrels like he had done to Reena Stanhope, the psyker appeared to have performed some kind of psychic acupuncture. Nothing fatal, but targeting all the right synapses so as to inhibit just enough reason and restraint, while focusing all that bitterness and resentment. Perfect motivation for carrying out precision tasks, such as activating bait profiles or passing on data on potential targets. Whether Rockfeather knew it or not, he was a puppet, a psychic slave, what Psi-Div called a 'Renfield.' Anderson had found her inside man. *Eat it, Hauser.*

Something was bleeping on the desk. Anderson opened her eyes and saw some kind of data stick flashing on Rockfeather's console. One of the applications on the screen read, 'Transmission in progress.'

She was about to ask Rockfeather what it was, when screams and gunfire erupted from the floor below.

Five

A POUNDING BASS line hammered Anderson's ears as she burst into the Rave Hall and aimed her Lawgiver. Spotlights swirled and flashed, sweeping over abandoned tables and chairs as the panicked guests crammed into the exits. Through the flickering gloom Anderson could see one of the suited security guys squirming on the dancefloor, clutching what looked like a gunshot wound in his leg, while two of his colleagues struggled to restrain a frenzied guest. The guest threw the first guard aside, then kicked away the other, before retrieving a pistol from the floor.

Anderson dropped to one knee and took aim for the centre mass. Then a flash of light revealed the gunman's face as he turned, staring strangely at his own weapon.

"Montana?"

He looked up. His mind thundered with hatred, joyous and unrestrained, fiercer than anything Anderson had heard before. He recognised her and his face curdled into a snarl. She dived as he fired at her. The bullet sang past her head and she landed behind an upturned metal table, flinching as Montana's next two shots punched twin dents into the metal shield, inches from her face.

Armour piercing, she heard him think.

As he uttered the words, she touched her temple and threw a blast of psionic energy into his head. He cried out in pain, barely audible above the rampant music. She peered out from behind the table. The blast should have been enough to drop him, but the rage that possessed him must have dampened her attack. He staggered as though drunk, wheeling to face the last of the fleeing crowd. Growling in pain and frustration, he took aim at a random panicked figure.

Anderson dropped her Lawgiver and sprang at him, grabbing his wrist with both hands before he could fire. She swung his arm back towards the empty Rave Hall, away from the crowd. He went to hurl her aside, but she kicked out his knee, still clutching his wrist as he dropped to the floor. He struggled, firing three times into the ceiling as she flipped him onto his back, landing beside him as she flung her leg down across his throat, pinning him. He choked and fired another armour-piercer. The bullet zipped through a rockcrete pillar, shattering a mirror behind it. Her ears ringing from the shot, Anderson could hear his thoughts bellowing above the deafening music.

Drokking bitch! I'll blow your head off!

Years of discipline consumed by an inferno of hate. The psyker must have hit him with everything he had.

Montana turned his head, grinning as he brought the barrel of his Lawgiver level with Anderson's face. She caught his neck between her legs and threw him back down, as he fired again. She felt the puff of air against her cheek as the weapon discharged. Ears still ringing, she wrenched Montana's arm and twisted the weapon from his grip. She tensed, squeezing his throat between her thighs until she felt his lights go out.

Anderson untangled herself from Montana's unconscious body and kicked his Lawgiver out of reach. Her hands shook with adrenaline as she retrieved a pair of cuffs from his pants pocket and secured him to the bar-rail. She hoped the effects of the hate-blast would wear off once he woke up, although she wondered whether such an overwhelming blast of psi-energy could be shaken off so easily. The battered security guys had recovered and were tending their buddy with the leg wound. The poor guy must have got to Montana before he could fire into the crowd.

Anderson sprinted from the room, leaving her Lawgiver behind. No sense scaring the already panicked guests or alerting the psyker that she was onto him. The creep would have no idea what she looked like. She dashed through an emptied casino, arms pumping at her sides, bare feet pounding the carpeted floor as she followed the trail of toppled furniture and frantic thoughts. The psyker had been in the Rave Hall only minutes ago. Now he would be heading towards the nearest exit, passing himself off as just another guest fleeing for his life. She could still catch him.

She caught up with the crowd feeding into the main exit. An automated voice chirped through the PA system, advising guests to calmly make their way towards the exits and await the arrival of the Justice Department. Staff and security were trying to herd guests through the emergency exits, but, having just heard shots fired, everyone was scattering through anything that looked like an escape route. Anderson tuned into the lower frequencies, figuring the psyker's thoughts would be the only ones in the block not wailing like a siren. The creep knew he had to get out of the building before the Judges arrived. She recognised a thought to her right and dodged a security guard. She emerged onto a landing edged with a balcony, which overlooked the city and the Meet Market lobby some hundred stories below.

Head down. Follow the herd.

His thoughts sounded as rich and melodic as his voice. They came from her right, where more Meet Market ushers were attempting to prevent a rush of citizens from piling into a huge glass elevator. These vessels carried fifty or so guests at a time, ascending and descending in a wide corkscrew around the inside of the block, and offering views of both the city outside and the attractions stationed at each level inside.

Anderson sprinted for the elevator as the doors began to close. She slotted herself through the narrowing gap, crashing into the citizens crowded within. The doors sealed and the elevator descended. The control panel counted down the time it would take to reach the ground floor. Less than five minutes.

Anderson gasped for breath, her heart hammering. He was somewhere in here with her. The terrified guests believed they had reached safety. Some collapsed into sobs or hugged each other. Others just stared into the middle distance and panted like dogs. Someone called out to see if anyone was hurt. Only a few Halos remained, all of them bright red and flickering. Anderson peered through the crowd, thinking she could use a pair of high heels about now. She gave up and listened instead, enveloping herself in a cloud of gasping thoughts.

Could have been shot...

Was standing right next to him...

Just get home...

How'd he get a gun in here anyway...?

One stream of thoughts flowed steady amid the rain of chatter.

Lawgiver. Undercover Judge. Never hit anyone that hard before. Killed him? Doubt he was alone.

The thoughts, slow and assured, emanated from somewhere in front of her. She peered through the press of bodies, looking towards the other side of the elevator as it continued its descent. She shouldered past two sobbing women, and saw a tall man wearing a white sports jacket embroidered with a pair of black wings. He stood motionless, gripping the handrail, and staring out the window as the floors rose past him. She tuned into his forebrain and, sure enough, it was full of crazy.

I am love turned to hate. I am spirit corrupted. I am Eros reborn.

This guy knew who he was alright. His addled brain was reminding him every second. This was the 'Eros' to whom Rockfeather had been praying.

An image flashed before her eyes: a black arrow, streaking towards her face.

She threw up her hands instinctively, as though reacting to a dream. He must have felt her probing him. She could already feel the toxic psi-bolt soaking into her mind. She stepped back into the two women behind her, as she fought to contain the fire now igniting her brain. Eros still had his back to her, still staring down at the lobby far below.

"You okay?" someone asked.

Anderson felt hands on her. She spun around, catching a man's wrist. He yelped in pain and she had to resist the temptation to twist his hand until she felt bones crack. She released him and he stared at her, horrified.

"What's wrong with you?" someone said.

Anderson looked into the frightened, bewildered faces surrounding her, people too stupid to even care that she was risking her life to protect them. She wished she had her boot-knife. That might wake these piggies up a little.

Anderson dropped to her knees, horrified by her own imaginings. She seized upon that moment of sanity and held her hands in front of her, as though pushing against an invisible wall. Aching with the desire to leap up and drive her thumbs into someone's eyes, Anderson curled her hands into fists and imagined holding a black arrow between them.

Psi cadets were taught to visualise every task. If you were on the shooting range, you had to visualise yourself hitting the target. If you were probing a resistant suspect, you imagined breaking down a wall. Without visualisation, you were just wrestling smoke. Anderson concentrated, ignoring the panicky voices surrounding her. She felt the arrow wriggle like an eel as it tried to escape and burrow into her heart. She had contained the negative psi-energy that Eros had fired into her head, but he was pushing from the other side, straining to visualise his arrow burning through her hands, swallowing her arms with beautiful black fire. The two psychics struggled like duellists locking swords.

Anderson shuddered and glanced up. The frightened guests were backing away from her, obscuring Eros. She could feel his energy, strong and steady.

I can't hear your thoughts, mortal, but I take it you can hear mine, he thought. *I hope you can hold out long enough for this elevator to reach the bottom. A young woman with your training should be able to kill her way through an elevator full of frightened citizens in less than a minute.*

His thoughts were so articulate. He did not seem to be breaking a sweat. Anderson found herself imagining the arrow consuming her hands, burning them to charcoal. She tried to push back as the blackness crept up to her arms, filling her with the desire to abandon herself to hatred.

I can feel your fear, fear for the safety of your fellows, Eros thought. *A rare virtue. I would spare you if I thought for a moment that you would understand.*

What's there to understand? Anderson thought, struggling to steady herself.

Eros replied. *I am trying to save our souls.*

Anderson locked her mind around the image of the arrow in her hands while reaching out for the mind taunting her from the other side of the elevator. The arrow twisted in her grip. He was turning up the juice, and making it look easy. The fire reached her shoulders now, filling her body with delicious rage.

You are in the presence of the city's saviour.

Anderson found his synapses, just as she felt the last of her defences give way.

And you're in the presence of Psi-Division, creep!

She let go and blasted him, screaming a torrent of psionic energy into his occipital lobe until she felt him go blind. The crowd turned as Eros howled and dropped to the floor. The arrow in Anderson's hands vanished and she toppled forward, her body exhausted. A couple tried to help Eros to his feet, but he shook them off. Seizing her advantage, Anderson touched her temples and rained psi-bolts into him too quick for him to counter, aiming to short-circuit his brain into shutdown. He was untrained, and could not raise any kind of psionic shield to defend himself. But his mind had been strengthened by madness. It was like punching a slab of beef.

Anderson looked up. Through blurred vision, she could see Eros reeling as the elevator settled on the ground floor and its doors slid open. The fearful guests abandoned the stricken pair and tumbled out into the lobby, where the uniformed security guards who worked the front doors were ushering a stream of guests outside. The disembodied voice on the PA system was assuring anyone who would listen that the Justice Department would arrive shortly. Anderson felt Eros weaken beneath her assault. Then he reached for one of the security guards, probing his mind.

She reined in her attack as she went to block him, but it was too late. Eros had already sent a black arrow screaming into the guard's mind. The man stared at the departing crowd, his hand wandering to the pistol at his hip. Eros staggered to his feet, taking advantage of Anderson's divided attention to wrench himself free of her psionic grip. Her body still exhausted, she gathered her mind to land one last blow, just as the guard drew his pistol and took aim at the fleeing crowd. She released Eros, threw out her hand towards the guard and shrieked into the man's mind, flooding it with deafening static. The guard collapsed, his pistol clattering to the floor.

Her energies spent, Anderson felt nauseous and dizzy, then

realised someone was stroking her cheek. She looked up into a pair of unblinking green eyes.

"This city will need people like you to protect it after I'm gone," he said, brushing a strand of hair from her eyes. "So don't follow me. It would pain me to have to kill you."

Anderson touched his hand, pressing it to her cheek, as though moved by his words. She sent a trickle of psi-energy into the man's mind, working like a thief probing the coat pocket of an unwary citizen. The guy was too crazy to know his own name, but he must have an address, a vidphone number, some fragment of a clue that she could work with. She found only a babble of short-term memories, nothing that looked or sounded useful. She must have tapped the wrong synapse. She let Eros' hand slip away as a Judge elbowed him aside.

"Move, citizen," the Judge said.

Anderson tried to speak, but the words refused to arrange themselves in her head. She watched the man who called himself Eros disappear into the fleeing crowd. She tried to push the Judge aside as he checked her vital signs, but she fell back and the ceiling of the elevator spun into blackness.

MONTANA.

She awoke to find herself laid out on a stretcher in the Meet Market lobby. She rolled to one side, landing on her feet, then dashed towards the elevator, ignoring the cries of the Meds chasing after her. She threw herself into the elevator and hit the button for level 106. The doors slid shut before the Meds could reach her. She slumped into a corner as the elevator rose and she watched the men disappear beneath her.

Anderson timed her breathing, slowing her heart rate, fighting the sickening feeling of panic as she reviewed the situation. Justice Department PR would not allow a Judge to be implicated in tonight's events. Van Doren would be forced to tell the press this was the work of yet another futise who had slipped the net. Unable to tell their subscribers the truth, Meet Market would be discredited even further, and would have to shed hundreds of employees as the company took another step towards complete collapse. All thanks to a failed gamble on Anderson's part. She thumped the back of her head against the window. *Stupid, stupid, stupid rookie.*

Minutes later the elevator *dinged* to a halt. She limped back through the pleasure suites and into the Rave Hall. The music had been shut off and the lights were up. Montana was still cuffed to the bar-rail, fighting a pair of Med Judges. He punched one of them across the dancefloor, while the other grabbed Montana's arm and tried to wrestle him into submission. Clearly, it would take more than a catnap to clear the overload of poison from Montana's mind. Anderson identified herself and ran over.

"We've shot him with two rounds of suppressant," the Med said, as he fought to restrain Montana, who bucked and snarled like a crazy refusing to return to his kook-cube. Anderson caught his face with both hands. His mind writhed with visions of violence so ecstatically obscene she had to stop herself from letting go. She could feel the force of his hatred creeping into her own mind. Eros must have hit him with twice as much as he had given her, and, if Montana's frenzy continued, his heart would give out long before his mind. He spat in her face, cursed her, threatened her, craned his neck and snapped at her wrists.

Anderson held his face and screamed, unleashing a torrent of psi-energy into his fevered mind. She imagined a tidal wave sweeping across a fire, plunging into every crevice of Montana's being, quenching his tormented mind and washing away every impurity. She could feel him beneath the cleansing flood, sinking beneath it. She was drowning him. She released him and saw his eyes roll back as he slid from her grasp and into the arms of the Med Judge. The one Montana had laid out on the floor caught Anderson as she stumbled back.

"What the drokk happened here, Anderson?"

Nothing much. Only risked the lives of thousands of people, caused a PR disaster that will cost the jobs of a thousand more. Then I let my partner get psi-bombed by a creep who I let escape. And when I tried to reboot my partner's mind I may have turned him into a vegetable instead. Pretty good for a night's work.

But she still had Rockfeather. The guy was an accessory. He was in contact with this Eros guy, maybe even knew who he was and where he lived.

"I got a guy cuffed to a desk upstairs who can explain everything," she said.

The Meds exchanged glances.

"You mean the guy who caught an armour-piercer through the melon?" said one. He indicated the ceiling.

Anderson looked up. Three bullet holes punctured the ceiling from where she had fought to restrain Montana. One of the holes was dripping.

Six

ANDERSON SLUMPED IN the chair beside Montana's bed. A med-bot was applying a patchwork of speed-heal plasters to the lacerations on her feet, none of which she remembered sustaining. Montana lay motionless, eyes closed, barely breathing. Solution feeds trailed from his arms while a network of wires had been attached to his freshly shaved scalp. An array of bleeping monitors crowded the other side of the bed like attentive relatives. Anderson could see nothing inside his head but darkness, and heard nothing but deep, dreamless thoughtwaves, heaving like an ocean. She had succeeded in driving the poison from Montana's mind, but had she extinguished him along with it?

Hauser would soon be looking for her, demanding she submit her report on last night's debacle before he banished her from his Sector House. She eavesdropped on the thoughtwaves emanating from an office on the floor above. Hauser was yelling into the vidphone at Psi Chief Ecks.

So she proved the perp exists, so what? What good is that if she let him get away? She's left us with a dead accessory, a promising young Judge in a coma, and no leads.

Ecks was trying to argue, but Hauser was on a roll.

Face it, Ecks. Your star pupil is as much a screw-up as the rest of your goofball Division. I've already submitted an application to the rest of the Council that she be withdrawn for re-evaluation.

Anderson tuned out as a Med Judge barged into the room, typing notes on a holo-pad. Anderson winced as he switched on the light.

"Shouldn't you be upstairs in recovery?" he said. "And where did you get caff? I thought the machine was broken."

Anderson sat up.

"The psi-doc said he was in a coma. Is that right?"

The Med saw the look on her face.

"It's not your fault," he said. "Judge Montana suffered a condensed charge of toxic psi-energy. And if it weren't for you blasting his mind clean he'd be dead already."

The med-droid at Anderson's feet retreated as she stood up, scowling in pain.

"So instead of saving him I just switched off his lights permanently?"

"We're gonna transfer him to the ICU, but don't get your hopes up."

He shone a pen-light into each of Montana's eyes.

"The psi-link is the only thing keeping him alive right now."

"Psi-link?"

The Med consulted his holo-pad.

"We figure it must be between him and the psyker who attacked him. Most likely a residual energy trail."

"Traceable?"

The Med shook his head.

"The psi-specialist already tried. Montana will remain in a coma until the psyker who attacked him dies."

"Then he'll wake up?"

"Then he'll die," the Med said. "Once the source of energy

sustaining Montana is cut off, brain death will follow and we'll have to terminate resuscitation."

Anderson steadied herself against the wall. Eros had told her that the city would need people like her after he was gone. Was the creep going somewhere? Was he planning a suicide mission? A guy who believed himself to be a god reborn might easily believe himself capable of being born yet again. Was that his trip? All that stuff about a corrupted world? Did he figure he would be reborn again having somehow cleansed the city? These messianic types were usually big on 'cleansing.'

"Is there some way of disconnecting this link without killing Montana?"

"Possibly," the Med said. "We'll just have to wait and see."

"What about the psyker?" Anderson said. "What if I bring him in alive? You think the psi-doc can figure something out?"

"I understand you're no longer working this case, Anderson," the Med said. "Besides, every Judge working the parade today will be on the lookout for this guy."

"But the parade spans the entire sector. He could pop up anywhere along the route. They don't even know where he might be right now."

"And you do?"

Anderson said nothing and rubbed her temple.

The Med called out after her as she limped from the room.

"Hey, if you're getting another caff, can you get me one?"

ANDERSON SQUINTED INTO the dawning sun as her Lawmaster sped along a busy overzoom that fed into the upper levels of Lauren Bacall Block. She had slipped out of Med Bay before Hauser could find her, but stopped off at the morgue. The pathologist confirmed that the stray armour-piercing round had entered Rockfeather's skull just below the cheekbone and evacuated most of his brain upon exit through the parietal wall. In other words, there was no way a Psi-Judge could retrieve any port-mortem information from this particular stiff. Anderson had only one place left to look for clues, but she would need some time to herself if she were to have any hope of finding anything.

She turned off the overzoom and onto a Judges-only lane that wound for hundreds of kilometres around the outside of the building, and pulled into an open-air watchpost that overlooked the eastern part of the city. There was a clear view of the rising sun from up here, unobscured by the smoking factories that crowded the blocks downtown. She took out her earpiece and relaxed, feeling the warmth of the sun on her face and the wind playing with her hair. She needed to relax if she was to remember anything.

She breathed in, closing her eyes, trying not to think about the possibility of wasting precious time. She ignored the thump in her temples, the pain in her feet, and the fact that she did not feel capable of remembering what she had for breakfast, let alone recalling an image that she had seen hours ago for about a nanosecond inside the head of a delusional psyker who thought he was the reincarnation of a Greek god.

She breathed out, sinking inside herself, retreating into her memory of last night's events. She saw Montana lying on the bed. She worked backwards until she could see herself fighting Eros in the elevator. She zeroed in until she recalled a pair of pale green eyes peering curiously into her own. He had brushed a strand of hair from her face and told her that the city would need her after he was dead. Had those been his exact words, or had he said something a little more poetic?

Anderson remembered touching his hand, pressing it to her cheek, as though moved by his words. She had then sent a trickle of psi-energy into the man's mind, working like a thief probing the coat pocket of an unwary citizen. The guy was too crazy to know his own name, but he must have an address, a vidphone number, some fragment of a clue that she could work with.

Anderson recalled the flash of short-term memories that she had seen inside Eros' mind, slowing her focus to a crawl, studying each fragment of memory in turn. There were three fragments in all. The first was definitely part of a dream; it had that unmistakably hazy quality, unreachable, humming with hidden meaning. The dreamer had been soaring above a storybook landscape of rocky hills and white pillared temples beneath a scorching Mediterranean sun. Dreams could be useful in profiling suspects, but had no grounding in terms of evidence. Scratch exhibit A.

Anderson moved on. Exhibit B was some kind of poem that Eros knew by heart.

Love in fantastic triumph sate
Whilst bleeding hearts around him flowed,
For whom fresh pains he did create
And strange tyrannic power he showed:
From thy bright eyes he took his fires,
Which round about in sport he hurled;
But 'twas from mine he took desires
Enough to undo the amorous world.

It was from an ancient play entitled *The Moor's Revenge* by someone called Aphra Behn and, judging by the angelic tenor in which Eros sang these words in his head, the creep was quite a fan. Very nice, but again not very helpful. Eros could have read this anywhere, at any time. Scratch exhibit B.

Anderson approached the final image: something about a butterfly. It appeared to be a memory, but felt too perfectly arranged to be real. It could have been one of those snapshot moments life threw at you from time to time, a flash of serendipitous beauty or perfect horror encoded in your memory forevermore. Then again exhibit C could be a nostalgic daydream or a scene from Eros' favourite movie. This creep was so deluded, everything she found in his head could be fantasy. How could she trust any of it? Her final line of enquiry appeared to have come to a dead end. Overwhelmed by anger and frustration, she felt the image slip away, and she was back in the elevator in the Meet Market lobby, watching Eros disappear into the fleeing crowd.

Anderson let her anger dissipate, clearing her mind before recalling the image of the butterfly. She absorbed herself into the scene that surrounded it, until she could see it through Eros' eyes. She was sitting on a bus, reading a book of poems. She could perceive only the memory of sounds and smells, but from the clarity of the scene it could not have been more than a few weeks old. A garbage truck swept past the window on her left, ploughing through a deep puddle by the kerb.

As far as she could tell, the bus was crowded. A sour-faced juve with pockmarked cheeks and a shark's fin of blue hair leered down at her, dripping rainwater onto the pages of her book. She reached out with Eros' slender fingers and brushed the drops aside. Something glimmered to her left. A butterfly was softly battering the misted window, wings of sapphire and lime glowing like stained glass, illuminated by sunlight bursting through the dark clouds. She watched, enchanted, until a hand slammed the insect against the glass. The hand withdrew and crumbled shreds of blue and green onto the pages of her open book. The fin-haired juve sneered down at her, daring her to respond. The image faded.

Anderson recalled the scene again. If only she had sound, she could have heard the robo-driver announce the stops along the way. And if only she was not restricted by Eros' sightline she could have craned her neck to catch the names of the city blocks outside. The garbage truck passed the sun on her left. A garbage truck. On its morning pickup? So the sun was rising, not setting. She must be heading south. Big deal. She needed more information. Where had the butterfly come from?

She replayed the scene a third time, but the more she concentrated, the more distorted the scene became, shaped by her own memories and expectations. The butterfly appeared even more brilliantly coloured, less like any insect from the real world and more like a fairy made of jewels and gold, an image she had seen in a storybook as a child. She looked again at the juve, but this time he appeared skinnier, almost skeletal. Had his hair really been that shade of blue, or had it been purple? Had he had pockmarks or just really bad acne? His face somehow blurred to accommodate the likeness of every punk she remembered facing on the street. The scene turned to gloop in her head, none of it reliable. Gone.

She surfaced in her own body, sitting astride her Lawmaster on a watchpost in Lauren Bacall Block, with nothing to show for this morning's labours beyond a pleasant view of the city. She shook the handlebars and swore, feeling herself sink inside at the thought of surrendering the case. Then inspiration washed over her like a gust of cold air.

The butterfly ranch. One of the first victims had been killed in the Meet Market butterfly ranch, an indoor park decorated with insects created by some of the city's top gene-designers. She activated her Lawmaster's computer and ran a search. Perhaps the insect had become trapped inside a fold of clothing before being released on the bus. Anderson scrolled through the visitor pages of the Meet Market website until she found a butterfly with wings of sapphire and lime, glowing like stained glass.

"Nav-com. Show me all bus routes heading south from Meet Market Block."

The screen revealed several routes. Eros could have been on any one of them, heading into a dozen different areas downtown. Anderson felt her heart racing.

"Show me all juve gangs associated with every block on these routes. I want to see colours. Anyone with blue hair."

The computer picked out five composite images, one of which was of a juve with a blue mohawk shaped to resemble a shark's fin. The Hammerheads. A small but vicious crew with records for dealing zizz and running enforcement errands for a nearby cartel.

They operated out of Lou Reed Block, the third and final stop on an express bus route heading south from Meet Market. Eros had been on that bus route when he saw the butterfly and would have disembarked at one of those three stops.

The juve with the pockmarked cheeks might know which one.

Having processed Anderson's description, the computer presented the rap sheet of a hollow-eyed youth with cheeks like the back wall of a firing range. Bart Merkin, aka 'Pube.' No address. Operated levels one through ten of Lou Reed. Backup advised.

If Anderson could find this kid, she could get the name of the block in which Eros lived. That was still a building the size of a city, but if she was fast and lucky she could capture Eros before he got himself killed doing whatever he had in mind for today's parade.

Her data-screen flashed up an incoming call.

"Van Doren?"

The Meet Market CEO looked weary behind the crimson heart-shaped beard and glittering pink hair. Anderson fumbled for words, but Van Doren spoke first, his voice drained of anger.

"Is it true you're off the case?"

"Yes. Another Psi-Judge will be in touch with you shortly."

"Judge Anderson, I'm expecting a stream of crippling lawsuits to arrive this morning. In the meantime, every newsfeed in this city is screaming about my company becoming a futsie free-for-all. Unless we can prove this psyker of yours is targeting my company, we'll be out of business by the end of the year."

"We're doing everything we can."

Anderson started up her Lawmaster.

"But right now I have to be somewhere."

"Did they tell you what Mr Rockfeather was transmitting when you found him last night?"

Anderson paused.

"It was an activation code," Van Doren said. "Miss Falcone overheard a member of your Tek Division. They believe Rockfeather may have built something, and they're crawling all over my block right now looking for explosives."

A bomb? Anderson doubted it. She had seen inside Rockfeather's head. He liked coding, not chemicals, and Eros liked to get his hands dirty, flourishing his 'godly' powers by destroying people's minds. He was far too much of a romantic to off his victims with the banal efficiency of timed explosives. Okay, so Rockfeather had been poisoned into building something for Eros. But what?

"I've only just convinced them to release my parade float," Van Doren said.

"Wait, you're not still taking part, are you?"

"Given how much I've spent on this blasted float, I'd rather be killed than see it go to waste. Besides, as I've said before, Meet Market is a sanctuary. We don't surrender in the face of fear."

"Citizen, I'm ordering you to sit this one out. This creep's still out there."

"Then find him, Judge Anderson."

Van Doren signed off before Anderson could answer. She checked her timer. The parade would not be starting for another few hours. She swung her Lawmaster around, then gunned it towards Lou Reed Block.

Seven

ANDERSON PROWLED ALONGSIDE the citizens of Lou Reed Block as they made their way towards the bus and elevator depots. They were heading down to the 'Tunnel of Love,' known for the rest of the year as the Mark Knopfler Underpass. Linking several neighbouring territories and spanning the whole of Sector 7, the cavernous passage had been designated by the Justice Department as the official route for the Valentine's Parade. The Department's strategists felt this was the best way to contain the annual 'festivities.'

Anderson continued to scan the crowds.

Gonna drink 'til I pass out...

Can't wait to see the Sambarettas' float. They're gonna wear even less than last year...

Her bag's open. Vidphone. Could fence to Gurney Rollins on Three. Wait 'til that Judge moves on...

She looked up. A furtive-looking man in a dark jacket was eyeing a group of college kids waiting at a bus stop. The creep jumped a mile as Anderson turned her Lawmaster towards him and revved the engine; seeing her coming for him, he bolted

83

down a side street. The crowd scattered as Anderson plunged after him. She could hear his mind screaming at himself to sprint for the narrow alleyway he knew lay up ahead. Anderson accelerated and booted him head-first into a pile of garbage bags. As he struggled to rise, slipping in filth on his hands and knees, she swung the Lawmaster around until the barrel of one of her bike cannons stood inches from his face.

"Intent to steal. That's six months. But if you tell me where I can find the Hammerheads, I'll think about taking a couple of weeks off your sentence."

She heard his brain fumbling for a lie.

"Don't bother," she said, thumbing her Psi badge.

He looked nervously about him.

"They're in the squats down on level four, opposite the Go-Mart," he said. "Would you take off another week if I warned you not to go down there alone?"

ANDERSON KICKED OPEN the back door and aimed her Lawgiver at four startled men seated around a kitchen table.

"Psi-Division. Hands on your haircuts."

A fifth man standing at the kitchen counter dropped a frying pan on the hob. His buddies looked at each other before dropping their forks onto their plates and placing their hands either side of their shark's fin mohawks. They were a lot older than Pube. Bigger, too, and Anderson could hear from their rumbling thoughts that they were not going to cooperate. Maybe a surprise attack had been a bad idea.

"I'm not here for the drugs you're gonna be slinging today, fellas. I just need to talk to one of your guys named Pube. Tall kid, skinny, cheeks like moon rock?"

Las-pistol. Charged, last time I checked.

She aimed her Lawgiver at the guy by the counter, whose hand had been moving towards an open drawer.

"Back up, fat boy."

The chef lunged for the drawer as one of the other Hammerheads leapt from the table. Anderson maintained her aim at the chef and fired, the blast deafening inside the cramped kitchen. The chef took a round in the chest as the lead Hammerhead grabbed her wrists, raising her arms above her head and driving her backwards. As he slammed her into the wall, she drove her knee deep into his groin. He doubled over in pain, and Anderson peeled away and jabbed an elbow into the man's temple, stunning him.

One man dazed, another dead, the remaining three Hammerheads charged at her. She dropped the Lawgiver, useless at close quarters, and drew her side-handled daystick as the next Hammerhead swung a ketchup bottle at her head. She dodged out of reach, swinging her daystick into the back of his skull. He fell forward, senseless, as his buddy's fist crashed into her jaw, jerking her head to one side. She fell against the wall and snapped a kick into the man's groin, pushing him backwards into the third Hammerhead, who was struggling to retrieve the chef's las-pistol from the kitchen drawer. She ran at him, kicking the drawer shut and trapping his hand as she smashed his collarbone with her daystick.

As the gunman dropped screaming to the floor, Anderson felt someone clutching at her legs. She looked down to see the guy she had kicked to the floor, his features contorted with rage as he caught hold of her belt and hurled her onto the linoleum, slamming the breath from her body and knocking the daystick from her hand. He pounced on top of her, teeth gritted, pinning her throat with his left hand as he drove a punch into her face. Pain exploded inside Anderson's skull. She gasped and caught the hand pinning her throat. He punched her again and she hooked her foot around his leg, trapping it. As he went to land the third punch, she bucked her hips, still holding his arm, throwing him off balance. It was just enough to tip him over.

As she landed on top of him, she drove her elbow into his nose, plunging her entire bodyweight behind the strike. Blood burst across his face and he went limp.

Someone behind her snatched her hair and dragged her backwards. She flipped herself onto her knees, her hair twisting painfully in her attacker's grip. She felt his thoughts writhing like snakes.

Gonna stomp in your skull, bitch.

She grabbed his foot and launched herself into his right leg, driving her shoulder into his knee. His leg snapped like a breadstick, folding backwards as he fell on top of her, flailing and screaming. She dragged herself free and caught his arm, twisting him onto his belly. It was the lead Hammerhead. His four buddies lay sprawled about the kitchen floor, either dead, unconscious or squirming in agony. Anderson almost laughed. The left side of her face throbbed. She tasted blood and quivered with adrenalin. She wrenched the man's arm up behind his back.

"As I was saying," she said. "I need to talk to a kid named Pube."

The Hammerhead laughed.

"Pube's dead."

His thoughts rang clear. He was not lying.

The lead she had fought so hard to track down was dead? Her anger flared at the injustice and she twisted the Hammerhead's hand. The man squealed.

"He was getting off the bus. Driver ran his ass over. Guy went futsie."

Anderson recalled Eros' memory of Pube sneering down at him, daring him to do something about swatting that butterfly. But there was at least twenty minutes between each bus stop. If Eros had poisoned the driver into crashing the bus, then Eros and Pube must have got off at the same stop.

"Which block?" Anderson said.

"Azealia Banks. Level two-one-two."

*   *   *

ANDERSON CREPT ALONG a vacant corridor in Azealia Banks Block, her Lawgiver drawn. She had shown images of Eros from last night and of Rockfeather to the caretakers of level 212. Neither the chief nor his maintenance crew recognised Eros, but one of the guys was pretty sure he had seen Rockfeather a few times.

Where?

Westside.

Anderson had knocked on some doors, and one of the neighbours recalled passing Rockfeather a couple of times. The neighbour believed he may be friends with that dude at the end of the hall, the one who never leaves his hab. The caretaker said the place was registered to Nate Givens, unemployed, a shut-in on account of a bum leg. That did not sound like the guy Anderson had seen flee so quickly from the Meet Market lobby.

Anderson paused outside hab 387. This could be it. The creep could be inside right now sleeping off the effects of last night's excitement. She smiled at the thought of getting the drop on him. That look of baffled defeat on a perp's face was always a pleasure. How much sweeter would that feeling be if she could drag this creep's unconscious butt down to the Sector House and see an equally startled look on Hauser's mug?

She listened for thoughtwaves emanating from behind the door. She calmed herself and listened again. Nothing. She was too late; he must have left early. She punched the wall. It was a safe bet he would be attending the parade, but he could turn up anywhere along the route, and that spanned the entire sector. The guy was on a suicide mission and would not be coming back. No point staking out the place. At least if she checked out the hab, she might find a clue as to what Rockfeather had been up to, anything that might help the Jays pick out Eros at the parade.

She holstered her Lawgiver, feeling weariness settle over her shoulders like a cloak. She had treated herself with meds after her scuffle with the Hammerheads, but her jaw still ached like hell. She hit the judicial override and the hab door slid open. She stepped inside and snapped on the light in the hallway. The curtains were closed and the place reeked of disinfectant. The air conditioner hummed on full blast. Unopened mail had been stacked in a niche by the door. A Meet Market summer catalogue addressed to Mr Givens. Nice of someone to set this to one side for the guy. She checked again for thoughtwaves. All she could hear was a woman three doors down preparing to leave and meet her friends at the parade.

Anderson stepped down the hallway into the living room. A lone armchair sat before a caff-table and a Tri-D set. The chair had been patched with duct tape, and the carpet where the owner's feet had rested was threadbare. The occupant had made no attempt to conceal his exotic porn collection. Whoever lived here was not used to visitors. And yet the shelves had been thoroughly polished and the ancient aeroball trophies replaced in a perfectly straight line. It felt to Anderson as if this hab had been inherited by someone who did not like mess. Maybe time to put out a 10-65 on poor Mr Givens.

She checked the rest of the hab, looking for clues to Eros' current whereabouts and current appearance. The bed did not appear to have been slept in. In the bathroom she found several pots of something called 'Baker's Wonder-Wax.' It appeared to be some kind of pliable mortician's wax, perfect for altering one's appearance. She also uncovered a set of sculpting tools, along with several hi-def prints of Meet Market profile pictures.

The spare room was lit by a bare bulb. The blinds were drawn and the floor appeared to have been recently cleaned. A swivel chair had been replaced neatly behind a desk freckled with scars and dents. It looked as though someone had been using it as a workbench. Anderson opened a toolbox and removed a tray full of electrical utensils and coils of wire. Beneath she found a box containing surgical equipment, swipes, latex gloves, tiny screws. She examined a screwdriver, stained brown at the tip, and removed a tiny bottle from her belt pouch. She shook the bottle and sprayed a puff of mist over the tip of the screwdriver. The stains turned green, positive for blood. She noticed stains on the chair and misted those too. More blood. What the heck had Rockfeather been doing in here? Torturing someone? DIY surgery? What was Eros hiding under those sculpted wax masks of his?

In the toolbox, she found several foil packets bearing the Meet Market logo. She tore one open and shook the contents into her hand. Halo discs, the same as the one Anderson had worn on her forehead last night. Miss Falcone had said the devices were basically tiny psionic amplifiers. Van Doren said that Rockfeather had been transmitting an activation code; Falcone had done the same in order to activate Anderson's Halo.

Anderson looked from the Halo discs in her hand to the toolbox. What if you strung a whole bunch of these things together, linking them with wire and screws, placed the resulting contraption in the hands of a skilled psychic, and then activated it with a transmitted code? Would you not have one big psionic amplifier?

Yes, you would.

Anderson spun around, drawing her Lawgiver. The doorway was empty. She scanned the hab for thoughtwaves. Nothing. Even the woman three doors down had left to meet her friends.

Don't panic, Cassandra. You're not alone.

Anderson went to call Control, and an avalanche of psi-energy crashed into her head. She fell back against the light-switch, plunging the room into darkness. She stared at the Lawgiver in her shaking hands, barely resisting the temptation to place the barrel between her teeth and pull the trigger. She threw the weapon across the room as she slid down the wall and onto her knees, fighting the urge to tear open her wrists with her teeth.

I have one of my arrows poised inside your head, Cassandra. I can either withdraw it or I can plunge it so deep into your being that your body's very cells will begin eating one another. I really am very much stronger than when last we met. Now I can hear what you're thinking, as well as feel every emotion you're experiencing. It's like we're in love.

The amplifier. Rockfeather must have implanted it into Eros in this room some days ago. And now Rockfeather's code has activated it. Anderson remembered seeing a psionic amplifier at Psi-Division, a huge coffin-shaped slab. Her tutor had explained to the class that the devices drained the psyker's life force to sustain the amplified psionic energy, resulting in the user's body eventually crumbling to dust. Not a pretty way to go for a romantic like Eros.

Oh, I'm not a vain god, Cassandra. I am merely love's messenger.

The thoughtwaves sounded impossibly close. Had the amp made Eros strong enough to cloak his thoughts? Having assumed no one was in the hab, Anderson had conducted only a casual search. The creep could have been hiding in the broom closet for all she knew. *Psi talents are no substitute for procedure, rookie.*

"Don't be hard on yourself," called a familiar voice from the living room. "I was planning on dying today, in the process of delivering a message to this blasphemous city. But you may have inadvertently saved me the trouble."

Anderson looked up, still struggling to shield her mind, as a blue glow approached the door. A tall naked man entered the room, shafts of sapphire light radiating from his muscular shoulders like wings. His features were obscured by lights dotted about his face and head, glowing beneath his flesh. The Halo discs. Rockfeather had implanted his makeshift psi-amp into Eros' flesh, working with scalpel and screwdriver, and hiding his workings beneath a layer of sculpted wax.

Eros knelt before her.

"I've been reading you all the while you've been searching this apartment, and I'm beginning to think I may not be the only god reborn within mortal flesh."

He reached down and unhooked Anderson's badge.

"You are worth so much more than this," he said, tossing the badge aside.

Anderson fought the urge to grab her boot-knife, unsure whether she wanted to drive the blade into herself or the figure knelt before her.

"When we fought last night, I felt something within you, Cassandra. Compassion. Pure and precious."

He touched her temple. The lights radiating from his body intensified and Anderson felt psi-energy cascade through his fingers and into her body, pushing her into unconsciousness.

"I'm going to give you what you want," he said. "I'm going to help you save this city."

Eight

ANDERSON AWOKE TO find herself in a body that was not her own. She was watching someone else's memory through their eyes. She sat at a desk in a brightly lit classroom as an antique robo-teacher explained a passage from a poem written on the screenboard. Anderson could not hear what the 'bot was saying, but the words on the board sang in her head.

...Whilst bleeding hearts around him flowed,
For whom fresh pains he did create
And strange tyrannic power he showed...

She was viewing one of Eros's memories. Through his eyes, she was staring at a girl of around sixteen, seated a couple of rows ahead. Her blonde hair shimmered in the summer sunlight beaming through the window beside her. The memory was so suffused with nostalgia it was practically a fantasy.

Anderson heard Eros' thoughts booming like fireworks as he gazed at the girl, one Shannon Weissmuller. He was not thinking about the sort of thing most boys his age thought about when they looked at girls. He was imagining the stuff of ancient poetry and romantic melodrama: what it would feel like to take her slender hands in his, to smell her perfumed hair. It was all laughably effete, but Anderson felt his every thought scream with want, with an intensity that was powerful, even for an adolescent.

Anderson felt a pang of sympathy. It was traumatic enough for any breed of psychic to grow up within the sanctuary of the Psi Academy. What must it have been like for a psychic who could experience the feelings of others to grow up on the raucous streets of the Big Meg? To Eros, everyone around him was a cloud of emotion, drenching him in rage or angst, sending his own feelings spiralling or crashing like a sailboat caught in a storm. But the cloud that was Shannon Weissmuller radiated only indifference.

Anderson heard Eros' thoughts wander into whimsy. He was envisioning himself as his mythic namesake: Eros, god of love, winged bowman of legend, whose caprice and cruelty had struck such a chord in the boy when he first read the fables of Apuleius in the school library.

He imagined himself selecting a white arrow from a quiver at his hip. Having armed his bow, he sent the missile deep into Shannon Weissmuller's heart. He imagined that arrow dissolving inside her like wet sugar, sweetening every ounce of her being with nothing but pure love for him.

Shannon turned and looked at him. Eros looked away, embarrassed, his eyes meeting hers for an instant. Shannon threw back her chair and ran at him, shoving aside the other desks before leaping on top of him. Eros sat transfixed, convinced he was dreaming as she grabbed his face with both hands and bit down on his nose.

Furniture scraped and clattered as the other pupils backed away in horror. The girl shook her head like a dog, her hair whipping Eros' cheeks until she tore his nose free. Anderson heard a chorus of screams as Eros struggled to push Shannon away, the two of them crashing to the floor as she clawed bloody furrows into his face and neck. The robo-teacher eventually prised her away, kicking and spitting.

"I hate you! Die! Stop staring at me and die!"

Anderson had seen enough. She pushed herself away and fell back into her own body, her heart thumping.

She went to get up, but her body refused to move. Her arms lay stubbornly by her sides; her legs refused to shift. She stared up at the ceiling and blinked. Then she took a deep breath. Thankfully, her body responded. She could roll her eyes and breathe, but that was it. She appeared to be paralysed.

Eros' voice spoke in her head.

Your body is asleep.

Anderson's eyes darted about the room, searching for the speaker. She appeared to be alone, lying on the bed in Nate Givens' hab. Something was sticking to her forehead and temples. Whatever it was, she felt it leaking a steady stream of psi-energy, leeching her ability to raise a psionic shield or wake her sleeping body. Halo discs. Perhaps some kind of prototype amplifier put together by Rockfeather.

I have your consciousness trapped between two bodies, yours and mine. Close your eyes and you'll see.

Anderson did so and the darkness behind her eyes brightened, then focused into a view of a busy pedway. She was looking again through Eros' eyes. But this time the scene was no memory. She was watching as he hurried through a crowd elsewhere in the city. Anderson opened her own eyes and found herself once again staring at the ceiling above the bed.

My amplifier has established a temporary psychic link between us, Eros thought. *A true meeting of the minds.*

Thanks, Anderson thought. *I love to spend my Saturdays sharing repressed memories with a psycho.*

Eros replied. *I want you to see the world through my eyes. I think it's the only way you'll understand the sincerity of the offer I'm about to make you.*

Anderson closed her eyes again. Eros was threading his way through a dawdling crowd on a walkway descending below street level. The sound of clattering drums and piping whistles enveloped him.

He emerged into a cheering crowd and a blizzard of streamers. A huge parade float surged into view, comprising three huge replica pizzas stacked like the tiers of a wedding cake. An enormous Fatty sat in the centre of each revolving platform, like a wad of clay on a potter's wheel. Each wore a wig of blonde curls and was naked except for a white sheet wound about their bulging loins. They frisbeed fresh pizzas into the crowds clamouring behind the rockcrete barriers that lined the tunnel. A banner running down the side of the float read *Pucker Up For Paunch-O Pizza!*

Anderson wondered how long she had been unconscious. It must be around noon if the parade had started. By now a separate procession would be snaking through every sector in the city. Millions of citizens would be getting tanked on drink and drugs, daring each other to break the law without getting busted, while the Justice Department struggled to contain the mounting frenzy.

Eros had paused to take in the full horror of the Paunch-O Pizza float. The Fatty rotating at the top looked decidedly unwell. He lurched forward and vomited, dowsing the crowd either side of the road as the platform continued to revolve. Eros turned away, disgusted, and moved up the tunnel, towards the head of the parade. Anderson spotted a sign beside the walkway through which Eros had entered: *Exit 13*.

If memory served, that was only twenty minutes by road from Azealia Banks Block.

More like thirty, actually, Eros thought.

With that damn psi-amp, he could hear every idea that entered her head. She was also powerless to stop him should he suddenly decide to fry her brain with a long-distance psi-bolt.

Anderson figured the only way out of this situation was to not think about what she had in mind.

Every week at the Academy, Anderson and her fellow Psi Cadets had undergone 'White Bear' training. As their tutor had explained, if you tell most people not to think of a white bear, the first thing they think of will be a white bear. Psi Cadets, however, were taught to control their naturally disobedient minds. If a well-trained Psi Cadet told herself not to think about a white bear, then she would not do so on any conscious level.

Therefore, as far as Eros could tell, Anderson was not thinking about escaping. She was not thinking about what Miss Falcone had said last night about body temperature interfering with the Halo discs. And she was not thinking about the breathing technique she had used while trying to keep warm at Meet Market last night. Most of all she did not think about keeping Eros occupied.

So what's this offer you wanna make me?

She watched through Eros' eyes as he elbowed through the crowd, the press of bodies so tight he was struggling to overtake the floats.

Do you know the community support centre just off the Tommy Cooper Glidewalk?

I'm guessing I should, Anderson thought.

She did not think about holding each breath. She did not think about contracting her upper stomach muscles at just the right moment to increase the warming flow of blood around her body.

It's run by a charity I doubt you'll have heard of, but they provide counselling, support and recovery for those who need it. They offer hope, compassion. In other words, they provide the closest thing to love I've yet found in this city.

Anderson did not think about how the air conditioning was still running full blast. She did not think about how chilly it was in the bedroom in which she lay.

That place is all that's keeping hundreds of residents in that area from dying or going insane. And yet last week I heard on a newsfeed that the city is withdrawing crucial funding, and this centre is now due to close.

Anderson did not think about how she was struggling to heat up her body. She did not think about the importance of keeping Eros talking.

Can't they survive on donations or volunteers?

Not for any length of time, Cassandra. What they need is someone like you. Someone with a talent for mending broken minds.

Anderson replied, *So you want me to give up being a Judge and go work for a charity? A nice idea, but what good would that do if the place is closing?*

She did not think about her quickening heart rate or the warmth she could feel creeping across her chest.

What if I could turn money in your direction, Cassandra? With this amplifier, I can control my abilities like never before. I can reach those with money and position, and I can influence them into donating funds. I can needle these people against each other, stoke rivalries, jealousies until each is desperate to outbid the other. A touch here, a nudge there, nothing fatal, nothing lasting.

Anderson replied, *Then why aren't you doing it? You don't need me.*

Yes, I do. The city needs you. I've looked into your very core, Cassandra Anderson. And I found nothing but love and compassion for those around you.

Eros had caught up with a marching band whose uniform appeared to consist of little more than fishnet stockings and a leather waistcoat. A young man was pounding either side of a huge drum on which had been scrawled the words: *The Slabwalkers of Sector 7.* One of the women dancing behind the drummer got so carried away by the crowd's enthusiastic reception that she pulled off her waistcoat and twirled it around her head. Eros was jostled aside as two Judges leaped over the barrier to preserve her modesty. A fight broke out as the Judges made arrests. The crowd booed and hurled missiles.

You are living proof that virtue can exist in this wretched city. And yet you work alongside sanctioned killers. Does duty make you any less a murderer than I?

Anderson did not think about the shiver that had just run through her sleeping body.

With the level of donation I could instigate, volunteering would be just the beginning. You could build an entire company dedicated to helping others. You could become the city's greatest humanitarian. You could do what you've always wanted, Cassandra.

Oh yeah, and what's that?

You could prove the system wrong.

Anderson struggled not to think about sustaining her measured breathing.

Assuming the impossibility that you can survive another thirty years as a Judge, how many more people will you have killed? Can you imagine looking back, knowing that, had you chosen differently, you could have saved ten times that many lives?

Anderson wondered whether by agreeing, at least for now, she could keep Montana alive.

Surrender your badge and join me, and I will do everything I can to save your partner.

Anderson had always believed the city was worth saving, but until now had no idea how it could be done, or at what cost.

I've seen what the Justice Department has done to you. If only you knew the extent of their deceit. If only you knew how rare you are. No one else in the city possesses your level of compassion.

Maybe you're not looking deep enough.

True love does not exist in this city, Anderson. Not yet. Only desperation, only this travesty of love. People buying, selling themselves like chattels.

His thoughts screeched with rage as Anderson saw images of Van Doren and his carnival of a dating agency dancing like flames in Eros' mind.

Give me your answer, Cassandra. Now.

I'm a Judge. Anderson's involuntary response surprised her. Eros paused, reading her.

You tell me, Anderson thought. *Am I lying? Do I believe what I'm saying?*

Anderson did not think about the beads of sweat she could feel gathering on her forehead. She did not think about the fact that she could now move her fingers. Her body heat was loosening the Halo discs' grip on her mind, but her arm still refused to move and peel the devices from her head. Eros could still kill her if he wanted to.

He paused by the tunnel wall, facing away from the parade, as if he could not bear to look at it any longer. Anderson thought she could hear him sobbing. She willed her arm to move, straining as if attempting to raise a dumbbell.

What are you doing, Cassandra?

She felt him probing her mind. Her arm was barely raised as he scanned her subconscious. Her hand turned towards her face, her fingers straining, as she felt him rear up in confusion and rage.

A wall of black arrows filled her mind's eye.

Gasping with effort, she threw up her hand, freezing the psionic volley in mid-descent. Her body heat had dampened the effect of the Halo discs, closing the psi-leak just enough to regain some of her power. Eros threw the weight of his mind behind the arrows, and her shield buckled, her arm bending as the volley inched towards her.

His voice raged like an inferno in her head.

By the time you find me, Judge Anderson, I will be dust and

*the people on this obscene parade will be nothing but torn meat
and scattered bones. A thousand human devils consumed by
their own corrupted passions and visiting upon one another
such atrocities that this parade, this travesty, this insult that
mocks the very spirit of love, will never return to this city.*

Anderson felt her focus return and she heaved the arrows
aside. He was too far away and their link was weakening. She
managed to shake her head and a tangle of wires and Halo discs
fell away from her warm, clammy skin. Eros' words trailed
away like smoke as she rolled off the bed and onto the floor.

Anderson grabbed the bedpost and rose to her feet, her head
spinning. The creep had looked into her soul alright. What had
he meant about the Department's 'deceit'? Had he believed her
brainwashed? Or had he seen something inside her of which
even she was unaware? A forgotten memory? Some kind of
dark potential? She did not think about it.

She had pissed off Eros as much as she thought possible. Pissed
off enough to start hate-bombing people right there and then?
She did not think so. His vendetta was focused on the mocking
figurehead of Cupid Van Doren. Right now, Eros would be
heading towards the front of the parade where he would most
likely poison the crowd into killing Van Doren. Then he would
turn up the juice on his psi-amp, reducing himself to dust as he
gathered an unstoppable hate-fuelled mob. The crazed citizens
would proceed to murder their way back down the tunnel,
killing thousands. Eros could not be too far from Exit 13, which
was just under a mile from her current position. Was it near
enough to stop him before he reached the Meet Market float?
Anderson doubted it, but it was her duty to try.

Eros had placed her badge on the bedside table. She snatched
it up and looked at it.

"You'd better be worth it," she said, clipping the shield back
onto her uniform.

Nine

"ANDERSON? REPORT TO Psi-Division immediately," Control said. "You were due to contact them over an hour ago."

Anderson swerved to avoid a group of shoppers as she cannoned through the kitchenware department towards the mall's exit doors.

"Scratch that," Anderson said, ducking as her Lawmaster exploded through the glass doors and skidded a hard left onto a lane of racing traffic. "Can confirm the Meet Market killer is at the parade, last seen heading north from exit thirteen. Am in pursuit, but not sure I'm gonna reach him before he makes his move."

That short cut through the Mollie Sugden Mall might have saved her ten minutes—as well as earned her a formal complaint for smashing through that crystalware display—but she still doubted she could reach Van Doren before Eros.

She yelled at Control, straining to make herself heard above the bellowing wind.

"Get psis down there right now. The suspect is armed with a portable psionic amplifier. He can cloak his thoughts and fry a bunch of targets at once."

"Roger that. Replacement Judges Hunter and Gifford are en route. Should be there in an hour."

"An hour?"

"Best we can do today, Anderson."

Another catch-wagon sirened past, as Anderson swung down onto a main road leading into exit thirteen of the Tunnel of Love. From here, a queue of floats were feeding into the underpass, flanked by hordes of cheering onlookers. A heart-shaped façade had been erected over the entrance, festooned with hearts and flowers.

A gigantic gravy boat was entering the tunnel, swaying precariously, sloshing gallons of steaming brown ooze. Clambering over a huge logo that read *Bleasdale's Alcoholic Gravy*, Judges were fighting off several citizens attempting to dive into the savoury sludge. One of the attackers disembarked, triumphantly waving a Judge's helmet. A furious, helmetless Judge gave chase and the pair disappeared into the cheering crowd.

Anderson checked her timer. It was at least another fifteen minutes from here to Van Doren's float at the head of the parade. There was no way she could reach it before Eros. The creep may even have closed in already. If not, maybe she could slow him down.

A couple of maintenance guys stood by the generator that fed the decorations around the tunnel entrance. One of the guys laboured with a set of cables, while his buddy whistled at the scantily-clad girls on the Veronica's Mysteries float. Anderson pulled alongside and both men snapped to attention.

"This tunnel have any kind of ventilation system?" she asked.

"Uh, yeah," said the cable guy. "We've been told to turn up the chiller after all those people got naked last year."

His buddy grinned wistfully.

"I need you to turn it down, way down," Anderson said. "I want that tunnel as hot as you can safely get it."

"Whoah. I'll need to talk to my foreman."

"And I'll need to talk to him about the two guys who got drunk one time and peed in his gas tank."

Their faces dropped.

"Okay, Judge. But people are gonna get real sweaty down there."

ANDERSON RODE AS fast as she could through the tunnel, ignoring the jeering crowds on her left, trying not to get distracted by the enormous parade floats on her right. She passed a vast pink cauldron from which Valentine's hearts rose like bubbles. Ahead of that was a marching band made up entirely of amputees. The musicians hopped and twirled their artificial limbs in lieu of batons. An Aztec pyramid loomed next, lined with gyrating men and women wearing clothing that would undoubtedly have got them busted if the Judges were not busy elsewhere. The air glittered with streamers and confetti until the dazzling floats seemed to merge into their surroundings. The sound of squawking trumpets and rattling, booming drums was inescapable.

The thoughts of the crowd were just as feverish. No two brainwaves sounded the same. Jazzed on every known intoxicant, stimulant or psychedelic, the crowd's thoughts sounded like howler monkeys fighting a brass band. How could she distinguish the thoughts of one man amid this racket? She had clipped an extra two stumm grenades to her belt, uncertain she could withstand a close-range attack if Eros's psi-amp was still working.

The air felt oppressive as she sped through the tunnel. She unzipped the neck of her jumpsuit and looked up. Through the cascade of streamers, she saw that the ceiling fans were no longer spinning. If she could raise Eros' body temperature in time, his connection to those Halo discs should weaken. Maybe then she could run in and punch the drokker's lights out. She needed to take him alive if she had any hope of saving Montana.

Through the ceaseless, hammering drums, Anderson heard booing up ahead. She accelerated, until she reached the head of the parade. The Meet Market float appeared to be in one piece. Had she beat Eros to the punch or was the psyker somewhere nearby, struggling to connect with his amplifier in this heat? She rode past the float, then turned her Lawmaster to face the oncoming parade. Her jaw dropped.

"Grud on a greenie."

Half a dozen muscular men emerged from the snowstorm of confetti, huge feathered wings spreading from their backs. They each pulled a length of golden chain slung over their shoulder and wrapped around their heaving body. They swayed in unison, their feet pounding the road. Seemingly dragged into view by his 'slaves,' Cupid Van Doren appeared before a Greek temple that materialised through the rain of streamers like a galleon parting a sea mist. Van Doren's hair and beard had been dyed yellow for this occasion and teased into a ring of spikes so that his face resembled a beaming sun. Around his chest he wore a golden harness fashioned to resemble a huge pair of breasts, the chains of his slaves tethered to each nipple.

The crowd continued booing, but Van Doren was unperturbed. He waved imperiously from a chariot car fixed to the rest of the temple, the pediment of which was shaped in the double 'M' of the Meet Market logo. Huge cherubs formed the columns beneath, urinating what Anderson assumed—hoped—was shampagne into the baying crowd.

As the cherubs turned from side to side, hosing the crowds, a man vaulted the rockcrete barrier and sprinted towards Van Doren's chariot. Anderson leapt from her Lawmaster and ran to intercept the citizen, whose thoughts she could hear boiling with hatred. She tripped him with a sliding tackle and rolled onto the man's back, pressing his face to the ground as she cuffed him.

The Meet Market float moved on unmolested as she reached into the man's memory, and retrieved the fleeting image of a black arrow. The psi-bolt had been no stronger than the one she had found in the head of Reena Stanhope. Was this all Eros could manage? Had her plan to inhibit his amplifier actually worked?

She detected a trail of psi-vapour leading into the crowd. She left the man where he lay and leaped up onto the side of the Meet Market float, closing her eyes as she followed the psi-trail into the crowd. Once she zeroed in on its source, she opened her eyes and saw a man with a mop of black hair, his fingers straining at his temples.

As Anderson went to jump down and engage Eros, the crowd surrounding him suddenly surged like an army over the barrier and charged towards the head of the Meet Market float. Anderson scrambled up and around one of the urinating cherubs and drew her Lawgiver. The cheers and roars of the uninfected crowd on the other side of the road were indistinguishable from the snarling of the poisoned citizens now closing in on Van Doren.

Anderson dropped to one knee.

"Rapid fire."

She felt her Lawgiver click as the RF mechanism locked, then she fired a few bursts of standard rounds into the slab—a safe distance from the slaves, but close enough to let them know someone was shooting at them. The slaves screamed as sparks danced by their feet. With no obstacle ahead of them, they fled down the tunnel. The chains wound about their bodies snapped taut, yanking Van Doren from his perch just as the mob reached out to grab him. The slaves continued to flee, dragging a flailing Van Doren behind them.

The mob pelted after him like dogs, as Anderson popped two of her three stumm grenades and hurled one after the other at the head of the pursuing throng. She grabbed the respirator from her belt as the canisters bounced along the ground, streaming noxious yellow smoke. The berserk citizens ran straight into the billowing cloud, making no attempt to cover their faces. Anderson watched as every one of them fell choking.

The Meet Market float continued to advance, its wheels grinding towards the unconscious citizens now sprawled beneath the thinning fumes. Anderson looked about her. The temple appeared to be mounted on a huge automated truck. She jumped down into the control pit behind the pillars and searched for the brakes. The controls appeared to have been modified, and it took her a few seconds to locate anything that resembled a brake lever.

She wrenched it back with both hands, and the float lurched to a halt. The cherub columns toppled forward, headbutting each other as the polyfoam pediment crashed to one side. Anderson ducked as gallons of shampagne fountained into the air from the float's ruptured pipes. The sparkling rain drenched her as she replaced her respirator in her belt and clambered from the cockpit. All thoughts of the stumm gas now forgotten, the uninfected citizens were vaulting the barriers and dancing in the alcoholic shower.

Anderson pushed through the ecstatic crowd and found one of the poisoned citizens lying inches from the float's front tyre. He was already waking up, revived by the sweet-tasting rain. She took his head in both hands and could feel that the hatred Eros had fired into his mind was already dispersing. If Eros' psi-amp had been working at full capacity, the effects would have been as indelible as they had been for Montana, and Van Doren would have been murdered by an army of unstoppable madmen.

As Anderson ran for her Lawmaster, she could see a couple of Judges further up the tunnel attending to Van Doren and his runaway slaves. The dishevelled CEO was on his feet and gesticulating wildly. At least he was safe.

Anderson mounted her Lawmaster and charged through the frolicking crowd, heading back down the tunnel. She passed maintenance personnel in lumo-jackets hurrying to investigate the cause of the parade's blockage, as the queue of floats behind Van Doren had been forced to come to a stop. Not that the partying citizens seemed to have noticed. A woman leaped out in front of Anderson, playing chicken with the oncoming Lawmaster. Anderson swerved to avoid her, ignoring the jeering crowds as she sped onwards.

As the floats began rolling forward again, Anderson slowed to a cruise. She pawed the sweat from her eyes and scanned the crowds. All she could see was a wall of bodies wilting in the heat, peeling off sweat-soaked clothing, glugging at bottles of water. Their thoughts were also succumbing to the heat, slowing down, melting into a single primal pulse. Amid this thumping chorus, Anderson could make out one set of brainwaves piping like a flute.

Must cool down. Escape this heat.

She sped towards the source of the thoughts, searching the crowd, placing her hand on the last stumm grenade attached to her belt. He was in there somewhere, but the throng was ten bodies deep and she was not tall enough to see over their heads. She needed to take him out before he cooled down, if she was to stand any chance of bringing him in alive.

As she continued to scan the crowd, she felt a bolt of psi-energy lash out. A black arrow. He must have felt her presence. But the missile had not been aimed at her. She looked around. The dart had been intense enough to cause madness almost instantly, but whom had it struck?

The crowd screamed as a huge truck carrying a vast structure covered in dancers veered towards them. The vehicle blocked Anderson's path as it mounted the pavement. She stood and flung her hand towards the driver, slinging a psi-bolt into his head. He fell to one side, turning the wheel, narrowly avoiding crushing the citizens as they shrank from the barriers. The driver re-emerged behind the windscreen. Anderson's shot had been unfocused, and the driver had already shaken off the effects. She leapt from her Lawmaster as it was crushed beneath the wheels of the advancing truck. The crowd roared their approval.

Anderson ran to one side of the vehicle, leaping onto the driver's door as he accelerated towards a marching band some distance in front of him, intent on mowing them down. Anderson heaved open the door, threw herself across the driver's lap, and wrenched the handbrake. The truck lurched to a halt, as the driver grabbed her hair with both hands and slammed her head into the dashboard with stunning force. Bracing her hand against the dash before he could do it again, she saw a lunch pail on the passenger seat. She grabbed it and twisted onto her back, swinging the metal canister at the driver's head. The blow caught him on the temple and he fell from the cab onto the road outside.

Anderson saw Eros standing amid the crowd, facing the stationary truck. He had stripped off his shirt and was dowsing himself with bottled water, touching his temple with his free hand. His face drooped at the jowls, the pervading heat melting his waxen mask, although he had cooled himself down enough for one good blast.

Anderson raised a psionic shield as a volley of psi-bolts sizzled past her head. She scrambled for the cab's open door, curling her finger through the pin of her last stumm grenade. The cab's rear window shattered and a flurry of hands grabbed her from behind. Her unseen attackers hauled her backwards through the broken window, tugging her arms and freeing the pin from the grenade before she could drop it. Frothing yellow smoke filled the cab. Her attackers retreated before the emerging fog, leaving Anderson to wriggle the rest of the way through the window, straining to hold her breath as the cloud enveloped her. She fell onto a pile of plasteen rocks, as she got her respirator into her mouth and sucked in a lungful of clean air.

She peered through the yellow mist, trying to locate an escape route. Eros would now be fleeing back up the tunnel towards the Meet Market float. The last of the stumm gas dissolved, revealing the entirety of the parade float that had been built on top of the truck. Anderson found herself surrounded by the coils of a towering replica snake. Instead of a head, the huge creature's neck terminated in a reptilian fist aiming a semi-automatic pistol into the air. A number of muscular women perched like vultures about the snake's coiling body. All had long black hair, their bodies painted to resemble patterned snakeskin.

Anderson recognised them straight away: the Diamondback Sambarettas, a famously psychotic dance troupe originating from Ciudad Barranquilla. Anderson could hear their thoughts raging with inexplicable hatred for this trespasser. She estimated well over a dozen of them glaring down at her. There would have been more, but Anderson presumed the rest were still in the cubes after last year performing a raunchy dance number that involved them hospitalising everyone from a rival dance school. These women had been psychotic long before Eros pumped their heads full of psi-venom.

As the stumm gas cleared, the crowds either side of the Sambarettas' float hollered and whooped in anticipation. Anderson went to draw her Lawgiver, but a foot came out of nowhere, slamming into her cheek, knocking the respirator from her mouth and throwing her onto her back. Her Lawgiver landed somewhere nearby. Anderson drew her daystick in time to block another kick, then another, before punching the weapon into her attacker's knee, dropping her.

The other Sambarettas howled and descended towards Anderson. She searched for her Lawgiver, but found only a tool-rack concealed on the back of the cab. She snatched a tyre iron and turned, a weapon in each hand, to face the maddened women charging towards her.

As the first turned to launch a kick, Anderson smashed her daystick across the woman's face, then broke her outstretched leg with a chop from the tyre iron. The second Sambaretta flung a kick at Anderson's chest. She dodged and struck the woman's chin with an upward swing of the daystick. She then spun around and smashed a third dancer in the teeth with the tyre iron. A fourth closed in, about to drive an elbow into Anderson's throat. Anderson popped a psi-bolt into her attacker's head and watched, unmoved, as her assailant crashed to ground.

The boos of the crowd filled the air as Anderson looked up. The other women had disappeared. She sent out a psi-pulse, scanning her surroundings. They were flanking her, cutting off her escape. She looked behind her to see several of the women vaulting over the serpent's coils towards her. A ferociously beautiful woman wearing a headdress of snake skulls had climbed onto the roof of the cab. She snapped a whip at Anderson's face, slashing her cheek.

The woman snarled as the others bounded towards Anderson.

"¡*Muere, puta*!"

Anderson hurled the tyre iron at the nearest Sambaretta, the tool bouncing off the woman's skull, toppling her. Anderson then turned and fled towards the rear of the float. She knew her only hope was to outrun them, dismount the float and maybe lose them in the crowd while she somehow doubled back to search for Eros. She tumbled over fibreglass coils, snagging her uniform on imitation cacti, constantly losing her footing as her feet plunged into troughs in the scenery concealed by stage-smoke. The Sambarettas closed in behind her, bounding with effortless grace. The crowd were in hysterics, their voices a chanting roar.

"Samba! Samba! Samba!"

As Anderson neared the rear of the float, she saw two more Sambarettas climbing aboard, blocking her escape. She sprinted, then launched herself past the two women and towards the float parked behind them. She landed on the side of a tower made of pink stone and began clambering up a line of embossed lettering that read, *SPARTAN CONDOMS*. The pursuing Sambarettas leapt after her onto the tower as Anderson reached the top, scattering a group of half-naked bodybuilders dressed as ancient Greek warriors.

Daystick in hand, she grabbed a shield from one of the men and shoved him behind her as the Sambarettas swarmed onto the roof of the tower. Anderson lashed out with her daystick, catching the nearest dancer on the side of the head and hurling her from the tower. She swung back, breaking the arm of another who was reaching for her hair, then slammed her next attacker aside with the shield. She turned and kicked away the snarling face of another Sambaretta clawing her way onto the roof.

Anderson raised her shield to block a kick aimed at her face, but the force of the blow shoved her backwards. Another attacker plunged a kick into her side. Ignoring a stabbing pain that could only mean a cracked rib, Anderson spun around and drove the edge of her shield into her attacker's throat. The woman staggered back, choking, as another Sambaretta sprang at Anderson. She batted the woman aside with the shield, mule-kicked another in the stomach, and elbowed her daystick into the face of a third.

As she raised the weapon to strike an overhead blow, she heard the crack of a whip and the daystick vanished from her hand. She saw the Sambarettas' troupe leader, Miss Snakeskull, standing on the rear of her float, smiling up at Anderson and twirling her whip. Anderson was horrified to see the woman had a pistol in her other hand.

Two more Sambarettas grabbed Anderson's shield. She tried to shove them away, but they were too strong. Someone landed a kick into her stomach. She gasped and doubled over just as a well-aimed knee slammed into her face, flinging her onto her back.

The remaining Sambarettas closed in, raining kicks and stomps at her head and body. Anderson had no choice but to curl into a ball. She could see, in the black rage boiling inside the heads of her attackers, that they would not stop until she was dead. Ignoring the blows pounding her ribs and head, Anderson snapped out a pulse of psi-energy.

The Sambarettas staggered back, their minds stung, as Anderson rose to her feet, teeth clenched in fury. She caught the first woman by the hair and rammed a knee into her face, snap-kicked another in the chest, and delivered an explosive spin-kick into the knee of the woman behind her. She grabbed the last Sambaretta by the shoulder and threw a right cross at her face. But the punch went wild as Miss Snakeskull's whip snapped around Anderson's throat and yanked her onto her back. As the last Sambaretta recovered and attacked, Anderson threw up her legs, catching the woman's neck between her boots and slamming her face-first into the floor.

Anderson felt herself dragged by the throat towards the edge of the parapet. Below her stood Miss Snakeskull, cackling as she aimed her pistol at Anderson's head. The crowd screamed. Anderson struggled to free herself. Then she recognised the pistol as her missing Lawgiver.

She winced as Miss Snakeskull squeezed the trigger. Having identified an unregistered user, the Justice Department weapon exploded in her hand. The Sambaretta's leader dropped to her knees, staring in disbelief at the ragged stump of her arm. Anderson disentangled the whip from her neck and climbed down the side of the tower. She ran to Miss Snakeskull and wound the whip around the stump of her arm, stemming the flow of blood, before calling for a med-wagon.

Anderson left the float and staggered back up the tunnel after the rest of the parade. She felt as though she had half a dozen knives sticking out of her body. She had lost every weapon save her boot-knife, while her Lawmaster lay crushed beneath the back wheels of the Sambaretta's float. Meanwhile, Eros had long since headed back up the tunnel.

Anderson was drenched in sweat, the air thick with heat. Eros would himself be sweltering by now, rendering his psi-amp useless. Her head throbbing hard enough to make her feel nauseous, she jogged up the tunnel, her aching feet scuffing through a carpet of debris and confetti. Every step sent jolts of pain into her cracked rib. She ignored it and broke into a run, wiping confetti from her eyes, spitting it from her lips. She scanned the crowds either side of her. Had Eros disappeared down a side tunnel and fled back into the city? Had he doubled back? No, even though Van Doren had evaded him, he still wanted to destroy the parade. But in order to do that, he would need to cool himself down long enough to get his psi-amp working again.

She caught up with the marching band that had preceded the Sambarettas' float. She managed to overtake two more floats before the pain in her rib became unbearable and she stumbled to the ground, gasping in pain. A young woman wearing a pale blue swimsuit ran to her side. She set down a bucket full of canned drinks, which she had been handing out to the crowd.

"You need me to call someone?" she said.

"I could use a good-looking masseur right about now," Anderson said. "And tell him to bring pizza."

Anderson winced and grabbed the girl's shoulder, hauling herself upright. The girl reached into the bucket and offered Anderson an ice-cold can of soda. Anderson read the label: *Frostbite: Puts Ice In Your Veins.*

She looked up at the float the girl was accompanying, which comprised a huge glass water tank, decorated to resemble an iceberg. Young men and women in fishtail costumes, with aqua-respirators in their mouths, somersaulted through the fizzing water, beckoning to the passing crowd.

Anderson grabbed the ice-bucket and emptied the contents

over her head. She gasped at the refreshing cold and wiped her eyes. The bemused girl watched her leap aboard the Frostbite float and grab a ladder leading up the side of the pool. Anderson paused to examine one of the rungs. It was smeared with a flesh-coloured paste. Melted wax.

She scanned the area for thoughtwaves, but could hear nothing aboard the float except the five swimmers in the tank and about half a dozen attendants handing out drinks nearby. Eros had found a cold place to hide and get his little toy working again. He was up there right now, cloaking his thoughts, perhaps unaware that she had found him.

She scaled the rest of the ladder and crept onto a ledge spanning the pool. Another attendant wearing a Frostbite jacket stood on the other side of the platform, his back to Anderson, tossing bottled drinks into the crowd. Spots of melted wax dotted the floor behind him. Anderson sprang, locking her arms around the man's neck and throwing him to the floor. She went to choke him into unconsciousness, but the bearded young man trapped behind her forearm was not Eros.

The lid of the chest freezer beside them flew open, and a tall figure erupted from beneath a mound of ice and canned drinks. Anderson felt something like a bomb go off in her head. For a moment, she thought she had been shot. The young man she had mistakenly attacked scrabbled away down the ladder.

She fought to raise her psionic shield, but Eros was already inside her head. His waxen mask had completely fallen away beneath his dripping black curls, revealing what remained of his face. The glowing Halo discs had been screwed into his cheekbones and skull, connected by wires running the length of the claw-marks that streaked his face. His lipless teeth chattered with cold. His round, lidless eyes stared as she squirmed at his feet.

"I have something special for you, Judge Anderson," he said, every word a dart of hate.

The wings of blue light flaring from his back shone like the sun as Anderson felt herself pinned to the floor by the weight of his fury. She felt a rain of black arrows prickling her body. The corners of Eros' mouth tightened into a grotesque smile as she gagged and writhed. She felt her muscles vibrate, every cell in her body turning on its neighbour, every natural molecular function overwhelmed by pure mindless aggression.

I've never seen a body eat itself before, Eros thought.

Anderson screamed.

Ten

ANDERSON FELT AS though she were being fried in oil. She could feel her insides writhing, as though maggots swarmed around her bones. Eros peered down at her, like a juve burning an ant under a magnifying glass.

"Stop pretending you're still a person, Judge. You are a machine, a heartless product of the Justice Department assembly line."

His ruined face twisted even further into a grimace.

"You could have saved this city."

He knelt until Anderson could hear his teeth chattering in her ear.

"You could have saved *me*."

The wings of light radiating from his shoulders intensified. Anderson convulsed, tasting blood in her throat, as her vision clouded and her brain bubbled into unconsciousness.

Eros grunted as someone hit him across the back of the head.

He staggered to his knees, his wings flickering like faulty strip-lights. The pain sizzling throughout Anderson's body vanished. She gasped, dragging breath into her tortured lungs as she felt herself dragged to one side. Her limbs fizzed with pins and needles as she struggled to gather her thoughts. She looked up into the familiar face of the young woman who had offered her a can of soda.

"It's okay," she said. "We got this."

Nearby a young man was attempting to threaten Eros with half a mop, the handle of which he had just broken across the psyker's head.

"Whatever you're doing, dude," he said, "back off."

It was the bearded young man whom Anderson had mistaken for the killer. Several more swimsuited attendants joined them from below. They were around the same age as Anderson and held their ground nervously as Eros rose to his feet, his wings reigniting. Anderson clutched at the arm of the young woman who now stood between her and Eros. She tried to scream at them all to run, but a strangled whisper was all she could manage.

Eros threw himself into the minds of the surrounding youngsters. They stiffened as if electrified, but the psyker did not consume them just yet. Instead, he fired one volley after another of psi-bolts into the crowd either side of the float. His wings turned a dazzling white as his flesh wrinkled and sagged.

Anderson closed her eyes and reached for him, but her mind was a mess. She fell face down. In her mind's eye she saw swarms of black arrows descending into the crowd. He must have hit hundreds of citizens by now, an army ready to plunge from one end of the tunnel to the other, murdering everyone in their path. She looked up and saw Eros convulse, his chest sucked into his ribs.

Anderson felt him gathering the last of his life-force, preparing to send out a psychic pulse that would ignite the minds of everyone his psi-bolts had struck. She rose to her feet, moving like a robot standing to attention. Eros' curly black hair fell away, revealing a bald skull.

She fell towards him, grabbed his shoulder and thrust her boot knife into his heart. His wings vanished and she felt him let go of the crowds. The Frostbite youngsters fell to the floor, released.

Eros clapped his hands either side of Anderson's face, the bones of his fingers piercing his crumbling flesh as he went to drive a final, lethal psi-bolt into her head. She hooked her arm around the back of his neck, hugging him as she pushed the knife up to the hilt. His eyes rolled back and dropped from their sockets, his teeth nearing her lips as if closing in for a departing kiss. She turned her head away as he slumped on top of her and they both fell backwards into the pool below.

Anderson let the cold water envelop her, swelling her boots and uniform. She watched the trail of bubbles leave her mouth and wriggle to the surface. Eros left her arms as she sank. He rose to the surface amid a cloud of ash and powdered blood, arms aloft as though he were taking flight. She closed her eyes and thought of Montana lying in a bed, beside a machine that would now be showing a flat, humming line. Water gushed down her throat as the last of her strength disappeared.

She awoke to feel someone pounding on her chest. She opened her eyes as water hurried up her throat and out of her mouth. She rolled onto her side, choking and gasping at the feet of the youngsters who had saved her.

"Thank Grud you're okay," said the Frostbite girl, who was kneeling beside her.

Before Anderson could draw enough breath to thank her, a Judge clambered aboard the float.

"Anderson, right?" the Judge said, shoving the girl aside.

Anderson nodded and coughed as she rose to her feet.

"Stay put. The Meds are on their way."

The Judge turned to crouch beside the pool, now covered with a scum of ash.

"That's your Meet Market killer, huh?"

Anderson did not respond. She had already clambered down the ladder and jumped aboard the nearby Lawmaster. The Judge yelled after her as Anderson sped down the tunnel towards the Sector House.

MONTANA'S CHEST ROSE and fell beneath the covers. The machine by his side registered a strong and steady bleep. Eros was dead, the psychic link that was supposedly sustaining Montana's life-force had been severed. And yet Montana still lived.

"How?" Anderson asked the Med Judge.

"I had the psi-specialist in here earlier asking exactly the same thing," he said, trying to sound nonchalant. "We ran another psi-scan over Judge Montana and it seems there's been a misdiagnosis."

Anderson swayed on her feet, but shrugged off the two other Meds who were trying to usher her into an exam room. The first Med Judge shifted uncomfortably, unnerved by Anderson's intensity as he explained further.

"This connection that's been sustaining Judge Montana this whole time? It's actually some kind of powerful emotional bond, not a psychic one. And it turns out he wasn't sharing this bond with the man who attacked him."

"Then who is he sharing it with?"

Montana stirred.

"Anderson?" he said.

ANDERSON SAT ON a bench facing a fountain in the Meet Market butterfly ranch. She watched several of the dainty insects flexing their golden wings as they settled on the sleeve of her yellow sports jacket. She enjoyed the warmth of the afternoon sun glowing through the glass dome arcing above her, the heat leavened by an artificial but no less refreshing breeze. She watched Meet Market's office workers eating their lunch and chatting on the other benches.

A young woman approached, nodding a greeting as she sat down next to Anderson and unwrapped an expensive-looking sandwich. She bit into it and let out a moan of pleasure, then glanced at Anderson, embarrassed.

"That good, huh?" Anderson said.

The girl laughed.

"I've been on homemade for so damn long now, I thought I'd splash out."

She took another bite.

"You saw the news, right?"

Anderson nodded. Hauser himself had attended the press conference, stating that, following a full investigation by the Justice Department, Meet Market had been cleared of all wrongdoing. The true perpetrator had been judged to the full extent of the law.

"Thought I'd be out of a job by the end of the week," said the woman. "We all did."

A hologram fizzled into life from the top of the fountain, resolving itself into an image of Cupid Van Doren's face, his hair and beard exploding into a flock of white doves as he appeared. The head revolved, addressing each bench in turn.

"Good afternoon, lovebirds. This is your matchmaker speaking, still alive and kicking, and we're now officially futsie-free since 2094. Well, almost..."

His head spun into a Tri-D commercial contained within a holographic sphere. The scene was a caff-bar in which a Judge had just gunned down a perp.

"I don't know what happened, Judge," said a confused-looking man in glasses. "She just went crazy."

The Judge blew smoke from the barrel of his Lawgiver.

"Well, with prices like these, citizen, I'm not surprised. A third off all subscriptions and a free caff-maker if you sign up before the end of February."

"But that's insane," gasped the man, clutching his head as he foamed at the mouth. The Meet Market logo fluttered onto the screen as the Judge beat the man into submission.

Anderson sighed.

"I never thought I'd be happy to see another of those stupid commercials," said the woman.

Anderson turned at the sound of an approaching Lawmaster.

"Move along, citizen," Montana said, waving away the woman as he pulled up. She shot Anderson a fearful look before hurrying away with her sandwich.

"Med bay told me you were on R&R up here," he said.

Anderson went to speak, but Montana held up his hand.

"Look, before you say anything, I know you can hear what I'm thinking. So there's no point me saying anything other than what I mean, right?"

"Go on."

"I have to ask," he said. "Do you..."

"No," she said.

He sat back. "Wow. Don't spare a guy his feelings."

"We're Judges," she said. "We can't afford to feel."

"That doesn't sound like you."

"It's the truth," she said. "You need to keep a clear head out there unless you wanna get killed."

"Would it bother you if I was?"

Anderson looked away.

"You can read me, Anderson. But I can't read you. Kinda frustrating."

"I'm telling you what I'm thinking, Montana."

"No you're not."

The butterflies on her sleeve scattered as she got to her feet and glared at him.

"We could both face an investigation just for talking about this," she said. "We're Judges, Montana."

He caught her arm. *We don't have to be*, he thought.

Anderson pulled away, pretending not to hear.

"I gotta go," she said, making a show of checking her timer. "I'm due back at Psi-Div by 14:30."

Montana said nothing, his thoughts seething.

"Take care of yourself, Montana."

He looked away and snarled at a couple smooching on another bench. "Keep it clean, citizens," he said. "This is a public area."

Anderson gave him a look.

Montana shrugged. "Hey, hearts and flowers won't get you far in this city, right?"

He revved his Lawmaster and rode away.

Anderson let him go.

PART TWO
THE ABYSS

Psi-Division, Quarterly Psyche Evaluation
Subject: Psi-Judge Cassandra Anderson
Date: 14.03.2100

"I MADE FULL eagle less than three months ago and I can say for sure there's one thing the Academy *can't* prepare you for, and that's the level of full-on crazy this town can throw at you. What you see on the crime scenes is nothing compared to what I see in people's heads—delusions as real to them as rockcrete. The Academy taught us not to fall in, right? Don't let the abyss gaze back at you and all that? It's weird. I'm not scared of getting shot. I can tell if a perp's gonna draw on me before he knows himself; I know exactly who's waiting for me around every corner. There's not much chance of anyone surprising *me*. Grud on a greenie, I can't imagine what it's like for Street-Div walking into hell every day with just a Lawgiver and a prayer.

"With an edge like ours, it's easy to feel like you're invincible, right? That's why the instructors kept telling you Resyk's full of Psis who thought they were bulletproof. Heh! What they *didn't* tell us is how many of us will end up in a kook-cube by the time we're forty. So here's... Okay, *here's* what scares me, alright? I'm scared that one day all those voices in the city are gonna get a little too loud, a little too many and a little too real. They're gonna start crowding in until I can't breathe, until I can't tell what's me and what's them. I'm not scared this city will kill me, Doc. I'm scared that one day it might drive me crazy..."

MEGA-CITY ONE
2100 A.D.

Eleven

THE COLD AIR stank of piss and garbage. Streaming water splattered the floor somewhere nearby. Judge Gurney figured he must be below ground. A disused parking lot, maybe? Some kind of linen—a pillowcase probably—covered his bare head, with his helmet replaced on top. Gurney angled his head until he could just about see through a split seam in the fabric. His visor shaded his eyes against the glare of the torch-beams, but he could distinguish little about the figures who held them as they peered up at him from the surrounding gloom. They had smashed the micro-computer inside his helmet, killing his comm relay and retinal tac-display. Gurney could feel the tiny broken circuit-board stabbing his scalp. His wrists were bound close behind his back. The cords felt thin through his gloves. Cable-ties? Someone stood behind him, their hand on the cross-section of his wrists, steadying him as he wavered on tiptoe, straining against the cord that tethered his neck to the ceiling.

It had been the rookie's fault. All Judges had been advised to vary their patrol routes ever since the Department started receiving direct threats, but Higgins had insisted on grabbing a burger from his favourite munce-joint on the way back to the Sector House, and Gurney had been exhausted enough to indulge him. Around 02:05 they spotted a white two-seater Hamasaki parked outside the munce-house. Someone had been pretending to be asleep inside. Before Gurney could stop him, Higgins had approached the vehicle without hailing the driver first. Despite fifteen years in the Academy, a hotdog run, and several months on the streets, some rookies still believed they could get by on nothing but swagger and a shiny badge. Higgins took a stun-bolt to the chest, while three guys had run at Gurney from the shadows waving tools. He managed to draw and get a single shot into the chest of the nearest perp, broke the jaw of the second and the neck of the third before a sizzling pain flooded his body. And here he was.

"The Justice Department," announced one of the figures, swishing his arm, "has failed to take us seriously."

The speaker sounded young, educated. He was trying valiantly to maintain a sense of drama, his voice breathless with nerves.

"They have ignored our demands to release Moriah Blake from custody. They have also underestimated how many citizens of Mega-City One are ready to fight in her name. And now, Bedlam begins."

Bedlam. Six months ago these dorks were just another anti-Judge movement, like the Social Justice Commandoes, the White Suprezmoes, Simps Against Shoulderpads. Low-level agitators easily frightened back into the woodwork with a few strategic arrests. Only this time, the crime-blitzes, the lockdowns and the beatings only seemed to encourage them. They had graduated quickly from flash-riots to sabotaging Department property. They were organised, committed and—worst of all—the cits seemed to like them. Fear was the Department's most reliable deterrent, but sometimes a pack of dweebs would actually grow a pair and, judging by tonight's shenanigans, Bedlam's balls weren't gonna shrink any time soon.

Gurney wobbled on whatever it was they had him standing on and he felt the cord tighten around his neck. The guy standing behind him caught his arms and steadied him. Gurney had already managed to work his tongue up through the tape pasted across his mouth, and was pulling at the fabric hood with his lips and teeth, chewing at the cloth until the seam tore a little more. He turned his head carefully, peering through the narrow gap. Higgins stood beside him, illuminated in the torchlight, full of muffled curses, his head straining blindly about him, a white line of what looked like plasti-cord connecting him to a thick overhead pipe.

"They're holding Moriah at Psych-Block Six in Sector Thirty-Two," the boy said. "Imprisoning her alongside murderers and maniacs. And yet her only crime has been to voice the truth about the Judges, about the degradation they inflict upon us every day and the madness they have driven us to. All she has done is remind us that we're human, that we're not alone, that we're not powerless."

Gurney looked up. From what he could make out, the plasti-cord around his neck was tied to another overhead pipe, stemming from a heavy downpipe scaled with rust and way out of reach.

"People of Mega-City One," the boy said.

Drokk, thought Gurney. *Are the creeps broadcasting this? Am I on camera? Better make this look good.*

"The only way to win back our sanity," the boy continued, "is to embrace the madness the Justice Department has inflicted upon us."

"Bedlam begins!" yelled the others.

"We're not terrorists," the boy said, his voice now soaring with confidence. "We're just citizens who have decided to no longer live in fear. We're the slaves finally turning on our masters. If you hate the Judges, then join us. If you want to help build a future free of fear, then join us. There are already more of us than the Judges can ever contain."

Gurney's heart pounded. He might be able to snap the cable-ties around his wrists, given enough leverage, but the cord around his neck was another matter. If he could speak to them without a mouthful of tape and pillowcase he might be able to scare them into backing down. Grud help them if he got within reach of a weapon. They were punks, whereas Gurney was a Judge, trained from childhood to fight, to endure, to react with the ruthless logic of Department protocol in the midst of panic and insanity. Gurney felt a surge of pride; he was eager to teach these callow revolutionaries what it meant to threaten the life of a Judge.

"To the Justice Department, we say this: Judges are dying tonight and more will die tomorrow, and the next night, until you release Moriah Blake. We know it's pointless to ask for your surrender, so consider tonight's execution the opening shot in a war you can only lose."

Gurney grabbed the thumb of the hand that steadied him, twisting it until the joint popped and a man screamed in his ear. Bracing the muscles in his neck as the crate rocked beneath his feet, he turned and whipped an enormous padded boot into the man's body, feeling the density of sternum and ribs. The linen had twisted over Gurney's eyes, blindfolding him once again, but he heard the man crash backwards into the corroded downpipe, the impact reverberating through the overhead pipe to which he was tethered. Cries of outrage arose and Gurney felt the crate kicked from beneath him. The cord snared his throat as he fell and Judge Gurney hung suspended for a moment, snorting, blood churning in his ears, his heavy boots stamping emptiness.

Then the pipe above him collapsed, dropping him to his knees as it sheared away from the downpipe and slammed across Gurney's shoulders with a hollow clang, driving his face into the floor and knocking his helmet off. He ignored the pain in his shoulders and hammered his bound wrists upon the anvil of his spine. Once, twice and the cable-ties snapped, freeing his hands to loosen the cord around his throat.

He dragged air into his lungs as someone tweaked the pillowcase from his head, unveiling a stained asphalt floor.

"Leave the noose on, Judge," the boy said.

Gurney convulsed, coughing, and squinted into the torchlight. A hooded young man was aiming a pistol at his face. Gurney slowly raised his hands, letting the noose drop to his shoulders. The weapon was a Kleestack .50 las-pistol, an expensive home-defence piece probably stolen from someone's dad. The boy's eyes were a brilliant blue above the patterned scarf that covered his nose and mouth. He gripped the Kleestack with both hands, trying to hide the fact that he was shaking like a virgin about to get laid.

Gurney surveyed the darkness of whatever corner of the Meg's sub-terrain these guys had selected for their ritual, and figured the boy had at least eight buddies, all wearing dark gymwear and ready with baseball bats, hammers and tyre irons, clutching them like they were trying to hide behind them. One of them wore a vid-visor, the green light above his eyes indicating the camera was still rolling.

"Gurney," he said. "My name's Titus Gurney. That there's my partner Reedus Higgins."

The boy shifted uncomfortably as Gurney indicated Higgins, still poised atop his crate with the cord around his neck, but quiet now, trying to listen.

"You're not gonna pull that trigger, son," Gurney told the boy, placing his hands on the ground as he went to rise. "You're too smart for that."

"Stay where you are," the boy gabbled. "On the floor, I mean. Stay on the drokkin' floor."

Gurney remained kneeling, hands on his thighs.

"Pre-med murder of a Judge during the execution of his duties carries a life sentence, kid."

"It isn't murder if what you're killing isn't human," the boy said. He sounded like he was reciting scripture.

"C'mon, Robbie," said one of his buddies, a young woman. "What are you waiting for? Just do it. What do you think we came here for?"

"Shut your gruddamn yap, creep!" Gurney's snarl echoed through the chamber. "You wanna win him more cube-time?"

The boy recoiled. He was scared. Good.

"You're not a killer, Robbie," Gurney said, rising to his feet. The boy's hands were shaking so much his crappy little piece might go off any second.

"Which is why you're gonna put that gun down and let my partner go."

The boy was struggling to summon his resolve.

"I'm not gonna pretend we're not talking sentences here," Gurney said, moving towards snatching distance of the pistol. "But I'm willing to take time off if you co-operate."

The boy edged back towards his buddies.

"Believe me," Gurney said. "It'll go worse for you guys if you string this out. Trust me when I tell you this. No matter how well you think you've planned this, how carefully you think you've covered your tracks, we'll have you on surveillance somewhere. We'll have your records, and the minute Tek-Division get here we'll have your DNA too. Hell, they've got this gizmo now that can tell what you ate for breakfast just from the air you've breathed. And when we find you, it'll go bad for your families, too, and for anyone else we decide may have covered for you."

The boy was glaring at him now.

"There's no escape from the Justice Department, Robbie," Gurney said. "No way outta this. Now drop the gun."

Robbie shot Higgins twice, bright red laser bolts disappearing into the man's chest. Gurney launched himself at the boy, but something lassoed his throat. His legs ran out from under him and he fell onto his back, jerked into submission like a dog on a leash. The noose. Gurney had been so focused on the boy he had forgotten about the noose resting on his shoulders, still anchored to a heavy length of pipe. The creeps were laughing at him as he struggled to free himself. Higgins' corpse sagged nearby, still tethered to the ceiling by his neck, his feet still resting on the crate. The cord around Gurney's own neck tightened like a garrotte around his fingers, trapping them. Someone was reeling him in like a fish.

Robbie stepped after him, followed by the creep with the vidvisor.

"You're right," Robbie said. "There's no escape for any of us."

He pulled the scarf down to his chin, revealing a young face distorted with rage.

"We're always under curfew, under surveillance. Our homes are blitzed for crimes we know nothing about. Our loved ones are dragged away for questioning and we never see them again. We get fined so hard we can't afford the rent, then we get cubed for living on the street. We can't protest. We can't speak out. You've taken everything from us."

Gurney continued struggling as he was dragged to a stop and a foot pushed down on his shoulder-pad, pulling the cord even tighter.

"You've driven us to the point of madness," Robbie said, almost in tears. "You've driven us to this."

He pointed to the body of the Judge he had just murdered, the boy's expression somewhere between horror and awe.

"Madness is all we have left."

The others crowded about Gurney as Robbie knelt before him, the las-pistol shaking not in fear but with fury. Gurney choked, his eyelids peeling back from his bulging eyeballs as he raised his hands as if in surrender.

"So don't tell me you're human," Robbie spat. "Don't tell me how much you sympathise. You are a machine; Justice Department hardware. You are—"

Gurney slapped the inside of the boy's wrist with one hand and snatched the gun with the other. Robbie stared for an instant, as though he had just witnessed a magic trick, and Gurney shot him in the eye.

The cord squeezed savagely around Gurney's throat as the others wrestled the pistol from his grip, breaking his fingers. He felt the cord slicing his throat, numbing him to the kicks and blows now demolishing his body. A ceiling of faces snarled down at him, consumed by hate and fury. As Judge Titus Gurney's consciousness melted into oblivion, he wondered what he had ever done to deserve such malice.

PSI-JUDGE ANDERSON TURNED away and held her breath as a hulking tanker-truck thundered past, enveloping her in a cloud of grit. She squinted through the haze of dust, watching the chain-link fences billowing like sheets either side of the road as the tanker rumbled away into the darkness. She ruffled the dirt out of her hair and looked again at her watch. She had been standing beside her Lawmaster on this lonesome road for the best part of an hour, feeling gradually sickened by the fumes of the nearby munce-packing plant, its chimneys bleeding columns of brown smoke into the night sky. Another vehicle was approaching, the headlamp array and the panther-like growl of its 4,000cc engine unmistakable. *Finally*, she thought.

She waved the Lawmaster down and its rider pulled in, the bike purring to a stop, the benighted city-blocks of Sector 32 a glittering mountain range in the background. The rider removed her helmet.

"Grud on a greenie," Anderson said, throwing up her hands. "You've gotta be kidding me."

Psi-Judge Zeinner retained her customary look of elegant indifference.

"Sorry I'm late, Cassie," she said. "The riots have got everything diverted around Kubrick Block."

"Psi-Div figure I'm not up to this, right?" Anderson said. "So why did Chief Ecks let me take the call?"

Zeinner was already raising her hands placatingly, giving Anderson that superior, older-sister look that always made Anderson want to throw something at her.

"I've been to Psych-Block Six several times before, Cassie," she said. "I know what it's like in there and I know how to help you handle it, okay? I'm here tonight as your partner, not your therapist."

Anderson was so used to seeing Zeinner in the formal surroundings of her office at Psi-Division, legs always crossed, hands always folded, that it felt intrusive to see her walking around in the outside world. It looked as though Anderson had found yet another reason to curse herself for losing it during her last psych-exam.

Like all Psi-Cadets, she had been subjected to these interrogations every three months since she was a child, but her confidence, directness, and the insight of her responses always seemed to earn her a pass. But her most recent interview had also been her first after making full eagle, and she had sweated through the whole damn thing. Sat in the armchair before Zeinner, Anderson had found herself suddenly, inexplicably terrified that her next answer might somehow jeopardise everything she had earned in the Academy. It was as though her first few months on the streets had weakened her. She had always been so open during her time at the Academy; she had never had secrets before now.

She had to tell Zeinner everything. A girl had no choice when her examiner was a telepath. She had told her about the nightmares, the feelings of listlessness, about the voices in her head. And what was the point leaving out all the stuff about Judge Montana during the Meet Market case? Zeinner had assured her that everything she disclosed was done so in strict confidence. Yeah, right.

During the weekly sessions incurred by the exam, Zeinner had advised her to get as much natural rest as possible and avoid using a sleep-machine. But after hours of staring at the ceiling, listening to her bunkmates mumbling and farting in the dark, she would head to the gym and take out her tension on the bags or whoever was dumb enough to spar with her in the ring. Or she'd go make some doilies out of the targets on the gun range. Zeinner had called these aggressive nocturnal pursuits a 'coping mechanism.' A mechanism. Like Anderson's mind was a machine ready to pop a spring. She dismissed the thought before Zeinner could hear it, which she probably already had.

"A shield-partner is standard protocol when visiting a psych-block," Zeinner said. "Everyone else was on assignment. I was free. That's all."

Anderson couldn't tell if she was lying. She never could. Zeinner was shielding her mind, just as she did during their sessions, and Anderson couldn't hear a thing. The woman's concentration was seemingly effortless, her placid expression both unwavering and maddening. Anderson's most excruciating secrets stood bare naked before a virtual stranger. She wondered how anyone could stand being around a telepath longer than five minutes without wanting to shove them out of a window.

Faced with Zeinner—she didn't even know the woman's first name—Anderson's only option, as always, was surrender. They were late anyway and Anderson's eyes felt hot and tired. She wanted a shower and something other than a bowl of E-Z paste for dinner.

"Then how about we grab a pizza on the way back?" Zeinner said.

Anderson threw her a look.

"Sorry," Zeinner said.

Anderson climbed onto the saddle of her Lawmaster and rolled the throttle, coaxing a snarl from the monstrous machine.

"Pizza's cool, Doc," she said. "But I'm warning you. If I see you writing in that gruddamn notebook of yours it's going straight in the chem-lake."

Zeinner said nothing and Anderson took off down the road, past the torn metal fences and the towering factories they guarded, and towards the raucous crowds gathered ahead. A crackling electro-cordon ran along the road, herding the citizens like unruly cattle onto an expanse of scrubland in the grounds of some forgotten industrial ruin.

Street Division had stationed a checkpoint on every access road, but that hadn't prevented the protestors from gathering here in their thousands. Their thoughts zapped through Anderson's head like lightning, galvanised by adrenalin. She could distinguish the genuine protestors straight away. Their thoughts were strong and steady, bright with hope and conviction. There were opportunists lurking in there too, of course, emitting selfish thoughts of gain and petty payback upon anyone wearing a blue-and-gold uniform. The overall chorus sang of coiled tension, an explosion awaiting a signal, a justification, a cause, some outrage that would finally stir them to violence. The slogan daubed onto blankets and placards echoed the chant the protestors bellowed into the night.

"Bed-lam begins! Bed-lam begins!"

The Judges ignored them, looking almost amused as they patrolled in pairs along the road on the other side of the cordon. Anderson knew the Department would be happy to let the protestors congregate for as long as the situation was containable. Let the creeps come and bawl their little hearts out in the name of protest. The Department's got drones in the air watching them the whole time, clocking IDs to make arrests later on. Maybe even score a couple of big fish who couldn't resist the temptation to come out of hiding and join the party.

That was always Street-Division's problem, thought Anderson. They always underestimated the citizens, their pain, their ingenuity, their capacity for spontaneous madness.

How easy it must be for a person to lose themselves in all that. Anderson felt something stiffen in her chest and she realised she was breathing hard, her heart a familiar rhythmic wallop, her stomach clenched tight.

She heard Zeinner's Lawmaster approach behind her and pulled away quickly before the woman could hear her thoughts. Anderson brought herself out from behind yet another derelict factory and there it was, wearing its famous numerals—06— like a badge.

Anderson felt almost disappointed. For all its gothic reputation, Psych-Block Six resembled nothing so much as a big white egg, planted on an island of rockcrete in the centre of a glimmering green chem-lake.

The stories that surrounded the place had been started by guys in Street-Division. They called it 'the Big Zero Six,' said the place was haunted, cursed, that it was built upon some sinister patch of New England from before the Atomic Wars. It was true the place housed a pantheon of legendary criminal lunatics, including the Sector Seven Strangler, the Eel Woman, and Timmy the Mallet. The presence of these celebrities only served to attract ever more fantastic stories, despite the fact that Psi-Division had never detected a single supernatural event in the block's history. Then some kind of chemical leak occurred a few years ago, devastating several wards. The Street guys wouldn't shut up about the place after that, and the more mischievous Psi-Judges would tell them all kinds of occult nonsense just to see the looks on their faces.

The Department accepted sponsorship from a pharma company to help fund the rebuild, although it seemed even re-branding couldn't obscure the block's sinister reputation. But for Anderson, and the rest of Psi-Div, it was just another kook-block full of crazy-ass perps, incarcerated for however long it took to unravel their pathologies and figure out what to do about them. Terrorist guru Moriah Blake was simply the latest acquisition, just another creep in need of psychic interrogation: associates, addresses, plans, the usual.

"You been psi-shielded before?" asked Zeinner.

She pulled alongside Anderson as they broke off from the main road and left the protestors behind.

"Not since the Academy," Anderson said, guiding her Lawmaster towards the gates of one of the four bridges that spanned the chem-lake, radiating from the island like the spokes of a wheel. A couple of Street-Judges had been stationed by the gate. They scanned the Psi-Judges' badges before the hatch yawned open to reveal a straight two-lane tunnel with a high vaulted roof of electrified mesh that ran for over a mile directly onto the island.

"This'll be exactly the same," Zeinner said as they passed through. "I'll project a dampener around your psionic field. Range about four metres. So don't go wandering off."

"What if I need to go to the bathroom?"

"I'm sure you already know this, but I need to repeat it so I can tick a box when we get home."

"I'll pretend I'm listening."

Zeinner took a deep breath.

"Many of the patients within the block will be in a state of permanent psychotic breakdown," she began. "Prolonged and/or concentrated connection can therefore cause psionic shock. Do not attempt to reach through the psi-shield and connect with any patient other than the one designated for interrogation."

"Yeah, like I want any more voices in my head."

"You must immediately report any feelings of nausea, dizziness, stomach cramps, any and all unusual feelings of hunger, thirst, sexual arousal, or emotional distress or euphoria, and any and all sensory, auditory or visual phenomena you suspect may be hallucinations."

"Aw, man. I feel like we've earned that pizza already."

The gates crashed shut behind them and they started down the tunnel towards the Big Zero Six.

* * *

ANDERSON PRESENTED HER badge to yet another security scanner and could feel Zeinner's psi-shield like a big bubble inside her head. It made her feel like she had a cold.

"You'll get used to it," Zeinner said as the doors hissed open and they stepped into the ground floor lobby.

"Welcome to Psych-Block Six, sponsored by Pharmville," said a spindly droid, unfurling from behind a desk. The walls and floor of the reception area were an ocean of cream. The ceiling panels glowed a heavenly white. A set of identical brochures lay fanned on the reception desk, untouched. A full-size animated hologram of a woodland glade covered the back wall like a portal into another world. Holographic deer grazed, untroubled by the lobby's dreamy muzak, which piped a tune Anderson couldn't quite place.

"We're passionate about the safety and security of both you and our residents," the droid said, running a UV light over the Psi-Judges, then indicating the drawers emerging from the wall beside them.

"Could you please place your firearms and ammunition in the trays provided, along with your belts, knives and daysticks."

Anderson looked at Zeinner, who had already popped the clip in her Lawgiver.

"Sorry, Cassie," she said. "They can't risk the patients getting their hands on so much as a paperclip."

Anderson scowled and placed her gun in the drawer, looking down at the weapon as though she had just laid it to rest.

"So where is everybody?" Anderson said.

"We are a fully-automated facility," the droid said. "Our control hub is located on level one hundred and fifty and is operated by a staff of thirty highly trained professionals who are passionate about healthcare."

"Thirty staff covering, what, three hundred levels?" Anderson said, unclipping her belt. "Don't you guys have any trouble from your patients at all?"

"Our sponsors, Pharmville, are passionate about enabling our residents to live comfortably without danger to themselves or those around them," the droid said, "allowing us to maintain a safe and stimulating environment for all."

The droid paused. The muzak played on.

Anderson turned to see Zeinner scribbling something in her notebook. Anderson snatched it out of her hands and tossed it into the loaded drawer as it merged into the wall.

"Let's go, doc."

"WHAT THE DROKK did you guys do to her?" Anderson said.

She stared through the observation window at the dark-haired young woman whose mind she had been sent to read. Moriah Blake sat back in her chair, unmoving, her hands cuffed to the metal table before her, her face slack, her dark eyes unfocused, a generous bruise enveloping one side of her face. Her baggy green jumpsuit made it difficult to detect the rising and falling of her chest, without which Anderson would have pegged her for a corpse.

Swanson, the Med-Judge who had been assigned as Blake's primary nurse, had pulled the headphones from his ears, but continued eating synthetti from a cafeteria cup.

"Relax," he said, chewing his food. "She looks like she's dead, I know. Freaks everyone out at first."

"What happened to her face?" Zeinner said.

"She didn't respond to standard interrogation," Swanson said. "Why d'you think we need you guys?"

Anderson folded her arms, thinking about the two Judges on security detail standing in the corridor outside. They had given her and Zeinner the stink-eye before nodding them through.

Anderson touched her temple, gently piercing Zeinner's psi-shield as she tuned into Blake's thoughts. The subject hadn't been doped, but what little was going on in her head sounded as languid as a harp, placid and deliberate, as absorbed in the moment as if she were meditating. Most detainees' minds were frantic with hopes of escape, but Blake merely contemplated the composition of the empty chair opposite her, wondering what kind of mechanism had enabled chair and table to rise up out of the tiled floor the way they had.

Most sane minds—or as sane as you got in Mega-City One— were an eternal firework display, thoughts constantly streaking and bursting. Minds in the throes of psychosis tended to blaze monotonously like a city on fire. Blake's mind looked like a starfield, every pinpoint of thought a certainty. Whatever passions she harboured, whatever charisma had sparked the fires of rebellion in her followers, presently lay in darkness. Anderson could hear her register the dull throb in her cheek where the bigger of her two guards had backhanded her, but she seemed only to observe the sensation rather than feel it. She was more concerned about the fact that she was mildly hungry.

"Remember, Cassie," Zeinner said. "Don't connect too deeply to a psychotic. Don't let their voice too far inside your head or you might never get it out again."

Blake turned towards the observation window, staring directly at Zeinner. The abruptness of the movement caused the Psi-Judge to flinch. Anderson couldn't blame her; it was as though a corpse had just come to life.

"I am hungry," Blake said, her voice a husky monotone.

Swanson sucked down another forkful of synthetti, whipping bright orange sauce all over his blonde beard. His white shoulder pads were spotted with the stuff.

"Control said you'd give us her full background," Anderson said.

"Don't know what they want me to tell you," Swanson said.

"A complete spook, this one. Nothing on facial recog. No idea who she was before she came here."

"No records at all?" Zeinner said. "How's that possible?"

"Tek are looking into it. Think maybe her followers hacked her records. Wiped everything. Doubt 'Moriah Blake' is even her real name. You guys must've heard her vox-casts? 'Kill all Judges?' 'Take back the streets' and all that?"

"*That's* what landed her a room at the crazy house instead of an iso-block?" Anderson said. "An opinion?"

Swanson laughed through a mouthful of protein-ball from an open sandwich-box beside him.

"You wanna broadcast that kind of opinion in this town, you *must* be crazy, am I right?"

Anderson wondered how many more of Mega-City One's influential dissenters were languishing in cubes throughout the Big Zero Six, personalities deleted by drugs, voices forgotten.

Anderson could hear Swanson thinking: *Man, I heard she was a bleeding heart, but really?*

"What evidence have we got that those Judges were executed on her direct orders?" Zeinner said.

"We got surveillance intel that she's a fully paid-up member of this thing she's inspired," Swanson said. "She's been seen in the company of a bunch of known anti-Judge extremists who're jumping on the Bedlam bandwagon."

Whatever the heck it was the catering droids in this place put in the synthetti sauce, it had stained his beard an almost fluorescent orange.

"You got pictures?" Anderson said. "Can we see them?"

"Look, we have them, okay?" Swanson said, annoyed now. "Jovis! Do you second-guess every damn thing the Department tells you?"

"It's one of my many outstanding features."

"Trust me," he said. "This one's a bona fide bad guy. Now is whatever you're here to do gonna take long? I wanna get her cubed and doped so's I can get outta this creep-farm."

Zeinner nodded at Anderson, who brushed past Swanson as he slurped another forkload of of synthetti.

"Hey," he called after her. "Where you going with my sandwich-box...?"

"Hope you don't mind sharing," Anderson said.

She let Swanson's sandwich-box swing from her finger as she sat in the chair opposite Moriah Blake. The woman stared, her mouth hanging open, her lank black hair hanging in curtains either side of her face.

Anderson was surprised how unnerved she felt as she made a show of opening the lunchbox and rummaging through its treasures. She scanned Blake's thoughts, waiting for a response. So far, zilch.

"Jelly and munce-paste sandwiches?" Anderson said, addressing the mirrored window. "What are you, twelve?"

Anderson heard a tremor of recognition in Blake's thoughts. She had clocked the Psi badge. That was usually the moment when the subject started thinking about all the interesting stuff they wanted to hide. It was always easier to let the subject *show* you their secrets rather than having to chase them down.

Anderson tossed Swanson's sandwich back into the lunchbox and stared at Blake. The woman stared back, her eyes unblinking, her expression immobile as her blackened mind swallowed the rest of her secrets.

"A bomb, huh?" Anderson said.

She stared at Blake, letting the word 'bomb' sink in, hoping it would startle other thoughts into revealing themselves. But nothing bubbled up out of that swamp of a mind.

Anderson switched on the communicator built into the back of her glove. A tinny male voice responded.

"*Control receiving, Anderson. Go ahead.*"

"Telepathic retrieval in progress," she said. "Subject Moriah Blake. Can confirm Bedlam have a Code Ten in play."

"*Location?*"

"Gimme a second, I'll find out..."

Moriah Blake remained motionless as a storm of gunfire erupted in the corridor outside.

Twelve

ANDERSON SPRANG FROM her chair as bullets stabbed the observation window beside her. She threw herself against the wall beside the door and realised the bubble inside her head had popped. Clarity had returned to her senses. The psi-shield was down, which meant Zeinner was dead. The shooters in the corridor were still firing, guns on full auto. By the sound of it, they were holding position and leaning on those triggers until they were sure as hell the two Judges guarding the door were not going to get up again.

Blake continued staring at nothing in particular, unmoved by the riot outside.

The barrage of gunfire ceased and Anderson heard the shrieking thoughts of the men and women outside.

Can't believe this is happening...

Get her outta there...

One more inside...

There was a single woman in the observation room on the other side of the fractured window. Anderson saw through her eyes that she was staring at the bodies of Zeinner and

Swanson, transfixed by the blood cascading down Swanson's white shoulder-pads. Anderson locked onto the woman's thoughts, targeting her position. She could hear the other shooters stampeding across the corridor towards the door of the interrogation room, their minds screaming thoughts of murder. Anderson took a run-up and bounded onto the table.

The gunmen burst into the room as Anderson launched herself through the observation window, bursting through the wall of toughened glass and crashing into the woman standing in the adjacent room, slamming her into a surveillance desk against the opposite wall.

Anderson scrambled to her feet, scattering cubes of broken glass as the startled woman aimed the assault rifle with both hands. Anderson shifted to the left as she rushed in close and slapped the barrel aside, feeling the weapon spasm against her hand as it fired, illuminating the look of surprise on the woman's face. Anderson darted a straight punch into her opponent's mouth, feeling teeth give way, before snatching the rifle, twisting it from the stunned woman's grasp and slamming its butt against the side of her head, knocking her to the floor, senseless.

Anderson ducked beneath the surveillance desk as a torrent of bullets flew through the ragged window-frame and ripped into the wall above her. Zeinner's corpse stared at the ceiling open-mouthed; she had taken several rounds to the chest. The hatch through which her killer had entered remained open. Anderson could hear a gaggle of thoughts surrounding Blake in the interrogation room. Three more shooters lingered in the corridor.

Clutching the assault rifle with both hands, Anderson crawled towards the exit on her elbows and knees. One of the shooters appeared in the doorway, startled by the sight of the Psi-Judge crawling towards him. She fired, watching the blood bursting across his chest before her weapon clicked empty.

She gathered herself as the shooter toppled backwards and another replaced him. Charging into the corridor, she drove her weight behind the spent rifle, ramming the stock into the shooter's face. The man staggered backwards, blinking through a mask of blood. Anderson caught his rifle as it fell and shielded herself behind him as she found the trigger and opened fire at the other shooter standing behind him. Her new assault rifle bellowed and the other shooter collapsed.

Anderson shoved her shield aside and fled down the hall. There was no sense forcing a shootout against superior firepower and with no cover. She heard gunfire behind her and felt bullets hissing through the air either side of her as she charged through a pair of swing doors, glad to have at least a little cover between her and her pursuers. She gasped into the communicator on her wrist, holding the heavy rifle with one hand, ready to turn and fire at any pursuers.

"Control receiving, Anderson."

"We have a Code Thirty in the Big Zero Six," she panted, glancing over her shoulder at the empty corridor lengthening behind her. "Bedlam terrorists have entered the block. At least seven confirmed. Two wounded, two down. Armed with Zee-27 assault rifles. Zeinner, Swanson and two security, all down. Hostiles have secured Blake. Code Ten still in play. Location still unknown."

She crashed through another set of swing doors.

"Copy that, Anderson," Control said. *"What's your position?"*

Her boots squealed on the tiled floor as she took cover behind a vending machine, steadying the barrel of the Zee-27 against the snack dispenser as she aimed the weapon at the double doors. Her finger rested upon the trigger as she waited for targets to come running into her sights. She closed her eyes, still fighting to control her breathing, and opened her mind, listening for the thoughts of any approaching pursuers. Silence. They had evidently given up trying to kill her.

She detached herself from the vending machine and caught her breath. They must have known they were too late to stop her alerting the Department. She wondered whether they would be dumb enough to try and high-tail it out of here, knowing half of Street-Div would be waiting for them on the shore. She thought of Zeinner and booted the vending machine.

"*Anderson?*"

"Control, security here is tight as a Judge's butt," she said. "I don't think they could have made it in here without securing the Control Hub, and that means hostages, plus a bomb for leverage. I have a hunch where this is going. Maybe I could—"

"*Judge Anderson, I'm ordering you to exit the block immediately,*" said a familiar voice: Chief Ecks, patched in from Psi-Division. "*We're aware we could be looking at a siege and are assembling a tactical team right now. We need you out of there.*"

Anderson felt a surprising sense of relief.

"*Repeat, what's your current position?*" Ecks said.

Anderson slung the assault rifle and surveyed the corridor.

"Level one-six-seven," she said. "Somewhere between Pete Rogers and Gerry Thomas Wards."

She hurried over to a circular hatch in the wall marked *Emergency Exit*. The gravity-chute on the other side would carry her all the way to the ground floor in a heartbeat. She opened a plexi-glass lid and hammered the button behind it.

"I've got grav-chute 484-A," she said. "I'll be outside in a few minutes."

She opened her mind again, steadier this time. Still no one. No sign either of the crazy vibes Zeinner had warned her about. It looked like she might get out of here with both her butt and her sanity intact. She listened to the strip-lights buzzing overhead and realised the hatch hadn't opened. Punching the button again, she noticed a red light blinking on the control panel. A mechanical whirr sounded above her and she saw a spherical camera, socketed like an eyeball in the frame of the hatch. She saw the iris constrict as it focused on her.

Turning away, she spoke calmly into her comm.

"Chief," she said, her mouth suddenly dry. "They've locked the door to the grav-chute."

"Do you have a weapon, Anderson?"

"If you can call it that."

She dropped the mag in the Zee-27, a tacky 'spray-and-pray' assault rifle printed out of cheap resin, legendarily prone to jamming, but popular with street thugs on a budget. She had about two good bursts left in the mag, then all she had was a club that would probably smash to pieces on the first swing. She thought of her Lawgiver pining for her in some locked drawer in the lobby far below, and cursed whoever had come up with the security protocols in this place.

"I don't think a gun will make much difference, Chief," she said, feeling woozy now for some reason. "It's likely they control every door in the block. Plus they'll have an eyeball on me wherever I go."

Anderson struck the grav-chute's button yet again, but the hatch remained shut. The surrounding corridor looked smaller than it had before. She imagined it branching off into a labyrinth of endless passages. The air felt uncomfortably warm. Had the creeps done something to the heating? The atmosphere felt as though it were thickening into steam. She felt a mounting need for air and an even more desperate need for escape.

"Okay, Anderson," Ecks said. *"Just stay calm."*

Anderson felt a sting of annoyance. She curled her shaking fingers into a fist and punched the wall, letting the pain in her knuckles anchor her in the real world. She forced herself to breathe, to focus on the reality at hand as she watched the blinking red light on the grav-chute's control panel. Gravity chutes operated on a mechanical release, separate from the rest of the building. That much she knew. Which meant that if she could somehow unlock this hatch she could still get out of here.

"Chief, I need to speak to someone in Tek-Div."

*   *   *

"WHAT DID SHE just say?" Heep asked.

"She said we're staying," replied the tall blond guy with the assault rifle. He didn't seem unduly concerned by the sudden change of plan, much to Heep's horror. First, talk of a bomb, now this? Whatever *this* was going to be?

Heep had dreamed of a life of adventure and excitement far beyond anything he had experienced during his weekends in the Citi-Def, which seemed to consist of little more than bureaucratic squabbles over training regimes and who stole whose sandwiches from the refrigerator.

Blondie still had his gun pointed at Teri, the woman with whom Heep had shared a control desk for the last two years. She was cowering before her holo-screens, one of which showed security footage of a Justice Department Manta prowling the air above the perma-gardens outside.

Heep had witnessed Moriah Blake's bloody liberation on the monitors and felt the first tingle of panic when the little Psi-Judge had managed to get away. Shortly afterwards, he loitered near the elevators, wondering if he could catch the same one as Blake when everyone was ready to make their escape in the tanker-truck awaiting them in the basement. No one had told him that Blake had already been escorted to safety and was now addressing her troops in the Hub's central surveillance chamber. The block's entire control staff had been herded here, where they each manned a surveillance desk guarded by a dour Bedlamite wearing a dark jacket and brandishing either a pistol or an assault rifle. Heep stood at the back of the crowded room, trying to hear exactly what Moriah Blake had planned for them all, but it turned out she was as softly spoken as she had been in her vox-casts. Heep pushed past several more gunmen before he reached a railing and could actually see her.

She stood a few feet away from him, the woman whose

voice had so bewitched him, whose truths had so inspired him, galvanised him, articulated everything he sensed was wrong with his world. She looked like the ghost of the woman he had imagined. She was thin and flat-chested, with glowering eyes and cadaverous cheeks, her black hair hanging straight down as though she had just been exhumed from a lake. She cradled her arms as she spoke, looking almost shy.

"You are scared," Blake was saying, that strong, syrupy voice unmistakable. "Your old lives are gone. You are part of a greater plan. We were poised to win a battle tonight. Now we are poised to win the war."

Heep had no idea what she was talking about and jumped with fright as the rest of the room hollered, *"Bedlam begins!"*

One of the gunmen offered her what looked like a bulky handheld vox-corder, perhaps the same device through which she had broadcast her famous speeches. She examined it as though it were a precious relic.

Heep's stomach churned and he found himself wondering how tonight's undertaking had ever seemed like sanity. Until now, doubt had been a whisper drowned out by the mantra, 'I'm doing the right thing.' He had always known the Judges were monsters. He saw the suffering they caused, the world they had created. But what had he ever done about it? Nothing. He felt haunted by his own timidity until the comfortable existence in which he had found himself began to feel like a curse.

He had endured a tense, hurried meeting with Blake's 'people' and risked arrest in obtaining the sequence of codes that would allow them access to the Control Hub. His reward would be entry into the ranks of the righteous, true adventure, the freedom of life lived off the grid, scurrying from hiding place to hiding place, fighting alongside those who shared his beliefs, lending whatever he could in the way of brains, muscle and courage to a cause that could achieve what most believed impossible: change. But now Heep's dream had collapsed into chaos and no one seemed to care.

"The bomb," Heep said, his voice sounding more like a squeal than he would have liked.

Everyone looked at him.

"What about the bomb?" he said.

Moriah Blake stared at him and he felt almost ashamed.

"We all heard the audio in the interrogation room?" he said, searching the puzzled faces surrounding him. "We heard the Judge contact the Department."

Blake gawped at him, frozen in time.

"You never..." Heep said. "I mean, no one ever said anything about a bomb."

"Who are you?" Blake said.

Heep felt a glimmer of rage.

"I'm Heep Brillantyne," he said. "I let you guys in here?"

"You're wearing an eagle," she said.

Heep looked down at his Department-issue jumpsuit, confused as to why that should matter.

"I used to work here," he said as Blake continued addressing the room.

"The less you all know the better," she said. "But there is a device. We have it located somewhere in the city, somewhere where it will hurt the Judges the most."

Everyone was nodding. Heep felt he should probably nod too.

"You have faith in me," she said. "Fear is too great an opponent to overcome with a single blow. We will conquer it step-by-step, hand-in-hand."

One of the gunmen called out from a surveillance desk.

"She's moving," they said. "She's heading towards Ken Williams Ward."

Heep looked back at Blake to find her staring at him.

"The inmates in this facility are drugged," she said, moving towards him. "Your badge says you are Head of Dispensary. You can give them something to wake them up."

Heep swallowed.

"The inmates," she said. "You know what they are. You know why they are here. They are monsters, just like the Judges."

Heep felt her voice envelop him like oil and his resolve crumbled, but with it came a strange kind of release. He was afraid, that was all. He recalled a passage from one of Moriah's vox-casts, words that had haunted him: 'Crazy is clinging to the notion that the world is sane. True sanity is the courage to face the truth that the world isn't perfect, that happiness is a lie.' It was just as Bedlam had taught: one must embrace the madness inflicted upon them. Heep felt something like pride. These were his people. They trusted him and he was a fool for ever doubting them. Together they would do the right thing.

"Which inmates do you want me to wake up?" he said.

"All of them," Blake said.

ANDERSON HAD ARRIVED at the entrance of Ken Williams Ward. It looked eerily identical to every other ward she had passed on the way here. The floor and ceiling were impossibly white, the matching doors of the kook-cubes lining each wall and a second row stacked above, accessed via stairs and a balcony. Anderson could just make out a double-door hatch at the far end. Maybe the creeps who had taken over the Control Hub had locked it; maybe not. Surveillance orbs lined the walls.

Anderson caught her breath and spoke into her comm.

"Now where?"

"*According to the blueprints, the entrance to the kitchen is on the other side of the door at the far end of Ken Williams,*" said Tek-Judge Simmons. "*You can't miss it.*"

Simmons sounded like a chipper little fella, like a friendly plumber or the host of a home improvement show on the Tri-D. For some reason, Anderson imagined he had a moustache.

"*The junction box you're looking for is in the kitchen,*" he said. "*Just pop a couple of fat ol' cables in that bad boy and you'll cut the power-feed to the entire level. Surveillance orbs too. But you'll need to make it back to the grav-chute within four minutes before the re-route kicks in. Sound good?"*

Anderson was trying not to think about Zeinner's corpse staring at the ceiling, or the miasma of whispers that seemed to fill the corridor between her and the door at the far end. She could hear the slow, steamy thoughts of the men and women lurking behind those cell doors. It was way past their bedtime and their sleeping, sedated thoughts sounded like a lapping tide. Hiccups of rage or lust occasionally broke the surface, stinging her with their intensity. The passage of countless patients over the years had left the corridor drenched in psionic residue. Anderson felt a wealth of anguish rising from the floor like a heat haze.

Don't connect too deeply, Zeinner had said. *Don't let the voices too far inside your head, or you might never get them out again.*

Anderson could see why. Hearing more than two or three psychotic minds in full meltdown was like sticking your pinkie in a plug socket.

"Sorry, Simmons," she said. "What was that last part?"

Simmons happily explained again and Anderson sprinted down the corridor, the Zee-27 tight across her back. She ignored the whispers, keeping her eyes focused on the door far ahead of her. She tried to absorb herself in the rhythm of her limbs, the coursing of her heart and the feel of her boots hammering the floor. But it was like running through a thickening fog, the whispers intensifying as she ran. She counted every snorting breath, stamped the floor harder, strained the muscles in her thighs and arms until they screamed. But the whispers only grew louder, filling her head with a ghostly choir. She felt a sudden ache in her ears and the corridor shimmered like a mirage. She stumbled and fell.

Cool it, Anderson, she told herself. *You got this, girl. Just shut them out. No biggie. It's like working street duty. Just keep your distance.*

She touched her temples and purged her own mind with a psi-blast. The rush of psionic energy swept the voices away like smoke, but more only swirled and gathered to replace them, stronger and more insistent than before. The whispers were becoming voices. This wasn't right. She detected another sound, a low gaseous hiss. It took a moment for her to realise that the sound wasn't coming from inside her head.

Anderson opened her eyes, trying to push away the gathering voices as she located the source of the sound. She stumbled over to one of the cells and placed her hand upon the bundle of pipes than ran the length of the corridor, feeding the cells with a mist of whatever pharmaceutical cocktail was required. The pipes were hissing. Anderson could hear ugly lucid thoughts piecing themselves together like regenerating tissue. The inmates were waking up.

She stumbled from door to door, steadying herself before launching into another run for the door that stood seemingly miles away.

A uniform *click-clack* rang through the hallway, like a thousand shotguns pumping fresh rounds in perfect unison. The cell doors flew open.

Anderson raced past, not daring to see what lay inside, but noticing a surveillance orb tracking her as she fled. She could hear a thousand minds slowly comprehending the fact that their doors had vanished and the outside world of the corridor now beckoned. She reached the hatch, almost crashing into it as she slapped the release button. It bleeped and refused to open. The red light registered *Locked*.

Moans, yells and screams arose behind her. Footsteps rang on the metal walkways above. Someone was laughing hysterically. Her heart bounding in her chest, Anderson tore off her glove and placed her bare hand over the keypad of the control panel.

She ignored the clamour of thoughts coalescing around her as she tried to absorb the psionic residue on the keypad, struggling to distinguish which buttons had last been touched by living fingers and in what sequence. The psi-prints were old, tough to read accurately.

The corridor was filling with wandering figures. She unslung the Zee-27, her fingers trembling as she jabbed at the keypad, entering the access code she had managed to assemble in her head.

One, Eight, Seven, Two, Zero, Zero, Four.

She hit the release, but the 'locked' light remained red.

Where did the wall go...?

Bright out here. Make it red again...

Shutupshutupshutupshutup...

Anderson held her breath as she jabbed the keypad again, slowly this time, trying to keep her finger steady. She slammed the entry button. The light bleeped green and the doors of the hatch slid apart a few feet before the control panel bleeped red again and the hatch began to close. Someone watching her from the Control Hub was trying to outmanoeuvre her, but Anderson had already jammed her rifle between the doors of the hatch. She heard the weapon's resin casing crack above her as she wriggled through the gap, then the rifle shattered entirely and the doors of the hatch bit down on her, pinning her, slamming the breath from her lungs.

She struggled to prise the doors open, her feet slipping as they fought for purchase on the polished floor. The corridor was crowded now with men and women, juves and eldsters, faces of every ethnicity, all wearing bilious green jumpsuits with black slippers and white socks. Many ambled like sleepwalkers, barely comprehending their surroundings, wondering what miracle had delivered them into this strange white world. Others had crumbled into psychosis already, their fevered brains ignited by whatever stimulant had been sprayed into their cells.

Anderson managed to shift herself enough to brace her knee against the edge of the door. A skeletal man with wild hair was blinking as he stared at her, not quite comprehending what he was seeing.

Is that a Judge...?

She felt his mind brighten with recognition and saw his lips peel back, revealing yellow teeth filed to triangular points.

Anderson got her foot against the door and grunted with effort, shoving the hatch open enough for her to tumble to one side before it slammed shut behind her. A smaller door stood to her right, just as Simmons had promised. She laid her hand against the control panel beside it, hearing the doors to the ward fly open once again behind her. She managed to decipher the psionic imprint on the keys when strong hands caught her by the hair, hauling her backwards.

The white mothers are coming, Judge, her attacker's mind screamed. *I need to hide in your skin. Don't let them hurt me again.*

Anderson caught his hand, pinning it against her scalp as she spun around and shot a punch into the jaw of the wild-haired man. His thoughts vanished as he sprawled upon the floor. Several other inmates were staring at her, the gold eagle adorning her shoulder kindling memories of hatred and fear.

Anderson's fingers darted over the keys and the door slid open. She hurried inside the darkened room and hit the door switch on the other side, but the door refused to close behind her. The lights fluttered on, revealing a huge kitchen. Whoever was watching her from the Control Hub was clearly keen to see what she was up to.

Well, drokk it, she thought as she weaved between the gleaming metal workstations. *Let 'em watch.*

"Chief," she spoke into her comm. "They've just released every inmate in this ward, maybe the entire block. You're gonna have a hell of a time getting a tac-team through here now."

"*Copy that,*" Ecks sighed.

"Simmons?" she said. "Where's this junction box?"

"*It's on the far wall.*"

She paused to try the drawers for knives, but everything was locked. She hurried past storerooms, sinks the size of bathtubs and a wall of zapp-ovens, then rounded a corner. She upset several bottles of synthetti sauce as she jumped, startled by the sight of a row of deactivated catering droids standing against the wall. She could hear the thoughts of the inmates filling the corridor behind her, voices a cacophony: pleas for salvation, songs of joy, wild threats and sinister promises. Driven by raw, unfettered feeling, the voices gnawed at Anderson's mind in a frenzy. She felt sweat snaking down her back and her scalp tightened with a sudden chill.

Just keep them out, Cassie. You can handle this.

She had managed to reduce the noise to a tolerable murmur when she reached the far wall and saw a large cabinet exuding cables from all sides.

Simmons, Grud bless you!

She tore the panel open, revealing a confusion of cables and cords, wiring and conduits. Simmons directed her attention to a plump green cable and the small black one running alongside it.

"*Unplug those suckers and you'll take out all the power in this section,*" Simmons said. "*That's surveillance orbs, lights, door locks, the whole caboodle. But you better be quick on your feet on the way back, though, y'hear?*"

Psi-Chief Ecks cut in.

"*We've got a Manta circling, awaiting your pick-up,*" he said.

Anderson seized the cables.

"Sir," she said. "Does the Department have any idea where this bomb might be?"

"*We've got some theories,*" Ecks said.

Anderson frowned and tore the cables from their housing in a burst of sparks. Blackness descended and Anderson heard distant screams.

"*Now move it, Anderson,*" Ecks said.

"Okay, here's the thing, chief," Anderson said as she felt her way through the blackness towards to the entrance of the kitchen, towards the cries in the corridor. "I'm going to stick around."

"*Anderson,*" Ecks said. "*Get your butt out of there. Now!*"

She reached the wild-haired man still sprawled outside the kitchen door, his fluorescent jumpsuit casting a vivid glow that illuminated the floor around him as other radiant green bodies stumbled past, howling in the darkness. Anderson felt practically invisible in her uniform as she dragged the unconscious man back inside the kitchen.

"Chief, that bomb could be planted in the Hall of Justice for all we know," Anderson said. "Only Blake knows for sure. If I can get close enough to her, I can find out exactly where it is. Get a long-range telepath outside and I can relay the intel from in here."

"*Anderson, you'll be dead before you get anywhere near Blake.*"

"Not if she can't find me," Anderson said, opening a storeroom and dragging the unconscious inmate inside. She unzipped his jumpsuit.

"*I'm not talking about Blake,*" Ecks said. "*You know the psi-field in that place is toxic. Stay longer than an hour in there and you'll lose it.*"

"Better to risk losing one Judge than however many more will die when that bomb goes off. I can handle the inmates long enough to get what we need."

"*No, you can't, Anderson,*" Ecks said. "*You're under probation. Did you know that?*"

Anderson stopped pulling at the inmate's jumpsuit.

"I know I failed my psych-exam," she said.

"*Your score placed you at risk of withdrawal from service,*" Ecks said. "*That's why we sent Zeinner along with you on this one.*"

"*Anderson?*" Simmons said. "*You have three minutes to reach the grav-chute before the power comes back on. You can still make it.*"

"*You can't do this, Anderson,*" Ecks said. "*And there's no shame in that. If you stay in there you won't be able to keep the voices out and your head will unravel. The nightmares? The anxiety? We all feel it, Cassandra. It'll all come flooding in and it'll never leave you.*"

You can't do this. The words rankled her. Anderson didn't fear death. It was inevitable, part of the job. But losing control? Over herself and her abilities? The notion was obscene.

"*It's suicide, Anderson,*" said Ecks.

"But it's the right thing to do," she said.

She switched off the comm before Ecks could respond, and finished undressing. She hid her shoulder-pads inside boxes of ingredients and stuffed the rest of her uniform down the garbage shredder, which would churn the whole lot to shreds the instant the power returned. She considered her badge for moment, then plopped it in a huge cauldron of what looked like oatmeal. She watched the heavy gold shield sink from view.

The luminous green jumpsuit glowed like a lantern in the darkness. She tried to ignore its mingled aroma of sweat, urine and worse as she pulled it up over her legs. The material felt starched and heavy, the folds of it pinching and poking her as she moved. She zipped it up to her waist for now, leaving the sleeves to hang by her sides as she heaved a bottle of synthetti sauce onto the draining board beside one of the sinks.

"Always wanted to be a redhead."

Thirteen

HEEP SURVEYED THE collection of holo-screens on his control desk, transfixed by the spectacle of the inmates roaming the wards outside the Hub. It had taken him a while to reprogram the automated dispensary, a system he had been charged with maintaining until today. Pressed for time, he had decided to simply flood every cube with an adrenal stimulant. A number of inmates now lay dead in their cells, their in-cube scanners diagnosing a miscalculated drug interaction resulting in either heart-failure or pulmonary embolism. Other than that, Heep's choice of medication appeared to be having the desired effect.

Most of the inmates were fully awake and storming about the wards, their psychosis once again in full swing. Clothes and bodies already lay strewn about the place. Blood streaked the walls and pooled on the floors. Patient 427-ZW, Henrietta Skullkiss, the woman the news-feeds had dubbed 'The Peeler,' had already amassed an impressive number of trophies with which she was busy redecorating her cube in Chuck Hawtrey Ward.

Several more holo-screens on Heep's desk suddenly blinked back to life. The power re-rout had evidently kicked in and the eastern sector of level 167 had sprung back to life. Several of the Bedlamites began yelling orders at the hostage surveillance crew, ordering them to find the runaway Judge. Heep ignored them, absorbed in the chaos he had created, marvelling at the disappearance of his old life.

He realised Teri was sobbing beside him, her eyes squeezed shut, both hands over her mouth. On the monitor before her, one of the inmates was biting the ears off another. Heep could sympathise, of course. Teri probably considered the inmates human. She had yet to realise they had crossed the line into monsterhood long ago. Maybe this was an opportunity to explain that, maybe win her over to the cause.

He reached for her along the control desk and went to speak. She pinned him with a look of hatred and spat in his face. Heep felt the saliva dot his lips as he stared at Teri in bewilderment. He hadn't even said anything.

"There a problem here," Blondie said, rifle in hand.

Teri switched the view on her monitor, only to recoil at some fresh horror.

"Find whatever's left of that Judge," Blondie told her.

Heep wiped his face on his sleeve. The inmates were awake, just as Blake had asked. Having surely proved himself, he wondered when he might receive a *thank you*, then inwardly admonished himself for expecting one.

Unsure what to do with himself, he left his seat and wandered the central chamber. Most of the outlying surveillance suites had been abandoned, their crews having been moved here where Bedlam could keep both an eye and a gun on them. The room was crowded yet unnaturally quiet. The Bedlamites were doing all the talking, and even then only in whispers, as they loomed over their seated hostages. Heep's former co-workers cowered over their surveillance desks, silent save for the occasional whimper or tearful sniff.

Heep figured he should have a gun, and wondered whether

he should ask for one. He certainly knew his way around a rifle from his time in the Citi-Def. Maybe he could show his fellow Bedlamites a few tricks.

He sauntered over to where Blake was sitting. Two women with guns slung over their shoulders were talking beside her. He overheard one of them say that none of the grav-chutes had been jettisoned, and that the Judge had most likely been killed before she could reach any of them. There was nowhere to hide in the Big Zero Six, not with surveillance orbs everywhere. All they had left to do was find the Judge's remains.

The comm had rung several times. The Judges, for sure. The Bedlamites had ordered the surveillance crew to ignore any calls. Blake clearly wasn't planning to negotiate just yet. What, then, did she have in mind? The Bedlamites didn't seem to care.

Blake still hadn't changed out of her green jumpsuit and was plugging audio cables into that homemade vox-corder of hers.

"Whoah," one of the women said, putting her hand on Heep's chest. "Can I help you, buddy?"

"I'm Heep Brillantyne?" he said.

The women looked unimpressed.

"So," he said. "The inmates are up and running and I was just wondering if there was anything else I could do for you guys. I guess, though, what I wanted to know, really, was just what the plan is here?"

"I'm going to make an announcement," Blake said, tweaking a dial on her vox-corder.

So that was what the device in her hands was for. He was going to be present during one of her famous vox-casts? Okay, if nothing else, that was awesome.

"Reinforcements," she said.

"Good," Heep said, wondering exactly what she meant. "Well, I just want you guys to know that I'm ready, okay? Whatever you've got in mind, I'm in. I mean, I'm in this for the long-run."

The two women glanced at each other. Blake ignored him.

"Look," he said. "I've sacrificed my life letting you guys in here. I'm yours now. I'm ready to pitch in and do whatever it takes to help bring down the Jays. Whatever you want me to do, I'm in."

Moriah looked up, as if touched by his words.

"I want a synthi-caff," she said. "Cream, no sweetener."

ANDERSON STRUGGLED TO remain on her feet as she burst into the unlocked recreation hall, carried along by a tide of howling inmates. With her fluorescent green jumpsuit and her bright orange hair, still slick with synthetti sauce, she figured she must look like a traffic light. Without a mirror, she couldn't tell whether she had made a convincing job of the disguise. It felt laughably phoney, plus she stank of tomato flavouring, but none of the inmates had given her a second glance when the lights returned five minutes ago. If she remained within a crowd, she reasoned, it would probably be enough to conceal her from the surveillance orbs.

The inmates were setting about the chairs and gaming tables. The charge had been led by the biggest of the inmates—two guys the size of Kleggs—and a green-haired woman. Anderson made sure to hang back among the carnival capering in their wake, inmates young and old, male and female. Together they poured into the room. Some ranted. Some sang. Some merely stared about them in a daze or were trampled underfoot. Some had stripped naked and were clawing at their bodies.

Traffic violations, section one, Anderson thought. *Driving under the influence of alcohol or narcotics: one to two years. Ongoing restrictions at Judge's discretion.*

Section two: Dangerous driving...

Anderson recited the Department's sentencing codes as a ward against the cacophony, but the inmates' thoughts still wriggled through the gaps in her concentration. She heard serial murderers, kill-addicts, spree-shooters, rapists, trolls and torturers, along with a bank clerk who had filed the wrong tax form and been driven to claustrophobic mania inside an iso-cube. Deprived of medication, therapy never even attempted, the inmates had reverted to baseline psychosis, their 'coping mechanisms' abandoned or forgotten. Whatever humanity they had once possessed, however they may once have been saved, all were now lost to madness.

The green-haired woman had already torn the Tri-D set from the wall and was now gathering lengths of shattered plasti-glass. A man lay dead on the floor, crushed beneath a toppled vending machine, while others wrenched it open and stuffed snacks inside their jumpsuits. Anderson ducked as a pot-plant sailed over her head and crashed into a holographic waterfall. The scenic view vanished, revealing a shattered screen and the barred windows behind it. Anderson kicked over a caff-table, feeling strangely self-conscious.

A young man cowered nearby, screaming in terror at the surrounding chaos. His petrified thoughts screeched in Anderson's head as she strained to shut them out.

Driving under a ban and/or without a satisfactory permit: One year.

Parking violation: Maximum 500 credit fine or up to twenty days imprisonment...

Anderson looked away, but could still hear him screaming. She had wanted to reach into his mind and banish his terrors, but opening herself to the sea of psychosis around her would risk drowning in it. She had to stay on point.

"Jessie!" someone grabbed Anderson's sleeve. "Jessie, you're alive!"

The man's thoughts wailed like a siren. She shoved him away, stifling the impulse to hold him and drive the nightmares from his mind.

Anderson shoved her way past several others as she followed the ringleaders from the room, their thoughts swishing like blades as they scanned the corridor beyond for something to destroy. She heard one of them think to look in her direction, but she had already slipped past them and down stairwell towards level 166.

She hurried down the stairs and into the lobby of Sidney James Ward, where another group of maniacs were tearing the limbs off a deactivated reception-droid. She hurried on, descending the next flight of stairs and the next, scenes of joyous carnage awaiting her on every landing. Her legs were already quivering with exertion and she paused to hurl a chair across the room in a manner she hoped looked convincingly demented. She kicked away a man clutching at her legs and head-butted a woman who came running up the stairs wanting to wear Anderson's face.

Anderson moved on, trying to recite the sentences for contraband. She stumbled on the stairs, her chest heaving. She had over a dozen more flights to descend before she reached the Control Hub on 150 and still had no idea what she was going to do when she got there. She needed to get close to Blake, close enough to reach into her head and find out the location of the bomb. Tek-Div would be scouring every Sector House in the city for devices, but their search would be futile without further intel. She realised she had forgotten which code of sentencing she was meant to be reciting and could hear the thoughts of the inmates clear and unrelenting. Maybe Ecks was right; maybe she couldn't do this.

Possession or manufacture of an illegal substance with intent to trade: Seven to ten years. Or was it twenty?

She staggered down the stairs, her thighs aching as she heard squeals of laughter coming from the lobby below.

Possession or trade of restricted publications: Six to twelve months.

Anderson halted as she rounded the bend in the stairs and

beheld the scene below. Giggling inmates were painting a mural of blood upon the white walls. The acrid stink of it made Anderson's gorge rise. A dark lake radiated from a pile of torn bodies in the centre of the room upon which crouched a naked muscular figure. The inmates were so absorbed in their devotions that they took no notice of Anderson as she moved past them, her eyes averted, trying to ignore the frantic thoughts of the crouched man, who was struggling with slippery fingers to tear the tongue from one of the corpses.

If you let him keep it, he'll put a curse on you...

She couldn't recall the correct number of years for possessing an illegal or unlicensed firearm, and could feel the man watching her walk past. Her resolve slipped and she risked a glance.

His name was lost to him, his eyes rings of white in a face drenched red, a single terrified thought screaming from his mind.

Help me!

Anderson felt her stomach lurch and thought for a moment that she had tripped, so acute was the feeling of sudden descent, as if the world had opened up beneath her.

Help me, he thought. *I want to stop...*

Anderson stood transfixed as he hunkered towards her, reaching for her with glistening red hands.

She felt herself yielding to her own compassion, overwhelmed by the need to do as the man pleaded, reach into his mind, help him find a way to live with what he was, embrace him, cure him.

Help me!

Vertigo spiralled through her as she opened her mind to receive him, just a crack, just enough to reach into his psyche and help strengthen it and by doing so perhaps strengthen her own.

It was like opening the door to a flood, as every voice within telepathic earshot descended upon her.

Heads rolling towards me beneath the floorboards... Can feel my teeth cracking, hatching tiny little birds, I swear... Rolling towards me and laughing... Gave him a present wrapped in skin... When it's quiet I can hear them telling me... There was light under my fingernails... They put the cameras where you can't see them... I had to break it open to get the thoughts out... Don't cry, little one... Screaming in the wind on the way down... Smells like Billy's lipstick... Faces swell up like fruit if you beat 'em hard enough... Bullet-holes full of bugs... All strangled and black... Veins and veins and veins and veins and whispers inside every one of them... Raining squirts of blood... She wouldn't stop laughing when I killed her... He was all wires inside... Like the back of his head was throwing up...

Anderson saw lights flashing around her, her body pummelled from every angle, screaming as she tried to drive the voices out of her head. She landed breathless and battered at the foot of the stairs, the man with the red wet hands hurrying down after her. Other inmates began crowding her as she hauled herself to her feet.

Look at the strings in the backs of her hands... She's rotten with it. Poke her and your finger will go straight through... Why's she calling my name...? He's still following me. Maybe she can help... Snakes in the blood... Another one without a head...

Anderson shoved them aside as she ran, hurling herself from wall to wall as she plunged down corridors, stairs, through doors, rooms, shoving past cackling, jeering inmates, every turn revealing another chorus of voices, each one clawing at the inside of her head. She skidded into a wall in an empty corridor and finally collapsed, vomiting again and again.

She tried to rise, spitting the bitterness from her mouth, striving to tame her breathing.

You can do this, Anderson. You're a Psi-Judge. You've trained for things a thousand times worse. This is nothing. You're trained to perform miracles.

Bullstomm and you know it, Cassie. Like you have any drokking idea what you're gonna do if you even reach the Control Hub. Any idea how you're gonna get inside?

I'll think of something.

You can't cope without Zeinner. And if you were any kind of Judge you wouldn't have let her die.

I can do this.

She thought she could feel the floor crumbling beneath her hands and imagined whispering blackness beneath. Her pulse throbbed angrily in the side of her neck, chill sweat trickling down her face as she shivered. She looked up and saw another surveillance orb.

How's this for a performance?

Hair-dye and a jumpsuit might fool the cams, Cassie. But you think it'll fool Blake if she gets up close? You'll go crazy long before you get anywhere near her. And let's face it, this little freak-out of yours has been a long time coming. By the time this show's over, you'll be in a kook-cube alongside the rest of these nuts.

Littering: 100 credit fine or six months.

You can't cope, Cassie. Looks like your brain-box finally popped a spring.

I can cope, thought Anderson. *I'll find a way.*

"Anderson."

It took a moment for her to realise that the voice was real.

"That's you, right?"

Anderson was startled to see an inmate standing a few feet behind her: a young woman, smiling as she reached inside her jumpsuit.

"I think you dropped something," she said, flaunting Anderson's psi-badge, the gold embossed letters smeared with oatmeal.

Fourteen

"FELLOW CITIZENS OF Mega-City One," Blake said. "I am speaking to you from inside Psych-Block Zero-Six."

The Bedlamites stared at her, weapons at ease, spellbound, as if bearing witness to the voice of God. Even the hostages appeared mesmerised by the sight of her hunched in a swivel-chair, clutching her vox-corder with both hands as if in prayer.

The huge holo-screen that dominated the Hub's central chamber had been tuned into a dozen Mega-City news-feeds, broadcasting views of the legions of Bedlam supporters amassed on the shores of the chem-lake, Justice Department Mantas probing their faces with searchlights. Phalanxes of Judges stood ready in riot-gear. Citizens with scarves and hoods concealing their faces pressed phones and radios to their ears. Heep looked away, silently cursing as he handed out yet another cup of synthi-caff.

"My followers," Blake said. "Regular citizens, just like you, have attempted to rescue me. They have penetrated one of the most well-protected blocks in this sector and made a mockery of Justice Department security."

Thanks to me, thought Heep.

The listening crowds on the holo-screens cheered, waving their banners in triumph.

"But their efforts have been thwarted by the actions of a single Judge," Blake said. "And now we're dead."

Heep almost dropped his tray, feeling his innards freeze. A couple of the Bedlamites fidgeted, but otherwise they all remained unmoved. Blake gazed into nothing, perhaps contemplating oblivion. The crowds on the news-feeds had erupted in protest.

"In a short while, the Judges will despatch their stormtroopers and we will be dead within the hour."

The Judges on the news-feeds braced themselves, Mantas flashing overhead, as crowds seethed on the other side of the electro-cordon. Heep set down his tray, wondering whether he could make it to the service elevator and into the basement car park before anyone noticed.

"Unless," Blake said, her voice stilling the crowds. "Unless you can save us. You, out there, listening to this. Ordinary citizens, like those standing beside me right now, who value their freedom, who oppose tyranny, who despise the Judges for the insanity they have inflicted upon us. You need to make a stand, and fight them. Tonight."

Her voice was like black magic, thrilling in its intensity. Heep recognised that same stirring he had felt when he first caught one of Blake's vox-casts on an illegal radio band. Again, he felt somehow rejuvenated, sensing his future reaching far into the horizon, his life boiling with possibilities once again.

"We've talked for too long," she said. "Now Bedlam must begin."

The crowds on the holo-screen were chanting, fists pounding the air: "*Bed-lam! Bed-lam! Bed-lam!*"

Heep knew she was right. It was the truth he had always feared, that there must come a time when words have run their course and the need to take violent action becomes unavoidable.

"Mega-City One stands on a knife edge," Blake said, her hands trembling as though she were trying to crush the vox-corder in her small white hands. "You have run the Judges ragged with riots and protests. They know they cannot contain us."

Several news-feeds offered images of the chaos unfolding around the city, of blocks alight, Lawmasters burning, citizens braving Lawgiver fire, a dozen bodies piling on top of every Judge. If the news was to be believed, the entire city was ablaze.

To Heep it felt like Bedlam's promise of rebellion against the Judges was finally hardening into a certainty. But it felt somehow greater than that, more like destiny. Surrounded by men and women armed with nothing more than cheap guns and adamantine belief, he envisioned the gears of fate finally grinding in his favour, as he—thirty-seven-year-old Heep Brillantyne, failed philosophy major turned failed retail manager, turned failed pharmacist and weekend Citi-Def—now stood in the vanguard of an army that was to change the course of history.

He watched the crowds on the shore charge the Judges as one of the news-feeds swung aside and burst into static. Blake continued regardless, her black hair veiling her face, her voice intense with a private rage.

"Can you allow your children to live through an age of terror knowing that tonight you had a chance to end it? You know the extremes to which the so-called Justice Department will go to silence us. Don't let them. Win back our city. Your future is in your hands. I have faith in the people of Mega-City One. I have faith in their courage, in their power; and if everyone..."

She paused to examine her vox-corder. A red light was flashing on several surveillance desks.

"We've been cut off," someone said. "Something's interrupted the signal."

There came a commotion at the back of the room and Blondie struggled to the front, clutching a startled Teri by the arm.

"She's done something," he said.

"She has done something," Blake said dreamily, her fury vanished.

Heep shoved his way to a surveillance desk, tapped a sequence of commands into the holo-screen and scanned the read-out.

"She's activated MATRON," he said with authority. "It's a security protocol."

"Should we be worried?" said Blondie.

"Not unless you're down there with the inmates," Heep said.

Blake unplugged her vox-corder and approached him.

"You can shut it down," she said.

"I've tried," Heep said. "But she's locked the system with a randomised code. I can probably crack it, but it'll take too long."

Teri was sobbing an apology, the courage she had summoned in attempting to thwart Bedlam abandoning her.

Blondie looked confused.

"Have we got any rope, or handcuffs or anything?" he said.

"It's wearing an eagle," Blake said.

Blondie comprehended her meaning immediately and unslung his rifle as he pulled Teri towards the exit. She screamed, tugging, clawing at his massive arms, crying out to the rest of the surveillance crew who sat rigid in their seats, guarded by grim Bedlamites.

"Heep," she screamed. "Please! Help me!"

Heep caught Blondie's arm and called out to Blake as she returned to her chair. "Wait!"

Blake and the Bedlamites turned. Heep stood his ground, gathering his words. His lips felt parched, his throat rigid, the eyes of everyone in the room upon him.

He forced himself to watch Teri's expression collapse into one of horror as he spoke.

"Let me do it," he said.

Blake nodded at Blondie.

"Can I have a gun?" Heep said, as Teri screamed anew.

"You can have one when you're finished," Blake said, returning to her chair.

ANDERSON MOVED INTO a crouch, careful not to startle the girl. Her own shakes had subsided, her fear steadied as she focused on the inmate. She looked as though she might flee at any moment and Anderson was too far away to snatch the badge, which looked enormous in the girl's trembling hand. Surveillance orbs lined the corridor.

The girl's thoughts were tight with fear.

Don't hurt me...

Get ready to run...

It's her job to help you...

From what Anderson could tell, the girl's head was a mush of confused memories. She could remember her name was Aerial, but that was about it.

"What's your name?" asked Anderson, clinging to the wall as she climbed cautiously to her feet.

"Aerial," Aerial said. The girl was too scared to play tricks.

"Okay, Aerial," Anderson said. "You're going to need to put that badge away before someone sees it."

"Help me," Aerial said.

Anderson shuddered.

"Say you'll help me and I'll put this away," the girl said, still holding the badge. "You're a Judge. It's your job."

"I'll do what I can," Anderson said quietly. "But first you better put that thing away before the orbs catch sight of it and think you're the one they're looking for."

Aerial considered this, then replaced the badge inside her jumpsuit.

The girl's thought processes felt too reasoned, too anchored in reality, for her to be a psychotic. Perhaps another regular citizen transported here on a technicality?

"It's okay, Aerial," Anderson said, her hands held out in front of her as she performed a deep scan. "I'm not gonna hurt you."

A rush of images as Anderson dived through Aerial's memory core. The girl had been among the inmates woken from their cubes when Anderson broke into the kitchen on Ken Williams Ward. She had believed herself to be dreaming when she saw the Judge, illuminated by the glow of the wild-haired man's fluorescent jumpsuit as she dragged his unconscious body inside the darkened kitchen. Aerial had slipped in after her, crouching behind a catering-bot and listening as Anderson argued with Psi-Chief Ecks. She had watched, half-frightened, half-fascinated, as Anderson pulled on the jumpsuit and dyed her hair with synthetti sauce.

Anderson figured she had been too busy shutting out the thoughts of the waking inmates to have heard those of Aerial. The girl had only fully comprehended what she had seen after Anderson had left and Aerial had retrieved the Judge's badge from the vat of warm oatmeal, awed by the weight of the golden shield in her hand.

Anderson felt calmed by the story, reassured by its logic. In the wake of her emotional collapse, it was comforting to find herself in the presence of someone from the outside world, whose rationality helped quieten the cavalcade of voices in her head. Here was a citizen: vulnerable, afraid, in need of protection. Anderson felt ashamed to think that here was something to focus on, a lifeline that could help her cling to her sanity.

Anderson withdrew from the girl's mind.

"What are you doing?" Aerial said. "Are you in my head? Please, just help me get out of here. I don't even know where I am."

"You're in Psych-Block Zero-Six," Anderson said. "You're in the middle of a patient break-out and I'm guessing you're not supposed to be here any more than I am."

"Can you radio for help?" Aerial said. "Are other Judges coming?"

"It's just me for now," Anderson said. "The cavalry will be here soon and they're gonna get you out of here, but there's something I need to do first."

Given the lives at stake, Anderson knew that Department protocol would probably dictate she restrain the girl somehow, perhaps even kill her if she threatened to compromise the mission. Anderson could put her into a nice deep sleep with the right kind of psi-blast, but she doubted she could find anywhere to keep Aerial out of harm's way before she woke up. Right now, Anderson reasoned to herself, if she was going to be a Judge she needed her sanity, and having Aerial by her side would help her keep it. She could analyse the decision when she got out of here.

Distant screams echoed through the corridor and Anderson caught Aerial by the arm.

"Okay," she said. "Let's not look too sane for the cameras, huh? Do you know what level we're on?"

"Uh, one-five-three, I think," Aerial said. "Why? Where are we going?"

They could hear frightened yells coming from beyond a corner at the far end of the corridor, followed by a mechanical female voice.

"*I've never seen such* outrageous *behaviour,*" the voice bellowed in an exquisite Brit-Cit accent. "*You shall return to your cubes* at once!"

Anderson turned and ran as a rush of inmates rounded the corner.

"Get to the stairs," Anderson yelled, pushing Aerial ahead of her. As she glanced over her shoulder at the inmates hurtling towards her from the end of the corridor, another mass of them ploughed into her from the side. Flailing, clawing, kicking bodies collapsed on top of her, scrambling to escape. Through the swarm of limbs, Anderson glimpsed something vast and white hovering after the inmates down an adjacent corridor.

"*How dare you!*" it roared, as if the inmates' terror was a personal affront.

A small steel dart whistled past Anderson's cheek and appeared in the neck of a bearded inmate. Anderson watched his eyes roll back and heard his panicked thoughts decline into sleep. He collapsed, and an immense egg-like body loomed over her. She grabbed the unconscious inmate with both hands and hauled him on top of her, feeling another dart thud into his back. She threw him aside, wrestling free of the tangled, grasping heap. Aerial caught her hand and they fled down the corridor together, just as the first group of inmates collided with the others on the floor behind them, creating a pandemonium of thrashing, yelling bodies.

Anderson and Aerial ran for the lobby at the end of the corridor, but another horde of panicked inmates appeared, cutting off their escape, forcing the women to turn and flee into another ward. More inmates joined then, racing alongside them, appearing from adjoining hallways. They were frantic, gibbering with fright, obeying a primal impulse to flee the great white monsters that pursued them. Anderson pulled Aerial close, swatting at hands that snatched at their hair and clothes, the inmates desperate to claw their way past.

Anderson sprinted ahead, dragging Aerial with her. The girl stumbled, threatening to disappear beneath the avalanche of stampeding feet, but Anderson yanked her upright. They turned a corner and sprinted down a short hallway ending in a scrum of inmates piling through a doorway and into the room beyond. Anderson accelerated, Aerial struggling to keep pace. Anderson grabbed the girl's jumpsuit at the shoulder and charged at the doorway, just as the last of the inmates disappeared inside the room and went to haul the sides of the hatch closed.

Another dart whispered past Anderson's ear and struck the sliding door as a riot of screams erupted behind her. An appalled mechanical voice rang out. Anderson slammed into the door and wrenched the dart free, stabbing it into the arm of a burly man trying to shove her back through the narrowing gap. His eyes closed and he fell forward, his body blocking the hatch doors as Anderson fought her way through the gap, dragging Aerial behind her. The inmates pushed the unconscious man clear and the hatch doors closed with a clang.

Anderson held Aerial tight as they sprawled onto the polished floor of a cavernous hall. The inmates dispersed to reveal a vast sports court with ranks of bleachers rising against one wall. The place was swarming with bewildered inmates, the rubber soles of their slippers creating an undercurrent of squeaking. The hall echoed with their sobs and cries. Anderson sensed she and the others had been herded in here, like cattle.

"What were those things?" Aerial said, dazed.

"They were shooting tranq-darts," Anderson said. "Security droids maybe? I'm not sure."

She pointed across the hall.

"We need to get through there," she said, grabbing Aerial and pushing through the milling inmates towards a door topped with a glowing *EXIT* sign. If they were on level 153, the Hub was just three floors down that emergency stairwell. Two inmates were tying a jumpsuit around the door-handles, while the jumpsuit's owner lay curled up on the floor, shivering in his underwear. Others stood by, brandishing metal pipes and lengths of broken furniture, yelling curses at whatever waited on the other side of the door.

"If those things are security," she whispered to Aerial. "Anyone with a weapon will be a priority target. Stay by me and we'll slip past if we can."

Aerial nodded, clutching Anderson's arm as the hatch opened a few centimetres. A small whizzing circular-saw emerged through the gap and sliced down through the knotted jumpsuit.

The hatch doors flew aside and the inmates retreated; a huge, white-enamelled robot hovered into the doorway like a battleship. Its bowling-ball head was crowned with a Justice Department eagle shaped to resemble a nurse's cap. The droid bulldozed several inmates aside, revealing lettering printed across the expanse of its belly: *CALL ME HATT•E.*

Anderson recognised it as some kind of modified riot-bot, based on the TR-20 model developed in Brit-Cit. She had submitted a term paper on the disadvantages of mechanised riot-control a few years ago, earning herself a grade of 29%.

"This is MATRON," announced a dozen voices at once.

Identical droids had barged into the hall, standing sentinel at every exit, surrounded by shrieking, hollering inmates. The droids were hive-minded, somehow working off a relay separate from the rest of the block, otherwise Bedlam would surely have deactivated them by now.

"Drop your weapons at once and return to your cells like civilised human beings," the droids echoed.

The inmates fell upon them like feral children. Anderson pulled Aerial back, watching the inmates clawing at the smooth white belly of the droid before them as it blocked their escape. The droid looked down at them, hatches opening either side of its head, and dispensed a volley of tranq-darts into the clamouring mob. Dozens of inmates slumped to the floor, trampled by others now snatching at the droid's huge arms.

"I've never seen such outrageous behaviour, and I shan't stand it a moment *longer!"*

Anderson couldn't help shivering at the authority in that voice, its tone and vocab-banks no doubt calibrated to trigger a maternal fear response in the inmates.

"Since you appear incapable of behaving like civilised human beings," the droids declared, their voices dominating the hall like thunder, *"we shall be forced to take a less civilised course of action."*

The droid hovering before Anderson and Aerial shrugged its left arm, throwing several inmates aside as it activated a glowing blue force-shield, while an enormous daystick slid into its hand from a porthole in its wrist.

Good old Department programming, Anderson thought, backing away. *If at first you don't succeed, pull out a big stick and hit something.*

Anderson ducked on top of Aerial as inmates flew overhead, hurled into the air by a sweep of the droid's daystick. She told the cowering girl to stay down, grabbed a discarded length of pipe from the floor and ran at the droid. Dodging the inmates fleeing past her, she went to aim an overhead swing at the droid's wrist. The glowing blue wall of its shield intervened, slamming into Anderson's face and lifting her off her feet. She crashed onto the floor, the pipe clanging beside her.

Struggling to clear her head, tasting blood on her lips, she rolled onto her hands and knees. She tried to rise, but an inmate tripped over her, pushing her back to the floor. More inmates surged past, fleeing the droid's lashing daystick.

She couldn't see Aerial. Had she lost her already? Anderson reflexively searched for the girl's thoughts, but found only those of the inmates screaming and dashing about her, their minds hysterical, inescapable. She rose to her knees and the walls seemed to lurch to one side. She looked down at the blood spotting the floor as it dripped from her nose and lips. It looked as black as pitch, as if it were dissolving the floor and revealing an impossible emptiness beneath. She tried to hold back the maddened thoughts of the inmates, but it was like trying to arrest a tidal wave.

Anderson gave in and the maelstrom filled her head, a whirlwind of shrieks, laughter, whispers promising all manner of horrors. She welcomed them, added her own screams to the deluge as she hauled herself to her feet, no longer fighting to steady herself as the hall and its combatants reeled around her. What a glorious sense of release. Never mind Aerial. Never mind duty. What did it matter now?

She spat blood and snatched the pipe from the floor as she glared at the mountainous droid blocking her escape from the hall. She saw that imperious golden eagle mounted upon the droid's head and felt rage ignite her. She ran at the droid like a wild animal, loping over the bodies of the unconscious inmates piled about her. She abandoned herself to fury and instinct, her thoughts unclouded by any notion of strategy or self-preservation. Her anger was all that mattered.

The droid had departed from the doorway, chasing the scattered inmates, dropping two more with tranq-darts as they tried to run for the exit behind it. As she ran, Anderson sprang onto the chest of a startled inmate, slamming him against the droid's back and running up his body as though he were a ladder, before leaping from his shoulders, launching herself into the air.

She screamed as she swung the pipe at the droid's head, smashing it to one side before landing on its broad white shoulders like a cat. The droid swerved to one side, its arms struggling to interpret the commands relayed from its damaged head. Recovering her balance, Anderson screamed again, raining blows onto the droid's head, her wrath tireless as she hammered that eagle into warped, golden scrap. There was no holding back, no shame, no fear of retribution, nothing but glorious freedom. She vibrated with energy. The inmates below had caught hold of the droid's arms, encumbering its shield and daystick. They cheered every blow, hailing their berserker queen, matriarch of the madhouse.

Anderson looked into the cracked lenses of the droid's eyes as she drove the pipe between them like a sword and levered open its skull, reaching inside and tearing out a fistful of sparking wires and circuitry, her psi-senses feeling the electrical pulses wriggling within. She gathered the inmates' thoughts, weaving them like the currents of a cyclone into a single psionic scream before unleashing it into the robot's circuitry.

Gloriously spent, her mind purged, Anderson watched the walls tip to one side as the MATRON droid toppled and threw her to the floor. She lay there, still gripping a handful of wiring, her throat raw, her head swimming and her chest heaving as the hall echoed with the sound of crashing droids, their hive-minded circuits rendered lifeless by the deluge of psionic static.

Anderson realised she was laughing uncontrollably, her ribs in agony. Her head was so full of voices she could no longer distinguish her own. Someone was tugging at her arm, a young woman. Anderson pushed her away. The few inmates who weren't tranquilised or concussed were swarming over the deactivated droids like ants, prising open their white carapaces and tearing out their insides. The girl was clutching Anderson's face now, imploring her.

"Anderson," she was saying. "Let's go. C'mon. You can do this."

Anderson looked about her as if waking from a dream. She winced at the cuts in her fingers, bewildered for a moment as to how they got there. The girl pulled her upright and helped her stagger through the exit and down the emergency stairwell. Anderson tried to banish the crazed voices that lingered inside her head, but it felt as though they had taken root.

You've gone and done it now, Cassie...

Fifteen

ANDERSON STUMBLED DOWN the last few stairs, barged through a swing door and spilled into the ruined lobby of level 150, her head still hissing with voices. She landed on the floor, hands pressed against the sides of her skull, fighting to drive away the inmates' thoughts. She knew that having welcomed them into her head she had established a permanent connection, just as Zeinner and Ecks had warned her she would.

The voices pressed in so tightly they were indecipherable, just a tumult of words, sobs and laughter, so loud and insistent Anderson was deaf to the sound of her own footsteps. Aerial looked desperate, pleading words Anderson couldn't hear. The more she focused on the girl's face, the more the room seemed to whirl sickeningly.

Anderson felt a hot sting in her cheek and the voices went quiet for a moment. Aerial had slapped her and was now dragging her towards the reception desk. A deactivated MATRON had fallen head-first through a holo-window, still gripping the ankles of two tranquilised inmates. Flickering waves of a holographic sea washed over the three bodies. The pain behind Anderson's eyes throbbed so hard it seemed as though the room had a pulse.

Aerial dragged her behind the reception desk, out of sight of the surveillance orbs. Anderson simply couldn't close her mind. The flow of voices was constant, drowning her every thought. The girl kneeling beside her looked unfamiliar; Anderson wondered what she wanted. She could recall trying to get somewhere and carry out some kind of important task.

The girl—Angel? Aria?—slapped her again.

"You're a Judge," she hissed. "You can deal with this. You *have* to deal with it. For me. You're gonna make sure I get out of here. Because that's your job, right?"

Anderson fumbled for a response as the girl placed Anderson's hands either side of her own face.

"You can read minds, right?" the girl said. "Then read mine. Focus on me. Nothing else. Just me. Now tell me. What's my name? Who am I?"

Anderson winced as her fingertips touched the girl's temples, feeling something like a snap of electricity as she tumbled into the girl's consciousness. The voices of the inmates mellowed, then evaporated as she bathed in the girl's mind. Her rationality soothed Anderson's tortured psi-senses. Her thoughts were like the strings of a violin, high-pitched but speaking of reason and comprehensible emotion, not demented fantasies or primitive urges run rampant.

"Aerial," Anderson said. "Aerial Adeyemi."

Anderson felt the words steady her and sensed Aerial breaking into a hopeful smile.

"You were a student at Zarkov U," Anderson said, reaching further into the girl's memory core. "Med student. You were gonna do well, judging by your grades. Then..."

Anderson frowned and pulled away.

"Then what...?" Aerial said. "Are you okay...?"

Aerial's boyfriend had been a Political Science major. The day after he was arrested, Aerial was summoned for questioning and learned that his latest stand in the school debating society had been classed as 'democratic platforming.' Anderson had seen a memory of Aerial yelling something at two Judges and slapping a desk in outrage. She knew, as the Judges exchanged looks, that they figured they had a future troublemaker on their hands. Unable to pin anything on Aerial straight away, they submitted her for a psych-exam, then told her she was to be remanded at a Psych-Block pending further questions. Aerial had been waiting in a kook-cube the best part of a year for those questions to be asked.

Anderson stood up, steadying herself against the reception desk, her head no longer spinning, her heart no longer hopping inside her chest. The inmates' voices now sounded like they were coming from behind a closed door in her head.

"I'm gonna get you out of here, Aerial," she said, eyeing the surveillance orbs. "But I need to make a stop-off first."

She knelt beside the girl and explained what she had to do and why she needed her to lay low. Anderson couldn't open her mind too far without drowning in another deluge of voices, but she could hear Aerial's thoughts as the girl tried to make sense of what she was being told.

A bomb in the city...

People will die...

I need to get out...

Aerial nodded.

"You go," she said. "I'll be fine right here."

Anderson smiled. If only Street-Div could hear what she heard inside so many citizens. So much decency and compassion, such willingness to help others. What was Bedlam if not a perverse derivative of those impulses? She moved to the fallen MATRON, reading the words printed on its butt: *Medbot Assisting in Tranquilisation, Retrieval, and Obstinacy Neutralisation.* She shook her head and stamped several times at its back until a tray popped up, revealing a rack of tranquiliser darts. She removed the magazine, punched out three steel darts and handed them to Aerial.

"MATRON here will have taken a chunk out of the number of inmates running around," she said. "But if anyone shows up and gives you trouble, make sure you stick 'em with one of these."

Aerial took them, trying to maintain her courage.

What if she gets killed...?

What if she's lying...?

Can't trust a Judge...

They'll put you back inside...

Anderson knelt beside Aerial and took her hands.

"Not all Judges are monsters, Aerial," she said.

Aerial tried not to look doubtful.

Prove it, she thought.

ANDERSON APPROACHED THE sealed doors of the Control Hub. Her continuous effort to keep out the voices had severely reduced the range of her telepathy. She knew she was going to have to get close to Moriah Blake—real close, maybe even hands-on—to have any hope of retrieving the bomb's location. Without extending her mind too far, she could tell the reception behind the frosted glass wall was empty. She moved past it, down a curved corridor, maintaining a glazed expression for the benefit of any surveillance orbs that might be watching.

She was just wondering whether pretending to catch imaginary butterflies might be a little too much, when she found a bald inmate with a grey beard frantically licking the wall. He called out to her as she wandered past.

"All of this," he said, his tongue black. "This entire block, man. They want it painted by Thursday. Thursday!"

He returned to his licking and Anderson was relieved to find she could shut out his thoughts with little difficulty. She ran her fingers along the wall of the Control Hub, drawing on the psionic impulses inside through her fingers. She could hear plenty of rational minds inside, but they were distant, busy at their surveillance desks on the level above.

Back in the physical world, she could hear the echoing cries of other inmates and hoped they were far enough away from Aerial, whom she had left crouched behind the reception desk in the lobby with only a fistful of tranq-darts to protect herself. She tried not to think what kind of inmate might have been resourceful or strong enough to survive MATRON's onslaught.

She hurried up a short flight of stairs, trying to calm her impatience, then paused. In the restroom behind the wall, she could hear the thoughts of a guy named Hal. No, Heath? Wait, it was 'Heep.' He worked here but somehow wasn't a hostage, and he had just finished throwing up in the toilet. His ribs ached, his throat burned and he was watching the water wash over his hands as they lay in the sink. He kept glancing nervously at a pistol he had placed on the shelf below the mirror.

Whatever, Anderson thought. *Just skim this guy. Don't let the voices in again. Can't risk another freakout.*

She avoided the thoughts warring inside Heep's head, and scanned his temporal lobe for the location of the bomb. He came up clean, but had last seen Blake in the Hub's central chamber. She risked a deeper scan and managed to extract the layout of the entire Hub. Thankfully, Heep had worked here for some time; the memories were within easy reach.

The place appeared to be similar to the control room in an iso-block, with ten observation rooms each dedicated to thirty levels. Most of the rooms now lay empty, their crews herded into the central chamber along with Moriah and her buddies. There were rest rooms, cafeterias, med-bays and access lifts all over the joint, plenty of room to sneak around, but maybe not so much if you were wearing a bright green jumpsuit that screamed, 'Well, hullo there. I might be a cannibal.'

Anderson dug deeper. Where there any air ducts in there?

C'mon, she thought. *Everybody loves an air duct.*

Apparently not. The only thing Heep knew about for sure was some kind of crawl space behind the walls where the technicians got to go and maintain the innumerable cables and relays that fed the Hub. Heep had never been in there because Heep didn't like spiders. Anderson wondered whether the surveillance orb above her head was still operational, and if anyone was watching from the other side. According to Heep, probably not. Everyone seemed to think she had either been killed by the inmates hours ago or else tranquilised by MATRON.

Anderson realised she could hear the inmates' contained thoughts growing louder in her head. She sensed Heep sobbing at his reflection in the mirror now and wished she had Aerial beside her as she focused on another of Heep's thoughts.

So tired...

Just wanna sleep...

Wake up in a world where none of this happened...

She ignored the encroaching voices, anchoring herself with thoughts of Aerial as she reached into Heep's mind. She entwined her thoughts with his, sending out subtle pulses of psi-energy, just a dab here and there, caressing his mind as gently as a lover, directing him to close his eyes and succumb to the weight in his limbs, enticing deeper thoughts to creep out from his subconscious. She heard Heep wondering why everyone took him for granted, why he'd never renewed the gym membership like he'd promised himself he would, why he had never asked Mindy Boomhouser to the prom.

Anderson massaged his brainwaves until they purred, warm and slow. As she felt him slipping away she threw out spikes of alpha-wave energy, just enough to keep his motor functions awake. She could hear the voices grumbling once again as she wove a cat's-cradle of psionic threads, working her fingers like a puppeteer as she directed Heep out of the rest room and towards the door. A maddened voice shouted in her ear, as though the speaker were standing beside her. She shook her head, banishing the voice, and heard Heep snoring on the other side of the door. Since fine motor skills were a no-no, she had to coax him into bashing at the door controls with the back of his hand, hoping the noise didn't attract any curious sentries.

She slipped past him the instant the door opened and found herself inside another corridor with smooth white walls, a glossy floor and glowing panels in the ceiling. There were footsteps and voices coming from up ahead. Heep blinked and looked about him before Anderson put her fingers to his temples and guided him into what turned out to be an empty surveillance room. He was snoring again by the time she got him into a chair and laid his head upon a surveillance desk. She could hear the thoughts of several guards prowling nearby; she couldn't risk trying to retrieve the pistol from the bathroom.

Hoping the surveillance room itself didn't have surveillance orbs, she searched the walls for an access panel and pulled it open, releasing a cloying odour of dust and machine-oil. She quickly squeezed inside, thinking the Tek guys in this place must be contortionists.

The maintenance cavity inside the wall looked unbearably narrow, and Anderson was grateful that her fluorescent jumpsuit illuminated the place as surely as a great big glowstick. The walls seemed built entirely of machine parts: industrial canisters, loops of intestinal tubing, hissing vents, buzzing junction boxes, everything labelled with unfathomable codes. The cluttered walls plucked at her jumpsuit as she moved down the tunnel, her toes snagging on the nest of cables that carpeted the floor. She could hear thoughts whispering up ahead and a small ladder materialised before her as she picked her way through the murk. She scaled the ladder onto the next storey, brushing the cobwebs from her face with both hands before moving on.

She could hear the thoughts of the hostage surveillance

crew, high-pitched and fearful. They grew louder as she crept further down the tunnel, cursing the cables that snared her feet with every step. The tunnel branched off in several directions, blackness awaiting her down each one. She took note of her bearings and followed the sound of excited thoughts and voices coming from her left. She tuned in until she could envision the men and women on the other side of the wall watching news coverage of what looked like thousands of citizens rioting on the shores of the chem-lake outside.

"It's everywhere," someone said.

I can't believe it's finally happening...

"The Jays are overrun."

We're gonna change the world...

"Your plan worked, Moriah!"

Knew it would...

Anderson recognised the strange, plodding cadence of Moriah Blake's thoughts. She reached out after them, but the minds of Blake's followers were so agitated they kept drowning her out. Anderson was having trouble focusing. Where was Aerial when she needed her? The girl was far away. Dead, perhaps, maybe beaten to a twitching pulp by a wandering inmate. Anderson felt sickened, and clutched at the apparatus on the walls to steady herself.

She looked about her, hypnotised by the teeming shadows cast by the green glow of her jumpsuit. She flinched as something scuttled across her hand and realised she needed to quieten her breathing. Her mouth felt parched, her throat sticky as though thick with cobwebs. The voices and thoughts on the other side of the wall continued to ring loud and clear as Anderson stifled a coughing fit.

She reached once again for the thoughts of Moriah Blake, but heard only maddened whispers. It was as if the inmates of Psych-Block Zero-Six had somehow followed her in here, their bodies crammed into the tunnels either side of her, blocking her escape, concealed by the darkness. Anderson glanced to one side and thought she saw a figure stepping back into the gloom.

She steeled herself, recalling her training. She had spent hours at the Academy strapped to a chair while the gizmo on her head pumped her mind full of terrors to see how well she could stifle her fear response. Breathing was key. Let the body control the mind. Inhale. Exhale. Rinse, repeat.

Anderson reached out and caught hold of Moriah Blake's thoughts, hearing the voices in her head rise in pitch and urgency as she did so.

Better make this quick, she thought. *And get out of here even quicker.*

She braced herself as she dived into Blake's mind, probing the woman's cerebral cortex with tendrils of psionic energy and whispering a keyword.

Bomb...

Anderson felt the word pinball between Blake's synapses illuminating an associative pattern its wake.

Change...

Judges...

Martyr...

The word finally ignited a memory. Anderson absorbed it, knowing the bomb's location as she fell back into herself. But it was too late. The voices in her head had escaped.

AN ARMOURED JUDGE carrying a Lawrod rifle flagged down Psi-Judge Tzu as he approached the checkpoint on his Lawmaster. He could hear the crowds rioting among the factories a short distance ahead, their thoughts as deafening as their assembled voices. A Manta sat docked beside the road. More Judges wearing tactical armour were tramping up the boarding ramp.

"Heard you guys got a Psi-Judge stranded in the Big Zero Six," Tzu said. "She asked for a long-range telepath?"

"Sorry, pal," the Judge said. "Figure you had a wasted trip."

"How so?" Tzu said, removing his helmet.

A burly Judge with a fearsome red beard was striding towards them from the Manta. His name was Greaves, Tac-Command.

"Didn't you get the drokkin' vid-link?" he shouted.

Probably busy meditating or something, Tzu heard Greaves think as he approached, swiping at his data-pad.

Tzu went to reply when a message autoplayed on the vid-screen of his Lawmaster. The face of a young woman with sickly orange hair was screaming and slavering into the camera. The image shuddered as she hammered at it with what looked like a length of pipe. Her face a grimace of fury, her eyes lost in madness as she continued battering the screen until it turned into a square of static. Only then did Tzu realise who he had been looking at.

"Tek Div were trying to get an eyeball inside the block when someone tripped the riot-robos," Greaves said. "They managed to pick up a relay, and facial-recog found that. Looks like your girl's gone native."

Tzu watched the footage again, incredulous, as Greaves departed for the waiting Manta.

"Plenty of action around here, if you feel like pitching in," Greaves called out.

"Wait." Tzu climbed off his Lawmaster and scurried after him. "So you're gonna storm in there and blow Blake away?"

"That's the plan, son," Greaves said. "Now those riot-bots have cleared most of the inmates for us, we've ordered the power company to shut down the entire block."

"What about the bomb?" Tzu said, catching Greaves' arm as he reached the Manta's boarding ramp. "Your going in there could be just the excuse Blake needs to pull the trigger."

Greaves almost laughed.

"Frankly, the only evidence we have that this bomb even exists is the say-so of a Psi-Judge that's just gone nutso. In fact, the Chief Judge has just cleared her as a hostile target. She gets in our way, she's going down."

"But she's a Judge," Tzu said. "She's one of us."

"Not anymore," Greaves said. "Now go on home."

THE VOICES SWARMED Anderson like rats.

Bend them back 'til you hear the crack... Then the ants pour out... Coughing maggots again... I died years ago... Just sacks of blood, could drown inside... No one knows I'm dead... Looking at me through the cracks in the ceiling... An angel standing over my bed wearing an animal mask... Listen to the sound it makes when it cuts, like a whisper telling you what they don't want you to know... Sounds like daddy kissing in the dark... Lifted up his hat and there was nothing underneath... Little mouths in my gloves, sucking my fingers... I just peeled it back and the head popped out, full of teeth... He climbed out of the drawer in my room...

She braced herself against the walls, as if straining to keep them from closing in on her.

I am Psi-Judge Cassandra Anderson, she told herself.

And you're going to die in here...

Not until I've done my job.

Not unless you go crazy first...

I am not going crazy.

You already have...

The smell of dust overpowered her, tightening her throat until it felt like she was trying to breathe through a straw. She fought the sensation that she was about to pass out. She couldn't lose it here, not in the darkness. The voices weren't just in her head anymore. There were things in the shadows now, stalking her. She felt hands moving inside her jumpsuit, crawling up her body towards her throat.

Anderson's scream rang through the tunnels. Voices cut through the moment's silence that followed.

"What the drokk was that?"

"Came from behind that wall."

Anderson tried to run, gasping for air as she clawed her way back down the tunnel, her legs shivering beneath her, stumbling, ripping cables from the walls. She wanted Aerial, wanted to feel the presence of another human being beside her, to help her face the things in the darkness. Something on the wall struck her head and she toppled backwards, crashing into a tall vent. A slit of light appeared down one side of the grate where she had pushed it away from the outside wall. She put her shoulder to it, punched it, kicked her way to freedom as the figures in the darkness reached for her. With a final shove, the vent gave way, scattering her into another room, where she promptly slipped and tumbled down a short flight of stairs.

Anderson looked up to find herself surrounded by a crowd of startled men and women. Some wore Justice Department jumpsuits and stood before banks of holo-screens. Others wore dark jackets and were pointing guns at her, looking unsure quite what to do about the madwoman who had just appeared into their midst. Light. Fresh air. People. She drank it all in, hearing the voices quieten in her head as she laughed helplessly.

"It's you," said a familiar voice.

Her heart still galloping, Anderson looked up and saw Moriah Blake rise from her seat. She looked almost bored. She retrieved what looked like a bulky homemade vox-corder from inside her jumpsuit.

Anderson heard Blake's thoughts and felt herself focused in an instant.

The dark-haired woman flicked a concealed switch on the device, one that turned it from a vox-corder into a detonator.

Sixteen

BLAKE'S FACE REMAINED immobile as she thumbed back the protective cap on the detonator. Anderson sucked in a breath, fingers at her temples. She gathered thoughts of fleeing through the darkness, of the voices, the imagined horrors, every terror that still lingered in her mind, then screamed them all into the heads of everyone around her. The psionic blast was unfocused, but its strength was enough to push everyone away, shooters and hostages alike. They staggered back, arms up, weapons clattering to the ground. Blake merely twitched, as a rivulet of blood crawled from her nose, her thumb wavering over the button of the detonator.

Her mind cleared by the psychic outburst, Anderson sprang to her feet, snatching the detonator from Blake's hand and closing the protective cap back over the switch. Several of Blake's goons had already recovered their weapons, clutching their heads and looking for something to shoot. Anderson shoved past Blake and fled down an adjoining corridor, unzipping her jumpsuit and slipping the detonator inside.

She sprinted down the glowing white hallway towards double-doors at the far end. The doors opened, revealing two men who immediately raised their pistols. She swerved down another identical white corridor, her feet slipping on the polished floor as bullets sparked against the walls behind her. She halted, seeing more shooters taking up position at a junction ahead, blocking her escape.

Hearing the two men running up behind her, Anderson fell back against the corner and threw a palm-strike into the nose of the first of her pursuers to appear. He ran straight into the blow, his nose splattering like fruit, stunning him. She heard his gun clatter to the floor somewhere nearby. Before she could retrieve it, his buddy had raised his pistol and fired.

Anderson heard the shot ricochet off the wall behind her, the shooter too far away for her to attempt a disarm. Her arms struck like snakes as she jammed her forearm into the wounded man's throat, pivoting him and locking his skull with her other hand, shielding herself with his body. Dragging him helpless before her, she shuffled backwards through an open hatch into another room.

It was a large surveillance suite illuminated by banks of unattended holo-screens broadcasting views of the wards. Anderson cursed. There appeared to be no exit. Tightening her grip viciously every time her bleeding hostage tried to gain leverage, she searched the walls, then backed towards one of the surveillance bays. Her heart pounded against the man's back as half a dozen more shooters, men and women, followed her inside the room, pistols and assault rifles cautiously raised as they fanned out to surround her.

"Stay right where you are before I unscrew your buddy's head in front of you," Anderson said, giddy with adrenalin. The shooters paused behind the line of surveillance desks nearest the door.

"You all know about this bomb, right?" she said. "Don't bother pretending you don't, because I can hear everything you're thinking."

They glanced at each other, listening intently, although they had no intention of lowering their guns just yet.

"You wanna know what your glorious leader didn't tell you?" Anderson said, kicking away a chair as she retreated towards the far wall. "You wanna know where the bomb really is?"

"It's in the basement," Blake said, appearing in the doorway. She hadn't even wiped her face, the rivulet of blood drawing a perfect line from nose to chin.

The shooters wavered. Anderson could hear their thoughts struggling to comprehend what she had just said. Anderson's hostage choked as she tightened her grip again, her back now pressing into the line of desks furthest from the exit.

"She never intended to let any of you leave here alive," she said. "My turning up was just a happy accident as far as she was concerned. She knows that if this place blows, everyone in the city will believe it was the Justice Department who pulled the trigger, that we're monsters enough to destroy an entire block rather than let a single wanted terrorist escape. Nothing cements a cause like martyrdom, huh?"

One of the shooters lowered her pistol.

"Moriah?" she said.

Blake ignored her, while Anderson addressed the men and women who still had their guns raised.

"You're worth more to her dead than alive," she said. "Don't you think you deserve the truth before you agree to lay down your lives?"

"They don't need the truth when they have faith," Blake said, moving among her followers as she spoke. "That is something a machine such as you can never understand. Fear of death is too great an opponent to overcome with a single blow. We have conquered it step-by-step, hand-in-hand. Now we're ready to make history. Our deaths will become legend, the reason to keep fighting, an inspiration everlasting."

Anderson pulled her hostage between two surveillance

desks, her back to the wall as she heard the thoughts of Blake's followers.

Have come this far...

Nothing to go back to...

The city needs this...

"The citizens may be crazy," Anderson said. "But they're not stupid. The blast radius? Damage patterns? They'll find out it wasn't the Department. Someone out there will get to the truth."

"And they'll ignore it, in favour of what they already believe," Blake said.

One by one her followers raised their weapons, their eyes fixed on Anderson.

"Listen to me," Anderson said, struggling to maintain her grip around the man's neck. "You're not murderers. This isn't going to win you the future you want."

Anderson thought she saw the ghost of a smirk on Blake's face.

"None of us have to die," she said, fighting now to maintain her chokehold as she heard a thought ripple through the mind of her hostage.

"Bedlam begins," he said, raising his arms, welcoming the hail of bullets to come. Anderson released him and fumbled for the catch in the wall she had spotted earlier.

She tore open the maintenance panel as Blake's followers opened fire, shredding the body of the man behind her, spitting blood and shrapnel after her as she disappeared into the cavity behind the wall. Her jumpsuit illuminated the darkness as she followed the curve of the wall, crouching as the gunfire continued, spears of light appearing above her head. A shot exploded inches from her face, stinging her eyes with grit. She let the pain drive her forward as she felt the bulge of the detonator still bouncing around above the waistband of her jumpsuit. Light flooded the tunnel as another maintenance panel opened in the wall ahead of her.

She scrabbled towards it as a woman peered inside the cavity, pistol at the ready. Anderson pounced upon the intruder, slamming an elbow into her startled face and fumbling for the pistol in her hands. She caught it, pinning the woman's arms and jamming the gun beneath her chin before squeezing the trigger and closing her eyes. Blood and meat slapped Anderson's face like a wet flannel. She twisted the gun from the dead woman's fingers, squinted through the blood and fired a double-tap into the chest of the man waiting outside for his friend to emerge.

She retrieved the dead man's pistol and saw the other shooters fleeing behind the surveillance desks. Blake appeared to have left them to it. Her detonator gone, she would be playing her endgame now, most likely making a run for the basement a hundred and fifty floors down, where she'd detonate the bomb manually. Aside from her friends on the outside who'd helped her set this up, Blake must have been the only person in the block who knew about the device. If there was anyone down there guarding the thing, Anderson figured, Blake would have made the call by now and everything would be rubble. She needed to stop Blake before she could make it to an elevator.

Anderson withdrew inside the cavity, wiped her face on her sleeve and examined the two pistols. Both were nine-millimetre Kiryaks, reliable Sov-made street guns. Next to a Lawgiver they felt ridiculously light, like toys. Ignoring an outburst of assault-rifle fire that destroyed a nearby surveillance console, she removed one of the clips and slipped it under the strap of her vest and tossed the empty weapon. Only gangsters and cartoon characters thought they could go at it with a gun in each hand.

She listened for the thoughts of the shooters hiding in the room outside, trying to locate their exact positions, but her head flooded with crazy talk the second she opened up. They probably had people stationed at the other hatches by now; no sense making a run for it back down the maintenance tunnels, not that she wanted to risk over-extending her powers again. It looked as though she would have to make it across the room and out of here with nothing but a pistol and a lifetime's worth of firearms training.

Anderson fired a few shots, forcing a couple of gunmen to duck as she scrambled out from the maintenance hatch and hunkered behind one of the surveillance desks, each one a wall of cream-coloured plasti-steel. If her previous kills were anything to go by, the shooters were dedicated amateurs, inexperienced but driven and unpredictable. At least she had the potential for surprise. She had made it out of that hatch so fast, the shooters may not have even known she was in the room with them.

The lights vanished and the holo-screens powered down, plunging the room into a darkness full of startled, cursing voices. Anderson's jumpsuit lit up like a bright green beacon, illuminating the ceiling. She swore, unzipping to the waist and pulling her sleeves inside out in an attempt to dampen the glow. The Department must have cut the power, which meant a tactical squad was on their way. They would secure the hostages shortly, but Anderson knew she couldn't wait around to introduce herself while Blake was on her way downstairs to blow them all up.

Rails of fluorescent emergency lighting appeared in the floor, leading the way to the exit. She slipped the detonator inside one of the sleeves, which she knotted at her waist. The glowing jumpsuit still covered her legs, but that would help light her way out of here. Besides, there was no way Cassandra Anderson was going to be known forevermore as the Psi-Judge who fought her way out of the Big Zero Six in just her vest and panties.

She snatched up her pistol. People were moving behind the consoles either side of her. They could still tell where she was, and now they were trying to outflank her. Slithering from cover, she held her breath and zeroed in on the man creeping around the console to her left, holding another pistol. She popped two into his face, then turned and waited for the guy the other side of her to come rushing into view. There you go. Double-tap to the centre mass. It was like running a training scenario back at the Academy.

She retrieved another clip from the dead man's pistol and manoeuvred from desk to desk towards the exit, head down, eyes front, searching the gaps in cover for signs of movement in the darkness. Whoever had that assault rifle wasn't letting up on the trigger any time soon, its muzzle flare lighting up the darkness, helping to distract from the glow of her jumpsuit. 'Comfort shooting,' her firearms tutor had called it. When perps get scared they lean on the trigger, shooting at nothing. Makes them feel safe. Anderson rose from cover and shut him up with a headshot, then wriggled another console closer to the exit.

She had to admit, she felt invigorated. It was the surety of a weapon in her hands, the air a delicious chill against her sweat-soaked skin. The reality of it all helped drive away the voices in her head. She felt a predator's sense of command over her surroundings, the protocols of combat distilled into instinct by years of Academy training. She sensed movement to her right, turned and fired into the darkness. A volley of assault-rifle fire answered her, shattering the wall of dead monitors behind her. Anderson calmly replaced the clip as she waited for the shooter to waste the rest of her ammunition, then rose and shot her in the cheek before sprinting out into the corridor, following the arrowed rails of light towards the exit.

She rounded a corner and a man rose out of the dark like an apparition. He swiped at her. Anderson saw the flash of a small blade as it slashed her forearm. She gasped in surprise and pain, dropping her pistol. The creep stared in amazement at the wound he had caused. It was the sleepwalker who had opened the door for her. She snatched his wrist with both hands while he was still gawping and wrenched his arm until he dropped the blade. Still holding his arm, she jerked him forward, driving her knee into his stomach and snapping her foot into his balls.

She let him drop to the floor, the fight knocked out of him, as someone else loomed out of the darkness behind her and grabbed her in a crushing bear-hug as she spun to face him. He lifted her off her feet and slammed her against a wall, driving the wind out of her.

She clawed at his face, unable to breath, his flesh slippery with sweat, his hands locked behind her back as he ran and slammed her against another wall with shocking force. Her fingers found the blond man's eyes and he screamed as she twisted his skull at the neck, peeling him away from her. He fell to his knees, clutching his ruined eyes.

The last one was a lanky woman who almost caught Anderson on the chin with a decent right hook. From the way she was hopping about, this one clearly thought of herself as a fighter. But Anderson was a Judge. The woman darted in for an uppercut as Anderson flinched aside, trapped the arm and broke the woman's jaw below the ear.

Anderson could hear more of Blake's followers tramping through the darkness towards her. She retrieved her pistol and kicked Heep onto his back.

"Where's Blake?" she said.

"Bedlam begins," Heep said.

Anderson broke his nose.

"In the elevator!" he screamed. "She was on her way to the basement when the power went out!"

Blake was stuck in the elevator? Anderson laughed at the absurdity. At least the laws of chaos that dominated the universe could be counted upon to swing both ways. She turned and fired twice, one-handed, down the corridor at more gunmen running towards her, before heaving open the nearby exit and fleeing the Control Hub in search of Aerial.

The hall outside looked unfamiliar, despite looking exactly like every other hall in this place, and Anderson was unsure which direction she should take back to the lobby. The glowing rails of emergency lighting made the high walls seem to disappear into a benighted sky. She ran to her right, clutching the pistol with dripping hands. That cut on her forearm looked pretty bad.

She reached the lobby with the wrecked MATRON droid, a tranquilised captive still fast asleep in each paw. But the reception desk had been abandoned. Aerial had vanished. Anderson felt her heart step up a gear. She heard men shouting behind her, directing others towards her. Steadying her breathing, she opened her mind. The voices rushed in, but she heard Aerial's among them.

Anderson...

Where are you...?

I need you!

The girl's thoughts shimmered with anguish, prompting Anderson to break into a sprint as she focused on the source of the cries, barging through the double doors of Joan Sims Ward, and aiming her pistol at the body sprawled on the floor. It was the wall-licker she had met earlier, two steel tranq-darts protruding from the chest of his glowing green jumpsuit. Aerial ran towards her from behind a vending machine.

"Anderson," she said, her voice trembling. "Is he dead? He came after me. I thought he was gonna kill me."

Anderson said nothing and threw her arms around the girl, clinging to her like she was the only thing Anderson had left in the world.

"I'm fine," Aerial said. "You're bleeding."

"We need to get to the basement," Anderson said, holstering the pistol in her waistband. "There's a squad of Tac-Judges on the way, so stick by me. You still got my badge? I don't want us getting shot."

Aerial retrieved it from inside her jumpsuit and Anderson looped the chain around the sleeves knotted at her waist, clipping the links together so the badge shone at her hip. On her other hip sat the detonator. If they could find an emergency stairwell, and if they were lucky, Anderson figured she might stand a chance of reaching the basement before Blake could make her way out of that stalled elevator.

Aerial had ripped out the lining from a discarded seat cushion, tearing it into shreds that she wound about Anderson's dripping arm. Urgent voices spilled into the corridor behind them and Anderson hauled the girl to her feet.

"Don't worry, kid," Anderson said as they broke into a run. "My head's straight, I've got a gun with lots of bullets, and the cavalry's on its way."

HEEP HURRIED AFTER the trail of blood spotting the dim fluorescent rails in the floor, pain spiking his ribs with every laboured breath. Two of Blake's bodyguards jogged behind him, cradling assault rifles. He had been awoken by the sound of gunfire to find himself in one of the empty surveillance rooms. Grud knows how he got there. His hard-won pistol appeared to be missing, so he had grabbed a knife from the kitchen before joining the fray. He must have slashed that Judge pretty good for her to be bleeding this much.

This is what he had signed up for: hunting down those who deserved hunting, doing what needed to be done. When the smoke cleared, whether or not he would be counted amid the honoured dead, his name would be included among the monuments raised and the stories told, lest future generations forget.

The spots of blood appeared to lead into either Bernie Bresslaw Ward or Kenny Connor, the doors to which stood either side of him. Here had dwelt the 'ab-human' population of the Big Zero Six: plenty of homeless aliens, along with things that had wandered in from the Cursed Earth and whose pathologies had apparently been too interesting to send back to the wastes. There had been a few cyborgs in there, too, their mechanical appendages either deactivated or confiscated. But the ab-humans were largely a menagerie of curiosities cooked up at random in the cauldron of Mega-City life. A dank smell of manure and straw hung in the air.

"What the drokk did that?" said one of the bodyguards, indicating the remains of a MATRON droid lying further down the hall. It appeared to have been torn to pieces. Heep shone his torch at its armour plating and could see it was scored with claw marks, as if it had been mauled by a bear.

The three men froze at a clacking sound, like rattling castanets, then something enormous exploded through the double-doors of Bernie Bresslaw. Heep was running back down the corridor before he realised what he was doing. He heard gunfire behind him, then screams, then a sound like someone tearing open a pumpkin. Fear and shame cascaded through him, his sacred duty abandoned.

He raced back to the Hub, telling himself that fear was too great an enemy to conquer with one blow. He needed a gun, reinforcements. He rounded a corner, arms cartwheeling, and felt the floor shake as something huge bounded down the corridor behind him. Heep knew something was hunting him, some horror that had once lurked sedated in a kook-cube under his supervision.

He glanced over his shoulder and tripped, skidding onto the floor. Rolling onto his back, he kicked away an unconscious inmate with two tranq-darts in his chest.

The thing scooped him up from behind as he tried to scramble to his feet, its long claws enclosing his face, its bristly paws muffling his ears to the sound of his own screams. He felt it sniffing at his hair, heard the clacking of its teeth, and willed himself to remain calm. After all the sacrifices he had made for the world, the cosmic laws of karma would ensure he meet a swift death.

A hot tongue smothered the back of his neck as sharp flat teeth chiselled his scalp from forehead to crown. He tried not to whimper as blood wept down his cheeks and the creature began gnawing at his skull.

LICK. LICK. BOWL all clean. Nothing left. Head still hurts. Still can't remember. Need more pink treats. Sniff. Sniff. Spots on the floor. Sniff. Sniff. Lick. Tastes like... Lick. Lick. Tastes like lady-girl. Lots of pink treat in her head-bowl. Nice and warm. Sniff. Sniff. This way.

Seventeen

ANDERSON FOUND HERSELF at yet another intersection of identical corridors, each one offering a trail of fluorescent light that disappeared into obscurity. It was like running through a hall of mirrors. She could have sworn she had seen this ruined MATRON droid at least twice already. The adrenalin comedown had left her drained and shaky; she had stopped a couple of times to prevent herself from passing out. She figured they must be at least a mile from the Hub by now.

"Please tell me you know where you're going," Aerial panted.

"According to that map on the wall back there," Anderson said, trying to sound calm, "the nearest emergency stairwell is on the other side of Babs Windsor Ward."

Most of the signs had been torn from the walls, replaced with a confusion of words and symbols smeared in a bewildering array of bodily secretions.

"Are the elevators still out?" Aerial said.

"We better hope so," Anderson said. "Or else Blake will get to the basement long before we do."

"How do you know she hasn't got there already?"

"Because the block's still standing," Anderson said, and immediately regretted speaking.

She pulled the girl down the corridor that appeared least familiar. The floor was littered with wrecked auto-chairs, discarded jumpsuits and slippers, some of them with feet still inside. Of the bodies strewn among the debris, Anderson noticed the skulls of several had been torn open like soda cans, their brainpans emptied. She steered Aerial around them, but could hear from the girl's thoughts that she had seen them.

"Keep moving," Anderson said.

Reassured by Aerial's presence, Anderson found she could extend her psi-powers at short range while keeping a lid on the blizzard of voices that had taken up residence in her head. Yet the only thoughts she could detect in these ruined corridors were her own and the girl's.

"What's that?" Aerial said, hurrying towards a doorway cloaked in sheets of black plastic. Behind it was an alcove cluttered with a ladder and sheets of plas-board, and behind that stood a pair of old swing doors criss-crossed with yellow hazard tape, a loop of chain threaded through the corroded handles. Anderson ripped away the tape to reveal a tarnished sign that read *Chuck Dexter Ward*. Aerial showed her the replacement nameplate she had retrieved from among the building materials: *Babs Windsor*. The ward for which they had been searching was apparently yet to be built.

Anderson booted the door, tearing a rusted handle from its moorings and revealing inky blackness beyond. Fluorescent emergency lighting had yet to be installed. Anderson aimed her pistol into the void as she ventured inside, realising the weapon's grip had grown slimy with sweat. Aerial bumped into her as she followed close behind, their fluorescent jumpsuits casting a drowned green glow over what looked like a forgotten reception area.

"What is it?" Aerial said.

Anderson could hear voices muttering in the darkness and knew those who spoke were no longer alive. Psychic residue, a more elaborate manifestation of the psi-prints she had lifted from the keypads during her initial flight from the roused inmates. What she could hear were the echoes of the men and women who had choked to death on a toxic cocktail of pharmaceuticals years ago when some staffer had gotten sloppy and flicked the wrong switches.

Unlike the thoughts of the living, these sounded dry and thin, mindlessly scraping the inside of their cells like a swirl of dead leaves. She would have to shut them out as best she could. Keep Aerial close by. If she moved fast enough, they wouldn't get their claws into her already addled mind. Unless, of course, they did.

"Nothing to worry about," Anderson said, her mouth dry. "Now, c'mon. We haven't got time to take in the atmosphere."

Dust stirred in the air like snow as Anderson and Aerial ran towards an open doorway and into the ward itself. Their jumpsuits cast their glow only a foot ahead of them as they ran, stumbling on debris. They passed filthy glass-fronted cells either side of them; an identical row was stacked above them, fading into the gloom. Anderson ignored the whispers coming from inside the empty cells.

"Eyes on me, Aerial," said Anderson as they turned down another corridor. "If there was anything in here we needed to worry about, I'd hear it thinking. There's nothing between us and those stairs but a bunch of empty hallways."

Then why don't you put the gun away? Aerial thought.

The glow of their jumpsuits revealed a T-junction. They followed a discoloured sign directing them towards a flight of stairs that Anderson hoped were actually there. Voices filled her head like smoke.

It burns...

I can see the bones...

I'm sorry, daddy! I'm sorry...

The place was a library of broken records, phrases repeated over and over. The effect was almost hypnotic. Anderson felt her concentration falter and heard livelier, more imaginative voices join the clamour in her head.

She stumbled drunkenly to one side, crashing into one of the cubes. The plasti-glass window had bubbled like old paint, as if boiled from the other side by whatever corrosive concoction had seeped into that tiny room long ago. Anderson saw something that wasn't there shift behind the frosted glass.

"Keep it together," Aerial cried, tugging her away from the cube. "We're almost out."

Anderson rose to her feet, fighting the racket in her head. A clang echoed through the corridor behind them, driving the voices away.

Anderson aimed her pistol into the darkness.

Aerial went to speak, but Anderson hissed at her to be quiet.

"Did you hear that?" Anderson said, her heart pounding.

A tapping sound came from somewhere nearby. Something had followed them into the abandoned ward.

"I heard that," Aerial said, pulling at Anderson's jumpsuit.

Anderson shoved her in the direction of the stairs, aiming her pistol for a moment longer before hurrying after the girl.

They finally emerged through a broken door into a wider corridor with walkways barely visible above them. Anderson could hear a chorus of whispers, hundreds more than she had heard in the previous hallway, and guessed there must be at least another two storeys of cells up there. She touched her temple, trying to focus amid the rain of whispers and voices. She detected living thoughts, growling hungrily.

Sniff. Sniff...

Lady-girl near...

Lick her clean...

Anderson fought to locate their source, but every time she

reached out the voices reached back. She shut herself off and grabbed Aerial.

Something moved above her. There it was again. The sound of metal creaking beneath a ponderous weight. Something was moving stealthily along the upper walkway. Anderson backed away, pulling Aerial with her, her pistol pointed in the direction of the sound, the weapon now shaking in her hands. Aerial yelped at the sound of clacking teeth.

Juicy pink treats...

Wobbly and sweet...

Anderson fired twice, muzzle-flare flashing in the darkness. Something white darted away to her left as her shots pinged sparks from a metal grille. Darkness swallowed them once again.

Aerial was whimpering now, hugging her chest, curling up like a dead bug as her body succumbed to terror.

We're gonna die in here...

Anderson tried to focus on the world of black that surrounded them as they backed away. Behind her, revealed in the glow of their jumpsuits, a set of doors formed out of the ether. A nearby sign read like an answered prayer: *Emergency Exit.* Aerial had already flung herself at the doors, but they were fastened from the other side by a rattling length of chain.

"Open it!" she screamed at Anderson.

Anderson threw her shoulder into it, but the doors held fast.

"Open it!" Aerial screamed again.

Anderson reached through the gap between the doors and tugged at the padlock and chains.

Aerial sobbed as Anderson returned her attention to the surrounding blackness.

"Quiet!" Anderson said, pulling her back from the wall of darkness before them.

We're gonna die! We're gonna die!

"No, we're not," Anderson said, wondering how much nearer the predatory thing had crept towards them while they attacked the doors. She wiped her streaming nose on the back of her hand and shut out the whispers, silenced the voices.

It's nothing but protocol, she told herself. *It saved you in the Hub and it's gonna save you now. Breathe, aim, fire. Simple.*

There was nothing out there but another crazy inmate. That was the reality. And few living things in reality could stand up to nine-mil rounds at close-range.

Yeah, drokk you. Come get me and see what you get back.

Anderson steadied her pistol against the darkness as she felt for the golden shield at her hip, needing to remind herself that she was part of a world that existed outside this madness. But her badge wasn't there. It must have fallen off. She recalled the sight of it sinking from view in that cauldron of oatmeal.

She placed both hands on the pistol, focusing her attention on her surroundings, waiting for the thing that stalked them to betray its position. She heard a steady tapping sound and realised blood was dripping from the exposed slash in her forearm. She could have sworn she had bandaged that at some point. In fact, hadn't there been someone with her? Someone scared. Someone in need of Anderson's protection, a reason to keep fighting when all was lost.

Anderson almost laughed. Zeinner probably would have described that kind of thinking as a coping mechanism. With that thought, Anderson sensed the darkness suddenly deepen in pitch, as though a meagre light had been snuffed out.

Anderson spoke, her voice breaking.

"Aerial?"

She held her breath and reached out to one side.

There was no one there.

She heard nothing but the sound of teeth tapping in the darkness.

Eighteen

"I DIDN'T IMAGINE you," Anderson panted.

Aerial assured her that she had.

Anderson turned and fought the doors once again, but the chains refused to release them. She flung her arm through the narrow gap and tried to squeeze herself through. Talons rattled upon metal somewhere overhead. Teeth clacked in the darkness and Anderson raised her pistol once more at whatever horror was about to descend upon her. She tried to focus, on the floor beneath her, the darkness around her, anything, her senses battling to distinguish reality.

"You're not real," said Anderson.

Aerial told her she was as real as Anderson wanted her to be.

"I wasn't talking to you," Anderson hissed.

Kill lady-girl quick...

Sniff. Sniff...

Before she can bite you with her stinger...

"None of this is real."

Anderson thumbed the safety on her pistol and tucked the weapon into the waistband of her jumpsuit.

Aerial asked Anderson what the drokk she thought she was doing.

"Proving a point," Anderson said. "I'm not crazy."

This whole thing was a fantasy. She was being stalked through the dark by an imaginary monster, just as she had imagined those horrors inside the walls of the Control Hub. Nothing but her mind playing tricks, cobbling together childhood fears, maybe stalk scenes from an old horror vid. Perhaps her subconscious was subjecting her to some kind of moral punishment, the entire scenario fuelled by guilt and shame.

Aerial screamed at her that although she had not been real, whatever was out there most certainly was, and that Anderson was about to die unless she did something to protect herself.

Anderson's frail logic succumbed to instinct as she heard something launch itself from a walkway above. She dived to one side, narrowly avoiding the boulder of muscle and white fur that thudded into the floor beside her. Instinct still carried her as she rolled onto her knees, her pistol appearing like magic in her hands, safety off. She fired twice, muzzle-flashes exposing the huge bubble-eyed thing about to take a bite out of her. She kept firing, driving the monster back into the shadows, illuminating its retreat one flash at a time until the pistol clicked empty.

She dropped the clip, hearing it clatter on the floor as she fumbled at the strap of her vest where she had stashed the refills. They too had vanished. Anderson wondered whether they had been there at all.

Aerial pleaded with Anderson to listen to her, to accept what she was going through and stop acting like she was sane.

Galloping animal feet thundered towards her from the darkness. Hurling aside the empty gun, Anderson positioned herself before the doors, screaming defiance into the shadows as she goaded the devil to come and take her. Something like a speeding truck composed of bulbous eyes and long teeth erupted out of the shadows. Anderson dived to one side as 800 lbs of reality smashed through the doors, snapping the padlock.

The creature's claws raked the tiled floor, dragging it to a halt as it turned to charge back at its tormentor. Anderson had already caught both ends of the sundered chain, still hanging from one handle. She threaded one end through the opposite handle on her side, wound both ends around her hands, then pulled the doors closed, their edges biting down on the chain between them. The thing rammed the doors from the other side, pulling the chains apart and snatching Anderson forward, the force threatening to break her arms.

She threw herself back, tugging at the chains. Long claws probed the gap between the doors. Anderson wrenched the chain tighter, driving her heels into the floor as she closed the gap, trying to shut out the madness.

Aerial reminded Anderson that it didn't matter how long she worked her shoulders in the gym, or how hard she trained her will to become indomitable, both these strengths would quickly fail.

Several links of chain slid through Anderson's grip, greased with sweat, her arms and shoulders spasming as the creature pounded the doors, its barrage unrelenting.

Aerial told her she needed to let the madness in.

"I need to keep it out," Anderson screamed, heaving back the chains.

Aerial told Anderson that she needed to stop thinking like a machine.

"I'm a Judge," Anderson said.

Aerial told her she was human.

Why do you think you went crazy in the first place?

The chains finally leaped from Anderson's hands. She fell backwards as the doors flew open and madness incarnate entered the hall.

Whether it had been a white rabbit or a human being first, Anderson could not tell. Its huge weeping eyes were lidless bubbles, devoid of mercy. A rusty metal collar around its neck clanged against the lintel of the doorframe as it loped towards her, pausing to shake out a pair of long ragged ears. It clacked its bile-coloured incisors as if tasting the air, then hissed at her. Its breath stank of putrid meat.

Anderson lay prone on the floor, transfixed by the monster's thoughts. The tortured musings of the inmates were nothing compared to this gibbering stew of a mind. It was fired by something deeper than madness, so lacking in human rationality that it felt practically alien. She could do nothing to prevent it from closing its filth-encrusted paws around her throat and lifting her off the floor.

Sticky pink treats...

It's hidden inside...

Bunny can't remember...

The creature eclipsed Anderson's world, the bloodshot globes of its eyes staring blindly into her own. Anderson felt as if everything she had ever known, every certainty to which she had clung, was merely another expression of her psychosis. The notion infected her, consumed her. Order and happiness were an empty promise; horror and misery were the only truth. Who could look upon such an ugly world every day and not be driven insane by it, knowing that one was part of the system that created it? What then was madness, if not an expression of her courage to confront reality?

You're only human.

Anderson clung to the creature's paws as it sniffed her hair.

Why do you think you went crazy in the first place?

She let the monster's thoughts consume her, feeling her consciousness fly helter-skelter through the nexus of its mind. She cast aside all control, any attempt to impose her own definition of reality upon the creature's psychosis. Instead, she let its madness speak for itself.

A kaleidoscope of images flashed through her mind. A laboratory. Syringe after dripping syringe. Looming faces.

Squirting liquid that burned its eyes until the world became a quivering yellow blur. The clarity was heartbreaking, the countless tortures that had moulded it into a monster. Then Anderson found it, a fragment of humanity, gleaming like half-buried treasure.

"Manny Fezbach," Anderson said.

The creature's ruined ears twitched at their roots as it paused open-mouthed, stifling her with its acrid breath.

"Manny Fezbach," she said again, still caught in the creature's strangling grip, her feet still dangling. "That's your name, right? What you've been trying to remember?"

The creature looked away as though it had caught a familiar scent. It made a gulping sound, and Anderson could hear its thoughts.

Manny Fezbach...

Manny Fezbach...

Manny Fezbach...

Anderson felt him grasping for something more, for memories of a life forgotten, of a humanity stolen. His paws gradually loosened around her throat, dropping her to the floor. She scrambled out of the way as the enormous body loped past her. Rising to her feet, she watched Manny Fezbach trudge back into the dark, growling the syllables of his long-lost name, clutching his newfound humanity like a treasured gift.

As the ruins of Chuck Dexter Ward fell silent, Anderson realised the only voice she could hear in her head was her own.

She ran through the shattered doorway and through another reception area, at the end of which stood another set of double-doors. She threw herself at them, praying they had not been chained shut like the others. The doors flew aside like a bullfighter's cape and she toppled in a skidding heap on the floor of a passage that opened onto the landing of a stairwell.

A single desperate laugh escaped her as she yielded to great gulping sobs, pawing at the floor like a wounded animal. She savoured the moment of submission, fleeting and unfamiliar, feeling somehow refreshed by her own vulnerability, by the sense that some mysterious peninsula of her psyche had finally been charted. The anxieties that had plagued her, the crushing heaviness in her soul, all had been caused by her insistence that the world conform to her heroic ideal. How futile. What a childish hope. The world was chaos and she could accept that, finally.

Feeling restored, reinvigorated, she grabbed a handrail, rushing to her feet and out onto the landing of the stairwell. She glimpsed the armoured figures seconds before they shot her.

Nineteen

ANDERSON DETECTED THEM seconds before she appeared on the landing, their minds twanging like tripwires. They fired as she went to pull herself back behind the wall of the corridor, but not before her shoulder exploded and she slid down the wall to the floor.

She snarled with pain and fury as the two figures manoeuvred into view, rifles raised. Before they could finish the job, she projected a beam of psi-energy straight into their minds and held it there. Their rifles clattered aside as they dropped to their knees, clutching their heads as if trying to prevent them from exploding. She maintained the psi-beam as she got to her feet, her mind singing. There were no voices now, no holding back. Barely registering the pain in her shoulder, she touched her temple, broadcasting her voice into the minds of the men quailing before her, her every word ringing through their brains like the voice of an angered goddess.

"Anderson, Psi-Division," she said. "Tonight I've lost a partner, seen three other Judges killed and narrowly escaped being killed myself—by terrorists, a horde of psychopaths, robot nannies, and, just now, a giant brain-eating bunny rabbit. Then I went and lost my mind. All that and I'm two days into my period. So let me assure you, gentlemen, I am not in the mood to be shot at by guys on my team!"

She released them and slumped against the wall, clutching her bleeding shoulder as the men recovered.

"Sorry, Anderson," said one; *Reed*, according to the badge embedded in his tac-armour. "We thought you were a hostile."

"Well I'm feeling pretty hostile right now," Anderson said. "Now can one of you nitwits put me through to your CO? We're on the clock here."

"We've found Anderson," the other Judge—Hamlyn—spoke into his helmet comm. "We're in the stairwell behind the old Chuck Dexter Ward, level one-fifty... Well, she seems pretty sane to me, sir..."

Anderson snatched Hamlyn's helmet off his head, ignoring his protestations as she placed it on her own.

"Chief?" Anderson said.

"*Greaves, here,*" said a gruff voice at the other end of Hamlyn's comm. "*Is that Anderson?*"

"Psi-Division's finest and a model of sanity, I might add," she said. "Now listen up..."

Greaves cut her off.

"*Team Six, escort Judge Anderson to the ground level. We'll have a Manta pick you up there.*"

"The bomb, you idiot!" she yelled into the comm. "It's not in the city. It's in the pharma-station on sub-level one."

Reed and Hamlyn looked at each other.

"Blake is on her way to activate it right now."

"*I'm not interested, Anderson,*" Greaves said.

Anderson swore and retrieved something from inside the knotted sleeve of her jumpsuit, handing it to Reed.

"Sir, I think she's just handed me a detonator," he said, examining the device.

There was an agonising pause.

"*Team Six, escort Psi-Judge Anderson to the pharma-station immediately,*" Greaves said. "*We'll get reinforcements to you as soon as we can. All prior objectives stand. If you find Blake, execute her on sight.*"

"Negative," Anderson said. "You're gonna need to exercise caution on that one. She actually wants to die."

"*Then we're happy to oblige her,*" Greaves said.

"You don't understand," Anderson said. "If the cits see her killed by the Department it'll only encourage them. I don't think you realise just how much she means to them, what they're capable of."

"*We can handle a bunch of rowdy kids, Anderson,*" Greaves said. "*Reed, tell her what she needs to know. Greaves, out.*"

Anderson rolled her eyes and handed the helmet back to Hamlyn as the three of them hurried down the stairs.

"We've secured the Control Hub and the hostages," Reed said. "And we found Blake's elevator stuck between levels."

Reed removed a portable charger from his belt as they reached the landing below, punching the device into a socket beside a locked grav-chute. The capsule's interior lit up and the hatch hissed open.

"We're searching the lower levels for her right now," he said as the three Judges strapped themselves inside. "But there's still a lot of crazies running around down there."

Hamlyn peered inside his helmet and made a face.

"What's with your hair?" he asked Anderson.

"I soaked it in synthetti sauce," she said. "Believe me, it's the *least* crazy thing I've done all night."

She hammered the release button and hollered like a kid at a fairground ride as the capsule plummeted towards the ground floor.

* * *

A ROW OF bullets sparked along the asphalt, chasing Anderson into one of the huge maintenance troughs that ran the length of each parking bay in the basement pharma-station. She dived inside, her wounded shoulder striking a metal strut. The pain bit through the anaesthetic of the speed-heal paste Reed had squirted inside her bullet-wound. She hunkered down as best she could, as sparks and shrapnel danced overhead for a few seconds more, then abated.

Anderson, you okay? Reed thought. He was getting the hang of a psi-link pretty quick for a Street-Judge.

Fine, Anderson thought back.

This mind-link thing is too creepy, Hamlyn thought, his mind wandering. *I hope she didn't see me staring at her—*

Focus on the gruddamn shooters, Hamlyn, Anderson thought, crawling through a mire of oil and filth towards the far end of the trench. *Blake and her buddies could get here any second, and then you'll have even more to worry about.*

The two shooters occupying the elevated control cabin had been too far away from the pharma-station's entry ramp for Anderson to sense their presence immediately. By the time she had extended her powers far enough to detect them, it was too late. The lights were out down here too, the main reason she and her glow-in-the-dark jumpsuit had agreed to hold back and scan for hostiles. One of the gunmen had glimpsed an armed figure advancing over a rail of emergency lighting, and suddenly the air between the Judges and the cabin filled with a storm of tracer fire. And here Anderson was: running to assist Reed and Hamlyn without a gun in her hands, and too far away from the shooters to fire a solid psi-blast.

Her arms and vest were smothered in black muck by the time she reached the far end of the maintenance trough. Peering over the lip of the trench, she could make out the figures of Reed and Hamlyn. They were crouching behind separate rockcrete columns, the pillars battered by automatic fire from the two shooters in the cabin, which overlooked the vast subterranean forecourt.

The immense parking bays were empty except for a single tanker-truck, its sleek domed cab resembling the head of a giant beetle. It carried four enormous cylinders, each bearing a cheerful Pharmville logo. Hoses connected the cylinders to a docking unit through which the visiting tankers pumped gallons of pharmaceutical ingredients into the reservoirs beneath the Big Zero Six.

This is taking too long, Reed thought. *They've got too much cover.*

Switching to Hi-Ex, thought Hamlyn, thumbing the ammo-switch on his Lawrod. *The cabin's far enough away from the truck to make a safe shot.*

No! Anderson thought back. *We're gonna need that control cabin to isolate the explosives, remember?*

According to the intel she had retrieved from Blake's head, the tanker had already delivered its payload of volatile chems into the block's reservoirs. The explosive charges were rigged inside the tanker's now-empty cylinders. The blast would ignite the vapour inside the containers, feeding fire through the hoses and into the reservoirs, and the legend of the Big Zero Six would reach a fittingly devastating conclusion.

Reed was consulting his comm, bullets dotting the ground around him.

Greaves still hasn't cleared the hostages, he thought.

And we still need to disconnect those hoses and at least localise the blast, Anderson thought back.

We're open to suggestions, Hamlyn thought.

Okay, she thought. *Cover me.*

Before he could reply, Anderson vaulted from the trench, the legs of her jumpsuit still casting their radioactive glow as she sprinted through the darkness towards Hamlyn. An armed figure appeared at the window of the control cabin.

"Hamlyn," she yelled. "I need your charger."

The Tac-Judge fumbled at his belt and tossed her the charger as she ran past. She hugged the device like an aeroball as she continued her sprint across the pharma-station towards the end-zone of the cabin. Opening her mind, she instantly visualised one of the shooters struggling to level his crosshairs at the glowing green legs racing towards him on the ground below.

Now would be good, she thought desperately.

A shot rang out, the *crack* of a large-bore execution round, and the mental image of gunsights and glowing legs vanished from her mind. As she reached the stairs leading up to the cabin, a door flew open at the top and a young man in a check shirt pointed an assault rifle at her. Anderson had already flung out her hand to greet him.

He stiffened as she reached into his mind.

Monsters not people...

Kill her... Do it...

Why can't you just be a man, son...?

She went deep, dispelling every notion of the courageous freedom fighter he had convinced himself to be. In truth, he was Derry Garrett, a media studies student who just wanted to belong.

He dropped the assault rifle as though it had just appeared in his hands. Anderson caught it as she rushed up the stairs, grabbing him by the collar as she pushed him inside the darkened control cabin.

"Am I going to the cubes?" he said.

"Not if you help me unhook that tanker right now. Unhook it, then lock it."

"I can't," he stammered. "The power's out."

Anderson slotted the handheld charger into a power port and activated it. The console lit up and walls of holo-screens sprang to life, revealing monochrome views of the pharma-station and the nearby vehicle bay used by the block's employees.

"While we're young, please, Mr Garrett," Anderson said, checking the mag in the gun, another crappy Zee-27.

Derry obediently tapped and dialled at the holo-screens.

Anderson, Reed thought. *The light on the docking station's gone green. The hoses have fallen away. I think we're good.*

An explosion shook the walls of the control cabin.

Cold fear drenched Anderson as she ran to a window. Smoke billowed around the column behind which Reed had been hiding, as armed men and women poured through a hatch on a walkway above. One of them stood peering into the smoke, assessing the damage as she pumped the grenade launcher attached to her rifle.

Anderson raised her own weapon and fired through the broken glass, but yelped as the rifle punched her wounded shoulder, sending her only shot wide of the target. The woman fired back at her. Anderson grabbed Derry and dived behind cover, the stairs behind them erupting. Anderson recovered, her ears singing, as bullets began zipping through the smoke and dust.

Reed? Hamlyn?

At least she'd managed to isolate the tanker from the rest of the block, although those cylinders were still rigged with enough vapour and explosives to take out the pharma-station and everyone in it.

Reed's been KO'd, Hamlyn thought. *Can't see the shooter through the smoke.*

Anderson peered through the door onto the walkway, along which Blake's followers were already creeping towards her. The lady with the grenade launcher had left her pals to deal with Anderson while she resumed her search through the smoke for the two Judges on the ground.

Can you see the walkway? Anderson thought.

I can see where it ends, Hamlyn thought back.

She's standing around fifteen feet to the left. How good a shot are you, Hamlyn?

The woman with the grenade launcher seemed almost to hiccup as an execution round pierced her chest and she fell head-first over the railing, still clutching her weapon.

Now get out of here, Anderson thought. *I've got this.*

Copy that, Anderson, Hamlyn thought.

Gunfire shredded the door beside her, spraying her with shrapnel. Derry shrieked and cowered in a corner. Anderson had given the Bedlamites enough time to flank her, manoeuvring into position behind the pillars that intersected the walkway. The door destroyed, a renewed flurry of bullets tore into the room.

Anderson pulled back and braced her rifle against a control desk, levelling the sights at a dark-haired man moving out from behind a pillar. The stock tight against her bleeding shoulder, she braced herself for agony as she pulled the trigger.

Click.

The trigger was stuck. The gruddamn piece of crap had jammed. She scrambled behind the console, spitting every curse in the book as bullets picked at the walls. One of the holo-screens disappeared, its projector shattered. The screen beside it offered a serene view of the employee parking lot. Anderson looked over at the portable charger in the main console. The counter read 17 percent.

Bullets spat past her as she dived across the room and snatched the comm-handset from its cradle on the console. She skimmed the device across the floor to Derry, who had now curled into a whimpering knot beneath another console on the far side of the room.

"Get me a public address line into parking bay thirty-seven," she yelled.

Derry stared at the handset as if it were about to explode.

"Now!"

He grabbed it as Anderson ducked beneath the main console and touched her temple, deep-frying the mind of the dark-haired man taking aim at her from behind a pillar. His mouth gaped stupidly and he fainted onto the walkway as Anderson fired another psi-blast at the woman behind him. Her eyes rolled back and she keeled over. Anderson tried to gather herself for a third blast, but she was already dizzy with exertion.

The holo-screens were dimming. The charger's energy counter blinked from four to three percent.

Derry threw the comm-handset back across the floor as if releasing some repulsive creature into the wild. Anderson retrieved it, praying the boy had dialled the correct number.

"Lawmaster registration eight-two-three-zero-seven, Anderson," she said, wincing as a section of the console above her exploded. "Activation protocol alpha-nine-four. Proceed to pharma-station one, sub-level one of Psych-Block Zero-Six. Neutralise all—"

The holo-screens vanished and darkness descended. The charger had died before she could finish her call, and the batteries feeding the emergency lights had been shot in the barrage. Anderson reached for the minds lurking perilously close by, wondering if she could get near enough to grab another gun before getting Swiss-cheesed.

Light flooded the forecourt and Anderson heard the roar of a monstrous engine. Ordering Derry to stay back, she crawled over to the doorway where the stairs had once stood, and looked outside.

The tanker-truck was rumbling away from the parking bay. She glimpsed a thin white face behind the wheel as the cab swung around, crushing a deactivated maintenance droid beneath the wheels of its trailer as it accelerated out of the station.

While the Bedlamites cheered its departure, Anderson braced herself for a leap to the ground. Maybe she could reach cover before they spotted her.

She pulled back as light re-entered the forecourt accompanied by a familiar roar. Crouching beneath the ruined console, she heard the crackle of assault rifle fire answered by a relentless bellow of heavy-bore guns, the sound drowning every scream that followed. She managed to land on the ground without breaking an ankle, and found her Lawmaster parked miraculously before her. It was surrounded by a litter of corpses and spent cartridge cases, smoke still oozing from its twin Lawgiver cannons. The empty saddle beckoned.

Twenty

ANDERSON REVELLED IN the feel of the cold night wind washing down her bare arms and neck, whipping her matted hair, chilling the wound in her shoulder. She leaned her Lawmaster through a bend, headlamps flashing past artificial trees as she traced the road through the perma-gardens outside the Big Zero Six. The block itself outshone the moon, a sheer white wall looming beside her. She saw the tanker's tail-lights glaring back at her through the darkness some distance ahead, swinging left and right as the driver wrestled the wheel. Anderson twisted the throttle, summoning ever greater speed as she chased the runaway vehicle into the shadows.

The city rose into view on Anderson's left, glittering in the distance as she neared the tanker's rear. The immense vehicle was rumbling alongside the high chain-link fence that skirted the shore of the island. The road would eventually feed onto the bridge. The Department would have erected a barricade at the far end, a plug of rockcrete barriers and heavy Lawgiver emplacements awaiting any escapee. Blake still craved public martyrdom, a death at the hands of the Justice Department to galvanise her troops on the distant shore and throughout the city.

The vid-screen on Anderson's Lawmaster was alive with targeting data as the Lawgiver cannons whirred either side of her, trying to draw a bead on the trailer's rear wheels. She thumbed a switch on the handlebars, disarming the auto-targeting. She couldn't risk a stray round finding its way into one of those explosive cylinders. Casting her psi-senses towards the front of the tanker, she caught Blake's mind. The woman's thoughts were tight and intense, focused upon nothing but the headlamps shining on the road before her and the glory that awaited her at the other end of the bridge.

Anderson saw the cab turn into view as the tanker followed another bend, its lights revealing the gateway onto the bridge a short distance away. Anderson immediately steered off the road, the Lawmaster now soaring across a meadow of plastic grass as she accelerated towards the head of the tanker. She felt a surge of purpose beyond mere duty. No monster was beyond saving, and here was her chance to prove it, to herself, to the Department, to the entire city.

She set the Lawmaster to auto-pilot, commanding it to maintain speed as it pulled alongside the tanker's cab. If she could hop onto that little platform between the cab and the trailer, she figured she could sit there unmolested and work her psi-magic on Blake, providing she could concentrate with that great big explosion waiting to go off inside those cylinders.

As the Lawmaster carried her within range of the tanker, a spectral face appeared above the door of the cab. It vanished as the vehicle swerved towards her, heedless of the archway towards which it was heading. Anderson's heart leaped as the bike braked of its own accord, a network of computerised sensors reining the Lawmaster back to avoid a collision.

The wall of the archway appeared. The cab had swerved back, straining to realign with the exit. The trailer swung in its wake, a wall of gleaming cylinders bearing down on Anderson from behind.

Swiping off the auto-pilot, she wrenched the throttle, steering the bike alongside the groaning mass of cylinders as they grazed the flanks of her Lawmaster. The wall rushed towards her, shearing off a wing-mirror as the cab vanished through the archway. Anderson accelerated defiantly and leaned hard, the bike threatening to topple onto its side as she ducked and the trailer's immense underbelly swooped overhead.

She goosed the brakes just enough and grabbed the first thing she saw, letting the Lawmaster disappear from beneath her as she flung her arms and legs around whatever she had found. Debris somersaulted about her, as the tanker bulldozed the checkpoint hut along with the deactivated security droids standing around inside.

Anderson waited a moment for the air to clear before opening her eyes, not quite believing she was still alive. She was clinging to the underside of what appeared to be a maintenance walkway between the trailer's four cylinders. A freezing wind rippled the legs of her jumpsuit, as she groped and heaved herself on top of the metal platform, asphalt hurtling past beneath her.

As she crawled along the walkway towards the rear of the cab, a harsh light flooded her surroundings.

"*Stop your vehicle immediately,*" barked a loudspeaker.

Anderson looked up and could make out the familiar outline of a Department Manta, its searchlight gleaming through the tunnel of mesh that caged the bridge. It appeared Blake's welcome party had arrived early.

"*This is your one and only warning.*"

Anderson scrambled along the walkway on all fours, her greasy hands slipping, threatening to drop her into the road, which coursed like a lethal river beneath her. She reached the huge metal collar that holstered the cylinders and felt the wound in her shoulder tear as she pulled herself through, before landing on the coupling platform securing the trailer to the back of the cab.

"*I am now authorised to use lethal force,*" announced the Manta.

"Gruddamit," Anderson said, surveying the confusion of pipes around her. "Gimme a minute here!"

The only apparatus that seemed to present itself was a long lever encased in red rubber, but it refused to budge. The Manta climbed into firing position.

Half-blinded by sweat and grit, Anderson fumbled along the lever for an obstruction, her fingers discovering a stiff length of looped cord. She tugged it and something clicked. She swung her weight behind the lever and watched as the trailer and its four enormous cylinders departed like a ship being launched into the sea.

Anderson threw herself onto the deck behind the red lever as a cluster of connective pipes snapped above her, becoming a nest of crazed, hissing snakes. Hands clamped over her ears, she glimpsed the trailer skidding upon the road for an instant. She looked away before it struck the wall of the tunnel, squeezing her eyes shut.

The inside of her eyelids flared glorious orange and her bones shuddered, the blast stabbing her ears as the cab swerved from side to side. She grabbed the red lever before she could slide overboard and saw the Manta pulling away to avoid the rising cloud of fire. The explosion had ignited a blazing sheet that rippled across the surface of the chem-lake, spreading until the Big Zero Six stood amid a sea of flames like a hellish monument.

Anderson got to her feet, gripping an air vent in the back of the cab as she peered around the corner, squinting into the wind. The end of the bridge was still some distance away, but the roar of the cab's engine intensified as Blake accelerated. Anderson opened the hatch in the side of the cab and swung herself inside, landing on the carpeted floor of the driver's sleeping quarters.

A pistol-shot rang out, popping a hole in the wall beside her. She dived beneath a small metal table as Blake fired again. She was steering the cab from inside an elevated compartment atop a small flight of steps: too far to dash without getting shot in the face.

Blake fired again, punching a hole in the tabletop as Anderson reached into the woman's mind. Who was she? What had caused this woman to pursue such a single-minded quest for martyrdom? She dived into her psyche, intent on finding answers.

Anderson broke into the mind of Moriah Blake, and found... nothing.

She felt herself freefall into darkness, into a mind of endless black, as airless as space, stirred not by the winds of sensation, emotion or experience. It was as though Moriah Blake were a computer from which everything had been deleted. Her baseline thoughts were numb, brutish things that throbbed with certainty, empty of doubt or enquiry.

Dead inside...

The Judges...

Together we can break them...

Together...

That last thought seemed to twitch in Blake's mind like an exposed nerve, like an antenna seeking another living presence.

I know, Moriah, Anderson thought. *I've felt it too.*

The black world recoiled as if in pain, spitting Anderson back into herself.

She opened her eyes to hear a distant loudhailer screeching something about a final warning. Blake stood before the cab window, arms raised in welcome, braced for the rapture.

Anderson flew up the steps of the cab and flung Blake down into the living quarters as sniper fire cracked the windshield. She ducked and pulled the emergency brake, the wheels squealing in protest. Struggling to keep her balance as the cab swung to the side, she caught Blake, as limp as a doll, and braced herself before the side hatch. She saw the road still speeding beneath them, then jumped into space.

THE FIRST THING Anderson saw was the broken leg. It was bent at the knee in a sickening zig-zag. Next, she saw the insects glittering and darting about her, addressing her with tinny, urgent voices.

"*Judge Anderson,*" said one. "*You're being held hostage by terrorist mastermind Moriah Blake. What can you tell our viewers about how you're feeling right now?*"

Anderson blinked, pain bursting behind her eyes, and the insects turned into a cluster of hovering cameras. News-drones, each offering the stalk of a microphone.

"*Our viewers are loving your hair,*" said another. "*What is that? Auburn Sunburst? Power-Tower Eruption?*"

Anderson went to swat the drone away, but screamed instead. Agony seized her shoulder, her right arm apparently refusing to move. Something tightened around her neck, an arm, its elbow raising her chin. It took a moment for Anderson to realise the broken leg was not her own. It belonged to the woman in whose arms she laid, propped up against the wall of the bridge. The cab lay on its side some distance away further down the bridge, the night sky glowing orange above the blazing chem-lake. Anderson felt a pistol digging into her temple.

The Judges would come running any minute, on their way to fulfil Blake's objective, to murder her and inspire a war that would endure for generations. Anderson was familiar with the thoughts of those about to die; it was weird how many of them remembered their moms at the last second. Blake's thoughts were more sanguine, although Anderson thought she could detect a tremor of uncertainty.

"Tonight," Blake croaked.

The news-drones stopped circling and focused on her.

"Tonight, the city will win back its sanity."

"There's no sanity here to be won, Blake," Anderson said, wincing as a broken rib announced itself in the roll-call of pain. "All you're doing is turning madness into something even worse."

Blake didn't answer and Anderson clutched at her arm with her good hand, moving it closer to the pistol jammed at her head.

"Murder won't get you what you want," Anderson said.

"It's not murder if what you kill isn't human," Blake said.

Kill her...

Blake's thought appeared out of nowhere, catching Anderson by surprise.

Kill her...

Anderson's left hand shot up and caught Blake's wrist, holding it firm though her strength was evaporating.

"I could have killed you before your tanker left the island," she said. "And I just saved you from getting shot, twice. What kind of a monster does that make me?"

The news-drones above them jostled and whirred as Blake struck Anderson across the cheek with her pistol, knocking her back. The woman slithered on top of her, the bones in her broken leg grinding beneath her meagre weight. She gripped Anderson by the strap of her vest and probed her face with the gun, her features becoming molten with fury.

"Monsters!" she shrieked. "You are soulless machines. You have no feeling, no mercy, no empathy. You know nothing."

"I'm a telepath. I know everything," Anderson said, feeling somehow glad to see that dead face finally animated. "You're the voice of the city? You should try being the ears, sister, because I hear everything. Every fear, every fantasy, every memory, every secret. I hear everything and I can't stand it."

Blake looked defiant.

"And guess what I hear more than anything?" Anderson said. "The same thing I hear in you."

Kill her...

"I hear it in everyone, doesn't matter whether they're a Judge or a cit. They're all people. And you don't kill people, right? Only monsters. So shoot me. The news-feeds are watching. Go ahead..."

"The Judges," Blake said, placing her gun against Anderson's head. "They'll be here any second."

"And when they do I won't let them kill you," Anderson said. "You'll have to kill me to change that, which means you can't. I can hear what's inside your head, Moriah. I can hear the name of the woman you used to be, before you became who you are now. I can hear everything you went through that brought you here."

Blake swallowed.

"And you don't have to inflict that on the rest of the city," Anderson said. "You don't have to go on being a monster. You can give the city all the sanity it's ever going to get by ending this madness right now."

The young woman known as Moriah Blake lowered her head and stared at the gun in her hands, her eyes pits of shadow. She eventually tossed the pistol aside and looked up at Anderson, then two shots caught her in the back and she dropped to the ground.

Anderson caught her, staring in disbelief at the exit wounds in the woman's chest. The young woman stared back at nothing in particular.

Rising to her feet, Anderson punched the first Judge to emerge from the smoke. The huge red-bearded man staggered back: Greaves, the Tac-Commander, accompanied by several more of his team. They hurried to secure the body and wave away the lingering news-drones.

"Do you have any idea what you've done?" she screamed at

Greaves as he rubbed his jaw. "How many lives will be lost? Do you realise you've just started a war?"

"Really," he said with a grin. "I thought we just ended one."

He motioned towards the shore.

"Go take a look."

Anderson pushed past him as she limped to the ruined cab, her right arm still hanging by her side as she clambered on top of it. The flames on the surface of the chem-lake were dwindling and Anderson could see through the thinning smoke an army in the throes of defeat. The rioters had been lined up on their knees, hands behind their backs, as Judges bullied them one by one into the backs of pat-wagons. Torn and trampled, the rioter's banners lay scattered across the deserted battlefield.

"We got the hostages out and made it back here just in time to see the finish," Greaves said, looking up at her. "We picked out the ringleaders, made sure the news-drones saw us put the squeeze on them. And we won't need a psi to get them to tell us where their pals are hiding."

Anderson's legs buckled and she sat down hard on top of the cab. She tried to recall why she had ever believed the Bedlam riots would result in anything other than defeat for the rioters. It was as if she had just awoken from a daydream.

"But," Anderson said, "there were so many of them."

"Don't worry," Greaves said. "I hear there's plenty of cubes just opened up in the Big Zero Six. After all, these guys showed up to let us know just how crazy they were."

Anderson glared at him as she jumped down from the cab.

"They'll fight back," she said. "We can only push them so far. They're not as scared as you think."

"They will be after the show we laid on tonight," Greaves said. "Once they see the news-feeds they'll be too scared to even say the word 'Bedlam.'"

Anderson heard his thoughts, low, sombre, almost fatherly in their concern.

Tough kid...
Just a rookie...
She'll learn...

"Listen, rook," he said. "I've been doing this a heck of years, so lemme give you some advice."

"Punch the jackass with the beard harder next time?"

"You got too much faith in humanity," he said. "Seen a lot of Judges wind up dead due to that kinda thinking. Just saying, rook."

One of the Tac-Judges called Greaves over before Anderson could answer. Apparently Blake's life had not yet left her. She was trying to speak. Anderson rushed over and found her already strapped to a stretcher, groaning at the Judges surrounding her. She caught Anderson's arm, her eyes wild and pleading as she laboured to bring the words up out of her throat. Anderson could hear her thinking what she was trying to say.

Don't leave me...

Anderson placed her fingers on the woman's temple.

"You find any more intel in there, you be sure to report it now, y'hear?" Greaves said.

The men surrounding Anderson vanished as she reached into Blake's mind and gently led the dying woman out of the abyss and into the light.

PART THREE

A DREAM OF THE NEVERTIME

MEGA-CITY ONE
2101 A.D.

Twenty-One

JUDGE ANDERSON FLED into the storm, her boots plunging deeper into the sand with every desperate step. The whistling wind had obliterated the horizon, merging land and sky into a single orange haze. The sand whipped her face, stung her eyes, scoured her throat and sinuses. Her holster was empty, her boot-knife and helmet had vanished.

Something caught her foot and she fell to her knees, gloved hands sinking into the soft red sand. She squinted up with streaming eyes. The glowing murk yielded no route forward, the sand before her dissolving into nothingness a short distance away. She had tried using her telepathy to orient herself, scan the atmosphere for psychic frequencies from which she might glean some clue as to her whereabouts, but all she could hear was hissing static. The reason, she somehow knew, was that every particle of sand in the air was actually a speck of energy, a mote of life-force as vital as a star. She was trapped in a galaxy of white noise that confounded her senses, blinding her to any means of escape from the thing that hunted her.

A familiar sound struck in her a chord of inexplicable fear:

an urgent, rhythmic whooping noise, long and heavy, scything through the air towards her. Her limbs had become mired in the gathering sand, and she struggled to free herself, looking right and left, searching for the source of the approaching sound. But the moaning emptiness betrayed no clue.

She waded free, kicking up flurries of dust as she began pawing her way up the side of a steep dune. The sound grew suddenly more acute, as though something had picked up her scent. The source of the sound was a mystery to Anderson, but she knew somehow that it presaged a thing terrifying beyond measure.

The dune steepened as she climbed, seeming to gather above her like a tidal wave until she felt as though she were swimming.

She glanced behind her and thought she saw something slithering towards her through the mist. She bit down on a scream and continued battling up the sand, until she found herself clawing through the crest of the dune. Gasping, spitting, growling, she wriggled forward until she fell head-first down the other side. She rolled, letting her limbs flop this way and that, her aching muscles thankful for the moment's respite. She gently rolled to a stop, then floundered upright, seeking a new direction in which to run. She froze.

Something like a monstrous spider crouched nearby.

The squatting figure flinched, as though it had not meant to startle her, and Anderson felt her terror abruptly melt into wonder. The hazy silhouette was a nest of elbows and knees, limbs unnaturally long, cradling a strange curved spear. The weapon was thick and clubbed at one end, tapering to a sharp point at the other. The heavy, brutish thing appeared to be fashioned from some immense rib of polished bone and shone like a ghost in the gloom.

The figure rose, spinning the great weapon—whoop, whoop, whoop—before stabbing it into the sand with the triumphant air of an explorer planting a flag in newfound soil.

Anderson felt borne up by a strange joy.
The figure extended a paw-like hand.
She took it, willingly.

ANDERSON STRUCK HER head on the sealed lid of the sleep machine, dropping back into the padded interior with a groan. The flurry of spikes on the heart rate sensor beside her softened into a steady ripple as her breathing slowed and she fidgeted to release the tension in her joints. She felt cheated as she watched the machine's timer count down the remaining seconds of her precious ten minutes of compressed sleep.

That damn dream. The same scenario every time: the running, the sandstorm, the gnawing fear as something hunted her across an endless alien desert. But this was the first time she had actually *seen* the bogeyman.

As a trained, gifted psychic, Anderson was capable of entering dreams and manipulating them while in a lucid state. But when she entered regular sleep, the memory centres of her brain shut down like they did in everyone else's, which made dreams tough to remember upon waking. All she could recall about last night's was a sense of someone tall and thin, a man with something serpentine in his movements as he brandished that impressively huge and so very phallic bone of his. The vibe wasn't sexual, but it was certainly intimate, somehow familial, as if he were a brother or an old friend.

The dream had manifested shortly after her recent breakdown. Following her adventure in the Big Zero Six, which had landed her another psych-review, a post-traumatic anxiety dream or two was the least she could have expected. But the weird thing about this one had been her reluctance to describe it to her counsellor, a weary little empath who picked his nose when he thought Anderson wasn't looking. The dream felt so pregnant with meaning, so secretive, that she felt *protective* of it, for reasons she couldn't explain. Her counsellor had said it meant something about loneliness, but was clearly more interested in whatever he had just discovered on the end of his finger.

The excruciating sessions had been extended several times over: her dreams, her memories, every detail of the cases she was working on and how she felt about them, every part of her life, every facet of her character, dissected and examined by strangers who could read her mind and interpret her actions better than she ever could. The therapy felt increasingly like a charade.

When the old farts finally caved and signed her off, Psi-Chief Ecks had given her a stern talking to about having to call in a career's worth of favours to keep her on the street, and the ongoing importance of sticking to protocol and blah-de-blah-de-*blah*. If there was one thing her first year had taught her, it was that the Department expected you to be a team player. No. Questions. Asked. Any criticism, however reasonable, amounted to sedition. Any deviation in the program meant you had fallen off the rails. She remembered how reassuring that binary world had felt during her last couple of years in the Academy, and the eagerness with which she had attacked her first few months on the street. All of it seemed to have given way to a nagging disquiet that intensified whenever she considered the years ahead.

The merry ding of the sleep machine never failed to irritate her. It made her feel like a micro-zap dinner. She squinted as her surroundings flooded with white light and the machine chirped in her ear.

"*Psi-Judge Anderson, Cassandra,*" it said, as an array of holographic touchscreens materialised above her. "*As a token of congratulations on completing your first year as a Psi-Judge, enter discount code BB27/G for a free item at any Justice Department vending machine. Offer restricted to Munce Jerky, Vitamin Paste and Cheez-Wad.*"

Anderson grunted and started flipping through her Department mail. She banished the last of her briefings to the trash when the window of her dream-log appeared.

"*Your heart rate and brain activity indicate you were dreaming,*" said the sleep machine.

Being in permanent receipt of psychic frequencies known and unknown, Terran and alien, living and dead and everything in between, Psi-Judges were required to log their dreams, however seemingly trivial or downright embarrassing. These entries were fed into a computer somewhere in the depths of Psi-Division, where they were analysed alongside the Judge's psych record and the city's surveillance data. Certain trigger words in specific configurations immediately bought you a thinly-veiled interrogation with a specialist who would divine whether or not your dream contained any prophetic content of consequence to the city.

"*Please make your report after the tone.*"

Anderson had recited the events of her desert dream every time since it had first appeared, and Psi-Division had yet to call her in for a 'consultation,' even with her colourful psych-record.

She described it again: the alien desert, the dust storm, the figures, yadda, yadda, yadda. Nothing she hadn't logged a zillion times before, and with the same strange feeling of reluctance. She hesitated before describing the debut appearance of the spear-wielding stranger.

And there it was again. That sense of protectiveness, that resentment towards the Department. She wondered what Psi-Division might make of the willingness with which she had taken the stranger's hand? Might this new development be enough to finally earn her a consultation? Maybe another six-month psych review? What might the Department find in her head this time?

She tapped the button marked *End Recording*. The window vanished and she felt a pang of remorse. Failure to log your dreams was classed as gross negligence, which in extreme cases could win you a visit from the pitiless inquisitors of the Special Judicial Squad.

Fine, she thought. *I'll log it if he turns up again. Happy now, professional conscience?*

The sleep machine tilted upright as it hissed open, the stifled silence within giving way to the clamour of the outside world. Anderson climbed out into the Sector House dormitory. The hall looked like a mausoleum, with its rows of sleep-machines, their sarcophagus lids hissing as they rose or sank. Judges trudged along the aisles, exhausted from their shifts or still groggy from sleep. She nodded hello at a couple of weary, familiar faces, the air ripe with an accustomed brew of stale sweat and that cloying sanitiser the machine sprayed itself with once it was done with you. She sniffed the inside of her uniform critically, wondering if she had time to grab a shower before returning to Psi-Div.

"*Psi-Judge Anderson,*" chirped the comm-bead in her collar. "*Report to Bay Four, Level 82. Commanding Judge Deetz requires assistance with a riot in progress.*"

RAIN BEADED AND trickled down Anderson's visor, dribbling ice-cold down the back of her neck. The downpour formed a corona around the glare of the street lamps lining the skywalk, strands of rain whipped back and forth by the winds above the Meg. Anderson glanced out across the benighted city, but saw only a starfield of multicoloured lights, whole blocks reduced to hulks of shadows by the intense rain.

Anderson stood between two Judges carrying Lawrod rifles. Everyone else carried shock-batons and shields styled like huge judicial badges, each topped with a row of blinding lights. Encased in bulky blue and yellow tac-armour and lining the width of the skywalk, Anderson's squad resembled nothing less than a line of medieval knights awaiting the signal to charge.

Riot Squad Leader Judge Deetz stood to one side, busy confirming their position through her helmet-comm, deaf to what Anderson could hear coming from beyond the blast doors several metres in front of them. Even through the helmet, which muffled her telepathy, she could hear the rioters' thoughts spiralling like a hurricane, reason and individuality drowning in a vortex that threatened to devour Anderson at any moment.

Street Division were busy suppressing a pro-mutant sit-in apparently raging in a nearby park. Around two hundred of the fleeing protestors had snuck into Howard Hawks Block and broken into the Angie Dickinson Mall on the executive level, where they were now venting their frustration on anything that looked expensive, which was pretty much everything.

Deetz's voice crackled through the comm by her ear. "*The play's simple. We span the width of the hall, two men deep, then make a steady advance until we've pushed the hostiles back into the parking bay at the far end where they came in. All secondary exits are sealed. Street will pick them up as they disperse down the levels. We seal the doors, then go home.*"

Anderson had broken her arm and been stretchered off before completing the only riot simulation she had attended at the Academy, but she remembered the basics. Intimidate first, move to disperse second, crack skulls only when necessary. Give the part-timers a minute to realise what they were up against and let them run, along with any civilians caught in the melee. Anyone left hanging around was most likely a perp.

She tuned into the other Judges, trying to sync herself with the mindset of the squad.

Gonna serve these punks some serious beat-down...

Stomm, I think I need to pee...

Triple-mint gum... La-da-di-da...

"*These pro-mutant demos bring a lot of perps out of the woodwork,*" said Deetz. "*Agitators, pro-democracy creeps, people who know people. Surveillance says ninety percent of the hostiles in there are wearing hoods and masks... Blondie?*"

"Over here," said Anderson, raising her hand.

"*That's our headhunter from Psi-Div. Keep her safe. She's gonna ID as many lifers as she can so's the stun-team can bag 'em. Anderson, pick up anyone who knows anyone. Got that? Good.*"

The blast door rose, a groaning metal curtain slowly revealing pandemonium.

Caught in the blinding glare of the Judges' searchlights, most of the rioters bolted. Anderson heard their collective thoughts shatter into a mutiny of shrieks and hoots, like grazing animals startled by a predator.

Go, go, go... Judge bastards... What do I do now...? Dad'll find out... Where's Debbie...? No cubes for me, man... Bad idea, bad idea... Debbie, where are you...? Run...

Cries of "Jays! Jays!" reverberated down the darkened mall, summoning other rioters from inside the eviscerated storefronts, faces concealed behind scarves or Halloween masks as they abandoned the wreckage and fled into the gloom.

The Judges advanced through the blast doors.

Anderson took a second to match the squad's rhythm, armoured boots pounding the polished floor, crunching their way across a carpet of broken glass. The rioters formed a line as they backed away, shadows dancing like black fire as they flung debris at the advancing wall of light.

"*Targets, Anderson,*" said Deetz over the comm.

Anderson focused on a shaven-headed man pounding at his broad chest, bellowing behind the red scarf wrapped around the lower half of his face. She locked onto his thoughts, zooming in on the memory centres. A seam of chatter disclosed that he had been pinched several times for drugs and violence, including a measly four-month cube stretch for violent sexual assault. She cursed the lazy-ass Judge who made *that* call. This moron couldn't spell 'revolution' if you handed him a dictionary. No political connections. Just a standard-issue thug along for the ride. Pity.

The Judges advanced a second time.

A young woman with a bright blue afro pushed past Red Scarf, stumbling over a shattered Tri-D set as she screamed at the Judges. Her thoughts sounded like breaking glass, sharp with hate. Anderson zoomed in. The woman's younger sister had been born a mutant. Since the Law forbade genetic taint within the city's gene pool, mom had been forced to give up her child for adoption in one of the many mutant camps the city maintained in the Cursed Earth. Both mom and sister had been handed mandatory sterilisation.

Anderson couldn't stop herself from reaching further into the woman's mind. Broken by trauma, her mom had dwindled into addiction, then death, leaving her remaining daughter to seek a justice the city would never grant. This was a woman with every reason to want answers. In her search for those answers she had come across names of people, organisations; names the Department would want to know.

"*Targets!*"

Startled by Deetz snarling in her ear, Anderson made her call. "Creep in the red scarf."

The Judge beside her raised her Lawrod rifle and fired a sizzling blue stun-bolt into the guy's chest, knocking him off his feet as a crackling web of energy writhed over his body.

A little something to make up for that four-month charge, asshole, thought Anderson.

The girl with the blue afro retreated into the mob as they edged towards the exit at the far end, some of them staring at the man's twitching body. Anderson could hear their thoughts as they contemplated his fate: judicial interrogation, cube-time. Any one of them could be next. She heard the thoughts stiffen, not with fear, but with anger. Dozens of them were standing their ground.

The Judges advanced again.

Deetz gave the order and the squad drew their shock-batons. Anderson drew hers, thumbing the activation switch, feeling the weapon humming through her glove as it generated its crippling charge. The move worked its fearful magic upon the rioters, thoughts ringing with alarm at the sight of the weapons. Even the steadiest began backing away once again.

"*Anderson,*" said Deetz. "*I want more scalps before they start running.*"

Anderson caught the stray thought of a woman in a blue raincoat, a cap pulled low over her eyes. A man in a tracksuit beside her was filming the Judges on his vidphone.

Anderson hesitated. "Those two," she said, pointing.

The shooter beside her responded instantly. Two blasts, one in the woman's chest, the other in the man's ribs as he turned to run. The woman had attended at least one meeting of an underground pro-mutant group. The man knew someone who ran a support network. He had contacted them after his wife was arrested for concealing her brother's mutation.

The Judges advanced one last time.

Anderson swallowed hard as her squad approached the unconscious citizens she'd singled out. They were in for a week of brutal interrogation and a minimum six-months' cube-time.

Shock-batons or not, the rioters were now lining up, readying bats, tools, knives, lengths of wood and metal.

Let's do this... Drokk it... Show these bastards... Let's see how much you mean this... Time to really do something... For you, Eddie... Don't forget. Never forget...

It was as if Deetz could hear their thoughts too.

"*We go in on three,*" she said.

Anderson felt a rush of blood prickle her cheeks as she surveyed the line of civilians, braced for the violence about to descend upon them.

"*Three.*"

The squad charged, Anderson running alongside them, startled by her own obedience, shield locked, baton raised. Her nearest target was a young woman clutching a kitchen knife, her terrified face floodlit by the glaring shield-lights as Anderson crashed into her, slamming her to the ground. Anderson stabbed her in the ribs with the baton before she could rise, refusing to look at her face as the woman screamed.

Someone lurched into Anderson's periphery. She raised her shield to impair her assailant's vision as she poked them in the stomach with the baton, holding the weapon in place as the rioter jiggled and collapsed.

Chaos raged about her, battling bodies flickering in the light of the shock-batons, which struck the rioters without mercy. Anderson saw a middle-aged man groping numbly at his bloodied jaw with crooked, broken fingers. Deetz jabbed him in the back with a shock-baton to put him down.

Anderson looked away, feeling woozy and careless. She tossed a psi-bolt into the head of someone pounding on a Judge's riot shield, and took a moment to watch him drop. Something smashed into the back of her helmet, knocking her to the floor. She got to her feet, her visor askew as she tried to grab the baton now dangling from a strap on her wrist, the thoughts of her attacker screaming at her from behind.

Kill her... Kill her... Kill her...

Anderson planted her boot, spun around and launched a powerful uppercut with her shield. Still half-blinded by the tilt of her visor, she felt the rim of the shield hit flesh and heard her attacker's thoughts ring with surprise and agony before popping out of existence.

She straightened her helmet and stood over her fallen attacker, breathing hard. Rage and revulsion curdled inside her as she stared at the fatal dent she had punched into the throat of the woman with the blue afro. Every Riot Squad detachment was allowed a three percent fatality rate before the higher-ups started asking questions. It looked like this lady had made the cut.

The dead woman stared back at Anderson, her face frozen in a look of surprise.

Happy anniversary, Cass, thought Anderson. *You've spent the last year signing up for this, proving you can do it. Looks like you've got a real talent.*

Anderson was accustomed to horror and violence; she had seen its stories played out in countless crime scenes. She herself had killed dozens, brutalised hundreds, all in her first year, and felt not a shred of pity. Every one of her victims had been trying to murder or maim or worse. In those moments, empathy invited death. But what else did such ruthlessness invite?

The other Judges were advancing once more, wading through battered bodies as Anderson wandered ahead of them. Deetz had hoped her display of aggression would frighten the other rioters into retreating. Textbook Department fear tactics. The citizens who remained—maybe fifty or so—retreated further down the hall towards the exit, but refused to run.

Anderson could hear why: a chorus of outrage that announced their hatred for the Justice Department, for the hell it had created. This was no longer about venting their rage. It was about making the bastards *listen*, communicating with them in the only language they seemed to understand. Weapons gleamed in the rioters' hands. Deetz's brutality had inspired only defiance.

She then realised Deetz was yelling at her through the comm.

"Back in line, Anderson! Right now!"

Anderson squinted at the wall of shield-lights behind her, at the mob of rioters jeering before her. Now Deetz was threatening her with a report.

"Pick a side, dammit!"

Irritated, Anderson shook off the baton dangling at her wrist, picked at her chinstrap and cast off her helmet. The thoughts of the assembled rioters washed over her with refreshing clarity.

They seemed bewildered by the gesture. She dropped her shield.

The Judges advanced and the rioters' bemusement gave way to anger once more. They rained missiles upon their attackers. Something shattered against the wall beside Anderson, a fragment stinging her cheek.

A man stepped from the crowd wagging a baseball bat, his features knitted with fury as he geared up to take a swing. Anderson heard his thoughts snarling in her direction. His brother had been a mutant, shipped to some dirt-farm out in the wastes. But right now he was focused on the unarmed Judge pacing towards him, imagining the cheers he would summon when he smashed this bitch's skull, signalling the others to make their final charge. The rioters were thinking in unison, all on the same emotional frequency, every one of them committed to the same futile urge: fight.

Anderson opened a channel into the mind of the man with the baseball bat and poured her energies into him, feeling her psi-senses threading through his mind, wriggling through his cortex like a worm, then out again, branching into separate streams as she dived into the minds of several more rioters, riding that shared emotional frequency as she stitched herself into their minds and out again, branching out, breaking in, weaving a web of psionic energy until every rioter was ensnared. She lowered her hands from her temples, slowly and cautiously; this was delicate work that required a steady mind, impossible with that damn helmet.

She heard the man's thoughts crack like a starting pistol a second before he ran at her, his bat raised behind his head. The Judges immediately broke into a run, faltering over the bodies at their feet, but Anderson was too far out of reach. She raised her hands as if to embrace her attacker, ignoring the hymn of mayhem in his head. She stood her ground as he closed in, bunching for the swing. She closed her eyes, feeling the radiance of the man's life-force, knowing exactly where to move next.

The bat swooshed through the air as she sidestepped, catching his head with both hands, twisting him to the floor. She drove a psi-blast down through her hands, into the man's brain and out again, electrifying every strand of the psionic web she had sewn into the collective mind of the nearby mob. She felt the rioters' thought-streams flicker and vanish, absorbed by the darkness that followed.

Someone was shaking her, clicking their fingers, hands waving in front of her face. Anderson sat there, the unconscious man limp in her arms. Deetz's face swam into view.

"The next time you wanna pull a stunt like that, you clear it with me first!"

Anderson nodded drunkenly as Deetz strode away. She felt someone pat her shoulder as she got to her feet.

"Good work, Blondie," someone said.

Anderson blinked until her vision cleared. The other Judges were surveying the sea of unconscious bodies she had created. She stood, clutching her knees for support. The feeling of sudden exhaustion that always followed a psi-blast was taking longer than usual to dissipate. She caught her head nodding, her eyelids drooping. Her joints felt like they would give way any second.

Bodies rushed to her side. Someone caught her as she fell, but she seemed to pass through their arms like a ghost.

Anderson landed on soft ground. She looked down in confusion, her gloved fingers clawing warm sand. The sandstorm had intensified since she had last been here, the wind scourging her hair, blinding her. Something glittered in the air.

Her head cleared, as though this place somehow reinvigorated her. She lurched to her feet, trying to shield her eyes, then stumbled aside as she realised someone was about to walk into her.

The man no longer had his baseball bat, his empty hands hanging by his sides as he sleepwalked past her. From his mouth trailed a tongue of smoke, and she realised he was spewing dust, a continuous stream of the stuff smouldering up from inside him, feeding the storm.

She saw other figures shambling through the haze. Anderson staggered towards one of them and recognised another rioter. She saw another, and another, all of them sleepwalking, all of them breathing plumes of dust just like Mr Baseball Bat.

Anderson turned away, gasping. Something glittered in the air again, like she was seeing stars. Why was everyone dreaming her dream? What had she done to them? Was she even asleep? It took a moment more to realise that the glittering dust was of her own making. She breathed out, watching herself exhale a thick plume of her own life-force, enriched with psychic energy, that sparkled like ground glass as the wind drank it away.

From somewhere inside the swirling dust storm came a familiar whooping sound, and joyous laughter.

Twenty-Two

ANDERSON HEARD BIRDSONG. She squinted into a world of humming white and sat up with a start, wincing at an ache in the side of her neck. She caught a med-droid, red cross printed on its back, disappearing through a nearby hatch, which sealed behind it. Her eyes adjusted to the brightness of her surroundings as she swung off the bed. Bare feet touched cold floor. She had been stripped down to her jumpsuit, her shoulder pads, belt, boots and gloves gone. Dominating the room was a large holo-window looking out into Tri-D woodland. Birds chirruped through the window's speakers.

She felt groggy from what she presumed was sleep. She must have blacked out after discharging the psi-blast. Why? She touched her temples, projected, trying to steady herself. Her psi-senses found nothing: not even the soft hum of psychic silence, but a perfect, unnerving absence of sound. She pushed harder and felt a ripple of resistance in the ether. The walls were psi-shielded.

Why had the unconscious rioters been dreaming *her* dream? She remembered her incomplete log entry and panic plunged deep into her chest.

The woodland dissolved, revealing an adjoining room. A Psi-Judge sat at a table level with the window. She wore a Psionic Security uniform; her badge read *Brackett.*

"How are you feeling?" she asked, her voice devoid of concern, face a blank. She had short black hair, oiled and combed to one side. Anderson wondered what she would look like with a little square moustache.

Brackett's face twitched.

A telepath, huh? And here's me on the wrong side of a one-way psi-shield.

"I'll feel better once I know where I am," she replied, sitting down at the small table on her side of the window. "What the heck happened in the mall?"

"You're under quarantine, Judge Anderson," said Brackett. "I'm afraid you may be for some time."

Anderson shivered. "Quarantine? What the hell's wrong with me? Are those cits okay?"

"How do you feel?" asked Brackett, examining her through the glass.

"Does Chief Ecks know I'm here?"

Brackett touched a tablet beside her, dragging three holographic files onto the smartglass table. Anderson had been deprived of her psi-senses before during training exercises, but never in the field. She felt somehow deaf, blind, helpless. Unnerved by Brackett's attentions and terrified of whatever contagion she might have contracted, Anderson floundered.

"C'mon," she said, smiling awkwardly. "We're on the same team here."

Brackett looked up. "Why do you think you're here?" she asked.

Anderson composed herself. "Okay. I was called to assist a Riot Squad. We isolated a group of around fifty hostiles who refused to disperse. I pacified them with a nexus-pattern psionic blast in order to avoid unnecessary use of force. Then I seem to have blacked out..."

She paused, waiting for Brackett to feed her a clue, but the Psi-Sec Judge just tapped one of the holo-files on the glass table, releasing a slew of documents.

"...Next thing I know I'm in here," Anderson finished. "Look, I can help you if you just tell me what's going on."

Brackett magnified one of the documents, examined it.

"Your Academy records say you were in the top three percent at White Bear. That must come in handy when you're trying to hide things from people who can read your mind."

White Bear. She had used that technique during the Meet Market case. Tell yourself not to think of a white bear and the first thing you think of is a white bear, unless you're a powerful psychic trained in controlling your mind's unruly impulses. The trick was to not think about what you were thinking about.

Anderson didn't think about her latest dream-log, about her decision to omit the appearance of the spear-wielding stranger. She didn't think about the fact that by doing so she may have threatened the lives of the rioters she had been trying to protect. She didn't think about confessing right now to avoid further trouble.

She didn't think about her complete lack of trust in the Department.

"You've committed a lot of misdemeanours in your first year, Judge Anderson. Enough for *three* years. If you were Street Div, your career would be over."

Anderson didn't think about the possibility that Brackett may not know about the incomplete dream-log, that maybe she could get through this without condemning herself to an interrogation by the SJS or—worse—another psych-review.

"Let me speak to Chief Ecks."

Brackett opened the second holo-file.

"You made an entry in your dream-log last night."

Anderson didn't think about panicking.

"You've had a recurring dream about being lost in a desert.

Same dream logged a total of twenty-three times in three months. Are you confident you logged this dream accurately? No details you declined to include?"

Anderson didn't think about maintaining a steady heart rate as she considered her answer.

Brackett leaned in. "As operatives of Psi-Division, our minds can receive signals from dimensions and worlds that we have to assume harbour hostile intent; dimensions that can generate power enough to warp reality itself. Failure to accurately report a dream, vision or out-of-body experience is negligence, equivalent to a satellite crew failing to announce the presence of an enemy warfleet."

Brackett was studying Anderson's face, looking for a tell-tale crease in Anderson's brow, a twitch at the mouth: cues that would indicate she was lying. Anderson didn't think about how Brackett mustn't hold all the facts. Anderson did not think about her concerns, about the knot of doubt which refused to unravel, her distrust of the Department, her anxiety about the future. Whatever it was that was troubling her, it was hers to deal with, and hers alone. The Department would not have all of her.

"Are you confident your log entries are accurate?"

Anderson didn't think about the consequences of lying to a Department official.

"Yes," she said.

Brackett sat back and tapped the final holo-file.

"Psych-evaluation with Psi-Judge Zeinner."

Anderson felt her stomach tighten.

"You must have trusted *her*," she said. Anderson didn't think about the emphasis on 'her.'

"You confessed feelings of intimacy towards your partner on the Meet Market case. Judge Casey Montana."

Anderson shifted in her chair.

"But you didn't register those feelings with the Department..."

"Like I told Zeinner, I was confused at the time. It was my first big case. I judged those feelings to be of no consequence. They *are* of no consequence."

"Judge Montana didn't make any registration either. Are you sure feelings are as far as it went, Cassandra? I doubt the SJS would think so."

Anderson didn't think about her resolve suddenly melting.

"Perhaps I should file a recommendation that they bring him in for questioning."

Anderson involuntarily slammed her hands on the table.

"There was one thing," she said.

She was silent for a few moments, not quite believing her own outburst. Then she explained the appearance of the spear-wielding stranger in her dream. When asked why she lied, she told them, saying that she felt another psych-review—the sense of being under constant scrutiny, of having to prove her validity over and over and over again—was detrimental to her ability to carry out her duties. She didn't tell Brackett how much those duties had come to feel like a sentence.

Brackett rose from her chair and waved a hand. The forest reappeared. Anderson got to her feet and pounded at the window.

"Wait! You didn't tell me what's wrong with me!"

The holographic trees quivered as she slapped the glass.

"Let me speak to Ecks!"

The Chief of Psi-Division would straighten things out. He always did. He always showed up to bail her from a detention cell or review the latest complaint. But where was he now? Exactly how much trouble was she in now she had officially lied to the Department? Would Ecks finally run out of strings to pull? Maybe the Council's patience with Psi-Division would finally expire when they learned Ecks' star player wasn't on the team.

Enraged by her own helplessness, she grabbed the chair,

bounced it off the window and went to sit on the bunk. She may have relied too much on Ecks in the past. Maybe she wasn't the hotshot she thought she was.

Maybe she was still just a rookie.

She couldn't steady her spiralling thoughts. She was in trouble deep enough for them to place her in quarantine and, judging by Brackett's line of questioning, they wanted to build a case to keep her there. What kind of disease had she contracted? What was going to happen to her? Death was nothing. It was a cakewalk; one minute you're alive, the next you're dead. One state of being eclipses the other. No compromise. The brutal simplicity of it was comforting. That's why they drummed it into you at the Academy. Train hard, suit up and do the job. That's all you can ever do.

But for her it was different.

Psi-Judges patrolled a far more unpredictable beat, an arena on which human science had only a tenuous hold. Here be dragons. There were things living in Psi-Div's vaults that had once been Psi-Judges, things coiling in jars or preserved in stasis tanks and abstraction-field generators. Anderson had heard of Psi-Judges who had been warped into forms of existence that defied categorisation, which had driven researchers to obsession and insanity. There were Psi-Judges who had tuned into unknown psionic frequencies and been transformed into gods or reduced to a smear of thought. There were Judges who had fallen down the open manholes in reality and been erased from existence.

The astral researchers at Psi-Division had confirmed that countless dimensions existed alongside their own, containing who knew what. A Psi-Judge might one day reach out and find themselves sucked into everlasting hell.

Street Judges had to live with the knowledge that their lives could end at any moment; what kept Psi-Judges awake at night was beyond anyone's comprehension.

Anderson shivered, her brow cold with sweat.

"It's okay, Cassandra," said a familiar voice through the holo-window speakers.

"Chief?" She sprang to her feet as the woodland vanished to reveal Psi-Chief Ecks standing in the other room, with Brackett. He looked even wearier than usual; Brackett looked furious.

"Please, Cass. I need you to sit down."

Anderson remaining standing, her stomach in freefall.

"Why am I here?" she asked.

"Sir," said Brackett with admirable restraint. "The more she knows, the greater the likelihood she could invalidate the Division's research."

Ecks silenced her. "Cassandra, you've contracted some kind of psychic virus."

Brackett tutted. "As I understand it, they've detected a malignancy in one of her dreams. It's technically more like cancer."

Anderson gripped the edge of the table, feeling dizzy. She spoke slowly. "Go on."

"One of your dreams—presumably the one about the desert? It's infectious, somehow viral. It seems to transfer via deep or prolonged telepathic contact and results in—from what we can tell—a permanent sleep, in which the dreamers are all dreaming the same thing."

"Then why am I still awake?" asked Anderson.

"Because you're lucky," said Brackett. "Dream Research have been working on a new form of anti-sleep meds. They're in limited supply, and at this stage they're basically an experimental stimulant. They'll let you go without sleep for a week at most, before your body starts crashing. You'll receive one a day as we study the progress of the 'virus.'"

Anderson's mind filled with thoughts of confinement, interrogation.

"We need to find a way to cure it, Brackett," said Ecks.

Brackett went to switch off the intercom, but Ecks stayed her hand.

"We don't know *how* to cure it," said Brackett, angrily. "She's somehow tuned into a psionic dimension previously unknown to Psi-Division. We've yet to find any other psychic in the city who can access it. She's the only one."

Anderson smacked the glass. "Then let me help you."

Brackett ignored her. "I had to see if we could trust her," she said. "And she chose to commit perjury, unsurprisingly. You said it yourself: she's erratic, unpredictable." Ecks glanced at Anderson guiltily as Brackett continued: "Unless we can *guarantee* she won't jeopardise the security of this Division, we have to operate on the assumption that there is no cure."

"What about the guy with the spear?" said Anderson. "Lay off these anti-sleep meds and let me go back into the dream and find him, figure out who he is."

"Even if we trusted you enough to re-enter the dream," said Brackett, turning to Anderson. "It would start draining your life the moment you went in. Those citizens you infected with the psi-blast…"

"Infected?"

"They're already dying. And because no one in the Division can access this private frequency of yours, we can't see inside their heads to help them. Or you."

Anderson felt a pang of guilt as she remembered the dust she had seen rising from the mouths of the rioters in the dream.

Ecks had turned away. Ruthless though Brackett's logic was, no doubt the rest of the Council would concur.

"Even if we *could* cure her, we can't trust her to help us," said Brackett. "She's worth more to this Division as she is—infected. She could help us find out more about this dimension she's tapped into. It's possible we could even harness it, explore it, secure it. For the sake of this Division, I recommend we commit her to a full mind-scour, perhaps even a complete etheric extraction. I'm told the meds would keep her awake throughout the entire procedure. Even if she loses consciousness and enters the dream, we can bring her back round. That girl is the most powerful registered psychic in Psi-Division; as far as the Council is concerned, she *is* Psi-Division. But the researchers I've spoken to believe there are aspects of her powers that could further our understanding of psionics, if properly explored. What we learn from her could benefit every Psi-Judge on the street. We cannot afford to waste this opportunity."

Ecks—his expression boiling with rage—caught sight of Anderson. She was seated on the bunk, calm, hands on her thighs, breathing out hard, faster and faster, breaths tighter and tighter, gradually starving her brain of oxygen, pushing herself into a blackout.

"Cassandra, no!"

She held her breath tight as she heard Ecks cry out, stars already dancing before her eyes. The meds wouldn't let her sleep, but—as Brackett just pointed out—she could still lose consciousness, however briefly.

Thanks for the tip, bitch.

The world turned black and she was out cold, tumbling inside herself.

With every breath, she had been generating a small core of consciousness, like a scuba-diver preparing an oxygen tank before a dive. Standard procedure for lucid dreaming. She could feel the stimulants in her distant body reigniting neural signals, already dragging her back to consciousness. But she reached through the blackness and into the dream that was struggling to materialise before her. She could feel something flitting about inside it like a moth trapped in a light fitting. She could see nothing, but felt an outline buzzing with life-force, like the silhouette of a heat signature viewed in infrared.

It wasn't a figment of her dream. It was a person. Someone carrying a strange, heavy spear. She could feel the currents of energy swirling this way and that as the staff twirled and swung, stirring the dream into being.

The dream wasn't hers. It was his.

This creep with the spear—this dreamer—he was the source of her infection; the cure might lie with him. To stand any chance of finding it, she had to establish a permanent link with him, a trail she could follow. She went to project towards him, but her consciousness was hauling her back to earth like a netted fish. She lashed out, flinging psionic hooks into the dreamer, striking sparks of visual memory.

For an instant, she saw through the eyes of the dreamer and beheld a flash of some deeper memory. A body in agony, mouth parched, feet a bloody mess, shoulders roasted by the sun, hands moving across smooth rock. The boulders gave way as the viewer looked out across a ravaged world, a land of parched rock cratered like the surface of a desert moon, broken mountains crumbling beneath strange clouds, a toxic yellow heat haze steaming above the earth, nourishing the horrors that dwelt there.

Anderson awoke. "He's in the Cursed Earth!"

She convulsed into a fit of coughing, shoving aside the robonurse trying to examine her. Anderson sat up, feeling a strange pull in her lower belly. She had opened a subtle channel between her and the dreamer, a psychic trail that could lead her to him.

Brackett stared down at her through the window, dumbfounded. She informed Ecks that Anderson had just breached quarantine. "She must have accessed this private dimension of hers."

"Then she can't stay here," said Ecks, staring at Anderson. His helplessness infuriated Brackett, who pounded the table, her patience at an end.

"How much longer are you going to indulge this maniac, Chief Ecks? How many more times are you going to let her gamble with the future of our Division?"

Your future's not worth—

Ecks turned on Anderson. "No jokes, Cassandra!"

The edge in his voice made her shiver.

"She's right," he told her, looking away. "You've become too aware of what you mean to this Division. I've let you become arrogant."

Anderson elbowed past the robo-nurse and ran to the window.

"Arrogant?" Her ghostly reflection scowled back at her, eyes glaring, teeth gritted. "I've spent the last drokking *year* proving how good I am. If I'm the best you've got, then don't expect me to apologise for it." She turned away. "I'm done having to prove myself. To you, to this Division, to the whole drokking Department."

Ecks said nothing for several seconds, letting her rage subside.

"Compassion is what makes you exceptional, Cassandra," he said eventually. "But it also makes you unpredictable. And the city needs to be able to rely on you."

Anderson shook her head. "Whatever, Chief. Just let me out of here so I can go fix this."

"I know you're not a rookie anymore," said Ecks. "You no longer need to prove you're a Judge."

Brackett cut in. "But she does need to prove that we can trust her."

Twenty-Three

GEARS CHURNED IN the walls as ancient mechanisms locked and rolled, and the vast steel door gradually rose. Anderson turned her head as a hot gust of sand washed over her. Light filled the subterranean confines of the garage, revealing dozens of Tek-Div mechanics labouring amid the dismantled vehicles and piles of discarded machine parts. The grinding rumble finally stopped, the wind fell and Anderson squinted out into the Cursed Earth.

From here—somewhere in the Meg's eastern wall—a wide slope guarded by autocannon turrets plunged into a sea of orange sand. Distant mountains lined the horizon beneath boiling purple clouds. Anderson felt the pulse in her gut grow stronger at the sight of the strange expanse, settling into a deep, rhythmic pounding, tribal drums in her belly. It felt like earth energy, ley lines, geomancy, all that hippy stuff.

Ecks had concurred. The closer she stayed to the ground, the stronger the signal would be, which ruled out an aerial mission.

The connection Anderson had made in the dream would act as a psionic compass, a psi-trail to the man she had to kill, to save herself and the citizens she had infected.

As Ecks had put it: kill the dreamer, kill the dream.

Brackett had been insistent in wanting to know why Anderson alone could access the mysterious psychic dimension in which the dream-virus operated. Why had she been singled out for infection? Why no other psychic in the city? What was it about Cassandra Anderson that made her so damn special?

Well, isn't that the million-credit question? thought Anderson.

"Pay attention," said Psi-Judge Dini, his voice muffled by the dusty handkerchief he held to his mouth. He handed her a small case, containing a metallic tube with a switch at one end.

"Contact with the city will be patchy at best," he said. "This will emit a supercharged signal lasting thirty minutes. Activate it once you've located the target and we'll send aerial assistance."

Anderson stowed the case in her Lawmaster's storage pod, in between her rad-cloak, cans of water, ration tins, and the tightly wrapped bundle of anti-sleep meds.

Ecks freeing her from quarantine to go cure herself out in the Cursed Earth may have been only a stay of execution, of course. She'd counted five of those tiny glass vials of fluid, to be loaded into a jet-injection pistol and fired into the carotid artery in her neck every sundown. Run out of shots and her body would start shutting down as the infection dragged her to sleep and into the vampiric dream. Those five precious little bottles may be counting out the final days of Cassandra Anderson.

Her mouth felt dry as she fired up her Lawmaster. She fidgeted, feeling impatient, last night's shot of meds still working on her like a fresh pot of synthi-caff.

"You still want that droid, toots?" The Chief Tek lifted her goggles onto her forehead, leaving a perfect outline of clean skin in a face otherwise black with grime.

"Sure do," said Anderson. "I'm looking for scouts, exploratory droids, anything like that."

Dini removed the handkerchief from his tight little mouth.

"You'll be riding in a state-of-the-art 'Killdozer.' It's basically a fortress on tank tracks."

He sniggered to himself, as if amused by Anderson's naivety.

"These warbots," she said, unphased. "Do they come programmed with any kind of geographical data, possible routes, landmarks, weather patterns? I'll know which direction to take, but I could use someone who can chart the best possible route, maybe save us some time, even some lives. Or is the plan for me to just blast my way across the Cursed Earth and hope I don't run out of bullets before I get where I'm going?"

"They're called 'rounds,'" said Dini, rolling his eyes. "And I think you'll find the direct approach usually works best."

"For the Department, maybe," said Anderson.

She followed the Chief Tek to a back wall, where a lineup of droids reclined on a huge rack of revolving shelves, all of them in various states of disrepair or dismemberment. The Tek hurried along the line of battered, lifeless droids with the air of a librarian searching for a long-forgotten book. She paused to rap the dented breastplate of a faceless droid sprayed with chipped desert camo, with legs like a gazelle.

"Mittelmark 0.7, off-world exploratory droid," she said. "These things run like the wind. Three-sixty sensor array, full atmospheric processor, perfect for scouting. Wrist-mounted las-cannons if you run into trouble. She's yours if you want her."

But Anderson had stopped to examine another robot further back down the line. It was big, real big. You could park a Lawmaster on those shoulders. Several dents wrinkled the robot's forehead, giving it an expectant look, its dormant, hooded eyes fixed upon some private horizon. It had a huge horseshoe moustache: not a metal moustache shaped like a horseshoe, but an actual horseshoe riveted to its face. Between the prongs of the horseshoe a monolithic chin jutted out like a challenge.

Someone had once cared for this guy. They had dressed him in a plain waistcoat, now stained and torn. It was way too big for a human; someone must have had made it especially for the droid. They had also knotted a handkerchief around his tree-trunk neck, although the gift was now little more than a rag.

Anderson opened the waistcoat and read the words embossed on the robot's battered metal chest: *CALL ME MARION*.

"Who's this bad boy?" said Anderson, shaking out the waistcoat, releasing puffs of dust and sand. The stuff clotted every scar and recess on the robot's body.

"That? It's an old cowbot. Dunson Robotics, out of Texas City. Dino-ranchers used 'em out in the Cursed Earth before the GR-20s came along. Traders probably sold that one to us for parts."

"These things see much of the Cursed Earth?"

"Sugar, those things used to drive dinosaurs from one end of the Cursed Earth to the other. If there's a sight to see out there, that thing's probably seen it. But listen, the Cursed Earth does weird things to 'bots if they stay out there too long. They get obedience glitches, start acting up. Who knows why? Besides, your Chief's gonna have my ass if I let you outta here with that junker. So do me a favour and take the Mittelmark."

Anderson scooped something up off the floor: a cowboy hat made of ancient leather, plain and battered.

"Just fire him up for me, okay?" she said as she popped the dents out of the hat.

The mechanic sighed as she opened Marion's belt-buckle hatch and started fiddling with the switches.

Dini appeared, looking disappointed.

"I've just been informed your Killdozer's been requisitioned. Some kind of mercy mission to Mega-City Two. They're sending up a Land Raider instead, but it'll be another three hours before it's ready."

Just then, the Chief Tek cried out. Anderson turned as something barged into her, knocking her to the floor. Someone snatched the robot's hat from her hands. Dini was shrieking.

Anderson looked up to see the cowbot thumping across the garage towards her Lawmaster, towering over the mechanics as they scurried for cover. She scrambled to her feet, cursing herself for leaving her bike idling as the robot lumbered aboard, replaced its hat and launched itself into the Cursed Earth.

The Chief Tek picked herself up. "He ran for it the second I switched him on."

Anderson grabbed Dini. "You've got more of those anti-sleep meds, right?"

"Those were the last ones," he said, babbling. "They're in limited supply. It takes Med-Div *weeks* to create a batch."

Anderson was already running to his Lawmaster.

He called out after her. "I'll get a ship out after him."

Anderson leaped into the saddle, yelling back, "And by the time they mobilise, he'll be gone."

She pulled on a Judge's helmet, positional data glimmering before her eyes as sensors targeted the droid, already dwindling into the distance under a plume of dust. Dini ran to her side, but before he could speak, she told him to cancel the Land Raider.

"I'm sick of waiting," she said. "Tell Ecks I'm doing this my way."

Anderson wrenched the throttle, hours of frustration released in a surge of snarling machinery and whizzing rubber. Her front wheel rose as the Lawmaster leapt through the open gate, sailing several feet through the air before landing hard on the slope below, tyres screaming all the way down as she rode out into the Cursed Earth.

THE SUN WAS falling towards the mountains on her left. Anderson had been chasing the runaway robot for several hours now, along a well-used dirt road. The droid sure knew how to ride; he'd succeeded in putting several miles between them, despite the abundance of debris that littered the way. She finally lost sight of his dust trail in the grey hills.

The son of a bitch had her meds. She would need them before nightfall. A tired ache was already creeping into her shoulders and the drumming of the Lawmaster's engine was beginning to sound hypnotic.

She had visited the Cursed Earth once before, during her Hotdog Run, that final make-or-break field exam undertaken by all Justice Department cadets. She remembered the sense of exposure without the ever-present Mega-Blocks and their crazed web of skeds looming over her. Out here there was nothing to hide her from the strangely unnerving expanse of sky.

She zoomed past another makeshift signpost, this one crowned with a Judge's helmet, the skull of its owner grinning from beneath the shattered visor. The mutant population of the Cursed Earth had good reason to despise anyone wearing a badge. The Council of Five had reasoned that if humanity were ever to rise from the mire of the apocalypse, then genetic impurities must be declared illegal and mutants sentenced to expulsion from the city. Most of those exiled agreed to work under protection in the outlying farms and landfill sites that serviced the city; others took their chances in one of the ramshackle frontier towns that sprang up and burned down at an alarming rate. A minimum of Judges were sent to safeguard the larger, more durable towns, but in truth Mega-City One had enough trouble taming its own urban wilderness.

The holographic targeting rings shuffling around inside Anderson's visor detected a deviation in the robot's tracks. Anderson followed them as they veered off into a range of rocky hills where the smell of baked earth gave way to a cool, urgent wind.

She had been trying to reason with herself that once she caught up with the droid and retrieved her meds, maybe she could persuade him to help her now she was on her own. But her hopes had felt more and more futile as time passed. She could feel the psi-trail tugging her in the opposite direction, the pulse of the psionic beacon diminishing as the hours passed and she travelled further from her quarry. Even if she could retrieve her meds, how many more would she have to waste before she got back on course? She tried not to think what Ecks and Brackett would be saying about all this. The lowering sun burned behind the mountains, lighting the clouds on fire.

As she followed the targeting rings down a narrow rocky canyon, she heard a distant explosion, followed by a crackle of gunfire. It was hard to gauge distance with this damn bucket on her head, but it sounded worryingly close. The cowbot had almost certainly run into trouble. Typing on her Lawmaster's control screen, she armed cannons and maximised peripheral sensors.

She slowed the bike to a cruise as she stowed her helmet and listened. The gunfire continued intermittently, from somewhere a short way down the canyon. It sounded like cartridge rifles mostly, along with something bigger, some kind of booming high-calibre hand-cannon. A standoff, maybe?

Another explosion echoed among the rocks, but it was a flat electrical zap, sounding to Anderson more like laser-fire than an explosive round. An ion-cannon? If someone wanted to take down a machine without damaging it, that would make sense.

Best leave the bike out of harm's way, she thought.

She set the Lawmaster on sentry mode and parked it beside a boulder before hurrying down the canyon on foot towards the source of the gunfire.

The valley widened out to a plain surrounded by high cliffs, behind which the sun had vanished, leaving a radiant amber sky. For a moment she thought the acres of ground before her were covered with the remains of some kind of petrified forest, the wood bleached by years beneath the scorching sun. Then she spotted an enormous skull, its gaping jaws lined with fangs the length of combat-knives. Anderson gasped as she realised that what she thought were the bare remains of tree trunks were in fact huge ribs reaching into the air like claws. Immense femurs lay strewn about her like spilled lumber while empty skulls stared into nothingness. A field of dinosaur bones lay before her like an ashen sea.

She picked her way quickly and quietly through the macabre detritus, towards the source of the gunfire. A boisterous wind pressed her, urging her to leave this sacred place. She found her stolen Lawmaster lying on its side by a ribcage the size of a hill. The bike didn't appear to have suffered any damage, but the lights were out and she caught the bleachy smell of ozone in the air. Her ride had been ionised for sure; its electrical systems would stay blacked out until the charge had dispersed completely.

The cowbot didn't appear to have seen her. He was crouched a short distance away behind an outcrop of rock stacked with bones. The concealed shooters were picking at his cover from atop a nearby ridge. At that distance they probably had better accuracy with their rifles than whatever antique six-shooters the cowbot was carrying; and he couldn't break cover unless he wanted to get zapped by that ion cannon. The poor metal lug was clearly stuck, but first things first.

Anderson crawled over to her stolen Lawmaster. The saddle pod was still unlocked from where she had been stashing her supplies, which was a relief; otherwise, she would have had to wait for the bike to regain power before she could open it. She retrieved her bundle of meds: five little bottles, all unbroken. She selected one, loaded it into the jet-injector, and shot herself in the neck. Those synthi-caff jitters kicked in almost immediately.

She ducked. The cowbot had spotted her. She thought for a second that he might open fire, but he just stared at her, his eyes glowing blue in the gathering twilight as he leaned against the rock. Had he rebooted? Had his mind been scrambled during his years on the shelf? What program was he following? Computerised brains were a mess of static to Anderson, leaving her deaf to whatever was going on behind those steady blue eyes.

She had spent an entire a day riding into the Cursed Earth, probably in the wrong direction, and she had four vials left. Four days to find the Dreamer and blow a hole in his head. That was a big ask without a guide or backup. She imagined mountains to be skirted, ravines to be bypassed; not to mention rad-storms, quicksand, pissed-off mutants, hungry cannibals, and the world's greatest menagerie of B-movie monsters, all out there waiting for her.

She considered activating the homing beacon. Maybe they could get a transport out here. But how long would that take? Another day?

Small as she was, she could probably make it to the cowbot's position without being noticed by the shooters.

Probably? Screw it.

She scurried into the low crawl she had mastered in basic training, keeping her body flat against the ground as she wriggled between the lengths of scattered bone, careful not to displace them and alert the shooters that another player had arrived at the table. She emerged at the robot's big booted feet.

"You're welcome, cowboy," she said. "I save your butt from the scrapyard and you steal my ride?"

He said nothing as she crouched beside him, catching her breath. His dented brow lent him a quizzical look, his voice a commanding drawl.

"*You came all the way out here looking for a bike, Miss Piss-Eye?*"

Anderson dusted off her badge. "It says 'Psi.' I'm a Psi-Judge. You know what that is?"

"*Can't say as I do, or care that I don't,*" he said. "*Miss...?*"

"Anderson. Cassandra Anderson."

He tweaked the brim of his hat. "*Marion,*" he said.

"Actually, I'm looking for your help, Marion."

"*Only help I got to give is for my herd. That's my program. I get things where they need to go.*"

Neither of them flinched as a bullet whined among the bones behind them.

"*But I sure do apologise for borrowing your ride without asking, Miss Anderson. I needed to find my herd, is all. Thanks to you, I found them.*"

He nodded towards a massive three-horned skull that sat nearby like an abandoned car. Large runes had been branded along the bony frill that would have shielded the back of its head.

"*Rad-storm hit us near Crackneck Creek. Caught me at the head of a stampede. Next thing I know I'm in some city garage carrying a megaton of headache.*"

More rifle fire crackled above them, releasing puffs of white dust into the cooling air, the scavengers trying to aggravate the robot out of hiding now evening was closing in.

"*Good thing I know where three-horns go when they're done wandering,*" he said. "*I was just finishing up my inventory when these scavs jumped me.*"

Anderson touched her temples as she reached out to the top of the ledge. She could hear the scavengers' thoughts jabbering away behind the rocks.

Maynard's gone for back-up... Who's that thing talking to down there...? Junker's gonna buy me a new skinning knife...

"These guys have sent for their friends," said Anderson. "When they get here I figure they'll nail you pretty quick. But they don't know I'm here. So how about a deal? I help get these creeps off your back and you help me get where I need to go. That's your program, right? Do that and I can talk to someone at Texas City, get you refitted, set you up with whatever you feel like herding. I can do that. I give you my word."

The huge robot seemed to sag with regret.

"You seem like a civil woman, Miss Anderson. But experience has taught me that a Judge's promise ain't worth a plugged three-credit piece. You go on flashing that badge of yours out here and you'll find plenty of folks happy to testify the same."

"You'd rather shoot it out on your own with creeps who've already got you outgunned?"

"And when I'm done I'll be heading back to Missourah for a new herd."

"On foot? You know I'm not letting you take my bike again."

"Then a stretch of the legs sounds just fine to me, Miss Anderson."

Frustration welled inside her, the robot as inscrutable as a stone.

"I'll cover you as soon as you're ready," he said. *"And on your way home, be sure to cover up that bullet-magnet you're wearing."*

Anderson muttered angrily as she retrieved two smoke grenades from her belt. She popped the first and flung it back in the direction of her stolen bike. She tossed the second grenade after it, hoping to make it seem as though Marion were attempting to retreat under the smoke. She told the watchful robot to stay put as the grenades pumped dark billowing clouds into the air. She heard a flurry of excited thoughts as Marion's attackers took the bait.

The walls of the canyon flashed blue as a sizzling ball of ion-fire cannoned into the fog, dispersing it as the charge detonated into nothing but bones. The blast helped the evening breeze carry the smoke towards the cliff, where Marion's attackers were positioned. Anderson scurried towards them beneath the drifting fog, darting between huge bones, as the shooters directed their rifle-fire elsewhere. They were onto her now, aware that someone other than Marion was out there. They shot into the darkness, trying to coax return fire that would betray her position. They were still firing when she reached the foot of the cliff and crept towards the rocks at their flank.

The cliffs were lined with ridges of powdery rock, thick plates of sedimentary stone sandwiched over millennia. The stuff crumbled under her boots and fingers as she climbed, but the recesses in the wall were deep enough for her to move with confidence. She paused near the top, shoulders protesting as she clung to handholds she could already feel giving way, and tossed out a psi-pulse, reading the positions of the men above her like echoes on sonar. One had the ion-cannon mounted on his aching shoulder. His buddies were further away, peering through the fading smoke in the darkened canyon below, wondering what the hell was going on.

She hauled herself up onto the plateau and crept behind a large rock directly behind the big guy with the cannon. He and his buddies were swathed in desert wraps, complete with goggles and crude respirators.

Save the psi-blast, she thought. *You might need it if you screw up.*

She drew her knife as she gathered herself, gauging distance and approach, visualising herself sliding the knife under the big man's chin, kicking the back of his knee as she forced him to the ground and swung the cannon around to fire a concussive blast into his huddled pals.

Anderson whispered out from behind the rock and the guy with the shoulder-cannon turned in time to see her disappear behind him. She kicked him to his knees, but something caught hold of her wrist as she went to level the knife at his throat. The ion cannon crashed to the ground.

She thought at first that she must have snagged her arm on some part of the man's clothing, but as they wrestled, she saw something like a leathery brown worm tightening around her wrist. Another tentacle appeared from nowhere and whipped around her throat, choking her. She felt more of them catching her limbs, prising her from the big man's body and hoisting her into the air. She struggled like a puppet trying to free itself from its strings.

As the bandit turned to face his wriggling prey, his face concealed behind a rusty mask, she could see the tentacles protruding from between the folds of his clothing. The guy was a mutant. She felt another of his tentacles reach into her holster and watched it toss away her Lawgiver. Another appendage relieved her of her knife as the big guy dangled her above the serrated rocks some thirty feet below her flailing legs. A psi-blast now would spell her doom.

One of the other mutants had recovered the ion-cannon and was aiming it into the canyon below. Another lightning flash of ion-fire lit up the evening gloom. The mutants cheered. Dumb robot must have made a run for it.

They gathered around Anderson's captor, urging the big guy to throw her to her death. One of them lifted her goggles and stared at Anderson with huge yellow eyes, pulling her scarf down below her chin to reveal a long face patterned luminous green and blue, like the markings of an exotic fish. She caught the big guy's shoulder, engaging him in an urgent whispered exchange, pointing at her own breast and at Anderson's badge. The big guy looked at her, evidently confused.

The bright-faced mutant called out to Anderson.

"Hi, there," she said. "I'm Max, and this is my crew."

"What can I do you for, Max?" gasped Anderson, clawing at the tentacle around her throat.

Max grinned. "So, what kind of psychic are you, Judge? You make stuff move without touching it? You make fire? You see dead people?"

"Read minds," said Anderson, fighting for breath.

"Then what am I thinking right now? And please bear in mind that if I get so much as a headache, Bosco here is going to take immense pleasure in turning you into a pancake."

Anderson tuned in.

You're gonna help us...

"What... What kind of help?"

The answer arrived with the mutant's next train of thought.
*Our people are sick... They're falling asleep... They won't
wake up...*

Twenty-Four

"THERE'S RUMOURS IN Dogtooth Market. It's some kind of sleeping sickness, like a mutant plague," said Max, shouting over her shoulder at Anderson as their skimmer zoomed across the cold, benighted desert. "Mutants all over the Cursed Earth been dropping like whores' panties."

Anderson figured it best not to say anything just yet about her own infection; probably not a good idea to give these guys another reason to kill her. Chief Ecks had said the virus transferred via deep telepathic contact, as it had when she'd psi-blasted the rioters. All the same, Anderson tried to keep readings to a minimum.

But she could still hear the murmuring thoughts of those riding behind her: Max was crazy if she figured she could trust a Judge, they should have let Bosco kill her. But they clearly trusted their leader's wisdom enough to leave Anderson's hands untied so she could ride pillion. Then again, they also trusted the arsenal of weapons they could bring to bear should the Judge decide to play any games.

They were scavengers, relying on scrap, animal hides and

whatever else the desert could provide for trade in the local markets. They'd stumbled upon the cowbot rummaging around in the boneyard several hours ago while out hunting tusk bats. They'd ion-blasted Anderson's Lawmaster soon after they captured her. She had seen them loading the two bikes onto a hov-trailer, along with Marion, handling the machines with far greater care than she had been afforded.

"So you got any idea what's going on, Judge?"

"I'll know more once I've taken a reading," said Anderson.

Apparently some twenty of the seventy mutants under Max's command had succumbed to the dream-virus, although as far as Max knew they had fallen into some kind of coma. She had no idea their sleeping selves were wandering around a desert dreamland that was slowly draining their life-force. Anderson hadn't made any kind of contact with the victims; the dreamer must have found his way into their minds just as he had into hers. But how? Brackett had said the dream-virus operated within a psychic dimension apparently unknown to anyone except Anderson, a frequency to which these mutants must also be attuned. So what was the connection between Anderson and the mutants?

She dispersed her crowded thoughts. She needed to help the scavengers as best she could, as quickly as she could, then see if she could work the old Anderson charm and convince them to help her.

Tough sell.

They reached a stretch of lonely crags, their skimmers slowing as they weaved between the rocks in a dizzying configuration before entering a large cave crammed with junk and makeshift vehicles. Max told the biggest and surliest-looking members of her crew to watch Anderson as she went to announce the Judge's arrival and, presumably, to advise everyone not to shoot her on sight. The air was cold and damp; she could feel wet sand under her boots. A passing mechanic with horns curving down to his cheeks spat at Anderson's feet. Eventually, Max whistled for the guards to follow, and they shepherded Anderson at rifle-point down a tunnel and into a crowded cavern that appeared to serve as a courtyard.

There was a huge hole in the stone ceiling, its circumference dripping with moisture, feeding a garden of luminous fungi that glowed an atomic yellow, bathing the walls in its sickly radiance. It seemed as if every mutant in the caves had turned out, eager for a chance to see Max's captive. They closed in around Anderson as the guards ushered her through the mob.

The mutants were unmasked, free of any protective desert gear, revealed in all their tragic variety. A pair of bulbous green eyes glared at her on bobbing stalks as she was shoved aside by a gruff armour-plated thing that resembled a carnivorous armadillo, its tiny black eyes glittering like onyx. Towering behind it was something that looked like an abstract sculpture made of living flesh, its head a huge pale hoop studded with a single eye. Another stalked through the crowd on legs like stilts, while smaller mutants buzzed and flitted through the air like enormous bugs. A half-naked child looked up at her with radiant green eyes, the lower half of his face a fanged skull, jaws lashed together with strands of gristle. Eyes of a dizzying assortment glared at her from every direction, until she could no longer bring herself to look back.

Their collective thoughts were deafening, so full of venom they stung her senses. When travelling through the streets of the Meg, what a Psi-Judge heard more than anything was fear; but she heard not a trace of it here. Just a brazen outpouring of hatred, murderous wishes hissing and spitting like snakes.

Anderson remembered having to interrogate a young mutant shortly before the Meet Market case. The boy had resisted questioning, and she'd been ordered to extract the whereabouts of his fellow fugitives. In a hands-on reading, Anderson's subjects usually screamed and tugged at their restraints, terrified of what she might be about to do to them. Some whimpered helplessly, or sobbed. This mutant boy had just stared at her, both sets of eyes imploring, uncomprehending, trying to impart the enormity of the injustice she was about to inflict upon him. He said nothing during the reading, said nothing when she recited to the attending Judge the names of the boy's fellow fugitives, the doctors who had obscured medical records, the loving families who had sheltered their children from the Law. Anderson finally gave the name of the sister who had kept the boy hidden since birth. She heard him think to spit in her face. She found herself letting him, and the attending Judge had given the boy a concussion for the affront.

Max beckoned her up a short flight of steps into a hall. As she pushed through the crowd of mutants, she had never felt so ashamed of her uniform. It felt like she was taunting them with the shield gleaming proudly on her chest, with the flared eagle she had spent years at the Academy fighting to win, its claws bared in defiance. It felt obscene. She could hear their thoughts rising in anger. A single thumbs-down from Max was all it would take; they would tear her to pieces without hesitation.

Max hurried her up the stairs. From here she could see the two Lawmasters parked near the entrance of a nearby cave, which appeared to serve as a garage. Marion was awake but paralysed, plugged into what she presumed was some kind jerry-rigged diagnostics machine. The cowbot's blue eyes glowed at her from the darkness as she was hustled inside the hall.

She entered yet another huge cavern, lit here and there by bottles of that glowing fungus. The curved sandstone ceiling was awash with some kind of patterned mural, swirls of dotted lines and capering silhouettes. She presumed it was some kind of communal hall. The floor was lined with long tables, most of which had been made into beds, each one occupied by a sleeping mutant. She could hear their dreaming thoughts churning and bubbling. Tending the patients was a middle-aged woman with three legs under her ragged skirts. A stink like rancid cheese rose from whatever she had smouldering in bowls beside each patient.

Anderson asked to see the first person to have fallen asleep, thinking she could perhaps figure out the source of the infection, maybe gain a clue about the mysterious dimension to which they were all attuned. Max led her to a bench attended by an albino woman bound in dark rags. Her eyes were milky white, but she was not blind. Her face radiated fear at the sight of the approaching Judge. She threw herself over the figure on the bench, screaming at Max that she would kill the Judge herself should she come near her child.

"Tell her I won't hurt her," said Anderson, feeling a tightness in her chest.

Max ignored her, eventually indicating for Anderson's guards to pull the screaming woman aside. She kicked and swore, and Anderson could see mutants shuffling into the hall, threatening to overwhelm Max's crew.

The girl on the bench appeared to be in her early teens, her flesh greyer than her mother's. Anderson couldn't tell whether the awful pallor was part of the girl's mutation or down to the dream-virus draining her life-force. She slept, gently rasping, blanketed in scruffy furs crawling with lice, her eyes sunken, deep shadows in her cheeks. Her fingers were covered in something red.

"She's bleeding!" said Anderson.

Max shook her head. "It's paint," she said, waving at the mural above. "Anya here is our chief decorator. Now, come on. What's wrong with her?"

The mother screamed as Anderson lay a hand on the girl's forehead, focusing until she could feel the brain fizzing beneath the skull. She stroked it like a crystal ball and saw the dream straight away: howling wind, rushing sand, mountains looming through the murk as a trail of dust glittered before the dreaming girl's eyes. The trail tapered off as she breathed the last of it out. Anderson looked down through the girl's eyes to see a small pair of hands fading like a ghost's.

Anderson heard a colossal groan, like the walls of a building on the brink of collapse. She fell back into the real world as Max pulled her away. The girl was now wheezing violently, groping at her own throat as if fighting for breath. The mother was shrieking, trying to fight her way free of the guards and tend her dying child.

Max turned on Anderson, brightly-coloured features knotted with anger. "What did you do?"

Anderson heard the three-legged woman say the girl was crashing. The dream-virus had drained about as much of the girl's life-force as she had to give. To save her, they would need to wake her.

The other mutants were surging into the hall now, drawn by the turmoil. Claws and fangs were bared; knives and pistols drawn.

Anderson grabbed Max. "I can save her," she said. "I can't cure her, but I can keep her alive. I have meds in my bike. Let me go get them."

The girl fell back as if exhausted, her breath a dying rattle. The mother clung to her daughter's hand, howling a prayer.

Anderson shook Max's arm.

"Trust me!"

Max pushed her away and threw an order at the guards.

"Take her to the bike. Kill her if she tries anything."

The guards grabbed Anderson and charged through the mutants crowding into the hall, bellowing at them to make way. Barging their way back into the courtyard, they rushed her to the garage where the Lawmasters were parked, shoved her towards the vehicles and trained their rifles at her head. More mutants crowded behind them, watching eagerly.

"I have to activate the bike to unlock the saddle-pods," said Anderson, keeping her hands in sight.

One of the guards nodded, but shuffled forward, squinting at her along the sights of his rifle.

The Lawmaster was parked facing the crowd, the guns either side of the front wheel aimed directly at the guards. A thought flashed through Anderson's mind as she activated the machine. The control screen snapped into life, reading, *Hostiles detected. Engage guns?*

Anderson saw Marion, still plugged into the diagnostics machine, still paralysed. She was pretty sure he could read the screen from where he stood.

The option buttons read, *Yes/No.*

On 'Yes,' the guns would lock and engage, emptying the courtyard in seconds. The high-calibre shells could easily punch through the walls; it would probably kill everyone in the hall as well.

She tapped 'No' and retrieved the meds from the saddle-pod.

As she ran back to the guards who started pushing their way back through the crowd, the girl's mother appeared in the doorway of the hall and screamed into the courtyard.

"She's killed Anya! She killed my baby!"

The crowd fell upon Anderson in an instant. Strong hands grabbed her arms, hauling her away from the protesting guards. The meds fell from her grip, lost somewhere amid the mutants' trampling feet. She went to reach for them, but someone grabbed her hair, pulling her head back as a fist plunged into her stomach, driving every ounce of breath from her body, lifting her off her feet and dropping her to the floor. She fought for breath that refused to come as hands, claws and tentacles caught her shoulders, grabbed her arms, pulling her upright. A huge, horned mutant loomed before her, preparing to unleash havoc.

Anderson sucked in a sliver of breath, enough to cry out.

"Bike cannon! Stand by!"

The monstrous guns of the Lawmaster clunked to attention behind her, whirring as they tracked the horned mutant. His snarl vanished into a look of horror. The rest of the crowd backed away, pointlessly; the bike's sensors would have already calculated a pattern of fire that would destroy every one of them before they could reach cover. Anderson staggered to her feet, wheezing, feeling as though there was a cannonball lodged in her belly as she searched the floor for her meds.

She found them, crushed and leaking.

Anderson glowered at the crowd of fearful, hateful faces. An order for the Lawmaster to fire teetered on her lips.

"I could kill every one of you drokkers right now and high-tail it out of here," she said. "Remember that!"

She ordered the bike to stand down, then shouldered her way through the astonished mob.

She unwrapped the bundle of meds on the bench beside the dying girl. The fabric was wet and glittered with shards. Three vials left, minus one to save a girl who was going to die anyway. That left her with two days, and her mission hadn't even begun. Impossible.

Fighting back nausea from the ache in her stomach, Anderson attached the vial to the injector-pistol, praying the thing still worked. She turned the girl's head, straining to see the vein pulsing feebly in her throat. She wondered if this might kill her. Ready, aim, fire, pray.

The girl cried out, her white eyes wide awake as the meds went to work. She convulsed, clutching her heart as though she had just received a shot of adrenalin, then sank back, sucking nourishing draughts of oxygen into her starving body. Anderson had pulled the girl out of the dream before the virus could drain the last of her life-force. Remaining awake for another day would perhaps bolster her will to live, allow her to build up her strength again, to sustain her a while longer when the meds wore off and she succumbed again.

The mother had come running back into the room, flinging her arms around her dazed, bewildered daughter. Anderson saw the girl's blood-red fingers. So she had saved an artist. An artist just like the dreamer, sculpting his madness in the heads of those he infected. Anderson asked Max about the murals, and the mutant told her what they were.

Anderson blinked. "Did you say 'dream paintings'?"

"It's a mutie thing," said Max, frowning. "You wouldn't understand."

"I'm very understanding," said Anderson.

"Well, some of us are like you. They got the gift to see into other worlds, right? Like second sight? And some of 'em believe in a place where dreams exist, all bunched together. Every dream that was ever dreamt. They call it the Nevertime."

The Nevertime. Anderson traced the garden of interlocking rings on the ceiling, and pictured a universe of worlds all crammed together. Psi-Division had verified the existence of at least a dozen dreamworlds, each one occupying its own unique dimension in the psionosphere. Was this 'Nevertime' the plane to which she'd found herself attuned? A dreamworld accessible only to the mutants of the Cursed Earth? But then how could a city-dweller like Anderson be attuned to it as well?

"You've seen those woven mats and those grass dolls they sell as charms in the market towns?" said Max. "Same thing as the murals. Most folks have got something like this. It's a mutie tradition. By sharing our dreams, we're supposed to be changing the world for the better."

"Nice sentiment," said Anderson.

She was already stroking the painted walls, as Max and the other mutants watched her intently.

"This got something to do with the sleeping sickness?" asked Max.

"Show me the last thing the girl painted before she fell asleep."

Max took up a bottle stuffed with luminous fungus and showed her a picture by the doorway.

"That girl ever seen a Judge before?" asked Anderson.

"Anya? Hell, she's never left the caves she was born in."

Anderson ran her fingers around the spiral of colour containing three blue-and-gold monsters surrounding a tiny stick figure, its arms raised in alarm.

The girl had painted a dream that clearly did not belong to her. It might belong to the man Anderson was hunting. She recalled the unfamiliar visions that had infested her own sleep, prior to her first dream of the sandstorm. Maybe other, less lethal dreams bubbled into people's heads as the infection worked its way in.

She returned to Anya's bed and knelt beside her.

"This'll only take a moment, sweetie," she said. Anya's mother twitched, but said nothing as Anderson touched Anya's temples. The room vanished as Anderson darted into the girl's residual memory, searching, sniffing out mnemonic trails like a bloodhound until she found the dream that had inspired the girl's painting. She fixed the memory in place, then dived inside.

She saw a pair of small reptilian hands playing with coloured modelling clay, little three-fingered paws, padded like a gecko's. She was staring through the eyes of a little mutant boy, a boy who would become the man she must kill. The vision trembled with emotion, but the details were crisp. This was a dream forged not of whimsy but of vivid, probably traumatic memory. There was a room beyond the hands, a bedroom, a small Tri-D set in one corner.

The boy was distracted by a break in the cartoons, by a special announcement that construction had commenced on the Statue of Justice, Mega-City One's latest architectural triumph. A wave of star-spangled graphics parted to reveal a revolving holographic blueprint of the statue, its fists planted on its hips as it scanned the Black Atlantic, dwarfing the ancient Statue of Liberty beside it. Anderson remembered the commercial from when she was a kid. The Statue had eventually opened to the public in 2099, the year before last. The mutant boy must now be roughly the same age as her.

She felt a surge of wonder sweep over the boy, an awesome sense of presence, almost godlike in its omniscience, unmistakably paternal. It was a feeling the boy associated with the Judicial infomercials he loved so much, the patriotic cartoons that aired on the kids' channel and assured the little boy that heroes existed, dedicated to his safekeeping, and his mom's.

The feeling abruptly warped into a rush of anguished betrayal as the boy heard voices urgent with aggression in the room next door. One of them spoke his mother's name.

"Miss Najara."

The door burst open and monsters invaded the boy's sanctum. Cold light rippled across their black visors, their huge green boots trampling his modelling clay figures. The eagles on their shoulders bore vicious claws, as if to snatch him from the safety of his room. The brutes rampaged towards him, huge green-gloved hands reaching for him as he screamed, hysterical with terror.

Anderson fought to preserve the vision in her mind's eye, but the scene melted, the walls morphing into windows, passenger seats looking out over a land of dust and wind. The boy was seated beside his mother, who stared with dazed horror through the window of the bus, her silence only heightening her son's dread.

A sign juddered past, the letters beyond comprehension, but the numbers clear: *177X*

The memory of the dream finally wriggled from Anderson's grip and the underground hall rushed back into place. She pushed past Max, gulping back tears, saying she needed air.

She forced her way through the crowd of mutants and out into the courtyard, shoving her way out until she stood beneath the great hole in the ceiling, through which she could see glimmering stars and feel the night breeze.

"Okay, Judge," said Max, joining her. Some of the mutants gathered to listen. "Just what the hell are you onto here?"

Anderson explained everything: the dream-virus, the sleepers, how she could stop it by finding the mutant who was dreaming it. Kill the dreamer, kill the dream.

"I think he's in a mutant camp numbered 177X. That mean anything to you people?"

Murmurs rippled through the crowd, but nobody answered.

"Then maybe some of you can come help me find it?"

"My people won't be seen on the road with no Judge," said Max.

"177X *was a landfill site last I saw, Miss Anderson,*" said Marion, standing inert but conscious, still plugged into the maintenance station outside the garage. "*Reckon it's two, maybe three days, from our past position.*"

"Judge, we appreciate you helping Anya, but don't think we're gonna let you walk out of here with that droid. That fella's worth food and meds enough for a month. We need him if we're gonna survive."

Anderson saw several mutants moving to cover the exits.

"And *I* need him if you people have even a hope of surviving."

Max stepped forward, fixing her with a look. "And what if you do save us, Judge? You gonna keep saving our people? You gonna stop the city from throwing our kind out like garbage? You gonna save us from living like this?"

"Let me out of here with the droid, the bikes and no trouble. Then I'll do what I can. Trust me."

"Trust a Judge?" Someone shouted from among the crowd, a hunched, hooded figure with arms as long as his legs. "It was the Judges threw us out!"

Anderson shouted back, glaring at the mutant crowd. "If you can't trust a Judge, then trust *me.*"

Max looked at her, as if she were asking the impossible. "Trust you? We don't even know who the hell you are."

"I'm Judge Anderson," she said. "I'm the woman who could have killed every single one of you but chose not to. I'm the one who gave a day of my life to save that girl. And if you don't unplug that droid in the next five seconds, I'm the woman who's gonna put my foot up your ass."

The crowd muttered angrily, but Max raised her hand, then nodded to the mechanic attending Marion. Then, without looking at Anderson, Max motioned for her to leave.

Someone tossed a Lawgiver, belt and knife at Anderson's feet and she hurried onto her bike. Marion took the other one.

Anderson called out to the assembled mutants as she swung the bike around.

"If I cure this thing, I'll be back. No Judges, just me. I said I'll do what I can—and I will."

"Enough with the speeches, Judge," said Max. "Just get the drokk out of here."

Anderson turned to Marion. "I got these guys off your back, cowboy. You owe me. So never mind two-to-three days; get me to the guy I'm looking for by *tomorrow*. Do that and I'll get you that new herd, the best in Missourah."

Marion looked back at the crowd of bloodthirsty mutants who had just let them go.

"*There sure is something about you, Miss Anderson,*" he said.

Twenty-Five

ANDERSON'S SPEEDOMETER STILL read a steady 155, yet the dazzling white sea before her never seemed to shrink.

"*Careful, Miss Anderson,*" said Marion through her helmet-comm. His speeding Lawmaster drew level with her own. "*You're veering off again. Set your eyes on the tallest of those crags up ahead, and keep your speed up. There's nothing but dead ground in front of us and a fierce sun behind us. Makes the horizon look nearer than it is.*"

"I feel like I've been riding on the spot for the last hour," she said.

Marion chuckled. "*That it will, Miss Anderson. Just be patient. The mutant camp you're looking for's on the other side of those crags. Figure we should reach it before sundown. Just keep your eyes on that peak and keep riding.*"

Anderson went back to staring at the crags, which seemed to hover off the ground in the shimmering afternoon heat, as though nature was pulling off a magic trick. She had struggled to see beyond the snow-white brilliance of the desert floor, until Marion had showed her how rubbing a stick of charcoal under her eyes helped absorb the vicious glare that penetrated even her photochromic visor.

Sweat streamed down her chest and back and soaked the rag Marion had tied around her neck. She would have guzzled most of her water supply if he hadn't pulled them over to a cactus grove. Hacking off a branch with a Bowie knife the size of a machete, he had carved out a dollop of what looked like brilliant green snot. The stuff tasted like soap and gave her terrific gas, but Marion assured her it would keep her hydrated three times as long as water.

Since leaving Max's cavern-hideout that morning, Marion had led Anderson here, there and everywhere. They were like Cursed Earth rats scurrying through a secret network of roads and passages. She was the compass; Marion the pathfinder, avoiding merchant trails and townships where two Lawmasters would draw unwanted attention. They ducked through hidden valleys that shielded them from the midday sun, down deep ravines that concealed their dust trails from raider camps, through foothills to avoid a sandstorm that Marion could somehow tell was stirring nearby.

The robot's hooded blue eyes glittered like sapphires in the shade beneath his hat as he read the world around them. Like a sailor traversing a perilous sea, he could discern multitudes of information from the tiniest quirks in the wind and weather. He responded to every cue, telling her when to speed up or slow down, when to eat or stop for a pee-break. By midday, they had covered an incredible distance and done so without firing a single shot.

Hours ago the psi-trail had felt like a murmur, but now it was a steady thump. Anderson could feel it tightening, dancing in her belly like a line with a hooked fish wriggling on the other end. She had two days of meds left and—thanks to Marion— she now stood a chance of completing her mission within hours. Why then did she feel such reluctance to take the life of the man named Najara, whose lethal dream threatened the lives of so many? She had killed countless times before. Why was her resolve slipping now?

Anderson realised how much obeying Marion's directions felt like an act of defiance. It was proof that there was a way through this awful world that didn't require Killdozers, a way beyond the bullish tactics of the Justice Department, beyond everything she had been taught, everything she had fought to become and now found herself struggling so hard to believe in.

Her Lawmaster's roar was a monotone, the wind a soothing rush, yet she felt wide awake, wired into her surroundings. The anti-sleep meds were still working their magic. She would need to take another shot before she got the job done.

As the hours passed and the sun lowered, the severed crags gradually fused back into the horizon. Anderson slowed as the ground became rockier and Marion guided her towards a ledge on a cliff overlooking the site known as Mutant Facility 177X.

Dominating the compound was a vast circular pit, tiered like an amphitheatre and half-filled with trash. The pit was surrounded by a wall topped with auto-turret pillars, enclosing a comms array, a water tower and several large sheds where mutants exiled from Mega-City One laboured and slept. Expelled from the relative safety of the city, the mutants, along with any loved ones who chose to accompany them, could continue working for the very society that had rejected them.

Marion had already hunkered down behind a pile of toppled rock, his eyes whirring as he zeroed in on the scene below.

"*Can't see anyone down there, Miss Anderson. Gates are hazard-taped. Trucks and skimmers look like they're all missing, and those turrets look like they're asleep. Place is half-buried in the sand. Looks deserted. You still figure your boy's holed up down there?*"

"No," said Anderson, a dull weight settling in her chest as she removed her helmet. "He's not here."

She paused, reaching out towards the horizon as she focused on the thread emanating from her belly, pulsing like a wound.

"He's moved on, but I think he's close," she said.

"*Okay, then,*" said Marion, rising to his feet, his knees joints squealing. "*Let's get back on the trail.*"

"Wait a second," said Anderson. "This Najara, he and his mom lived down there for a while, probably years. There may be some clue down there as to exactly what we're dealing with. What this dream is. I mean, why it even exists."

Marion glared at her.

"*Who cares why? We find this fella and put in a bullet in him. Or are you forgetting we're on the clock here?*"

"I just need ten minutes. The place is deserted. You said so yourself."

"*Miss Anderson, the city doesn't leave a landfill pit half-filled without good reason. Looks to me like something happened down there, your boy high-tailed it and the place got left to rot.*"

"I just want more information," she said.

"*I think you got all the information you need. It doesn't do to complicate things, Miss Anderson.*"

"But what if I can find a way to cure this thing without having to fire a shot, without anyone having to die?" she said. "What if I can find another way? Isn't that what you've been helping me do all damn day?"

Marion stared again at the compound, his jaw grinding as he pondered.

"*Ten minutes,*" he said, without looking back at her.

"Atta boy," she said, playfully tugging his hat down over his eyes before returning to her Lawmaster. She administered one of her two remaining meds, rubbed away the sting in her neck and wrapped up the remaining vial. Najara couldn't have gotten far. Ten minutes, to search for what could be a crucial advantage. Worth the risk.

Marion had already remounted his Lawmaster.

"Okay, cowboy," said Anderson. "Let's go see where this dreamer did all his dreaming."

"OVER HERE, MISS *Anderson! Room 281.*"

Marion had found 'Najara' among a dozen other surnames stamped on a label outside one of the crate-like outbuildings that served as a dorm for the mutant labourers. As far as both Marion's motion sensors and Anderson's psi-senses could tell, the building was empty. Like everything else around here, it seemed.

Anderson climbed the sand-covered steps towards the open front door. A dozen more doors stood ajar either side of a short corridor also thickly carpeted with sand, lit by the dimming sun through a small window at the far end. Anderson ventured inside, counting off the room numbers until she found 281. She pushed open the door, hot, stale air welcoming her as she entered.

Two single beds with footlockers lay before her, a large woven rug covering the floor between them. The sheets of the first bed lay trampled on the floor. Judging by the closed window and the thick layer of dust on the trampled sheets, the occupant had fled several months ago. Keepsakes on the nightstand had been knocked over in his hurry to leave.

The other bed had not been slept in, its sheets smooth beneath the blanket of grit. A small framed photograph had been placed upon the pillow. Anderson blew the dust off the glass, revealing the image of a gaunt woman in her forties with a troubled smile: Najara's mother.

Anderson replaced the photo on the bed, wondering how the woman's death out here in the Cursed Earth would have affected her son. He had been out here since he was a child; plenty of time for a psychic to become attuned to this mutants-only 'Nevertime' Max had told her about. Had the mother's death provided some kind of catalyst? Had it turned her son's dream toxic, poisoning the Nevertime, like a cancerous cell in an otherwise healthy body?

The boards creaked behind her as Marion ducked under the lintel and entered the room.

"*Looks to me like everybody left this place in a hurry,*" he said. "*Any idea why? Maybe something your boy did?*"

"Maybe," said Anderson, scanning the room.

Marion harrumphed, sounding like pipes straining inside a faulty boiler.

"*Well, do you have any idea why we're still standing here, Miss Anderson?*"

"Gruddamit, just gimme a minute!"

"*You got five more before we're outta here.*"

Anderson went to argue, but the robot growled back at her before she could speak.

"*We had a deal, Miss Anderson. Remember? You get me a herd if I get you where you need to be—and where you need to be ain't here.*"

Anderson was already shoving him out the door.

"*I take it you want me to wait outside?*" he said.

Marion's footsteps thumped away down the corridor as Anderson began searching the room. She found suitcases under each bed and clothes still bundled inside the footlockers. Najara was travelling a tad light for someone hoping to survive in the Cursed Earth.

The comm-stud in her collar buzzed. "*Four minutes, Miss Anderson.*"

She ignored him, bending to empty one of the footlockers. She found a large rusty tin holding clods of modelling clay, along with a thick white stick about the size of a pencil: a scrap of bone, carved into a point. It was a miniature version of the huge spear she had seen Najara twirling in her dream. But this wasn't a spear; it was a sculpting tool.

Najara obviously had some kind of psychic talent. Perhaps this was it. He could channel energy, like an artist transferring an image from their head onto a canvas. Somehow the sandstorm dream he was creating from the life-force of those he infected was his masterpiece, a maelstrom of blinding rage that consumed all it touched. But for what purpose? Would anyone really go to all this trouble just to construct a big toxic snowglobe? Anderson couldn't help but feel there was some kind of plan behind the artistry, an ambition. Something driving that rage, shaping it into something she couldn't yet see.

Artists were people of vision. Writers kept notebooks, artists kept sketchpads, scribbling out their ideas on whatever came to hand. Najara would be the same, but if there was any kind of purpose to the dream, he wouldn't be able to contain it within a few hunks of modelling clay. She tipped the footlocker, searching for notebooks. Nothing.

Notebooks! What was she thinking? Najara's vision was grand, elemental. He would need something bigger, some kind of blueprint he could look upon in its entirety to help bring his vision into focus.

The walls were bare and Marion would be hollering at her any second to leave. Her eyes fell to the floor, to the large mat spread between the two beds. She hauled the mat aside and saw what lay beneath...

Gunfire barked outside.

MARION'S SIX-SHOOTER TWIRLED back into the hatch in his forearm as he strolled towards the headless dog-vulture at the foot of the water tower. Miss Anderson's alarmed voice sounded over the comm-chip in his head.

"*Sorry, Miss Anderson. Just a scavenger come looking for chow. Probably picked up your scent. You gotta nail these critters fast before they start yowling for their pals.*"

"*I've found something,*" she said, voice trembling with excitement. "*I just need another five minutes.*"

"*You got as long as it takes me to walk back,*" he said and switched off the comm before she could start yammering at him.

The great trash pit lay before him, bathed in pixellated crimson, sensor data scrolling down the edges of his vision. He looked up and dismissed his infrared filter, revealing a violet sky, stars already glistening beyond the clouds.

The ancient robot unclipped his hat and wandered a few paces, looking up at those stars. He wasn't triangulating his position, he wasn't calculating wind speed or temperature to gauge what the weather might have in mind. No, he just liked gazing up at that cosmic mess, like a spray of milk on velvet. Mighty pretty.

He recalled a sea of three-horns all hunkered down to sleep beneath a sky much like this one, the air filled with snores and muffled farts, all of them dinos sleeping soundly knowing that ol' Marion had their back.

He always felt an unsettling twinge of reluctance at the end of a drive, like a weight in his insides as he herded his precious charges into the Texas City slaughterblock. The feeling always registered as a glitch in his programming, an imperfection in his code that no software update could ever patch.

A warning struck his brain and infrared swished back across his vision, his pistol already in his hand, aimed at a siphon station, pipes feeding down into the depths of the trash pit. Something about the size of a man had just skittered out of sight behind a cage full of yellow barrels. Another dog-vulture for sure.

Marion replaced his hat and ambled over to take care of it.

ANDERSON KNELT UPON the huge graph Najara had carved into the floor. It looked like the inside of an old-fashioned pocket watch, a universe of cogs and gears connected by what looked like cables, every interlocking line meticulously scored into the plaswood floor. She imagined the years it must have taken him to create this, and the mounting anger that drove him. But what did this blueprint, so precise in its detail, have to do with the wild sandstorm of the dream-virus?

She tucked her gloves into her belt and tried to clear more of the sand away, snaps of residual psi-energy leaping from the grooves in the floor, nipping her fingers. She felt the psi-trail flinch inside her with every minute discharge, prickling her senses until she was dizzy. Marion would drag her out of here any minute. She didn't have time to ponder the meaning of the arcane symbol—she had to connect with it right away.

She retrieved the sculpting tool from the box of clay. The sharpened bone felt slippery, its psionic field reactivated until it pulsed between her fingers. This was the tool with which Najara had carved his vision, the conduit through which his ideas had flowed, channelling energy from the world inside his head and into the real.

She held the bone above the grooves of the carving, like the needle on a record player. She could feel the bone willing itself to reconnect with the carving and whatever meaning lay behind it, the bond forceful enough to override the effects of her medication. The hair on her arms and the back of her neck turned to pins in her flesh.

She was about to reconnect with the dream that infected her; as long as she remained there, it would drain her. Was this worth the risk? There were infected citizens slowing dying back in the Meg, along with who knew how many comatose mutants out there in the Cursed Earth, all of them slowly dying in the viral dream she was about to enter.

But it would only take a moment to find out what Najara wanted, to discover the purpose of the dream-virus. Maybe then she could find a way of ending this mission without murder. Maybe she could show the Department there was another way.

And maybe there was more to it than that. Maybe the reason she was so reluctant to kill the man she sought was because they shared some kind of bond. What had enabled her to enter the mutants-only world of the Nevertime? Was there some flaw in her psyche that had opened her up to infection?

It would only take a peek into the dream in order to find out. What was it Brackett had called her? 'The most powerful psychic in Psi-Division.'

Anderson took a breath and channelled her consciousness through the bone between her fingers as she scraped its tip down a groove in the carving. Her stomach flipped, streaking lights blinding her, a tidal roar filling her ears as she plunged into another world.

Twenty-Six

MARION CURSED AS he attempted to stalk the dog-vulture behind the siphon console, his parched joints squeaking like rusty bedsprings and announcing his advance with every step. But the sound didn't seem to disturb his prey. He could still hear a wet lapping sound from behind the wall of cages near the console. His atmospheric sensors detected a cocktail of airborne chemicals. The yellow barrels in those cages must be leaking whatever gunk had once been pumped from the bottom of the trash pit.

He neared the console, six-shooter at the ready, and kicked the nearest cage, hoping to spook the critter out into the open where he could nail it more easily. The lapping sound stopped. The cage trembled.

Irritated, Marion grabbed the cage with one hand and hauled it aside, revealing an oily black puddle and nothing more. The barrels rocked on their pallets beside him, his confounded sensors alerting him a fraction too late.

Something clung to the cage beside him, something pale and naked that spat in his face, blinding him.

Marion fired twice at the spot where the thing had been

hanging, but it had already leaped onto his chest, knocking him back towards the edge of the trash pit. His six-shooter wheeled back into his forearm as he tried to grab the thing now scrambling onto his shoulders, feeling it stabbing at his armoured chest like it was trying to drive twin stakes through his heart.

He caught hold of a thick bony leg as one of those stakes found the join above his breastplate and plunged deep, prising open the lip of his armour. Warning glyphs flashed across his blackened vision as acid rinsed his insides. Still blinded, he flung the thing aside with a grunt, smashing it dead against one of the cages, its leg coming away in his hand.

Marion tore away whatever gunk the thing had barfed in his face, and looked up in time to see a cascade of yellow barrels bouncing towards him from the cage he had just smashed open. The cylinders knocked him from his feet, carried him several metres, then flung him over the ledge of the trash pit and out into space.

His vision fizzed as the huge, stepped ledges of the pit sailed past him through the gloom, before he crashed waist-deep into the lake of trash. Tumbling barrels rained about him, bursting open in showers of toxic sludge.

Half-blinded by blasts of static, Marion struggled to free himself from the mire of rusted machine parts and broken furniture, fighting his own immense weight, which threatened to drag him deeper into the debris.

He hailed Miss Anderson several times, but she wasn't answering. What the hell was she *doing*? Was she deaf? Had something gotten to her? A fierce protective urge overwhelmed him, perhaps another glitch in his haggard programming.

He hauled himself onto a busted refrigerator, clinging to it like a life-raft as he tried to gauge the distance towards the nearest ledge. His vision swarmed with data as his internal systems assessed damage, survival protocols kicking in and re-routing power as best they could.

The trash ended a good distance below the next ledge, and Marion couldn't tell whether he would be able to reach it and climb up. Several of his sensors had shut down, and he felt dizzy.

As the garbage creaked beneath his shifting weight, Marion could hear the sludge from the ruined barrels leaking down through the sediment. Then he heard something else.

At first he thought his ravaged sensors were playing tricks on him, but the sound was rising, a rattling, scuttling, scampering sound approaching from deep below like a shoal of piranha rushing to devour him.

He made a run for the wall and immediately plunged into a bog of broken toys, shattered crockery and soiled nappies. The scuttling intensified beneath the robot's clambering feet as he tried to crawl free. He flailed for a moment, dislodging a mattress beside him, unleashing a landslide of trash on top of him, blocking out the night sky.

Marion managed to scoop some of the heavier debris beneath him, giving him purchase enough to crawl to the surface. His hand slipped in a patch of filth and a brown skull rolled into view, along with a litter of bones entangled in shreds of orange cloth that had once been overalls. One of the mutant labourers.

Something caught hold of Marion's foot and he fell onto his back, hauling his leg into view along with the horror that clung to it with long spidery legs. Its head was an eyeless wad of wrinkles that peeled open and ejaculated a thick rope of some sticky fibre; Marion had just enough wits left in his system to dodge it. Lightning-fast, the thing scrabbled onto his chest, a pair of enormous black fangs springing from among the folds of its head. Marion seized the ebony hooks before they could plunge into his already-smoking throat. He could feel the power behind them, strong enough to prise open his armour as surely as a couple of crowbars. Still gripping its fangs, Marion ripped the gruddamn thing in half like he was making a wish.

He cast both halves of the body aside as more of them

wriggled to the surface of the trash lake, pale, bony-legged bodies sprouting from the wreckage like sinister vegetation. Critters were plenty sensitive to the strange currents that circulated the Cursed Earth; maybe the vibes this Najara kid had been throwing around had attracted this grotesque swarm from whatever radioactive burrow had spawned them. They must have overrun the compound, the City abandoning the place until an extermination crew could be scheduled.

Marion summoned his six-shooters into his hands as he hurried on, clambering over the wreckage as fast as he could. He hoped he could still shoot straight; his gyros were fried to hell and back. The wall of the pit rose around him, but the swarm would be on him by the time he reached it. Miss Anderson needed to get the hell outta here. He hailed her again.

Nothing.

Gruddamit! What the *hell* was she doing?

ANDERSON HURTLED LIKE a comet through the Nevertime, an undulating mosaic of multi-coloured stars spiralling like footprints into worlds of dream and story, each fiction bound within a planetary bubble of swirling patterns and orbiting countless more.

The energy of the place was like nothing Anderson had ever felt before. It sounded like a chaos of ceaseless thunder, earthquakes, crashing waves; but a strange music played amid its currents, vanishing the moment she paused to listen.

She rode the rippling waves of psychic energy towards one dream, feeling her astral form burn with friction as she skated a razor's edge towards her destination. One less gifted in psychic ability would likely have succumbed to awe at the immensity of their surroundings, lost their focus and been dashed into oblivion. But the genius of Cassandra Anderson was a peculiar combination of tenacity and levity that enabled her to traverse the kaleidoscopic ether with the grace of a dancer.

She could feel the spike of bone far away, gripped between the fingers of her meditating body. While channelling herself through the thin conduit, she maintained a thread of consciousness between her body and her spirit-self, a rip-cord that would enable her to let go of the bone at any time, breaking the spell, freeing her from the grip of the infectious dream towards which she was now hurtling in search of answers.

The dazzling spheres before her parted, revealing a noxious black world lurking behind them, its surface coiling with a rainbow sheen, like oil oozing on water. As she entered the dreadful orbit of Najara's dream, its toxicity stung her ethereal flesh. She could feel the Nevertime straining against this awful place, isolating it lest its infection spread.

Anderson felt for the dream's epicentre, the spark that had inspired it, the portal through which this bubble world had expanded into existence. She wriggled through the gateway, feeling a fleeting resistance as she pierced the skin of Najara's noxious dream.

She felt her life-force rise within her, preparing to leak out the moment she opened her mouth to breathe. The wind and sand lashed her hair as she stood atop of a high shelf of rock, though the sandstorm had subsided since she had last visited this place. The maelstrom had coalesced, the swirling grains of stolen life become the terrible vista that now lay before her.

The shattered city blocks of Mega-City One stood silent and still beneath a familiar amber haze. The network of skywalks and overzooms lay broken, scoured of life and traffic. Rivers of ochre sand flooded the streets below, kilometre-high slopes that half-swallowed the deserted buildings. Infected dreamers wandered the derelict metropolis like zombies, trailing plumes of life-force that swirled in sparkling eddies above them and adhered to the surrounding ruins, gradually building the broken world that towered above them.

Constructed from the blueprint Najara had carved on the floor of his room, this was a vision of vengeance, the oblivion of the Cursed Earth visited back upon the city. No wonder the contagion had spread so quickly among the exiled mutant population; their feelings of outrage would have provided a fertile breeding ground.

Anderson let out a long glittering breath, feeling herself weaken as she did so.

There was a terrible clarity about this place. She didn't feel as though she were standing in a dream at all, but another reality, a reality that had been shaped with the utmost reverence. The Mega-City One that Anderson knew was a tempest of colour and noise and screaming thoughts, a cacophony of life in all its ugliness and contradiction. This place was as tranquil as a painting, every detail arranged to capture light and contrast. It was as though a skilled mortician had prepared the dead city for its funeral.

She found herself thinking that Mega-City One had never looked so beautiful, and the thought stirred something shameful within her.

Behind her, miles away across an expanse of crumbling harbour, stood the corroded husk of the Statue of Justice. This was the portal through which she had entered, the seed that had inspired this dream. Najara had seen the icon of justice as a boy, had fallen in love with its heroic ideal; and had been betrayed by it, the day the Judges stormed into his refuge and cast him and his mother out of their home. The statue gazed out into the grey mist of the Black Atlantic, a miasma of nothing that marked the boundary of Najara's creation.

Anderson despaired. Was the dream nothing more than a poisonous monument to injustice? Its energy felt too solid, too forceful to be a mere ornament. There was something that drove it. She could feel it straining at the ethereal bonds of the Nevertime, raring to exist.

Najara's rage, focused by his psychic ability, had turned this dream cancerous, made it go viral. But what was his endgame? The infected dreamers were still bequeathing their life-force to create the place, their labours nearing completion. But what happened when all that accumulated energy achieved critical mass? What happened when Najara's masterpiece was complete, when it achieved a weight of reality too great for the Nevertime to hold?

Max had told her that the mutants of the Cursed Earth shared their dreams in the hope of changing the world for the better.

Change the world.

Some dimensions can generate power enough to warp reality, Brackett had said.

The realisation struck her like a bullet, sending an involuntary shudder through the line connecting her to her sleeping form, causing her to drop the bone in her hand, breaking her connection to the dream.

Anderson felt herself stretching like a length of elastic as she was torn from the Nevertime and fired back into her waiting body.

She awoke sprawled on the now-darkened floor of Najara's room, shivering, sweating, drooling. She barely had strength enough to raise herself, coughing in the dusty air, still grasping the magnitude of Najara's goal.

He was going to obliterate Mega-City One. Once he had finished assembling his apocalyptic vision from the stolen life-force of those his dream had infected, that dream would materialise in the waking world. The living city would be replaced with the dead, one reality eclipsing the other. No compromise.

There was no way of warning the Department from here. No way forward except to kill Najara, to save not only herself and everyone infected by his dream, but also everyone in the city. She was a fool for trying to find a peaceful solution. Brackett was right; she was an arrogant daredevil gambling with the lives of others for the sake of a ridiculous ideal. She had gone in search of a reason not to kill Najara, but found only more reason to do so. Her judgements were clearly flawed beyond reprieve.

Anderson made to stand and nausea overwhelmed her, her knees giving way, spilling her back onto the floor. She had left the dream too quickly; now her psionic field was struggling to achieve equilibrium in the waking world, the stimulants in her system overwhelmed. Her eyelids drooped as strength melted from her muscles, ushering her towards the sleep her body had been denied for days. She needed to stabilise herself or she would fall asleep, slip back into Najara's dream and spend the rest of her dwindling life contributing to the dream that would eventually destroy her city.

A single vial of anti-sleep meds remained in her Lawmaster's storage pod.

Anderson groaned. She had taken her last dose less than an hour ago. Now she needed to take her last one just to dig herself out of the hole she had thrown herself into.

You've screwed up big-time, Cass. Even for you, this is bad. If you do make it out of this, how do you expect to survive another day in this job?

She hauled herself upright, crashing into the wall of the corridor as she stumbled from the room, and stood swaying.

A jet of grey paste flew past her face and struck the wall behind her. The strange cord stiffened, and she turned to see what looked like a spider the size of a man launching itself towards her, its thick legs spanning the corridor as it went to grab her.

Anderson threw herself back inside Najara's room, her head striking one of the footlockers as the creature bounced off the wall and onto the floor. Its gristly legs scrabbled crazily as it righted itself, while Anderson, still on her back, kicked the door shut, her booted feet holding it in place as the thing clawed at the other side.

She wondered whether she might be hallucinating, whether

some facet of her awareness still lingered in the Nevertime, when a pair of black spikes burst through the door by her feet. The huge fangs split the brittle plaswood as they slid forward, their points almost crossing. A sickly ichor wept from the tips, hissing where it struck Anderson's boot.

She heard a stampede of claws rattling in the corridor outside, shaking the walls, as she drew her Lawgiver. The door quaked beneath her feet as she steadied her pistol with both hands and fired two holes into the space between the black hooks. The dripping fangs withdrew, leaving gashes in the door. Upending the heavy footlocker, Anderson jammed it against the door, which shook as more of the creatures piled against it.

Her comm-stud bleeped as something ran across the roof of the cabin, the ceiling flexing under the creature's weight.

"Marion? Where are you?"

"*Miss Anderson, listen to me,*" he said. "*Cross the river and head straight west across the plains.*"

Anderson roared down the comm. "I said, where *are* you?"

"*Keep your speed up, and after a night's ride you'll see a bunch of high rocks. If I was a runaway mutant looking for shelter that's where I'd head. Now go.*"

"But—"

"*It doesn't do to complicate things, Miss Anderson,*" said Marion. "*Not when you got a job to do.*"

Marion signed off.

The walls trembled and the door cracked in its frame. A spindly shadow crossed the room as another of the creatures smashed the window behind her. Another pair of enormous black fangs tugged at the grille covering the window as she hauled the mattress from the nearest bed and crouched behind it like a riot shield. She stifled her ears as best she could as she aimed her Lawgiver at the wall beside the window.

"Hi-Ex!"

The blast shook the room, releasing a deluge of debris that

battered the mattress as Anderson hunkered behind it. Flinging the makeshift shield aside, she charged, half-blind, through the hole in the cabin wall. She stumbled into the cool air of the alley outside as Najara's room collapsed behind her.

She pelted down the narrow alleyway between the dorms and out into the compound, adrenalin and the night air refreshing her as a seething clatter of bony legs accumulated behind her. As she ran, she could see her Lawmaster parked nearby and heard booming pistol-shots coming from deep within the pit, illuminating the tiers beneath the rim. Marion.

She went to yell a command at her bike, hoping to activate its cannon, when something caught her shoulder and yanked her to the ground.

Anderson rolled as she fell, raising her Lawgiver and blasting the thing that had tried to tether her with its rope of gunk. She tore it apart in mid-air as it leaped, muzzle flashes revealing the flood of bodies racing across the ground towards her. She fired into the oncoming swarm as she got to her feet, but they continued their advance, swift and implacable, lacing the air with jets of webbing as she ran for the bike. There were too many of them, even for the targeting system of a Lawmaster.

She cried Marion's name across the compound. There were yet more thunderous gunshots, but a rescue attempt against such odds would be suicide, especially weighed against the demands of her mission.

The clatter of scurrying legs grew nearer as she screamed at the Lawmaster to activate and vaulted into the saddle, stowing her gun as the bike's engines growled awake. She wrenched the throttle and a jet of webbing slapped the eagle on her shoulder, tightening, threatening to drag her from the saddle. She pinched the release on her shoulder pads as she pulled away, feeling the heavy mantle slip from her shoulders as she accelerated, casting a cloud of dust over her pursuers as the bike boomed out of the gates of the compound.

A shallow river ran along the western wall. She sliced across it, climbed the rocky bank on the opposite side and flew away across the desert beneath an expanse of stars, the world before her reduced to a cone of light radiating from her headlamps. The adrenalin was subsiding, the shock of returning too quickly from the Nevertime was finally kicking in.

She switched the bike to auto as she rummaged with shaking hands in the storage pod beside her for her meds. Once she'd spent the remaining vial, she cast the jet-injector into the wind, feeling her senses brighten and a rush of focus clear her head. She set her nav-com due west before retaking the controls, intent on the earth just ahead of her, the psi-trail taut as ever in her belly.

She promised herself she would reach Najara by morning and she would kill him. Marion was right: no more risks, no more looking for excuses. No more faith in her own recklessness, not now the existence of an entire city was at stake. Thoughts of Marion, of his trust in her, of abandoning him to be destroyed by a mob of Cursed Earth horrors: they would lead only to madness. She could no longer afford to be the woman she had once been, not if she wished to serve the city as a Judge.

She gazed into the darkness, absorbed by its depth, promising herself that come morning there would be no compromise.

Twenty-Seven

THE HATCH IN Marion's forearm slid open and a speed-loader clamped his last round of bullets into the open cylinder of his smoking six-shooter. The robot fired before the loader was done retreating back into his arm, vanquishing another six targets, winning him the seconds he needed to haul his battered bulk the rest of the way onto the ledge.

The damn things were like angry termites, endlessly bubbling up through the trash lake, ceaseless reinforcements summoned from whatever tunnels they'd burrowed into the walls of the pit. He raised the rusted car door he'd retrieved from the trash for a shield, fending off the creatures' webbing. Exchanging his empty six-shooter for his knife, he slashed the ropes still stuck to his shield and the wall behind him, cutting the creatures loose as they went to reel themselves towards him.

It had been at least ten minutes since he heard Miss Anderson's engine rumble into the distance. Smart woman. He swung his makeshift shield at one of the creatures as it leapt at him, batting it halfway across the trash-lake. Another bared its fangs at him over the rim of the car door and he buried his knife in its blind, wrinkled head.

Marion glanced up at the half-dozen shelves of stone carved above him, along which dumpsters had once travelled on their way to tip bellyfuls of garbage into the abyss below. They were too high to climb, but Marion made out a wide ramp leading back up to the compound. Trouble was, it was all the way on the other side of the pit. Ignoring what his survival protocols calculated were his chances of escape, Marion began staggering towards it.

Something caught him and stabbed the side of his chest. He grabbed the creature and threw it away with such force that its fangs broke off in his body. He slowed, feeling the creature's acidic venom chewing into his already tortured servos. He shuddered as his primary battery cut out and he switched to auxiliary power. His right leg was almost numb as he limped along the impossible road before him.

A wrinkled head appeared over the ledge, opening its maw to snare him with a length of webbing as he crushed it under a metal boot and staggered on, slashing at anything else that came near him. His insides steamed, then smoked, his joints squealing as he slowed.

He felt another twitch in his code, a glimmer of regret at the thought of never finding another herd. Then again, maybe there were things in the Cursed Earth more deserving of his service than a crowd of doomed dinosaurs. Maybe there was another way to do what needed doing in this world. Not that it mattered now. He dashed another creature against the wall with his shield, slashed the legs from several more. Cords of webbing entangled his limbs, slowing him even more. He looked up at the majesty of stars above him and thought what a thing it would be to shut down under a sky like that.

Something flashed overhead with a snarl, landing like a pouncing lion before him, crushing several of the creatures to a smear beneath its wheels as it skidded to a halt, its cannon bellowing into the night. The woman behind the guns roared like a Valkyrie, guiding their fury, a turmoil of muzzle-flashes and spinning cartridge cases that filled the air with shreds of flesh and spurts of ichor. The cannon finally stilled, thick coils of smoke veiling Anderson's face as she looked up at him. Gruddamit if she wasn't grinning at him, a huge dimpled smile lighting up her face as if she couldn't help laughing at her own craziness.

"We're outta here, cowboy!"

"Miss Anderson, are you outta your gruddamn mind?"

"Get on! Now!"

Marion found himself doing as he was told, grumbling as he climbed aboard the Lawmaster behind her. The bike shuddered as the cannon opened fire again, popping the creatures one after another as they clambered over the ledge towards them. In all the excitement, she appeared to have lost her big yellow shoulder pads, making her look even smaller in just her dusty blue jumpsuit, even more like some crazy woman who thought it was a good idea to rescue a robot when so many real lives were at stake. The cannon ceased fire and Miss Anderson twisted the throttle, the rear wheel shrieking under his weight as they took off down the road, heading towards the slope that would lead them back to the surface.

Marion's head buzzed like flies on a carcass as his operating system assessed his internal damage. The acid appeared to have run its course, doing all the harm it was going to do, which was more than enough. In short, he was cooked. Even if he'd had any bullets left, he doubted he could have planted them now his targeting system was offline. He would have leapt off the bike and dived back into the trash pit to hasten Miss Anderson's escape, but he couldn't guarantee the lunatic wouldn't dive in after him again.

They made it onto the ramp, a smooth, steep slope lined up ahead of them ready to carry them all the way up to freedom. But

Marion could see a curtain of bodies scurrying in the darkness directly above them, streaming over the lip of the trash-pit and descending over the ridges towards them like a waterfall. They must have followed Miss Anderson down here, probably the same mob that chased her out of the dorm.

The bike cannons folded away as Miss Anderson fired the accelerator, the bike's engines fighting to gather momentum under his weight. They had almost cleared the deluge of bodies when one of them flung out a strand of webbing that caught the handlebars, jerking them to one side and threatening to pitch the bike into the wall as the creature yanked itself aboard. Miss Anderson wrestled with the steering, managing to maintain course as the thing landed on the handlebars in a jumble of thrashing legs and quivering pink flesh.

The impact knocked the Lawmaster off the ramp and onto one of the ledges that branched off of it. All three of them would have continued over the ledge and out into space if Miss Anderson had been any less fearless in battling to keep them on course. The creature wheeled around on the handlebars, the bike's headlamp array glowing red beneath its bulbous, veined abdomen, obscuring their descent back towards the trash-pit.

Marion went to lean forward and grab the thing, but Miss Anderson beat him to it. She grabbed fistfuls of its wrinkled flesh before the creature could brandish its fangs and slammed its head down across the handlebars, pinning it there as she jabbed its brains out with her boot-knife and shoved its remains over the front. Marion hopped in his seat as the Lawmaster turned the creature's body to mulch beneath its wheels.

Miss Anderson pulled the bike into a tight U-turn, its wheels grinding into the rock beneath them as the headlamps swept across the trash pit below. She braked, facing the horde of creatures now swarming over their escape route. Fresh monsters seethed up towards them from the ridges below.

She drew that spindly little iron the Judges called a 'Lawgiver' and took aim up at the water purification tower that stood over the pit, near where he had been damn fool enough to fall in. He comprehended her plan: if she could release the tons of stagnant water inside, it might wash most of the creatures off the slope. The two of them would be far enough away from the worst of the deluge, but this also meant the tower was too far for Miss Anderson to make the shot. The creatures would reach them in less than a minute.

Miss Anderson's hands shook as she cried "Hi-Ex!" and fired.

Hopeless. The shot sailed wide, dropping down over the rim of the pit and lighting up the sky with a distant explosion. Undaunted, hands still shaking, Miss Anderson took aim again, as death seethed towards them.

Marion cradled her hands, guiding her aim, his vision jittering with static as he re-routed all the juice he had left into rebooting his targeting systems. The swarm's innumerable legs hissed like rain upon the rock, rising to a crescendo as they neared the Lawmaster. Marion felt Miss Anderson's arms relax, her shakes subsiding as he helped guide her where she needed to be, his sensors calculating air temp, wind speed and the estimated propulsion of whatever explosive round it was these pea-shooters carried. She seemed to sense the correct course a split second before him, her finger putting that last ounce of pressure into the trigger just as his crosshairs shimmered over the target.

The Lawgiver boomed, jerking in her hands as the incendiary round hurtled into space. It landed like a miracle, blowing the tower's legs out from under it with an explosion that floodlit the swarming creatures, their legs scurrying, furrowed eyeless heads intent on their prey. The tower tipped high above them, disembowelled, and a deluge of water burst from its insides and poured into the pit, plunging over the ridges, forming rivers, obliterating everything in its path.

They ducked, Marion's weight helping anchor the bike as a wave of putrid water and drowned bodies engulfed them.

Miss Anderson hit the accelerator the second the tide subsided, launching them forward, skidding on wet rock and juddering, crunching over a carpet of twitching bodies. They found the slope just as the last of the flood surged into the trash-pit below.

Miss Anderson headed upwards, picking up speed, the brim of Marion's hat fluttering around his head like a victory flag. They reached the top of the ramp with a speed that carried the bike a foot off the ground as it leapt back into the compound. In seconds, they were through the gates. Marion took in the stars one more time, feeling himself deflate as he slumped almost on top of Miss Anderson, her filthy blonde hair fluttering like prairie grass before his eyes as they fled into the night.

MARION AWOKE ON his back looking up into a storm-grey sky, the sun struggling to break through a wall of cloud low to the east. Rising above him, appearing to float above a bank of heavenly white mist, was an immense crown of grey stone, towering columns of volcanic rock jewelled with vivid greenery.

Well, hell, if Miss Anderson hadn't made it to Weir's Rock just like he directed.

He stirred, feeling a welcome current surging through his injured frame, energising what few circuits remained undamaged. His operating system was waiting for him to regenerate enough energy to enable a reboot, and once that was done—though he was loath to admit it—he'd need a good mechanic with a bucket of spare parts. A cable snaked out from the port beneath his right arm, plugging him into Miss Anderson's Lawmaster, which stood guard among rocks nearby, cannons on full display.

He started at the sound of someone clapping a fresh clip into a pistol and rose to see Miss Anderson stumbling into the mist, holstering her iron as she clambered over the rocks towards a path winding up into the misty foothills. The storage pods of her Lawmaster were open, contents scattered about the ground nearby, perhaps as she had searched for a suitable power cord. It looked as though she had taken nothing but her gun and a flask of water. Then he noticed something gleaming among her strewn supplies. Intrigued, he crawled towards it and picked it up, calling after Miss Anderson as she went to disappear from sight.

She turned, startled as a deer, the morning light revealing deep shadows that haunted her eyes and tightened her cheekbones. Standing there amid the fog, she looked like a tortured phantom who had forgotten its way back to hell.

"*You forgot something,*" he said.

He held out a small silver cylinder with a switch at one end, the homing beacon her people had given her to summon air support once she had confirmed the location of her target. She had shown him how it worked during one of their pit-stops. The thing hadn't been switched on. Had she forgot?

She stared back at him for a moment, her face betraying a glimmer of fear. From the way her hollowed features twitched, he guessed she was figuring something out.

"I... I didn't think you'd be awake," she said. "Give that here. I don't have much time. I got a day of rock climbing ahead of me, and no meds left to wake me up when I reach the top."

She was stumbling back towards him, her hand outstretched.

"Give it here," she said, her voice sharp, with an eagerness that disturbed Marion.

"*You go on,*" he said, raising a hand to calm her. "*I'll activate it for you.*"

"I said give it here, dammit!" The shadows on her face darkened.

Marion examined the beacon for a moment, then popped the cover off the switch and placed his thumb over the activation button.

Miss Anderson's face lit up with horror and she ran towards him, tripped over something hidden by the crawling fog and sprawled on the ground before him. She glared up at him through a mask of dirt to see his thumb still hovering above the switch that would summon her ride back to the city.

"*So what's the plan, Miss Anderson?*"

"The plan is I kill the guy I can sense hiding at the top of that mountain," she said, rising to her knees. "I cure everyone he's infected, including myself."

"*Then what?*" said Marion, unconvinced.

Her eyes wandered, her whole body seeming to deflate in surrender.

"Then I don't go back to the city," she said. "I'm not a Judge."

Marion lowered the beacon, his internal power bar nudging past eighteen percent as his maintenance system geared up to shut him down and reboot.

"I risked the lives of millions to save you," she said, still gazing into the surrounding mist, retreading a debate she must have had many times on the ride over. "I couldn't help myself. All to save a…"

"*A partner?*" he said.

"A walking toaster," she said, looking back at him. "That's what you are, in the scheme of things."

"*Agreed,*" said Marion.

"And that's the problem. I can't see the scheme of things. I just can't. I can't think like a Judge. What kind of Judge can't stop herself from making a gamble like I made in going back to save you?"

"*Well, I reckon it feels a lot less like a gamble when you're as good as you are at what you do, Miss Anderson. When you're used to pulling off the impossible.*"

"I wouldn't have to try and pull off the impossible if the system wasn't the way it was. Don't you see? That's what my first year on the street has taught me: that I can't live with doing what a Judge has to do. I can't be part of a system that makes things the way they are."

"*I'm guessing folk don't become Judges overnight, Miss*

Anderson. You must have had a heck of years to realise you weren't the woman for the job."

She got to her feet, furious.

"You think I'm just whining about my lot in life, asshole? I'm good with what I am, with what I can do. No, this is me making a choice!"

She pointed at the beacon. "Now you hand that over, mister."

Marion looked up at her from his seat on the ground, still clutching the beacon.

"And then what?" he said. *"You think staying in the Cursed Earth's gonna change things? How long do you figure on surviving out here?"*

"I'm a fast learner," she said. "And there are people out here who could use my help, maybe *our* help. You saw how Max and her people have to live; and they had it better than most out here. I can help them, and I can do it my way."

"Maybe so, Miss Anderson. A woman like you, with sand, a good gun arm, and a notion of what's right and wrong. But if you go back to the city, as good as you are, being who you are, you'll set an example folk will notice, folk just as strong as you who want to make a difference. By doing what you do, you could help change a lot of badness the city creates out here."

She gave a tight smile.

"You don't know the city, cowboy," she said. "The Justice system—it's like a machine, it just follows the programme, right or wrong, everything in between just gets destroyed. No compromise. How can I change that?"

"We had a deal, right?" he said, cutting in. *"You help me out against those scavengers and I get you where you need to go."*

He activated the beacon and flung it into the fog.

Miss Anderson watched it disappear, incredulous, then stared at him with a look of honest-to-goodness hellfire.

"Figure you got about four hours before air support arrives to take you home, which is about the same time as it'll take you

to reach the top of that rock and do your job. And keep out of the tall grass as much as you can. There's rad-rattlers around this time of day."

For a moment, he thought she might just shoot him. Instead she booted him onto his back, grabbed his torn armour and shook him as best she could.

"That was *my* decision," she screamed in his face. "*Mine!* Why did you do that? Why?"

Her words crumbled into sobs and she let him go.

Marion felt a twitch in his system as it prepared him for shutdown, his power bar now at twenty percent.

"You think you've saved me?" she said, bitterly.

Marion's vision flickered, then went black.

"You and everyone in that city who's gonna need you some day, Miss Anderson."

Calculating...

Code corruption 100111010100

Reboot compromised...

Eighty-three percent chance of permanent corruption...

Reboot initiated...

Please wait...

CRICKETS SIZZLED AMID tufts of dead grass as Anderson clambered up the grey stones. The rich powdery earth of the tree-shaded foothills had given way to vast sheets of naked rock baking beneath the afternoon sun. The psi-trail felt like a rope of fire inside her, a blaze that overwhelmed every other sensation, her shaking legs, the torture of her blistered feet, the thwarted rage at the thought of the ship that would soon arrive to take her back to the city. She felt as though she were no longer following the psychic trail that led to Najara; rather, *he* was pulling her towards him, reeling her in as she hurried to keep up. She stumbled on between shoulders of stone that loomed above her like city blocks, frozen columns of volcanic magma squeezed out of the earth by the seismic violence of the Atomic Wars.

She lost her footing and slipped, cutting her bare hand on a seam of rock. Her heart throbbed and she felt sick. She dimly understood that her body was crashing, and without another shot she was slipping towards a sleep in which the dream-virus would finally consume her. She thought she could hear the rustle of a desert wind, and see distant figures wandering among the rocks behind her, exhaling glimmering smoke.

She hurried on, the psi-trail tugging her down a narrow rift, high walls of lichen-stained stone reaching into a rail of sky overhead. She drew her Lawgiver as she moved along the passage, feeling the heat in her belly spread to engulf her entire body as she neared her final destination.

She peered out onto a wide ledge overlooking the plains and mountains of the Cursed Earth, her attention riveted to a cave at the foot of a pillar of rock. A tide of psychic energy drew her towards it, like a drain.

Anderson allowed herself a simple shudder of fear before sidling towards the mouth of the cave as steadily as she could, clasping her Lawgiver with both hands as she scanned the entrance for any booby traps Najara may have laid to protect himself as he slept.

She saw him straight away, lying just inside the cave.

Her shots rang savagely around the confines of the cavern, five standard execution rounds in the back of the filthy orange jumpsuit he had been wearing when he escaped the landfill site. She hurried forward, still aiming her gun at the body as she rolled it onto its back.

Najara's reptilian skull gaped up at Anderson as if in awe, ants going about their business on scaled skin dried to a husk by weeks of desert heat.

A chill overwhelmed her and she fell to her knees, grabbing the long-dead corpse as if to demand answers from it. Why could she still feel the psi-trail? How could she still be connected to Najara if he was dead?

She could feel the eddies of psychic energy swirling about the cave like trapped smoke, churning around her insides. Najara was still here, not in body but in spirit. This channeller of energy had channelled his *own* life-force into the viral dream, become a permanent part of it. Perhaps he hoped to be reborn when his apocalyptic vision finally emerged in the physical world.

Kill the dreamer, kill the dream. But how *could* she, when the dreamer was already dead?

Anderson noticed something else lying beside Najara's remains.

Her own sleeping body, the Lawgiver still smoking in her hand.

Twenty-Eight

"CASSANDRA?" SAID A concerned voice. "You're back."

What appeared to be a giant lizard wearing baggy shorts and a *Pug Ugly and the Buggleys* T-shirt crouched beside Anderson. The cave had at some point become a city street flooded with sand, drifts and dunes climbing the walls of a derelict city block beside her. The sandstorm had abated; nothing more than a gentle breeze now stirred the air.

The creature gazed down at Anderson with eyes like huge marbles, rippled blue and green, divided by slitted pupils. Only when Anderson saw the bone spear it held cradled in its lap did she realise who she was staring at.

"Najara?" A plume of glittering steam clouded the air as she spoke, exhausting her.

"Of course," Najara chirped, cocking his head thoughtfully before grabbing his spear and twirling it wildly as he sprang to his feet with delight. "Of course you know my name! You're a psychic, like me. We must know everything about each other, right? Oh, man. It's so good to see you again. We met before, remember? Back when all this was just a sandstorm? Huh?

Remember? You took my hand? Back when you first joined the dream?"

Anderson struggled to summon energy enough to answer. She felt weary just watching the reptilian mutant scurrying about her, spinning that long whooping bone around like a cheerleader's baton, more energy within him than he knew how to spend, a dizzying contrast to the desiccated corpse he had left in the cave. It was Najara's spirit, his very soul, which capered around her, his sentient life-force manifested within the dream he had created, and it was dancing with joy at the sight of her having woken here only to die.

Kill the dreamer, kill the dream.

Anderson gathered herself and lunged at him, but her weightlessness startled her, and she stumbled on top of him. Najara caught her arms, gently, evidently thinking she had merely fallen in attempting to rise. Anderson clung to him despite herself, feeling as if she might drift off into space at any moment. Her astral form had manifested wearing her Judge's uniform as always, although her bright green gloves had turned to a drab olive as her life-force faded. She tried to reach out and read Najara's thoughts as he jabbered on, but the moment she did so, she could feel herself threaten to blow apart like the head of a dandelion.

"I thought I could sense you phasing in and out of here for a while," he said. "How come? Did they have you on some kind of medication? Never known anyone go without sleep for that long. For a while there I thought I'd lost you." He paused to moisten one of his eyes with a huge pink tongue. "Sorry. I'm rambling. I haven't spoken to anyone in a while, y'know? Ha-ha. Anyway, we haven't got long. Now you're here, everything's going to happen much quicker. I mean, look—ha-ha-ha! It's quicker if I just show you."

Before Anderson could protest, Najara grabbed her and vaulted effortlessly up the wall of the ruined city block. Her stomach lurched as she clung to his arm, the ground vanishing beneath her. The mutant landed nimbly on a ledge several feet off the ground, then slithered through a broken window with Anderson still under his arm. She held tight, feeling Najara's own psychic energy gather and release, gather and release as he bounded from level to level, his bare padded feet slapping the walls as he climbed, his spear stabbing fissures in walls and floors as he catapulted himself higher and higher up the crumbling building, eventually dropping her onto the shattered edge of a high storey.

Anderson panted great shimmering clouds as she looked across the ruined city towards the grey, misty horizon. She had beheld Najara's apocalyptic vision before, but never with such awful distinctness.

"Watch this," said Najara, brandishing his spear.

He stirred the tip of the weapon into the glistening cloud of life-force escaping Anderson's lips. The grains of psychic energy swirled like a miniature cosmos around the tip of Najara's spear, which glowed like a tiny sun. She watched, spellbound, reminded of the spiralling mosaic of lights she had beheld in the Nevertime. Then, with a vicious flick of his spear, Najara flung the light into the misty horizon, where it detonated like an atom bomb. Anderson shielded her eyes from the flash, as a panorama of ruined city-blocks fused into existence from out of the grey ether, an entire sector wrought upon the canvas of this imagined world.

Najara shrieked with delight, triumphantly lashing the air with his spear.

"A little of you goes a long way, Cassandra," he said, crouching beside her. "You're different from the other dreamers. Your life-force, your psychic energy. It-it-it..." He rolled his hands over and over like he was generating more words. "It's *way* more powerful! If I hadn't found you, all this would have taken me *years* to build."

Anderson watched another gleaming breath drift towards the horizon, another piece of herself sent to nourish the nascent world. Once she had nothing left to give, this terrible dream would be born in reality; if she stood any chance of preventing that, she would have to escape. She numbly accepted that she was beyond saving, but she could still give her city a fighting chance. She had to get back to the cave, to the real world. If air support hadn't arrived by the time she got there, then she would prevent herself from ever returning to Najara's dream by putting her Lawgiver to her temple.

"I guess I just wanted to thank you," said Najara. She let him touch her arm. "Before you go, I mean. I wanted you to know that you're helping to change the world for the better."

Anderson could see the renewed skyline through her fading hands. The grey horizon had retreated, forced back as Najara completed another part of his creation. She paused to gather her will, pondering that distant fog of the yet-to-be-created that bordered Najara's dream.

She went to speak, but stopped herself.

"What is it?" asked Najara.

"Did you mean for this to happen?" she said eventually. "No one would blame you for dreaming this place, but did you mean for it to become more than a dream, for it to infect people, to *hurt* them?" She sagged, weakened by the effort of speaking.

Najara's lipless mouth curled into a strange, sympathetic smile.

"The dream only shares itself with people who want to share it," he said.

Anderson had to stop herself from protesting out loud.

"As for the people in the city," Najara continued. "They won't feel a thing. They'll just pop out of existence. Like bubbles. We're not killing anyone, really."

Anderson imagined men and women clutching their loved ones, screaming in terror as reality was remade around them.

"It's weird, but after everything that's happened, what the

Judges did to me and my mom... you'd think I'd hate them, but I don't. Maybe I spent too long living away from the city, too long dreaming this dream, I dunno. Thing is, I don't really feel anything anymore. Sometimes it's like I've forgotten why I'm doing this. All those people in the city, all those Judges and norms, they're like machine parts, y'know? Stuff inside a machine that's busted. We're just putting it down."

He looked away and murmured, "We're breaking the cycle."

"What do you mean?" asked Anderson.

"Something my mom used to say, that hate and anger are like a virus. It can infect whole communities. People need to break the cycle if they wanna get better. I never really understood what she meant until I left my body behind and channelled myself in here. But that's what I'm doing, right? I'm rising above it. I am the dream now, and all I need to do is *be*."

His voice caught in his throat. "I don't have to feel anything anymore."

Anderson cupped Najara's face, turning his huge lidless eyes towards her. She saw in them a lurking rage the young mutant could barely understand or articulate. It was so strong it almost made her think twice about blasting him senseless.

Najara screamed like he had been plugged into the mains, as Anderson poured herself through her hands and into his head, torrents of blistering psychic energy electrifying his mind. She tried to maintain her grip on him as he fought back, but he was too fast. He somehow swung his staff into her with force enough to send her flying across the city.

She landed on a stretch of broken skywalk, rolling, light as a windblown leaf, her astral form almost emptied by the psi-blast. She could still hear Najara screaming from somewhere inside the shattered city block behind her, fighting to subdue the charge she had unloaded into him. The blast wouldn't be enough to kill him; she was too weak. She'd just wanted to give herself a head start.

Anderson gathered herself, feeling the air thicken with static, as if with the onset of a storm. Her body now ghostly, drained of energy, she ran towards a gap in the crumbled wall beside her, weightless as an astronaut as she leaped through the gap and out into space, landing on another skywalk far below. She rolled and leaped again, down, further down, skipping from precipice to precipice, gathering what little of her power remained, then releasing it as she jumped, propelling herself just as Najara had done. She skipped through the city, flitting like a fairy, leaking trails of golden dust as she headed towards a familiar landmark.

The Statue of Justice stood, tarnished and cracked, on a raft of manmade islands, towering over the remains of the harbour, fists on hips as if disapproving of the grey nothingness smudging the horizon.

Anderson descended onto an abandoned promenade as Najara's cry rang across the derelict city, like the bellow of an enraged god. It blurred her vision with its intensity as she leaped, dizzy, over a torn fence of wrought iron and fell several feet down a sheer rockrete wall, landing on a beach of stones a short way from the water. The ground quaked as she tried to rise. She could feel the dream's creator surging through the city towards her like some mythological behemoth, waking to bring about the end of days.

The stones barely shifted beneath her weight as she fled down the beach, feeling herself diminish with every breath, her eyes fixed on the dark water ahead, imagining the nothingness that lay beneath its surface. In creating this dream-world, Najara had focused on buildings and streets; everywhere people would have been, he imagined their absence, every empty street and deserted block a blow against the society that had rejected him. Why would he care what the bottom of the harbour looked like? Why spend precious energy creating something he couldn't see, which would exist already when this dream world merged with reality? Beneath those inky waters, no barrier had been created to prevent her escape back to the waking world.

Anderson scrambled, clutching, clawing at the stones, fighting her own buoyancy, feeling as though she were rising like a balloon the nearer she came to the water's edge. The stones stirred beneath her, clattering, rustling as they crumbled into glimmering streams of psionic pixels. Anderson lost her footing entirely as the ground slid from beneath her, weaving itself into great lengths of chain that caught her as she fell, whipping around her flailing limbs. Snatching her away less than a metre above the black waves.

Something pounced onto the iron fence above her. Anderson had felt a reservoir of rage simmering within Najara when she had touched his face, but it had been tamed, channelled by his artistry. Now the fury overwhelmed him, unleashed by her treachery. He had warped into something demonic, a line of horns sprouting from his cheeks, his eyes narrowed to yellow slits as he glared at her, his scales a livid red, as if engorged with anger. He was stirring the air with his staff, faster and faster, until the chains swirled about her like a hurricane, hoisting her high into the air, borne aloft by the heat of his wrath.

The chains teemed, rattling like endless streams of coins as Najara swung his spear under his arm, clamping it in place as he leaped aboard one of the links as nimbly as an acrobat. Anderson struggled weakly to free herself, but the chains around her limbs were fusing into her astral flesh, draining the last of her life-force, feeding the roots of the world. The chains rose into a great spire, with her at its apex, soaring into the sky. Anderson looked out over the ruins once again, wrecked city blocks glowing into existence before her, spreading like an infection. Najara appeared from beneath her, scampering up the spiralling chains. As he reached the top, he thrust his spear into Anderson's side, releasing a plume of gleaming dust from the wound.

Her astral body convulsed as he began draining what was left of her psychic essence. She felt as though she was being eviscerated, her insides dragged through the wound and released into the world. He smiled, revealing rows of tiny pointed teeth, satisfied by her screams. He leaned over her, his anger diminishing for a moment, long enough to satisfy his curiosity.

"You a spy, then? You must be. Deep cover or something. Sent to kill me."

Anderson said nothing, confused, too weak to answer.

"But don't you realise why you're here?" he asked, incredulous. "No?"

He shoved the spear deeper between her ribs, releasing another gust of sparkling energy. She felt no pain this time, only her connection to the city below as she brought it to life, its burgeoning walls tracing a line around the circumference of Najara's creation as it neared completion.

Anderson suddenly found herself marvelling at a beauty that had previously eluded her. The feeling stirred something she knew had been festering within her since her first week on the street.

"I told you," hissed Najara. "The dream only shares itself with those who *want* to share it."

The spite in his words seemed to ignite a malice of her own. She saw, now, not a vision of her city's destruction, but retribution for its crimes, against its people, against mutantkind, against her. This secret yearning for justice was why Najara's dream had chosen her, why no other psychic in Psi-Division could see it. The dream-virus could only take root in fertile ground, and she wanted to see the city punished just as much as the exiled mutants, just as much as the rioters she had infected.

Had she the energy, she would have laughed at the devastation, to see the Justice Department and the deranged city it had spawned scoured from existence, a world consumed by a wasteland of its own making. She thought of all she had lost in her lifelong quest to become a Judge—her childhood, her happiness, her humanity, a man she might have loved—and felt a terrible willingness to strike back at the cause of all her misery.

Damn them all.

Anderson surrendered herself, willingly yielding her own life-force, casting it down through the chains like shimmering rain, pouring her anger into the world, gladly feeding the dream that was killing her. She didn't want this feeling to end, this ecstasy of release, of striking back at the city she had secretly detested for so long, which was so much a part of her.

Najara held the spear firm as she gave him the last of her life-force. He smiled, eyes wide, wondering at her power.

Anderson thought of Marion, awed into placing his faith in her. In a Judge.

Najara erupted into a frenzy of laughter, a shrieking cackle of delight at the prospect of millions of innocent lives snuffed out to satisfy his vengeful whim.

What am I doing? thought Anderson. *What have I done?*

Focusing on the spear still lodged in her side, draining her, she forced her last ounce of psychic energy directly into the weapon. The psi-bolt was weak, but carried enough force to sting Najara's hands as he gripped the spear. His laughter broke off with a yelp as he dropped the weapon, and the spire of chains burst into a rain of shimmering dust, releasing them both.

The spear slid from Anderson's side and she fell backwards into a bottomless cushion of air. She felt like a dying ember, helpless, her astral form now little more than a whisper. Najara caught the spear as it tumbled through the air and clambered on top of it, riding it through the sky on a current of psychic energy channelled from the atmosphere. He circled Anderson, watching as she fell, and his laughter returned. He eventually darted away like a dragonfly as the buildings of the harbour rose steadily above her, crowding the sky as she fell.

When she finally crashed into cold water, its chill seemed to congeal around her, lending her weight and substance, filling her ears with a rush of bubbles as she sank, feeling herself dissolve into the darkness, feeding it. The rippling light above her dimmed as she willed herself to sink deeper into the gloom, knowing her descent would either drain the very last of her, or release her back into the waking world where she must quickly put an end to herself.

Death awaited her in both worlds.

HER HAND FLEW to the holster on her boot the moment she awoke, but her shoulders were restrained. She was buckled to a stretcher in the droning belly of an aircraft. A small med-bot unfurled from a compartment overhead and ran the blue light of a scanner up and down her body as she tugged open the buckle and sat up, pulling sensors from her face and throat as she reached for her gun; quickly, before she could comprehend the madness of what she was about to do.

But her holster was empty and more droids appeared around her, wrestling her back onto the stretcher. She struggled, trying to scream sense into them.

"You can't let me fall asleep!"

"*Easy now, Miss Anderson,*" said a familiar drawl. Marion's dented features loomed over her, a ponytail of cables feeding into a panel in the back of his head. She grabbed his arm as the other droids retreated.

"Marion, you don't understand. I can't go back to the dream. If I do, it'll drain me in seconds. It'll break through into our world, replace the entire city."

The med-bot was trying to tell her something.

"*Listen to the doc,*" said Marion. One of his chest plates was missing; a crew of tiny repair-drones crawled around his insides like bugs.

"*You no longer show any sign of infection, Judge Anderson,*" said the med-bot.

"What?"

"*Please remain calm,*" it continued. "*You are on board a long-range scout vessel and will shortly be arriving in Mega-City One, where all your questions will be answered in full. Please be patient.*"

One of the other droids spoke, a slender scout-bot with a small las-blaster mounted on its shoulders. "*We established contact with Psi-Chief Ecks just before your cowbot led us to your position. Ecks said to inform you that the infected citizens were now out of their comas. That was just over four hours ago.*"

Anderson groggily struggled to make sense of the world. If the cits were awake and cured, then so must be every other mutant in the Cursed Earth who had contracted the dream-virus, including Max's scavengers. The absence of the psi-trail throbbing in Anderson's belly confirmed it. She was no longer connected to the dream.

"*Looks like you're cured, Miss Anderson.*"

"But I didn't kill him," she said, feeling dizzy and cold as realisation sank in. "The dream's not dead..."

She trailed off as she recalled the brief moment in the dream when she had willingly ceded to her own subconscious desire to punish the Department and the city it had created. Had the glut of psychic energy she provided in that moment been enough to finally complete Najara's creation?

The ship trembled with turbulence as Anderson lurched to her feet and pushed past Marion. She hurried down the fuselage, barging through the scout-bots towards the cockpit, where two faceless droids monitored a confusion of switches and dials and peered through the window into an orange haze of sky.

The clouds parted.

Anderson felt as though she were falling, her stomach tight, tears welling as she stared across the sand-swallowed ruins of Mega-City One.

Twenty-Nine

"This is my fault, all of this," said Anderson, gazing across the sea of broken city-blocks as she comprehended the magnitude of her appalling achievement. "I wanted this."

"*Can we stop it?*"

Marion's voice was so deep it seemed to reverberate from somewhere inside her. She turned and looked up at him, feeling ashamed to meet his gaze.

The huge robot tossed away the charge-cable from the back of his neck and slammed his buckled breast-plate with a clang, slapping it several times until the thing stuck.

"*Well?*" he asked. His crumpled, concerned brow made him look expectant.

"Meg Central," Anderson said as she turned and broke up the pilot-bots now conferring in troubled chirps. "Get us to the Statue of Justice. Fast."

She wriggled around Marion's obstructive bulk as he replaced his hat, his eyes cobalt stars in the gloom of the ship's interior.

"The Statue's what inspired this whole dream," she said,

hurrying back to her seat. "It's the epicentre, the first thing Najara would have created. It's also the portal through which the dream will be entering this world."

One of the pilot-bots called after her. "*I'm afraid I cannot change course without proper authorisation.*"

One of the scouts caught Anderson's shoulder. "*Let us handle this,*" it said.

Anderson called back at the cockpit. "Oh, I'm sorry. Can you hail Psi-Chief Ecks and get us permission?"

"*Uh, we appear to have lost all communication with Psi-Division,*" said the pilot.

"Which makes me your commanding Judge. Now get us to Meg Central as fast as this thing can take us, which I'm guessing is pretty fast. You two!" She pointed at the scout-bots. "Sit your asses down, recharge, maybe do your nails, whatever. We may need you."

The engines rose to a steady whine as the ship accelerated, hull trembling. The scout-bots hunkered down into their docking stations. Marion buckled himself in as safely as his bulk would allow, while Anderson took the window seat beside him.

She zoned out, her perception of time fading as she absorbed herself in the city she could feel rushing below. It was like pancake batter pouring into a pan, one reality decanted on top of another, eclipsing it. She could feel the distant fringes of the dream still surging into existence, sweeping across the city like a rolling tide, its edges hissing with the screams of a terrified, bewildered populace bulldozed out of existence.

Anderson struggled for a moment with the mental math. On arrival at the Statue of Justice, she would have less than thirty minutes before this new reality enveloped the whole of Mega-City One. Once that happened, this new world was here to stay. But if she could cut off Najara's reality while he was still pouring it into this world, she would cause the transition to short circuit. The ruined city would revert to the stuff of dreams and hopefully dissipate—if the Preston/Logan theory on somnial field manifestations was correct.

Marion nudged her out of her trance. "*We got any kind of plan, Miss Anderson?*"

"Same plan as before," she said. "Kill the dreamer, kill the dream."

The pilot-bot's voice buzzed over the intercom by her head as the craft slowed. "*Coming up on the Statue of Justice now, Judge Anderson. Please remain seated and advise our next course of action.*"

Anderson unbuckled herself and hurried to the cockpit as the degraded monument emerged from among the shattered buildings. She could hear a ceaseless roar, like a burst dam, emanating from within the Statue's fractured head; the sound of stolen life-force channelled from the Nevertime into the waking world.

Najara was in the Statue's noggin for sure, reborn as flesh and blood, along with the rest of his world, shepherding his dream into existence with that goofy spear of his.

"Pilot, I'm gonna need you to blow the head off the Statue of Justice."

"*I am forbidden to open fire on grade-one municipal property without clearance from the Council of Five, Judge Anderson.*"

She detected a spike of energy, like a startled blip on a heart monitor.

"*Please suggest a legal target,*" said the pilot, deaf to the rush of psionic energy Anderson heard erupting beneath them like a geyser.

Anderson screamed, "Pull up!"

"*Target not recognised,*" said the pilot as Anderson shoved the droid aside and grabbed the steering yoke, heaving it hard to the right. The ship veered away as something crashed into it from below, throwing Anderson sideways. She collided with a bulkhead and barked in pain as the ship continued to careen to one side.

The pilots wrestled the controls as Anderson clung to the wall, the view from the cockpit window whirling like the world outside a merry-go-round. The droids finally regained control, throwing Anderson back to the floor as the ship levelled out. They maintained an unsteady course, circling the Statue of Justice.

She pulled herself up the cargo netting near a porthole and saw smoke and flames pouring from a wrecked turbine on the wing. As the ship yawed to the right, she saw the enormous spike of glittering psi-particles that had nearly impaled the ship. The huge barb was now sinking, its lustre dimming as it reformed into a ruined building.

Najara had detected their approach and managed to divert his attention enough to try and stab the intruders out of the sky. Had Anderson not reacted so quickly, the whole ship might have been destroyed.

The leaking turbine finally exploded, the vessel dived and the skyline sank from view. Anderson almost lost her footing as the floor tipped. Marion was lowering himself towards her, ignoring the protests of the scout-bots locked into their docking stations beside him. She yelled at him to get back to his seat as she ran uphill, her ears popping.

A hush of pure acceleration filled the air as she hauled herself into her chair, seatbelt clips rattling as her shaking hands struggled to connect them. Finally locked in, momentum pressing her deeper into her seat as blooms of white crash-foam pillowed around her limbs. She glanced through the porthole to see a slab of rockrete rushing up to meet her.

Her teeth clashed as the ship struck the ground, the impact blurring her vision, filling the interior with a blizzard of debris. The floor quaked with the ruthless crunch of tearing metal as something broke away from beside her, destroying the scout-bots in a shower of sparks as it bounced down the craft and crashed into the cockpit. Only when she saw the cowboy hat spinning through the air after it did she realise it was Marion.

The downed ship eventually ground itself to a standstill. Sand whispered through the ragged walls. The atmosphere thickened with warmth and the stench of kerosene. Marion stirred, extracting himself from the ruined cockpit.

The crash-foam unclenched around her, but Anderson made no move to unbuckle herself. Shaking, she stared through the shattered porthole at the immense stone boots of the Statue of Justice. It waited outside, anchored atop an abandoned gatehouse framed with the defiant Aquila of the Justice Department. The Statue's legs towered out of sight, veined with cracks, scoured by desert winds.

The monument's oppressive immensity seemed to crush the life out of Anderson. Exhaustion suddenly weighed heavily upon her, her face fanned by a stifling hot breeze that evaporated all sense of purpose. Everything she had achieved in her first year on the street felt suddenly trivial, every hard-won battle, every case she had pieced together, all she had gone through on the Meet Market case, her breakdown in the Big Zero Six, the woman—the Judge—she had proved herself to be this past year, every spectacular achievement dwarfed by the magnitude of the task before her. Never before had Anderson been expected to save the entire city.

Marion had retrieved his hat and waded through the wreckage towards her, her belt and weapons in his hand. Anderson spoke as he approached, the words escaping in long, shuddering gasps.

"I don't know if I can stop this," she said.

Marion took her trembling hand, gently, then slapped the Lawgiver into her palm. She gripped it, feeling the familiar whir of machinery in the handle as the palm-print sensors recognised the weapon's owner.

Marion tore open the crumpled hatch, releasing a sigh of hot air into the wrecked ship. Anderson realised that she had expected some kind of pep talk and felt a pang of shame. She unbuckled her seat-belt, holstered the Lawgiver, sheathed her knife, strapped on her belt, and hurried after Marion towards the gatehouse.

ANDERSON KEPT HER eyes shut, her arms locked around Marion's neck, her legs dangling above fathoms of emptiness. The robot's hands moved in a blur as they climbed the rungs of the narrow maintenance ladder, the ringing rattle of their progress up the darkened turbolift like an endless blast of machine-gun fire. Anderson's teeth chattered, her body juddering against Marion's back. It was like riding a Lawmaster over a mile of corrugated iron. She could have thought of more dignified ways of ascending the Statue of Justice, but none as quick.

Marion called over his shoulder, his arms still whizzing up the ladder. "*Figure we're in his belly now.*"

The beam of his shoulder-mounted lamp shook in the darkness overhead. The ladder was fitted inside a recess running up the wall, a web of steel beams and columns caging the lift shaft behind them. The air smelled of dust and axle-grease, the oppressive heat relieved only by the occasional breeze sighing through bright cracks in the corroded metal walls.

Anderson tuned into her surroundings, if only to take her mind off the lunatic ascent. The roar of psychic energy overhead made her feel as though she were climbing a waterfall. She was sure that even if Najara couldn't hear all the noise they were making, he would certainly be able to sense their presence, just as he had when they approached in the ship. She vainly tried to assure herself that his attention might be elsewhere, or that he assumed his pursuers had been obliterated when the ship crashed.

The walls of the Statue trembled with a majestic groan, resounding with the unmistakable scream of tortured metal. Anderson reeled with vertigo as the ladder shook, the walls swaying like a ship at sea. Marion ignored it, his hands still pounding up the rungs. Anderson tightened her grip around the robot's neck, a cold, helpless fear creeping over her as she sensed a shift in the psychic energy coursing above them.

Something hit the wall beneath them like a battering ram, sending a tremor up the inside of the Statue that tore the ladder from the wall in a shower of rivets. Terror seized Anderson as she felt herself slipping from the robot's back; the section of ladder to which they still clung swung to one side, pinned to the wall above them by a single rail. Marion tried to grab one of the steel supports behind them, but the ladder swung back before he could reach it. Another shudder echoed up the walls and the ladder fell away, dropping them both into the darkness below.

Anderson sprang instinctively from the robot's back, twisting in the air as she flung herself blindly at the supports. She caught one of the beams, bawling in pain as it slammed across her chest, the weight of her legs threatening to drag her back as she clawed at the ledge. Pulling herself onto the dusty metal girder, she gazed down the throat of the lift shaft to see Marion already clambering up the columns several stories below her, his torchlight wagging in the gloom.

Something moved through the huge tear punched into the wall beneath him.

As she fumbled for handholds, Anderson watched four great metal columns sliding through the gap in the wall. They curled like enormous metal worms around the lip of the tear and began slowly peeling the metal aside, tearing it further, filling the air with a toe-curling screech.

Anderson didn't wait to see what it was. She climbed, dripping with sweat, ignoring her racing heart, focusing entirely on trying to keep her feet and fingers from slipping as she groped for the next handhold. A haze of light flooded the shaft from below, revealing a blizzard of dust in the air. The ceiling was just a few stories above her. No, not a ceiling—the underside of a turbolift cabin.

She realised the cacophony beneath her had ceased; she could hear the steady clang of Marion working his way up the beams just beneath her. Then the scream of metal returned as something enormous barged through the tear in the wall below. She glanced down and saw the monstrous thing in its entirety, seconds before its bulk blocked out the light and darkness returned.

It was an enormous gloved hand, now driving inexorably up the turbolift shaft, the girders trembling as it climbed, fingers spread to seize her and Marion like the tentacles of the Kraken. As Najara directed his world into being above them, he had managed to divert his concentration enough to soften one of the Statue's limbs, animating its right arm and hand with his sorcery. She could feel the psionic current flowing through the beams. The Statue of Justice was reaching into its own chest, as if striving to tear out its heart.

The supports quaked, causing Anderson's foot to slip several times as she tried to scramble up the next beam, knowing there was no way she could outrun the thing. A metallic groan echoed above her, followed by a sharp clang, and something clattered and bounced down the girders towards her. She ducked as it flashed past her head. She peered, blinking up through the shower of dirt, at the turbolift cabin, now tilted to one side and outlined in light. One of the two rusted brake-clasps that fastened the carriage to a huge rail in the wall had come away.

"We're almost at the head, Miss Anderson. Keep going."

That remaining clasp was all that stopped the cabin from plunging down the shaft on top of them. Anderson drew her Lawgiver.

She turned to yell instructions at Marion, only to see the monstrous hand closing around him from behind. The robot refused to let go of the beam, shaking the supports above even more violently. Anderson locked her arm around one of the trembling bars and aimed her pistol at the thing below. She couldn't risk a Hi-Ex, so she peppered the great wrist with several armour-piercing rounds, strobe-lighting the crazy scene below as Marion tried to wrestle himself free of the monstrous hand. She had hoped to fracture something in the thing's steel skeleton, but the rounds did nothing except pop holes in its rusted skin. By now it had both of Marion's legs and was lifting him over the shaft; he clung to the beam, sparks spitting from his shoulder as cables and ligaments tore.

Marion looked up at Anderson, hat still fastened to his head, blue eyes glimmering in the gloom. He nodded.

Anderson aimed up at the turbolift cabin and fired five armour-piercing rounds in a row. She was sharpshooting in the dark in the middle of an earthquake, but she gave way to her training, slipping into unshakable concentration. Adjusting for recoil before each shot, Anderson was tranquil, letting the muzzle-flash guide her aim. Her fifth shot shattered the decayed clasp, releasing the cabin.

The shocking speed of its descent startled her; she swung herself around the column by which she stood, dodging the falling cabin, sparks grinding in its wake. She peered down through the cloud of grit as the cabin crashed on top of Marion and the hand that held him, shearing the robot's head at the neck and the huge hand at the wrist.

Amber light poured down, streaming through a slit in the half-open turbolift doors in the wall above. Anderson climbed the rest of the way up the supports, wincing when she eventually heard the crash far below, trying to dismiss the image of Marion's severed head bouncing on top of the cabin as it vanished into the darkness, his hat tumbling after it.

She noticed the silence upon reaching the doors. The roar of psychic energy had stopped, but she could still feel the weight of its presence in the room above. Lawgiver in hand, she peered through the gap. Beyond was the inside of the Statue's head, a domed, two-storey chamber dominated by a pair of huge broken windows forming the Statue's visor. Najara was in there somewhere. She had forced him to take a timeout. He would be crouched behind one of the broken display cases or deactivated holo-stands, catching his breath, getting his head together, trying to cloak his thoughts from the woman hunting him, knowing he would have to kill her before he could finish channelling his dream into this world.

Anderson quickly climbed up, shoving the doors aside as she elbowed herself onto the dusty tiled floor of the chamber, then scurried behind a row of seats as she drew her Lawgiver. A wild breeze cooled the sweat on her face and neck as she caught her breath, her mind assuming a predatory focus. Najara's world was beginning to congeal; it would take the mutant too long, take too much concentration for him to mould anything in this room into something that could kill her. If he wanted her dead, he would have to do it himself. Najara had animal strength and speed, but Anderson had a lifetime's schooling in the science of violence. He was good with his spear; she was lethal with a gun.

The Lawgiver leaped out of her hand, snatched away by a channel of telekinetic force that came out of nowhere and hurled the pistol through one of the broken windows. Her psi-senses locked onto a lithe figure slithering from cover on the other side of the room, twirling a great spear as it directed another channel of energy towards her. The blast caught her, paralysed her as she moved to flank him. She felt the tendrils of psionic energy constricting around her like snakes, lifting her off her feet.

The figure swung the spear up, launching her into the air, until she crashed into the ceiling, slamming the breath from her body in a cloud of dust and debris.

Najara stalked into view, reborn, still pointing his spear at her, pinning her to the ceiling. His scales glimmered blood red, the huge reptilian eyes devoid of mercy. He wore only a scrap of loincloth, rustic bangles clinking on his wrists and ankles.

No longer the gabbling young mutant she had first met in their shared dream, he had recreated himself as his ego wished him to be, a malevolent shaman, bringer of vengeance and death, dream and dreamer entwined.

Anderson wriggled, unable to push back the sheer weight of raw psychic energy Najara was forcing against her. She would have to get near him to have any chance of killing him, and he wasn't going to give her the chance. He could have flung her out the window, tossed her down the lift shaft, but he was possessed by rage, furious with the woman he'd believed to be a kindred spirit, and with himself for allowing another Judge to betray him.

Anderson sensed immeasurable pain behind those narrowed eyes, but all Najara wanted to do with that pain was to visit every ounce of it upon her before he killed her.

His mind hissed.

Throw her...

Keep throwing her...

Keep throwing her until there's nothing left but meat...

Anderson gazed at the distant floor, bracing herself as Najara went to swing his spear down.

Thirty

NAJARA CRIED OUT as the psi-bolts struck him.

Anderson had spat a volley down the channel of energy pinning her to the ceiling. The bolts, shards of focused psi-force, swarmed like venomous fish into Najara's brain. He reeled back, releasing her, screaming like a madman trying to drive the nightmares from his head. The decayed floor tiles collapsed beneath her as she fell, breaking her fall, along with a few ribs. She growled away the pain clawing at her side as she rose, blurry vision reducing Najara to a squirming shadow before her. She groped for the hilt of the seven-inch combat knife sheathed in her boot.

By the time Najara recovered, Anderson was on him, knife in hand, dazed but hungry for murder. She pulled his left shoulder, exposing his flank, seeking his ribs with her knife. She would have stabbed him repeatedly, shredding his liver, ending the fight in seconds, but the reptilian mutant somehow slithered out of her grip before she could land a single blow.

He appeared at her side like an apparition, swinging the blunt end of the spear into her nose, breaking it, spreading a hot sheet of blood across her face. Her vision fizzed and she gulped down a mouthful of her own blood, but rode the momentum of the blow, dropping to one knee to spin and lash out with the knife, hoping to catch the inside of her opponent's leg and sever the femoral artery. The blade swished through empty air.

The next blow came from behind, striking her in the side of the head. Again she rolled with the impact, rising to her feet in a boxer's stance, knife in hand, the pressure in her skull building to nausea. She maintained distance, keeping him in sight, using feints and footwork to crowd him into the wall, where she would finally kill him. He constantly licked at his huge yellow eyes as he jabbed at her with his spear, like a hunter cornered by an advancing lioness. She felt his terror of her ferocity, the realisation that, for all his agility, he couldn't hold her at bay forever. She cursed herself for listening to his mind, his fear diminishing her resolve.

"So what's the endgame, Najara?" she panted. "You wanna be reborn just so you can spend the rest of your life wandering the hell that killed your mom? You think that's what she would have wanted?"

Najara's reptilian features tightened and he bared his tiny serrated teeth. "She wanted justice."

"And you want revenge. Not the same thing, pal."

The mutant seemed to hesitate, his brow creasing with uncertainty. Anderson lowered her guard slightly. "And you're right to want revenge, Najara. But you can't break the cycle like this, not at the expense of millions of innocent lives." She spat blood from the side of her mouth and gulped another breath. "I know you don't want to feel anything. After everything that's happened to you, who could blame you? I know it's easier to be angry. It's less painful than the truth. But these are people, just like you. Just like your mom."

"But I've come so far," he said, bewildered. "I've endured everything, sacrificed everything, even my *life*, back in that cave. You think I can turn back now?"

Anderson felt a flicker of anger. "There's more to this than just you."

Najara's face hardened into a sneer, his scales turning an even more furious shade of red. "I've spent my whole life being angry, and whose fault is that? It's made me what I am. It's given me everything." He hissed the words, his grip tightening around his spear, and Anderson raised her guard. "After a lifetime of building yourself into something, would you turn back, Cassandra? Give it all up? Walk away?"

Anderson said nothing, breathing hard, her head spinning, her shoulders in agony.

"Me neither," he said.

Anderson rushed at him with the knife, criss-crossing the air, trying to overwhelm him with pure aggression, but Najara's spear blocked every blow. Every swipe at his scaled flesh, every jab at his ribs and eyes struck a bar of bone. He weaved the huge ivory spear through the air with superhuman dexterity and growing strength, pushing her back as he gained confidence, sensing her frustration. As he went to flank her, she spun the knife into a stabbing hold and launched herself at him again, aiming for the eye.

The blade *thunked* inches deep into the thick shaft of the spear, her weight on top of him now as she struggled to free the blade. She realised she'd over-committed just as Najara slammed the end of the spear into her cheek, smacking her into a row of plastic seats, the rusted metal frames collapsing as she crashed into them. As she freed herself from the wreckage she felt a sharp fragment of molar roll across her tongue. She spat it away and lashed out with her foot as Najara raised the spear, preparing to pin her to the floor. Her heavy boot caught the side of his knee, crushing the joint, almost snapping his leg. He shrieked in pain, the spear stabbing the floor by her head as he toppled forward.

Anderson lurched to her feet as though drunk, dragging

a rusted metal bar from the wreckage. She booted away the spear as Najara tried to rise, knocked him back to the floor and hammered the metal bar over his head. He slumped again with a grunt, but he caught her legs before she could strike him again, pulling her to the floor and scrambling on top of her.

Without his precious spear, Najara was nothing but strength and speed, driven by naked fear: fear of his precious dream being snatched away before completion. His weight crushed the breath from Anderson's chest as his jaws clamped around her throat. She yelled in revulsion as much as pain, feeling tiny, hook-like teeth sawing into her flesh.

Her right hand still clutched the metal bar, but Najara had her wrist pinned. She clawed at his bulbous eyes with her left, until he smothered her face with his paw, the rough pads on his fingers ripping at her hair, tearing at her skin, suffocating her with their acrid stink as he grabbed her head and slammed it back into the floor. Anderson's world went black for a moment, stars spinning behind her eyelids.

Seeing her go limp, Najara released her right arm and gripped her skull with both hands. Anderson saw clawed thumbs poised over her eyes and slammed the metal bar into the side of his head. The weapon broke, but knocked him aside; released from his crushing weight, she coughed, gagging on her own bloody breath. His blurred outline scurried towards the discarded spear.

It wasn't defiance or passion that made Anderson rise from the floor and stagger after him like an automaton; it was pure will, the Justice Department's relentless training, animating her when all natural strength had gone.

Anderson caught the spear with both hands as Najara turned to face her. His reptilian eyes widened in disbelief, as though confronted by some revenant bent on his destruction. Still gripping the spear, she kicked him in the stomach, a powerful, stamping blow mastered by a lifetime of practice, enough to bring down a door. He staggered back, still clutching the weapon. Before he could recover his wits, she slammed the shaft of the spear into his face, following him as he reeled backwards, still clutching the weapon, refusing to let go of the conduit through which his dream would be born.

Anderson slammed him in the face again, willing him to let go of the spear. He didn't, his jaws now a bloody wreck. She thought of the millions of lives the mutant yearned to erase, the children who might one day grow up to see a better world, a world that she could help bring about. She found herself hitting him over and over, anger lending her strength. Najara's head hung limp and dripping, but still he held on. She could feel the strength leaving his arms and she twisted the spear from his grip, staggering back under the weapon's enormous weight. It seemed to vibrate in her hands, as if eager to channel the rest of Najara's dream into the world.

Anderson aimed the spear at Najara's throat. The battered dreamers studied each other through swollen eyes, breathing in ragged gasps. Najara was the first to speak.

"Why?" he asked, drooling blood and broken teeth. "Why save a city you hate so much?"

Anderson thought better of protesting. Najara chuckled.

"We shared this dream," he said. "We built it together. You think killing me will banish that anger? You'll go on feeling it long after I'm gone. And you'll hate yourself even more for becoming part of the horror you've saved."

Anderson hefted the staff and began whirling it around her head.

Whoop, whoop, whoop.

Najara watched in helpless fascination as the circling spear gained momentum.

Whoop, whoop, whoop.

Anderson slammed the spear upon the floor. The weapon cracked, splitting to the marrow as it fell apart in her hands.

*　*　*

THE REST WAS like a bubble bursting in slow motion. Anderson had destroyed the link between two worlds: the half-real world Najara had conjured on top of the Meg and the reservoir of psychic energy still in the Nevertime. The connection broken, both worlds short-circuited, fizzling out of existence. The air quivered for a heartbeat, and Anderson felt pressure sucking at her body. Then Najara's world simply peeled away. The dream rolled back across the city, revealing the bright, teeming Mega-City One that had lain there before.

Najara sighed as he disappeared along with the rest of his world, dream and dreamer entwined.

"Oh, my Grud, Judge. Should I call someone?"

Anderson looked up at the concerned citizen standing beside her, wearing a plastic souvenir tiara in the shape of a Judge's helmet. The little boy whose hand she was holding stared at Anderson over the ice cream melting down his fist, his thoughts tingling with astonishment.

She just appeared out of nowhere...

Anderson looked around her. She was in the viewing chamber at the top of the Statue of Justice, surrounded by gawping tourists. The bloodied Judge who had suddenly appeared in their midst was of far greater interest than the view from the unbroken windows they had paid ninety-nine credits to peer through.

She could hear their thoughts babbling in confusion, gloriously alive, blissfully unaware of their temporary oblivion. Najara's reality had retreated into non-existence across all of space and time, fading into nothingness like a dream forgotten. No-one beyond Psi-Division would have any idea the city had been imperilled.

Anderson closed her eyes, enjoying a rush of gladness, glorious in its privacy.

*   *   *

ANDERSON THREW THE shovel aside and clambered out of the grave. The sun had melted almost completely behind the mountains, the cooling wind sending a welcome chill through her filthy, sweat-soaked vest. She sat on the piled earth beside the hole she had spent the afternoon digging and glugged at her canteen, the ice-cold water sending a vicious twinge into the roots of her new molar. Her aching muscles were plastered with speed-heal patches, which had itched like crazy all day long. But at least she could see through her left eye now, and her ribs didn't feel like they were stabbing her every time she drew breath.

Three days ago, Anderson had saved millions of lives. The private knowledge was a source of giddy pleasure, and she caught herself marvelling at her own determination and capability. She felt oddly guilty for doing so, as if the city might somehow vanish again in punishment for her pride. But something darker had been gnawing all day at the periphery of her mind, a lurking anxiety that neither labour nor meditation seemed able to banish.

The ceaseless, echoing hammering of the construction-bots labouring nearby had done little to improve Anderson's mood. The floodlights of the new township shone like a beacon in the twilight, busy with the sound of CHIP-E droids and Sparky-bots tinkering into the evening.

Anderson had taken a day's leave and visited Max's crew again that morning. The mutant scavengers gave her a reserved welcome, doing little to conceal their astonishment at her promised return. More of them had been infected by the dream-virus after Anderson left, but now everyone, including young Anya, had awoken and were recovering. The crates of food and medical supplies Anderson brought with her on a hov-trailer were received with rather more caution than she had expected. The invitation to join the independent township under construction was met with outright suspicion.

Anderson could hear what they were thinking loud and clear, despite her insistent reassurances: the devils in blue and gold never gave gifts without strings attached. Max's grateful smile was a disheartening contrast to the ugly suspicions Anderson heard brewing within. The mutant leader told Anderson they would think about it. As much as they liked clean water and food for their children, along with auto-turret protection from the roaming perils of the Cursed Earth, the mutants disliked the idea of placing themselves under the scrutiny of the Justice Department, who had cast them into the wilderness in the first place. Maybe Max would convince her people to move in; maybe she wouldn't. Anderson had left under a cloud of disappointment.

She groaned as she rose to her feet, wincing as she stretched her aching back, and opened the crate waiting beside her Lawmaster. Setting the lid aside, she heaved out something the size of a micro-zap oven. She placed it on the seat of her bike, plugged it into the console and adjusted the thing's position on the seat until she felt it had a good view of the darkening sky.

"Thank you, Miss Anderson. I sure do appreciate this."

Tek-Div had recovered Marion's shattered remains from the bottom of the turbolift shaft, along with the wreckage of the scout ship, which had mysteriously appeared at the feet of the Statue of Justice. Najara's dream-version of the city had been whipped away like a tablecloth, leaving behind only what was left of its interlopers. Marion's body had been broken beyond repair; only his severed head and his hat were salvageable. Anderson had nodded politely as one of the Teks had explained how Marion's damaged fusion somethingorother was too old, rare and expensive to replace. However, the robot's prime thingamabob drive could be hooked up to a battery for several hours before his central processing doohickey burned out for good.

Marion's enormous head rested on the Lawmaster's saddle, his monolithic features unreadable, the electromagnetic pulses that passed for his thoughts indecipherable. His gleaming blue eyes looked up at the stars he had asked to see one last time, his crooked jaw locking into something resembling a contented smile. Anderson saw that crazy horseshoe under his nose and the distinctively wrinkled brow and felt a pang of sadness at the loss of the robot's body, of those immense hands habitually clamped to his belt, of the way his lanky legs seemed to swing like pendulums as he swaggered.

Anderson built a small fire and sat on the ground beside Marion and the bike. They shared the cosmic splendour above them in silence.

It was Marion who spoke first, eventually asking Anderson what was on her mind. They ended up conversing long into the night. Talking to Marion was somehow like talking to herself. The mind of a human companion was a cascade of chattering thoughts, like endless tickertapes of breaking news: private judgements, shameful secrets, helpless lusts, Anderson had endured them all. Friends and enemies alike were naked before her. But Marion was like a chunk of rock. His mind offered nothing to respond to, his presence a welcoming vacuum into which she could pour anything.

"It's stupid, I know," she said, staring into the crackling fire. "It just feels thankless, I guess. This job, I mean. And I'm gonna need to do more than my job if I'm gonna go back."

"*If?*" said Marion.

"Relax," she said. "I'm gonna go back." Her smile faded, the words catching in her throat.

She had unravelled the dream-virus by surrendering to it; learning its weaknesses, finding leverage points by which she could change things for the better. But how long would it take her to do anything like that within the Department? How deep would she have to immerse herself, how much corruption could her soul endure before she could work out how to help break the cycle? If at all?

Anderson toyed with a piece of kindling. This was the heart of the uneasiness that had plagued her over the last three days. It was like part of Najara still lingered inside her, staining her conscience with anger at the Department, at the crimes it committed in the name of law and order.

"I'll do my job," she said. "I just don't know how long I'm gonna last doing it. Or whether I can make any kind of difference, y'know?"

Marion snorted.

"Fifteen years in your fancy Academy and a year on the street, and you still think someone can answer that for you? No-one can, Miss Anderson. All you can do is wear your badge and do the job. Let fate take care of the rest."

Anderson threw the kindling into the fire and started to her feet. "That's it?" she said. "But I wanna be more than just some cog in the machine. I can't be like the others. I can't be a robot— no offence. It's just not me. I don't wanna follow the damn program. In fact, I don't think I ever can."

Marion's hooded blue eyes simmered in the darkness as she stood before him.

"Miss Anderson," he said. *"You can't help trying to save people. You can't help caring. I've seen what you are, sure as you're standing right there. Now I don't know if you were born like that or whether these powers of yours have made you that way, but it's who you are. That's your program, Miss Anderson. Don't fight it. Stick to that, do your job, and you'll do as well as you can do in this world."*

Anderson sat down again, too exhausted to argue.

Silence returned, robot and human lost in contemplation.

Eventually Anderson laughed. "So, cowboy. You think I got what it takes to be one of the good guys?" She felt stupid for saying it.

Always with the jokes, Cass. Sheesh.

Marion replied in a voice of gentle thunder.

"Miss Anderson, I think you got what it takes to be a gruddamn legend."

Anderson laughed, and she turned to ask him if he was kidding. But the robot's head just stared into the stars, the hooded eyes no longer lit. He was gone.

Silence followed as she knelt beside him for another hour before bedding down to a dreamless sleep. She buried him at dawn.

Dirty, tired and aching from her labours, Anderson stowed the shovel and looked out across the Cursed Earth. The desert smelled of sandalwood and the promise of rain, bright green and purple clouds boiling on the horizon. The earth felt, for now, not cursed at all, but strangely blessed. She climbed aboard her Lawmaster, enjoying the savage thrum of its engine as she spun the bike around, its huge wheels spraying dirt.

The wall around Mega-City One ran the length of the horizon, the city-blocks beyond it trailing smoke like an orchard of volcanoes ready to erupt. Anderson wrung the throttle, coaxing a roar that carried across the desert as she charged towards the city.

"Okay," she said. "Let's see where this goes."

TOO MUCH INFORMATION

MEGA-CITY ONE
2137 A.D.

ANDERSON CAUGHT THE man's wrist, stopping the screwdriver inches from his own skull. He struggled as she threw her bodyweight into his arm, driving him down onto the rocking floor of the carriage. The screwdriver tore the arm of her sports jacket, piercing her flesh. She cried out.

ANDERSON CAUGHT THE man's wrist, stopping the screwdriver inches from his own skull. He struggled as she threw her bodyweight into his arm, driving him down onto the rocking floor of the carriage. The screwdriver tore the arm of her sports jacket, piercing her flesh. She cried out.

"I just bought this, Gruddammit!"

She twisted the man's arm, flipping him onto his stomach and locking his hand behind his back.

"Anderson, Psi-Division," she announced, producing her badge as she kicked the screwdriver out of reach and squinted at the other passengers. Sunlight flashed across her face through the windows of the bullet train as it hurtled through Mega-City One.

"Anyone hurt…? No? Groovy."

She was still out of breath after shouldering her way here from the other end of the crowded train. The precognitive psi-flash had been spot-on. This guy—a quick psi-scan identified him as a marketing manager named Dexter Sargassi—had suddenly decided to unscrew his own head. By the standards of Mega-City One, it was fairly standard.

Sargassi was still jabbering incoherently as Anderson placed her fingers on his sweating temple. His mind was like a snow globe, a zillion glittering ideas swirling after each other, whipping his mind into a frenzy as he tried to make sense of them. Anderson had no idea what 'quantum decoherence' might be and was sure that Sargassi didn't even know how to spell it. And yet the man's limited mind had been filled with ideas so expansive that he had felt the need to open his own noggin to make room.

She rifled through Sargassi's short-term memory, watching through the man's eyes as he got dressed, ate breakfast, and made a call on his vid-phone while peeing. He had been sat on the train reading the biography of some big-shot CEO on his holo-reader when *boom*—something had plugged him into the mains, some kind of reservoir of pure information, distilled into psychic energy. It was as though he had digested a thousand books at once. It was more than anyone could take, let alone someone who thought Einstein was that big guy from the horror-vids with the bolts in his neck.

Anderson could hear snatches of sanity from Sargassi's tormented mind. *Must let them out. Must. Must...* She performed a quick short-term memory wipe, probably saving the guy a fortune in therapy, and looked up at the abandoned holo-reader lying on a seat nearby. She prodded the device and a snap of psi-energy stung her finger.

"There goes my day off," she sighed.

An hour later she was in uniform and a big guy with a mop was showing her into a locked room in the basement of Sargassi's block. Illuminated by a row of humming strip-lights, the room was small, windowless and featureless, save for a tall white cabinet housing a computer server.

"Welcome to the block library, Judge," said the librarian, leaning on his mop. "Someone forget to pay their late fees?"

Anderson stared at the server from which Sargassi had downloaded the book he was reading when he was struck down. She heard the librarian wonder whether she was here about the—

"Ghost?" said Anderson.

The librarian's name was Penrod Curruthers. The name-tag on his dungarees read *Librarian*, but all he really did around here was keep the place clean and press 'reset' when there was a problem with the server. Penrod didn't get many visitors, so Anderson let him gabble.

"I swear it's the old guy who used to work here," he said. "The other guys say he was a real bookworm, always trying to get people to read better, y'know? Like the other night I sat down to watch the game on my vid-phone and the channel kept flipping onto this documentary about some famous architect."

"What was this guy's name?"

"Isambard Kingdom something…"

"I meant the old librarian."

"Uh, Fenwick," he said. "Quillium Fenwick. He practically lived in here. Drove everyone nuts uploading books all the time, scanning in old stuff he'd found in the lit-marts and Grud knows where else."

"Married to the job, huh?" said Anderson. "I can relate."

She removed her glove and ran her hand down the smooth white front of the cabinet. Another snap of psi-energy nipped her fingertips. She let the sensation course through her body, the brittle chatter of pure information, the same crackle she had heard inside Sargassi's head. Whatever had caused the man's breakdown was in here, and this sucker was connected to every citizen in the block with a library card. She was ordering Penrod to tell her how to shut it down when he grabbed her arm, nearly wrenching it from her socket as he hurled her across the room.

She slammed into the wall, cracking the back of her skull against the painted rockcrete. She clattered to the floor, trying to focus her blurred mind as she looked up. Penrod had flipped open a maintenance panel on the server and was slowly pressing buttons. His movements looked jerky and uncoordinated, as though he were struggling to remember how to use his limbs. She rose to her feet and staggered back against the wall as she reached out towards him. There were two people in there, one energy piggybacking the other in classic possession mode. Where was an Exorcist Judge when you needed one?

She zeroed in on the intruding spirit. It was Quillium Fenwick, all right. Death couldn't erase the memory of his name, although it had whittled the rest of his mind down to a single impassioned burble that crackled like static: *idiots, idiots, all of them, shut them up, open their minds, make them see.* The entity ordered Penrod's fingers to deactivate the firewalls that isolated the library from the city's internet. This digitised ghost was making a run for it.

Penrod turned as though Anderson had called his name. She instinctively launched a psi-bolt as he rushed towards her, but her aim must have been off, her head still ringing from its meeting with the wall. Penrod's eyelids twitched as he shrugged off the bolt and snatched her up by the throat with one arm, lifting her off her feet. Anderson heard the presence inside Penrod Curruthers order his fingers to squeeze. She slammed her weight down across Penrod's arm, trying to bend it enough to throw a knockout shot at his jaw, but his arm felt like iron. She pounded his chest with bonebreaking kicks, but the spirit inside Penrod's body held it firm. Penrod slowly lifted a finger to his lips.

"Sssssh!" he hissed.

The sound seemed to drain the world of colour; black sparkles danced before Anderson's eyes. She cursed to herself as she reached for her Lawgiver with one hand and flung out the other at Penrod's face. The tips of her fingers brushed his temple. It was enough. She felt that familiar tingle in her stomach, like she was about to plunge down the chute of a roller-coaster. The entity recoiled, as Penrod fought the urge to continue squeezing her throat. Anderson felt his elbow give momentarily and she slapped her hands either side of his anguished face. *Time to turn this sucker off at the mains*, she thought as the world around her rushed into a blur and she hurtled into the entity's mind.

Focusing her astral form into a body composed of pure psi-energy, Anderson materialised inside a cavernous library, even bigger and even stranger than the one in the vaults of Psi-Division. She looked up at bookcases three stories tall, overlooked by a swirl of ornately wrought balconies spiralling into infinity above her. Standing on the ground floor of this tower, Anderson examined a row of books beside her. She could read every title and discern every wrinkle on every spine. Anderson had seen so-called 'memory palaces' before, visualised maps of retained information, but never one built so meticulously.

She snatched a book and opened it. The words arranged themselves across the blank pages, forming ranks of sentences. Outside of Psi-Judges and tech-augmented humans, Anderson had only seen memories this legible in the heads of genius-level savants. Most citizens' memories were just a mush of fancies and random associations. Could it be possible that the old librarian was crazy or obsessive—or genius—enough to have memorised every book he had ever loaded onto the library server?

Anderson stared as the words began writhing on the page, then swarmed towards her bare hands. She closed the book with a thump that echoed up the throat of the tower. The sound prompted an agitated rustling from the surrounding bookshelves, as though each volume contained a horde of insects eager to escape.

"I know what you're doing, Quillium," she cried out, her words resounding through the empty library. "You've spent a lifetime collecting knowledge. Now you wanna share it, right? Make people smarter?"

Time passed slower in the psi-verse than it did in the real world, but not that slow. She needed to take this spook down fast before her throat got squished back in the real world. She shouted louder.

"We could all use a brain-boost now and then, but what you're doing? It's too much, Quillium. You're hurting people, and I figure—in your own way—you're looking to *help* people, right…?"

Anderson realised someone was standing beside her. The figure raised a finger to its lips and Anderson felt something like a cold wind course through her astral form, draining her. She suddenly felt like a frightened child, stripped of experience, of all she knew about the world, as every comforting shred of information she had gathered throughout her life had been blown away like dust. She caught a spark of anger and lashed out.

"Don't shush me," she snarled, flinging a psi-bolt at the entity's head.

The figure blew apart and vanished.

Anderson tapped one of the bookcases. The memory palace was still here, which meant so was the entity. Quillium Fenwick was gone. Only his murderous shadow remained, and it needed taking care of with something bigger than a psi-bolt. She could feel her astral form growing dim as her body lost consciousness. She needed to lure the creep out into the open.

"So information is your thing, right?" she yelled. "You can give it, or you can take it away. That's a neat trick, pal. Why don't you try it again…?" She grabbed a book from a nearby shelf, feeling the pages wriggle between the covers.

The floor shook. Anderson looked up to see the plasteel balconies tearing themselves free of the wall and lashing themselves together to form a huge, expressionless face. It bore down on her like a malignant stormcloud, raining dust and chunks of rockcrete, darkening the entire library. Anderson prepared a psychic shield and gripped the book tightly as another length of plasteel unfurled like the tentacle of an octopus to form a single immense finger. Metal squealed and groaned as the finger touched a pair of pursed plasteel lips, which issued a torrent of psionic energy that knocked Anderson to the floor with the force of a hurricane, toppling the bookcases either side of her.

She fought to maintain her psychic shield against the blast, feeling her astral form flutter and fade. She flung the book open against the floor and slammed her palm onto the flapping pages. The words swarmed off the paper and covered her hand, dissolving into her astral flesh, filling her with knowledge. The ongoing blast scattered books from the fallen shelves, whipping a blizzard of pages into the air. Anderson watched as a sea of words surged across the floor towards her in a bristling black tide. She let it wash over her, absorbing every secret, exploring every fiction, cherishing every detail, a world of answers for every imaginable question.

Anderson drank in the flood, then spat it out in the form of a brilliant white spear—a bolt of pure information—which she hurled at the metal face looming above her. The missile pierced its forehead. The huge face reeled and howled, a storm of writhing metal and crumbling rockcrete. The maker of the memory palace had built it, piece by piece, over the course of a lifetime; Anderson gave it back to him in a single, dazzling burst.

The library vanished in a flash of light and Anderson found herself lying on the floor of the server room, shielding her eyes against the fluorescent lights glaring above her. As she coughed and rubbed her throat, she realised the unconscious librarian was slumped on top of her. She gently pushed him aside and checked his breathing. He had a couple of broken ribs, but at least his mind was now his own. The entity had been blasted out of existence.

The geeks from Tek-Div arrived a while later, while a med-crew examined poor Penrod in the lobby outside. The two Teks conferred with each other over the library server, as though unsure what to do next.

"Have you tried turning it off and on again?" said Anderson.

"We're running a scan," said the Tek.

Anderson rolled her eyes, wondering if Tek-Div could ever download a sense of humour.

"How many books did you say were in there, Anderson?"

"Lets just say this guy collected books the way you guys probably collect action figures."

The Tek stared at her.

"A lot, okay?" she said.

"Indeed," said the Tek. "We've already found a lost Shakespeare play in there." He tapped at the screen of his holo-tab. "According to this, the last physical copy was obliterated during the Apocalypse War."

"Maybe you could print it out for me," said Anderson. "I could do with a little light reading on my way home."

"Oh, I'm afraid that's out of the question," said the Tek. "We've already detected several publications by banned authors. Plato, Marx, Brand..." His buddy muttered something to which the Tek nodded in agreement. "We're going to have to flush the server."

"Flush it? You mean delete it?" cried Anderson. "But there's a *lifetime's* worth of books in there. Books people can't read anywhere else. Do you have any idea what that means? Generations of knowledge, experiences, ideas?"

"They're just books," said the Tek, bewildered.

"Grud on a greenie, why don't you just build a bonfire and throw the Mona Lisa on there while you're at it?" yelled Anderson as he jostled her aside.

"For goodness sake," said the Tek. "This isn't the dark ages."

He tapped a button on his screen and a counter on his holo-tab dwindled to zero.

Anderson shuddered.

About the Author

ALEC WORLEY IS a comics writer whose credits include *Judge Dredd*, *Anderson*, *Age of the Wolf* and *Dandridge* (all for *2000 AD*), as well as *Teenage Mutant Ninja Turtles* and *Star Wars* (for Panini). He also writes fiction set in Games Workshop's *Warhammer* universe. *Judge Anderson: Year One* is his debut novel. (Well, technically, it's three e-novellas collected as a print omnibus, but it's all good, right?)

www.alecworley.com

FIND US ONLINE!

www.rebellionpublishing.com

/rebellionpub   /rebellionpublishing   /rebellionpub

SIGN UP TO OUR NEWSLETTER!

rebellionpublishing.com/sign-up

YOUR REVIEWS MATTER!

Enjoy this book? Got something to say?

Leave a review on Amazon, GoodReads or with your
favourite bookseller and let the world know!